THE GHOST LINE

A JACK WIDOW THRILLER

SCOTT BLADE

Black Lion Media

CHAPTER 1

Nora Sutton stared out a window at a giant stranger towering over her two daughters, five and six years old, at the mouth of their country-farm driveway. By the look of him, the giant stranger could simultaneously crush both girls' skulls with his bare hands.

Behind him, just past the end of her driveway, four lanes of a quiet highway and two lanes of a dusty country road crossed at an intersection, a literal crossroads. Part of the intersection crossed directly in front of her driveway, a dangerous threat to small children like hers. But Nora's girls knew better than to venture out into the intersection. When it came to cautionary situations like that, they minded her warnings. When it came to talking to strangers, especially a giant stranger like the one hulking over them, it was a different story.

Dust covered two of the roads at the intersection so heavily, even the paved streets looked like dirt roads. Suddenly, violently—two eighteen-wheelers barreled down the old highway, slamming through the intersection. One going one way, and the other going the opposite way. They roared past each other, shaking the ground. The trucks' momentum and enormous wheels kicked dirt up into the air, forming a dust cloud. It lingered above the intersection for a long moment, and then dissipated.

Unfazed by the intensity of the passing trucks, the little girls stared up at the giant stranger. No fear registered on their faces. Their fight-or-flight instincts warned them of nothing. Not a whisper from their young, still-forming brains that they should be afraid of the giant stranger. Perhaps living near such a dangerous crossroads numbed them to other things they should be afraid of. Or perhaps the giant stranger had perfected the art of camouflaging himself. Many predators in the wild have the ability to mask their true intentions. Leopards use their spotted coats to mimic the speckled sunlight as it's filtered through forest trees, making it difficult to see the predator in its natural hunting grounds. Tiger stripes blend these fierce hunters into tall grass, masking the animal as it stalks its prey.

Nora's daughters didn't scream for help. They didn't run from the giant stranger. They just stared up at him like they were both in awe of his stature, but also unintimidated by it.

The giant stranger stepped closer to the children. He talked as he walked, exchanging words with the girls, and the girls spoke back. A transaction was happening. *But what kind? What was he asking them?*

Nora was too far away to hear the exact conversation. Her first instinct was to grab her walkie-talkie and radio her girls. But that's when she noticed they didn't have their walkie with them. It sat on a side table by the front door. Unlike her daughters, Nora's brain was fully developed. Her fight-or-flight instincts worked just fine. She knew there was no fighting the giant stranger, not a man like that. A fight with him would result in catastrophe. Anyone who's ever been around dangerous men could see that.

In her rebellious years, Nora ran with a motorcycle gang in Honolulu. Most people wouldn't believe there was such a thing. But there was. The group she ran with was what her youngest daughter would call a group of *bad dudes*. So, she knew a thing or two about men like the giant stranger.

That life was way back in her past. Nora was far from Hawaii. Now she was a mother and a wife, living on a farm in Missouri. She possessed motherly instincts, which might be more powerful than just normal survival instincts.

At that moment, the powerful combination of her survival instincts and motherly instincts tingled in her brain, warning her to stay cautious, to keep watching the exchange between her daughters and the giant stranger. No red alerts sounded in her brain—not yet. Her brain told her that there may be nothing to worry about because the giant stranger might just be talking to her daughters for legitimate reasons. After all, they were offering lemonade to the public.

Earlier that morning, Nora's two girls had set what looked like a lemonade stand out in front of their driveway. *What're lemonade stands for if not to offer up lemonade to strangers?* That question was why Nora hesitated. The giant stranger could just be talking with her girls about their homemade lemonade. It was a hot Missouri day. The sun burned in the sky with full force. Summer days in the Ozarks were hot and humid. It was reasonable to think that the giant stranger was simply interested in lemonade and nothing else.

The other thing was that this lemonade stand wasn't actually a lemonade stand. Not technically. The girls offered lemonade, but lemonade wasn't the product they were pushing on unknowing passersby. Although it was the only consumable thing on the menu, it wasn't the main product. Lemonade was the bait to catch the attention of potential customers.

Nora's girls had set up the lemonade stand as a deception, a marketing trick—like offering people a free vacation, only to sell them a timeshare chock-full of expensive hidden fees.

The true purpose of the lemonade stand, and the lemonade, was so the girls could sit out in the blistering sun and give away what they really aimed to give away. Her girls were on a mission. It was a mission that she set out for them because they couldn't keep the real product. "We have enough mouths to feed," Nora had said to her girls. And so, they were given a very specific product that needed to be offloaded.

As the sun rose that morning, but after Nora and the girls fed the chickens, goats, and the two horses they hadn't had to sell off yet, Nora prepared for her moneymaking job and over-heard her daughters down in the kitchen, talking and scheming. They discussed what to do with the real product and how to give it away to the public. That's when the older daughter came up with the lemonade stand idea.

Business 101, as Nora's six-year-old daughter lectured the younger one, was to drive up demand and then people would beg for the supply. She followed the statement with an eye roll and a *duh*, like the five-year-old should've known this information because everyone knew it.

Although the whole operation hinged on a bait-and-switch, the lemonade was real. The girls picked the lemons from a lemon tree, using a stepladder to reach the limbs. After all that, they concocted the end result in their mother's kitchen. They squeezed the lemons themselves and mixed the juice with sugar and water. The final brew was never meant to be sold to people, but offered for free—the bait. As a bonus, the girls drank much of it themselves.

The sun beat down on the fabric roof of the small, makeshift lemonade stand. The girls' father had constructed the frame for them last summer out of PVC pipe, as part of a playhouse project that never got finished. The girls had draped a long stretch of unused fabric from their mother's collection over it. Nora liked to sew and make various clothing items from her own designs. She considered herself an amateur fashion designer.

The girls sat behind a short table that was covered by an old tablecloth, set back inside the lemonade stand's frame. The lemonade rested in a costly glass pitcher. It was the only pitcher their mother owned that was made from glass. She had asked them to use a plastic one, but the glass one symbolized *prestige*, her oldest informed her. Therefore, the glass pitcher made more sense, because her daughters aimed to attract upscale customers, not just the occasional *dirty people* who crossed the highway on foot.

Nora didn't like her daughters calling them that, but her girls could never remember the actual word for them. What they really meant was *transients*. That's the word the anchor on a local TV channel called them. He ranted about them at least once a month, sometimes more. Nora would turn the channel, but they only had two, and the other one was the Weather Channel. Now, thanks to getting an online job, she had fast internet, so she bought the kids a couple of the big streaming services. It made life easier with something else for them to watch.

The Sutton farm attracted transients due to its location near the intersection of that country road and the old highway. Occasionally, one or two transients might walk onto her property to ask if she needed workers. It was the reason Nora had staked a sign in the dirt at the edge of the yard, visible from the road. The sign read: *No Work Here*. Even with the sign, transients would venture up to the house, ring the doorbell, and ask about work-for-hire anyway. Every time they did, Nora opened the door with politeness and caution—plus her husband's rifle. It was a Marlin 336, a rugged and dependable lever-action rifle chambered in .30-30 Winchester—less stopping power than a .300 Magnum that could blow a man's head off, but definitely more punch than a chin-tickling .22.

Staring at the giant stranger from her window, Nora wished she had the .300 Magnum. She knew the .30-30 Winchester was enough to damage the giant stranger, *but would it be enough to put him down?* That was an entirely different question. One that she honestly couldn't answer.

Questions and worries swarmed Nora's mind. *What did the giant stranger want? Was he approaching her daughters to inquire about work, like all the usual transients? Perhaps he was asking them to fetch their father, so he could ask him about work on the farm?*

The giant stranger didn't look like a farmhand, however. He looked more like an out-of-work prizefighter, the kind of guy crime bosses used to intimidate their enemies, to collect on unpaid debts, or to send a violent message that included broken bones.

The giant stranger was dressed all wrong to be a farmhand. Normal transients wore trucker or cowboy hats and wore tattered clothes—which the giant stranger did, sort of. But the usual work-seeking transients favored a specific kind of worn, Western style: jeans, flannel shirts, and cowboy boots. Sometimes they showed up in overalls. Not this guy. He wore a t-shirt and jeans. Everything else about him was off too, and he wore no hat.

Nora couldn't hear what the giant stranger said to her girls, but she figured they were innocently trying to lure him to the lemonade stand, to help take the merchandise off their hands. They were good girls, and smart too. However, they were naive, as most five- and six-year-olds are. They talked with the giant stranger because they saw him as a potential customer, same as anyone else. They presumed he wanted the merchandise.

The merchandise was already free, which should be enough to attract customers. The problem was they lived out in the country, and, as the oldest daughter explained to Nora, *Retail is about location, location, location,* and, *This isn't Times Square,* when defending her and her sister's business choices. In part, she was right. Their operation was small-scale, in a place that was literally the road less traveled. There wasn't a large pool of upscale customers coming to their lemonade stand to begin with. In order to offset this, the girls had to offer upgrades, like premium lemonade served from a premium glass pitcher. That's where their mother's glass pitcher came into the whole scheme.

Regarding the location argument, the girls' geographical problem was that they lived in rural Missouri, in the Ozarks region. So, they didn't get a lot of vehicle traffic, at least not the kind that stopped at their driveway. Most of the traffic didn't stop at all. It flew through, like there was no reason to stop in the first place.

One road, the main one, led to the interstate, and it was the only way out of the county. People sped by so fast, they ran right through the intersection. To be fair, the state of Missouri didn't care about Nora's little country road, and, thus, they never noticed that two of the stop signs were completely missing. These were the important ones too. They were on the highway. Some local kids had stolen them, after using them for target practice. The stop signs had been missing so long that when they first vanished, Nora only had one daughter.

Nora complained about the missing stop signs to officials in Iron Crossing, the nearest town. She complained to the mayor's office, the county public works department, and all the way up to the governor's office. Nobody had ever done anything more than send her generic letters, promising to investigate. No one ever came out to look at the intersection. So much for *Let the welfare of the people be the supreme law,* the Missouri state motto. Which might not be totally fair to think, but Nora considered herself well-educated, at least compared to others in the county. And that's how she described it to her family and friends back home, the ones who still called her once in a while to ask how she was doing. Most of them followed up with: *Why don't you come home?*

Nora was originally from Hawaii. She's what the locals call *hapa,* which meant mixed heritage. She was half Native Hawaiian and half white. Her mother was born and raised on Molokai. Nora could trace her lineage back for eight generations, and probably further, though no one had ever tried.

Nora's father was a Navy man through and through. Although white, he was a third-generation Hawaiian, with roots in the islands stretching back to when his grandfather— Nora's great-grandfather—served as a fighter pilot during World War II. His grandfather took to the skies on the day Japan bombed Pearl Harbor, one of the few who managed to get airborne in defense of the islands. The US Navy awarded him the Distinguished Flying Cross for his bravery on that day. The medal still hung in her parents' living room.

That resilience and sense of service ran deep in Nora. With a hardened Navy father and a tough-as-nails mother, pride was part of her core. It was this pride that kept Nora from returning home, even after a year with no word from her husband, who had vanished.

Although they loved and supported her, her parents never understood why she came out here. But both of them understood being in love because, even though they were both stubborn, they loved each other deeply. They were glad she had married someone who made her feel that way.

Nora's friends were a different story. They never liked her husband. She was a firebrand with looks that could kill. Every guy wanted her. But she never loved any of them. She dated a few, sure, but never felt the feelings that she felt for her husband. He was a nerdy kid from her school who grew up to be a veterinarian.

After her husband vanished, Nora's friends pressed her hard to return home with her children. *Just forget that loser! He left you!* they said. But her husband wouldn't just abandon her and their girls. She knew it. And when she reiterated that to them, they dismissed it. Nora felt betrayed by them every time this happened, which was why she rarely returned their phone calls.

Nora's so-called friends didn't concern her at that moment. What concerned her was the betrayal by one of her own family members—the most loyal one at that. The worst kind of betrayal was the unexpected kind, the kind that felt like a knife in the back. This betrayal came from their dog—officially Joan-of-Bark on her registration, though the kids just called her Joanie. She was their Cane Corso—a very expensive one at that. According to her youngest daughter, Joanie's street value was a thousand-trillion-million dollars. Nora's daughters were smart; they got that from their father. Their imagination, however, they got from her. Of course, the amount was wildly off, but Joanie was indeed a purebred Cane Corso, and worth every penny they had spent.

Joanie betrayed the whole family, because instead of barking at the giant stranger towering over Nora's children, Joanie acted like they were best friends. She approached him, smelled him, and not only allowed him to pet her, but she rubbed her body across his legs like a cat. Nora wouldn't have been surprised if Joanie had purred as well. *Unbelievable!* Nora thought. She'd never seen anything like it before. Instead of acting like their protector, Joanie behaved like a schoolgirl with a crush.

Not that she could blame the Cane Corso. The giant stranger was breathtaking in a certain way. He stood six-feet and four inches tall—not the tallest man Nora had ever seen before; her brother was taller, and some of the boys local to Iron Crossing stood taller—but it wasn't just his height or build, which was like that of a lean NFL player. It was something about the way the giant stranger carried himself. There was something in the way he stood: stoic, relentless, and, she would say, timeless, like a gunslinger from the Old West. He stood tall like a man from legend, like he lived in the moment and nowhere else. Not a shred of him was anywhere else but right there with her children and their beloved protector, their dog. *Protector? What a joke that is!* she thought.

Nora saw the giant stranger, her kids, and their useless protector, and decided it was time for action. She grabbed her husband's rifle and ran out of the farmhouse and down the driveway, and confronted the giant stranger. The giant stranger didn't look in her direction at first. But if he had, it would've been impossible not to stare at her.

The vision of Nora running down the country driveway toward the giant stranger was something to behold. Anyone would stare. It wasn't Nora speeding down the driveway that made the sight a head-turner. It wasn't that she was armed, and barreling toward the giant stranger with a rifle. It was more due to what she was wearing, or rather what she wasn't wearing.

Before Nora noticed the giant stranger talking to her children, she was getting ready for her job, which required a certain kind of business wear. She considered this job her *paying* job, as her real job was being a mother and trying to get the farm back on its feet. But she had to do something to pay the bills until the farm was profitable again.

Her *paying* job was a job she took out of desperation. It wasn't something she wanted to do. But when her husband vanished, there were two little girls to feed, a farm to run, and bills stacking up, so what else could she do?

Her *paying* job required her to wear less clothing than other jobs. In fact, she practically wore nothing most of the time. And a lot of the time, she literally wore nothing at all. Nora ran out of the house wearing a black string bikini, tennis shoes, and nothing else. With her kids in potential stranger-danger, she had no time to put on more clothes.

Half-naked, Nora raced, rifle in hand, to the end of her driveway. Tiny dust clouds kicked up behind her. She ran track in high school, more than fifteen years ago. Even though it was so long ago, and her muscles didn't get the same relentless practice, she could still move fast. Her motherly instincts injected a boost of adrenaline to her old track muscles. She sped down her driveway, clocking in at her new fastest time. She cleared the fifty yards from her front porch to the mouth of her driveway in seconds.

She got there, startling her daughters and the giant stranger, who only just now noticed her. He stared at her like his eyes were caught in a tractor beam. His mouth hung open a bit.

She'd intended to scare him with her rifle. Only he wasn't scared of her or the rifle as much as he was confused by her choice of clothing. He thought the word *showstopper* was the best way to describe her.

The fast sprint winded Nora, but she had no time to worry about catching her breath. Not now. She stopped abruptly at the end of the dirt driveway, nearly sliding in the dust, and raised the rifle. She didn't point it at the giant stranger, but she held it so the barrel pointed at the ground and she could redirect and aim it up at the giant stranger's knees with a quick flick of her wrists and elbows. No problem. She'd had plenty of practice firing it over the last year. Living as a single mom on a rural farm in the Ozarks with two little girls to protect gave her the desire to get good at shooting at dangerous predators that might come around the farm. And the giant stranger looked like he could be a dangerous predator.

Nora, like a shifting gear, slipped into what her daughter, Violet, called *momma-bear mode*. She slid between the giant stranger and the lemonade stand's counter. Never taking her eyes off him, she said, "Violet, Poppy, I want you to get behind me!"

The two little girls plopped down off the milk crate they had been standing on together. The older one was Violet, and the younger one was Poppy. Violet frowned, like she was upset by the interruption of her sales pitch to the giant stranger. *How unprofessional*, she thought. But Violet could see that her mother was serious. So, she grabbed Poppy's little hand and led her sister out of the lemonade stand. The two of them shuffled out and over to their māmā. They stopped behind her as she had ordered.

Violet gave no protest, as she'd been alive longer than Poppy and was well aware that when Nora went into *momma-bear mode* it was a serious situation. Resisting Nora during *momma-bear mode* always resulted in her māmā crying and, probably, taking away Violet's outside time. The last thing the six-year-old wanted was to lose her outside privileges, or have her chores doubled. *What's the point of life on a farm when you're stuck indoors? Or doing chores?*

The giant stranger stayed where he was and stared at Nora. He kept his eyes locked on hers, only deviating to see where the rifle was pointed, to make sure it wasn't at him. He didn't want to get shot. And he especially didn't want to get shot out in the middle of the Ozarks.

The giant stranger kept his massive arms down by his side and his palms open wide and face up, showing Nora that they were clear of weapons, assuring her he was no threat to her.

The giant stranger stayed quiet, stayed calm.

Nora craned her head up slowly. Her eyes followed the giant stranger's torso up, past a muscular torso that looked like a Spartan warrior's metal plate of armor. She stopped on his face.

The giant stranger stared down at her with piercing ice-blue eyes. His face was statuesque in the way she might think of the Colossus of Constantine's giant face, only it wasn't a clear-cut resemblance; it was more a matter of the stature and the marble-like features. The giant stranger's face was covered in stubble. It wasn't a beard; it was more like what Violet called *whiskers*.

The giant stranger's clothes were a bit dirty, a bit dusty, like he'd either slept in them on the ground, or walked for a couple of days wearing them, or both. Neither would've surprised Nora.

The giant stranger wore a red t-shirt with writing on the front that read: *I'm weth Stoopid*, and a large white arrow pointing directly up at his face. Wrinkles creased the t-shirt, like he really had slept on the ground. He wore faded blue jeans and worn Timberland boots; worn either from him walking them to death, or they were that way when he got them. It was another question where neither answer would've surprised her.

The giant stranger's skin was tan, like he'd been out in the sun for days.

Suddenly, the giant stranger made his first attempt to defuse the situation. He closed his mouth, paused, and then smiled at her and her daughters. His dark tan emphasized his teeth, which were mostly straight and all white, like he took exceptional care of them. The mostly-straight perfection of his smile suggested that he might've spent time in the military. Nora was familiar because of her father. One benefit of service to country was socialized medicine. And one benefit of that was a dental plan. Apparently, the giant stranger had taken advantage of such a plan.

The giant stranger's jeans were dusted from the wind blowing dirt across the roads, like he hitchhiked to Missouri from somewhere out West, crossing the Great Plains of Kansas, where the wind blew hard like it does over open water.

She wondered if the giant stranger's Timberlands had been bought secondhand. Timberlands were a big fad for the bad-boy types Nora used to run with back home. She presumed they were still in style. She'd seen men around the Ozarks wearing them. But she couldn't be sure, not without a Google search from her phone, which she realized she'd left back in the house. Nora didn't keep up with men's boots, not since there was no longer a man around her house to wear any. Her focus lingered on the giant stranger's boots for a long second, like she was only just realizing that confronting him alone may have been a bad idea. Not that she had a choice.

Like the rest of him, the giant stranger's boots were massive. Nora was alarmed just by their size. They looked big in the way an NBA player's sneakers looked big. Deep boot prints were in her dirt and gravel driveway behind the giant stranger, like Bigfoot had left them.

A potential intense exchange unfolded right there on Nora's country driveway in front of her children's lemonade stand. Her rifle felt cold in her hands. For a split second, she questioned if it would fire—but only for a split-second, like some kind of irrational fear. She knew it would fire. She practiced with it every week. And not just to be able to shoot straight, but also because gunshots on her farm indicated to her neighbors that she wasn't some delicate, helpless flower. It told them that she wasn't to be trifled with. Some of her neighbors were less than friendly. And a couple of the local boys were far from neighborly. When she drove into town, sometimes they'd leer at her and make lewd comments. They all knew her husband had vanished. They all knew she lived on the farm alone. Most of them kept their vulgar thoughts to themselves, but not always. Like when she pumped gas at a gas station, and a truck full of local boys would pull up. They might be there for the same reason as she, but sometimes one or two of them would sidle over. They might play nice at first, like offer to pump the gas for her. But sometimes, the moment she'd reject them, they wouldn't go away. Sometimes they would take things too far. That's why she started bringing Joanie along with her when she went into town. When they saw a huge Cane Corso hanging out in her pickup truck's bed, the local boys stopped bothering her.

The next thing that Nora started doing was carrying her rifle into town with her. It was amazing how self-reliant she became without her husband around. She bought a gun rack for her pickup and installed it herself. Now, when going into town, she loaded up the dog and left her rifle on the rack in the rear window of the truck for the whole town to see. Adding to that form of deterrence, she also made it known that she practiced shooting her rifle every week. And she'd gotten damn good at shooting. At this close distance, she'd hit the giant stranger right between the eyes.

Even so, the giant stranger intimidated her. Adrenaline pumped through her veins. Nora feared him. She feared what he could do to her girls, and to her, if he got the rifle out of the way. She worried that her hands trembled, showing fear. But they didn't. Her hands stayed steady. The rifle stayed steady.

The rifle was the only thing standing between her family and this dangerous stranger. It protected them. However, the rifle wasn't supposed to be the family's first line of defense. Firearms were meant to be the last line of defense as far as Nora was concerned.

However, her family's first line of defense was doing everything but protecting Nora and her girls. Her family's first line of defense wagged its tail and stared up at the giant stranger. Their first line of defense was supposed to be Joanie. She was supposed to be standing between them and danger.

Instead of standing between Nora's family and stranger-danger, Joanie abandoned them and approached the giant stranger, wagged her tail, and picked his hand up with her head like a cat looking for head scratches. Joanie betrayed her family blatantly, right there in front of them, and wagged her tail while she committed this treason.

Nora barked, "Joanie! Get back here!"

Joanie grunted, stopped begging for head scratches, and sat at the giant stranger's feet like she was his best friend and had never seen this family before in her entire dog life. But even though Joanie wasn't barking at the giant stranger, Violet and Poppy's real merchandise barked at him from a box that had its lid wide open. Actually, they were too young to really bark; the merchandise puppy-squeaked at the giant stranger. The merchandise sounded like puppies because that's what they were. Puppies were the merchandise that the girls were trying to give away. Puppies were the switch in their bait-and-switch scheme.

Violet and Poppy had set up the lemonade stand to entice passersby to come over and try some homemade lemonade—albeit made by little girls —but their true aim was to give away Joanie's litter of Cane Corso mix puppies. Which they didn't really want to do, but Nora convinced them that if they didn't find homes for the puppies, then both of them would have to find proper jobs to pay for puppy food. Poppy, defiant till the end, claimed this was *no problem*. But Violet convinced her little sister that she'd *seen the world* because she'd been alive longer. Therefore, she knew that *jobs suck* and *working was for the birds,* all her own words. Poppy trusted her big sister more than anyone in the world. Therefore, it took little reasoning to convince Poppy that they were better off finding homes for the puppies than working hard-labor jobs.

Poppy agreed to this proposition, but on the condition that the new owners must be close enough for Joanie to visit her pups. In fact, Nora didn't know this, but Poppy had been interrogating the giant stranger about where he lived. She wanted to know how far they had to walk to visit the puppies he'd take in. She wanted to make sure he could afford to take care of them. "What kind of house do you have?" she asked. "Do you have a big yard? How far away is your house?"

In fact, the giant stranger was worried that the girls were about to bust out contracts they'd written in crayon and make him sign each page, like he was signing his life away at a Navy recruiter station somewhere.

Before Nora ran out of her house in a mad dash, half-naked and with her rifle, her girls had grilled the giant stranger about his intentions with their puppies. In fact, he had spoken very few words so far.

All the giant stranger wanted was some lemonade, because of the heat. He had walked most of the night and some of the morning. He was tired, thirsty, and overheated. The sight of a lemonade stand on the side of the road was like seeing an oasis in the desert. It lured him in. But the girls needed answers to their questions before they would pour him a glass of free lemonade.

"The lemonade is for customers only," Poppy told him. That was the last thing she said to him before Nora barged out of their farmhouse and charged down the driveway.

Nora looked at him and squeezed her husband's rifle tight, the way Violet squeezed her security blanket when it was too dark in her and Poppy's shared bedroom at night. Nora eased her finger into the trigger housing, but didn't put pressure on the trigger. Not yet. She merely brushed it with her finger.

Poppy clutched Violet's hand. They stood behind their māmā, confused. Poppy stomped her feet, angry, she said, "Māmā, we had him on the hook."

Nora ignored her daughter, and said, "Mister, you're not from around here. I've never seen you before. And I know just about everybody that lives here. I hope you understand that you look like a man I should be concerned about around my children. So, who're you? What're you doing talking to my girls?"

CHAPTER 2

Jack Widow kept his hands open, palms up—worn, rugged and covered with lines across his skin—the hands of a man who's worked hard and lived harder. Which was sort of true because, once upon a time, he had worked hard and lived hard, but not now. Not anymore. Now Widow lived a life of leisure. At least, that's the way he saw it. Widow hadn't worked for a living in many years, except for cash-under-the-table odd jobs here and there. Most of those, he worked simply out of boredom or the need to do something different, to mix things up.

Occasionally, Widow found himself needing money, so he'd locate and acquire odd jobs to help raise capital. Most people worked jobs for money in order to pay their bills, rent or mortgages, car and student loans, and taxes. Most people rinsed and repeated the daily cycle of work and spend, work and spend. But not Widow. Whenever he worked for money, it was to finance his life's blueprint, which was to wander, to nomad, to go everywhere and nowhere in particular—all at the same time.

Widow was a man without a plan. He wanted to go, to move, and to see it all. He was an explorer without a flag. He had no more missions. No more orders. No more undercover assignments. Life was short, and Widow wasn't going to waste a second of it living like most people. He did what he did. And he went where he went. That was the way Widow liked it.

Living this way opened up all kinds of possibilities. Widow never knew what adventure waited around the corner. Two nights ago it was no different. Widow found himself near a trainyard in Chicago on a dark night, where he stumbled upon a group of homeless vets playing dominos. They burned a fire in a city trashcan, but not for warmth. It was the end of a hot summer, and the nights were still too warm to need a fire. The trash fire burned to provide light for them because they were on a dark city street. Several of the nearest streetlights were either burned out or the city had just switched them off to save money. Except for around the trash fire, the street was dark and quiet.

The homeless vets laughed at Widow's t-shirt. He admitted to buying it at an Indiana truck stop because it was the only size that fit him. Thinking he was a hobo, the homeless vets invited him to hang out with them. Which he did, because Widow couldn't resist a good time. And hanging out with a few former service members and playing dominos for money sounded like a better than average weeknight.

One of the homeless vets, a young sailor, told Widow a tantalizing story about being discharged for having an affair with an admiral's daughter. Widow listened, but wrote off much of the story as embellishment and fantasy. However, he liked the guy. The guy was definitely a sailor at some point. Widow believed him about that part. That portion of the story was true, as well as the guy having been discharged. Widow believed him about that part too. Whether the discharge had been honorable or dishonorable was anyone's guess. But

Widow didn't care. The Navy was ancient history in his book. He lived a different life now.

Still, you can take the sailor out of the Navy, but you can't take the Navy out of the sailor. Even though Widow had been out for a decade at this point, he still recognized other sailors. He could tell the young sailor had been enlisted because the guy knew things that civilians got completely wrong. He had that sailor-look about him, like they could commandeer a ship right then and the young sailor would know exactly what station was his.

The young sailor was adventurous. He was a nomad, like Widow. They had the same restless spirit. Widow recognized that in the guy too. Widow had been nomading around the United States for damn near a decade. Sometimes it felt too short, until Widow stopped to think about all the faces of the people he'd met along the way—the friends he made, the families he impacted, the injustices he corrected, the villains he dispatched, and the innocent people they hurt before he got to them.

Widow thought about the women. He had met so many strong, amazing women in his life. In a way, Widow was that old cliché of a sailor who had a woman in every port. It wasn't something he'd planned, but it came with living the way he lived. It was an occupational hazard—only he had no occupation, just a way of life.

When swapping war stories with the young sailor, Widow left out the parts about taking out bad guys. He omitted the violence, crimes, and taking justice into his own hands. As he saw it, some men needed killing. In a way, Widow told bigger lies than the young homeless sailor did. Widow thought the young guy fabricated at least some, if not all, of the story about the admiral's daughter and was really discharged for some other reason. But Widow omitted information, which made him a liar too, in a way.

Widow had been feeling a little bitter lately, a little lonely, and maybe doing a little second-guessing about his life choices. Perhaps he had it all wrong. Perhaps he should open himself up to the possibility of a different kind of life. Maybe things weren't as grim as he'd been feeling. Widow thought again about all the women he'd met. He had been romantic with some of them—intimate. Some of them were really great, wife material even. Maybe he'd meet one who'd change his ways someday. Maybe some great woman would cross his path and make him want to settle down. Only time would tell.

For some reason, perhaps because they'd both served in the Navy, Widow shared his thoughts with the young sailor. The young sailor said, "My friend, I think you're experiencing a midlife crisis."

"I'm too young for a midlife crisis."

The young sailor looked Widow up and down. He said, "The average man lives to be seventy to seventy-five. If you're forty, which is what I would guess, then you're over the halfway point already."

The realization hit Widow like a ton of bricks. The guy was right. He was certainly on the young side of middle-aged, but he was still in the ballpark. *Where did the time go?* Widow thought. But he didn't linger on it. He concentrated on playing dominos with his new friends and enjoying the night.

Later, the young sailor told Widow another interesting thing. He said he was leaving soon, headed south to St. Louis. That wasn't the interesting part. The interesting part was when he said, "Well, it's been real, fellows. But I got a train to catch." Which confused Widow because the young sailor clearly had no money. And the trainyard they were next to wasn't a train station. It only had freight trains. There were no passenger trains around. Widow asked about it, and the young sailor explained, "I'm a hopper."

"A what?" Widow asked.

One of the older homeless vets said, "He means train-hopping."

"People still do that?" Widow asked.

"Sure. Lots of us do it. It's kind of a thrill. It's exhilarating, actually. Plus, It's a cheap way to get cross-country," the young sailor said, and paused a beat. His face lit up, like a lightbulb went off and he had a great idea. "Oh, you should come along. Come with me and find out. I'll show you the ropes."

Widow thought for a moment. Technically, trainhopping was a crime, he figured. He wondered, *What's the penalty if I get caught?* By habit, Widow tried not to commit crimes, but trainhopping was a victimless crime. Unless he considered how it might hurt rich corporations who ship by rail. Unless he sympathized with the uber-rich who used the rails for shipping goods, which he didn't.

The young sailor saw Widow contemplating the risks, and said, "No one gets hurt by us hopping on the trains. Trust me. Besides, they're already going the direction we want to go. Why not hop on and take a free ride?"

You only live once, Widow thought. So he went. The young sailor showed him what to do. First, they boarded a moving freight train right after it took off from the railyard. The young sailor told him to always board a moving train, and never a stopped train. Moving trains aren't being inspected or loaded or unloaded. A stopped train was likely being inspected. Which happened a lot. The train operators have ways of suspecting if hoppers were on board their train. Some of their tools were as advanced as heat and motion sensors to RFID scanners—radio frequency identification, using electromagnetic fields to automatically identify and track tags on train cars—to simply a guy on the ground whose job was to look for stowaways.

A lot of the time, the guys on the ground inspected with trained dogs. "Hiding from them is damn near impossible," the young sailor said. "You see a police dog, you better start running."

Widow and the young sailor boarded a flatbed and rode it for the first hour, leaving Chicago. An hour later, a pair of sisters close to the young sailor's age joined them for the ride. They hopped on at a section in Grundy County, Illinois, where all trains had to slow for a long stretch because other rails cross-sectioned there. It was too dangerous to pass through the multiple crossing tracks at high speeds. Once they passed the cross-sectioning, the train picked up speed again, and they were back in business, headed to St. Louis.

Before this experience, Widow had assumed it was old-timers who trainhopped. However, now that he'd tried it, he realized it was more of a young person's game because hoppers had to be agile, limber, and quick. It also helped to be small in frame because at one point they had to hide from a railway policeman. The train stopped a couple of hours later. The young sailor said it was a random checkpoint.

The sisters showed Widow and the young sailor an open car they had noticed earlier. The four of them transitioned to it and slid the door closed. The sisters showed them a way to make it appear the door was locked when it really wasn't. They bypassed some kind of old locking mechanism to do it. This tricked the inspectors, as long as they didn't look too closely.

The young sailor was impressed. He whispered to Widow that normally he had to crawl up under the train and hide inside the undercarriage, twisting himself into uncomfortable positions and using various axles and train parts to stay up there, out of sight. It sounded dangerous, and difficult to do. Widow doubted he could squeeze his bulk under there and stay out of sight the same way. Plus, Widow didn't know train parts from car parts. He might grab the wrong thing, something blistering hot. The intense and immediate pain might force him to drop from the train and be discovered.

The car they ended up in was half-packed with crates full of industrial machinery. It was enormous on the inside. A lot bigger than Widow had imagined. There was plenty of room for all four of them to spread out, which they did. The sisters sat together. Widow and the young sailor sat on the other side.

Once the inspectors were satisfied there were no stowaways on the train, it started moving again. After another hour passed, the young sailor yawned and mentioned it was still a long ride to St. Louis. Widow asked how long, but the young sailor wasn't sure exactly. He said more than six hours, but less than twelve. He set an alarm on his phone so he'd wake up before dawn. He said he'd ridden this line many times before, and when it arrived in St. Louis in the morning, they should be off it or take the risk of getting caught. There was a major railyard and security checkpoint outside the city, where they routinely opened all the cars to check them. Plus, they for sure used dogs at this checkpoint. He knew that from experience.

The young sailor told Widow he'd wake him up when his alarm went off. He yawned once more, and left Widow alone against the wall, venturing off toward the crates and vanishing in the darkness.

Widow woke before the kid's alarm went off. He'd slept well despite the cold steel floor and the rocking train. Widow had slept in harder spaces in the past.

Widow stepped quietly to the cargo door, unlocked it, and cracked it open. He peered out at the landscape. He looked and listened. The train groaned, like an iron beast surging across the Midwestern plains. Steel train parts rattled below the freight car.

The day's first light spilled slowly over the horizon, lighting up rolling plains and green treetops. Fingers of sunlight stretched out through the haze, illuminating the wide, endless expanse of Illinois farmland, the last of the state before Missouri. Endless stalks of corn rolled by in tidy rows, swaying in a rhythm set by the train's passing.

Ultimately, the cornfields became rolling green hills, which evolved into green flatlands, then gave way to gentle hills. The skyline was peppered with tall oak trees, their twisted branches reaching toward the sky like tall religious people worshipping the rising sun.

Roosters crowed, marking the waking countryside. It was peaceful, serene. Widow could see the appeal of trainhopping. Other than it being the cheap and easy way to get cross-country, there was the romance of it. It represented freedom—peace. For a man like him, it was symbolic of a cease-fire to the war that veterans fight within themselves.

For that fraction of time, it felt as if the world moved slower while the freight train barreled forward, carving its way south toward St. Louis. Widow watched the sun rise and allowed himself to get lost in it.

Eventually, the train slowed outside of St. Louis, and they had to hop off before the train passed through the trainyard where it would be inspected by the local rail police—and cars would be loaded and unloaded—leading to the possibility of them being discovered if they stayed on board.

Outside the city, the group got a ride in a pickup truck with Marine Corps bumper stickers plastered all over the back. The sisters and the young sailor rode in the cab while Widow rode in the truck bed. At about eight in the morning, they were dropped off outside the Soulard Farmers Market, where they shopped for breakfast. Widow ate pastries and drank some really great coffee, which tempted him to stay behind for more.

The four walked the city all morning, talking and having good times. Widow enjoyed it because he hardly ever had company on his travels. Mostly, he was left with his own thoughts nearly 24 hours a day, 365 days a year. It was nice to have new friends for a while. They ended up having lunch and dinner, spending the afternoon and some of the evening at the famous Gateway Arch, watching the riverboats.

All was well, until Widow started to feel that itch. It was partly because he needed to move on and partly because he'd had enough of them. They were fun and interesting, but young and immature. Widow was fifteen years older than the youngest of them, and more than a decade older than the other two. They reminded him of the younger sailors coming up when he was already an officer in the Navy. They were fun, but their life experiences were so different from his. He couldn't relate to them any more than they could relate to him.

Widow was ready to move on. Besides, the sisters were headed west to Santa Fe, and the young sailor wanted to follow. Widow had passed through Sante Fe less than a month ago, and he hated going backwards. He wanted to head south. It'd been awhile since he'd gone south in the summer. So why not spend the end of summer down there?

Normally, Widow followed the birds, heading south for the winter and north in the summer. The American South was hot in the summer. But Widow was from the South; born and raised in Mississippi. He could handle the heat.

Widow told the group his plans. He thanked them for showing him the ropes. He said he'd take the next train south. The older sister said, "That's going to be the MNA, or the Missouri & Northern Arkansas Railroad, which operates the freight route that runs through parts of the Ozarks and northern Arkansas. It covers more than five hundred miles of track, connecting several key locations. It's a beautiful route. Very scenic."

The younger sister glanced at the others, and said, "But it's dangerous for a newcomer."

The older sister looked at the younger one and slow-nodded in agreement, like she'd forgotten about how dangerous it was along that route.

The young sailor said, "Yeah, you want to stick with MNA Route 85."

Widow asked, "How's it dangerous? Aren't all the freight routes a bit dangerous? We're not supposed to be on them."

The older sister said, "It's different because the MNA passes Route 67. You want to stay away from that line."

"Route 67?" Widow asked.

The older sister said, "BNSF Route 67 is the technical name of the line. My sister's right, you wanna avoid going down that one."

"No problem. I'll just stick to the 85," Widow said.

"It's not that simple. Other trains go that way also. It's hard to tell which one you're on," the older sister said.

Which made sense. If Widow wasn't supposed to be on the train, how would he be privy to the route and destination?

The younger sister added, "Some hoppers call Route 67 *The Ghost Line.*"

Widow puzzled over this, and said, "Why do they call it that?"

The sisters stayed quiet. The younger sailor waited for them to speak, but when they didn't, he said, "The Ghost Line was once a frequently used freight route. It connected smaller, isolated Ozark towns, but it became infamous for passing through dangerous terrain and treacherous weather conditions. It rains a lot out there. And the canals and rivers flood all the time."

"So that's it? Bad weather?" Widow asked.

The young sailor said, "Not just that. The major railroads abandoned it. The rumors are that drug smugglers and other criminal organizations use it to smuggle stuff."

The older sister said, "It's sort of an urban legend now. No one ventures down those tracks anymore. It's best to stick to the main route."

Doubtful, yet intrigued, Widow asked, "An urban legend? Is it real, though?"

"It is!" the younger sister snapped.

The older sister said, "You should just stay on MNA Route 85. And don't deviate until you're out of Missouri."

"Yeah," the younger sister, calmer now, added. "And if you see the train turn onto that line, hop off. Don't take it. Stay with the right track until you're in Arkansas."

"But why? What happens on Route 67? Other than supposed drug smugglers?" Widow asked.

The younger sister said, "Hoppers go missing there."

They hadn't mentioned missing hoppers until just now. Widow thought for a moment, and asked, "How do you know they went missing?"

The three of them glanced at each other, like they were trying to decide which one of them had the best way to put it. "Everyone knows," the young sailor said.

"But how do you know it's true?" Widow asked, and looked at him.

"Hoppers talk," the older sister said.

The young sailor said, "People talk about horror stories of their friends vanishing after taking that track. They share it on message boards and social media."

The younger sister added, "And the *Hoppy* app." She took a phone out, swiped across the screen to open it, and showed it to Widow. She said, "This is an app that a lot of us use to keep up-to-date with what's going on and plan out routes. See here, it'll tell us what's ahead and best times to ride, etc."

Widow studied the app. He was amazed by how much he didn't know about trainhopping and, like many other things, how modern it had become. It's so 21st-century now. Widow guessed everything would have to become so in order to survive. In this life, you have to evolve or die.

Widow looked. The map on the *Hoppy* app showed freight routes and was updated with what times the trains ran, similar to the digital board at an airport, the one that showed arrivals and departures. The map also highlighted the areas the trains passed through and where it was best to board. An asterisk at the bottom of the map indicated that *all hopping times were approximate.*

The younger sister showed him Route 85 and where it forked off to Route 67, which was grayed out. But that wasn't all. It also had little symbols by it. The kids called them *emojis*. Widow didn't own a phone, but he wasn't stupid. He understood some emojis, but not all of them, not even most of them. But he recognized the emoji marking Route 67. It was the skull and crossbones, the universal symbol for danger.

The younger sister said, "That means do not travel it. See the warnings?"

Widow nodded.

The young sailor looked at the girls and asked, "Remember TrackHopper?"

Widow looked up from the phone screen and at the young sailor, confused. The young sailor said, "TrackHopper was his *TikTok* name. I don't know his real name."

Widow nodded, like he knew what that meant. He recognized the name *TikTok*. He knew it was some kind of popular app on a phone. He'd seen young people dancing in front of their phones in public places, and recording videos that he guessed were to be posted online for some reason. He didn't get the appeal. But *live and let live* was the first half of Widow's life motto. *Live and let live, and if you can't let live, then we got a problem* was the whole thing.

The sisters nodded, and the younger one said, "Alex was his name. Alex Hopper. We met him once. We rode with him from Boulder to Grand Junction a couple of summers ago."

The older sister said, "He was a nice guy."

"What happened to him?" Widow asked.

The older sister said, "No one knows for sure."

The younger sister took her phone back, tapped the screen, and pulled up *TikTok*. She showed it to Widow. She said, "Alex was a skeptic and an adventurer."

"A daredevil too," the older sister added.

Widow looked at the screen. It was a still image of a young guy, about their age. He was all blond hair and blue eyes, had that all-American look. The younger sister played a couple of his *TikTok* videos so Widow could get a glimpse of the kid. He was trainhopping in one, hiding from the rail police in another, and walking on a long railroad trestle in third. It was high up over a canyon somewhere that looked like it was in the western US. The bridge framework was all wood and steel supports.

The younger sister said, "He didn't believe the rumors. He wanted to see for himself. So he did a bunch of videos talking about taking Route 67 to investigate and debunk the conspiracy theories about all the hoppers who've gone down the line and never returned." Then she scrolled to the last video on TrackHopper's page and clicked it. Widow watched. The video went as she'd described it. The kid talked about his skepticism about Route 67 and the disappearances. He stated that he wanted to debunk the whole thing. He was riding a train that was on its way there while he recorded the video.

The video ended, and the younger sister showed Widow the date of the video. It was dated a year ago. She clicked away from it, showing him that there were no more videos after that.

Widow asked, "What happened to him?"

"No one knows. He never uploaded another video. Not on his *TikTok*. Not on his *YouTube*," the younger sister said.

"Anyone tried contacting him?"

The younger sister said, "Oh, sure. I texted him and even called him."

"And?" Widow asked.

"Nothing. No voicemail. No response. The number's disconnected," the younger sister said.

Widow sensed there was more between her and Alex than just friendship. Maybe there had been a spark, a connection that never got pursued. And now it never would.

They spoke no more about it. Despite their warnings, Widow wanted to part from them and head south. Although he liked each of them, they were young and were talking about urban legends and hearsay. For all they knew, this Alex guy may have just decided to quit making videos. Maybe he was living his life, happy somewhere, doing something else. Or maybe he got caught, and was behind bars somewhere. Maybe his lawyers told him not to post on social media anymore. That could be it. Maybe he was awaiting trial on charges of train-hopping, or whatever the charges are called for that, and his attorney told him not to post anymore because the prosecution could use it against him. It could also be that he entered a plea deal and got probation, and part of the deal was that he couldn't use any social media for a period of five years. Judges are given a wide range of latitude when it comes to sentencing and plea deals.

The sisters told Widow to take the MNA Route 85 outside of St. Louis, headed south to Newport, Arkansas. The young sailor warned Widow to make sure he got off before the railyard in Springfield. He said, "They check hard there. Then you'll have to traverse around it and board another train on the other side."

The younger sister said, "Make sure you get on the right train."

The older sister said, "You should be back on the 85. From Springfield, it heads to Newport. Get on that one and ride it through Branson. Stay on the main tracks. If the train you take veers east, it's the wrong one. Get off and go back."

Widow asked, "Is that Route 67?"

"Yes," the older sister said.

The younger sister said, "Route 67 forks off from it. It's unmarked. If you see a sign for a small town called Iron Crossing, then for sure you're on the wrong line. The Route 67 line runs through it."

With that, Widow said goodbye to them. They wished him luck, and he crossed the rest of St. Louis and climbed a train and rode into the evening, as the train's speed continued changing. It went fast in rural areas and slow in the more populated ones. Around Springfield, Widow nearly got caught by the railway police. He evaded them and hopped on a new train. It was a livestock train filled with various farm animals, mostly cattle. On the way to Branson, the train stopped in the middle of nowhere, but right at a fork in the tracks. It sounded like what the young sailor and the sisters had warned him about. He saw a mileage sign for Iron Crossing on a road that crossed the tracks but couldn't see the distance because the sign was angled a little off true.

The operators must've been onto him because they checked the entire train. They went from car to car, like they were searching for hoppers. Widow couldn't fit under the cars, not the way the young sailor had told him to. So he hopped off the train just before being discovered, and fled. He ended up following the darkened set of tracks that must've been Route 67. *So much for heeding the warning.* But the escape worked because the operators never saw him. They didn't follow him.

After he was well on his way, he saw the livestock train again. It barreled down the tracks, like the operators were behind schedule. Or maybe the operators didn't want to stop in the middle of Route 67, like they were also afraid of rumors of The Ghost Line.

The train picked up speed. It traveled much faster than it had when he was riding it. It was impossible to hop back on. So, Widow hid off the tracks in a forested area until the train vanished down Route 67. He stood on the tracks, in the middle of nowhere, with two directions he could go. It was probably smarter to go back the way he came, and try to board another train back on Route 85. But Widow hated going back. Plus, he was curious about Route 67 and this place called Iron Crossing. Still, he stood on the tracks and thought about it. He realized that curiosity killed the cat. And if the rumors were true, then curiosity also may have killed Alex, the TrackHopper TikToker.

At midnight, Widow faced Route 67, and walked in the direction of Iron Crossing, not knowing how far he had to go. It could be a few miles, or twenty miles. But he mentally prepared himself to walk all night.

Shagbark hickory trees overgrew the tracks, creating an eerie effect that made the line appear to vanish into a long dark tunnel of trees.

The one thing that the sisters were wrong about was the signage. There was one sign marking Route 67, only it didn't say Route 67 directly. It read: *Warning! This line closed indefinitely!* Which was weird, because he just got off a train heading down it. The sign was old. Maybe the information was outdated. Now Widow was more curious than before. He had questions. Maybe he'd find answers. Maybe not. Either way, he was going down Route 67, down The Ghost Line.

CHAPTER 3

I t was a good thing Widow was ready to walk all night, because that's what he did. He followed Route 67's tracks through the night and into the early morning hours, that space of time between late-nighters calling it quits and early risers getting started. Widow shadowed Route 67 under heavy tree cover and dark clouds. At one point he heard rushing water. It was distant, but loud enough to be heard from far away. Besides the streaming water, animal sounds filled the night, followed by early rising birds.

The tracks cut through the thick Missouri woods like an old scar that never healed, winding their way through dense forests. Oak and hickory trees surrounded Widow at every bend in the tracks. His heavy boots crunched the gravel laid beside Route 67's rusting rails, each step merging with the sounds of dawn creeping over the Ozarks. Widow moved forward steadily, his eyes scanning the shadows cast by the towering trees that arched overhead, forming a canopy dense enough to block out most of the emerging morning light. It reminded him of that line from the Battle of Thermopylae: A Persian boasted that their archers were so numerous their arrows would blot out the sun, and upon hearing of this, the Spartan replied, "Then we will fight in the shade."

The surrounding forest was so dense in places, Widow couldn't even tell that sunrays had crept over the horizon, not until he cleared the thickest parts of tree cover.

Along the way, about forty-five minutes back, Widow had crossed through a dark tunnel under an old highway—a four-lane strip, busy with long-haul trucks. The tunnel reverberated with each truck that blasted overhead. The sound echoed through the tunnel, bringing Widow back to the many times his mother took him fishing under a bridge. It was nearly the same resonating sound, like hundreds of wild horses galloping. Widow crossed through the tunnel and stepped back into the trees, the world gone quiet once again.

In the morning's pre-dawn glow, Widow passed remnants of old rail crossings, derelict signals, and broken posts overgrown by kudzu and wildflowers. If not for the occasional livestock train barreling through the territory, nature would've reclaimed the line long ago. Route 67 appeared to be a route rarely used, but that was all he could deduce. As for missing trainhoppers like Alex, Widow needed more information. So far, he'd seen no evidence of anything nefarious. There were no strange occurrences, no danger. No bandits waiting around the corner to rob a train, like there might've been 150 years ago. No one sprang out at him. There was nothing but the silent darkness of the forest.

Widow pressed on. Eventually, the woods thinned as the tracks veered southeast. He heard sounds just over a hill. As he got closer, the distant clamor of truck engines and muffled voices overshadowed the Ozark forest sounds. He stopped and listened. It sounded like some kind of rally was getting started, just over the horizon.

Widow kept walking. The ground tilted up. He crested a hill, and came out to a morning view he wasn't expecting. In front of him, about a hundred meters away, a busy railyard sprawled out across an open field. Route 67's tracks ran right into the railyard, and they didn't run back out. This was the end of the line. If Alex, and the supposedly missing others, had come this way, then this was where their line had ended too. However, there was no sense jumping to conclusions. As it stood, all of it was a big question mark. Widow had his doubts about the sisters' story. After all, they were strangers to him. What they told him was probably just a rumor. But what was the harm in looking into it?

A long service drive circled the front of the railyard, with a road leading out. Maybe it connected back to the highway where Widow had crossed through the tunnel. A huge metal sign chained between two rusty poles read: *Black River Rail & Stockyard*, and under the name, *A Brock Industries Company*.

Big open fields stretched out from the tracks. The fields were covered with trucks and trailers, each larger than the last, all parked in neat, calculated rows. The whole scene was bustling, and yet felt ominous somehow. The air was thick with the smell of diesel and animal smells, like the inside of a horse stable. Farmers and truckers gathered in large groups, shuffling in boots worn from age. They were preparing for something, but what?

The air was filled with early morning excitement, the kind of charge that only ranchers, farmers, livestock traders, and field hands knew intimately. But there were also truckers and rail-road workers. *What the hell's going on?* Widow wondered.

Widow decided to recon, and hung back in the shadows of the trees, watching as rail workers unloaded crates and animals from the same train that he'd ridden in on. They opened up the large, vented shipping containers and herded farm animals down ramps in clouds of dust that hung in the early morning light. The sun had barely risen, but the railyard was already alive. Men worked hard and quietly, like an active beehive. They moved in a fast, steady rhythm, like this was what they were born to do.

Widow wanted a closer look, so he stepped off the tracks. He moved to the forest's edge and watched. Immediately, he noticed the men ranged in size from big guys to bigger guys. Their lives were filled with backbreaking work, which required a certain kind of man. And these were all hard men.

Widow saw no guards, no one carrying weapons or walking the perimeter. No sentries. He figured he could just walk right out of the tree line and join the crowd, and no one would be the wiser. So that's what he did. He stepped out of the trees and hiked the length of the field and walked into the fray.

As he entered the outer perimeter of men, Widow started to piece together the differences in all of them, based on their clothes, hygiene, and trucks. Clearly, there was a hierarchy among them, a class system—ranchers at the top and workers at the bottom. Ranchers stood out because they wore expensive boots, cowboy hats, and sunglasses—in some cases the sunglasses were pushed back on their hats. They wore clean, ironed clothes and fancy watches. Some of them leaned against the grilles of their hundred-thousand-dollar trucks. Livestock traders were the next rung down. They generally hung around the ranchers, ostensibly conversing about life, but really feeling out their competition. The second-to-last rung was the farmers. They ranged from the newly rich to the struggling-farm types. The struggling-farm type stuck out because they were helping the workers, the lowest rung on the hierarchy ladder. Whereas the newly rich supervised, the workers—rail hands, farm hands, and animal wranglers—were the bottom of the ladder. Most of them were grizzled, tough-looking men. Dirt covered their faces. Many of them were hard at work setting up for something.

Widow passed a long line of parked trucks and ranchers and livestock traders. They gathered in knots, leaning against their vehicles and talking in low voices. Widow threaded through them, but not inconspicuously. Nearly everyone stared at him. He didn't exactly fit in with the rich and elite. He was dirty, and his clothes were in bad shape. And their stares made him feel it too. They stared at him like he was beneath them. A few of the wealthier ones snickered at him, like he had stumbled through their golf course and country club.

Widow didn't stick around to make a big deal about it. You have to pick your battles. And challenging the opinions of some old rich snobs wasn't a battle worth fighting. He opted to move on and find men he could relate to better. Maybe he could talk to one and get some answers about what was going on.

As he threaded through the crowds, the parked trucks, and the various pieces of heavy equipment, Widow saw the train he'd been tracking. It moved slowly, like the operators were moving it closer to the fields, adjusting its position. It came to a halt, creaking and groaning. Doors banged open, and wranglers climbed up and herded more cattle out. The animals shuffled out, blinking in the harsh morning light like they'd been crammed into their train cars for long periods of time.

Widow moved forward, slipping into the edge of where the workers were. He took it all in—the ranchers, farmers, ranch hands, and the cattle—the whole setup. It was a very foreign experience for him. In a way, it reminded him of gathering with his platoon at the crack of dawn, to be briefed by a higher-up about the deadly operation they were about to conduct.

A big man brushed past Widow. It was one of the wranglers. He paused a long beat and studied Widow's clothes. He stared at Widow with suspicion in his eyes. Widow nodded at him. The big man nodded back, with no smile, and carried on.

Widow continued, taking everything in, trying to piece it together. He moved slowly, but not too slowly—just enough to seem casual, like he belonged there. His hands stayed by his sides and his eyes scanned everything he could. Even the lower-tier men looked at him at least once. Although he matched them in ruggedness, they all wore country-western-style clothes. And he didn't. Most of the lower-tier men were craggy and unassuming, dressed in worn, mud-streaked boots, frayed flannel shirts, and old cowboy hats, whereas Widow wore a gas station t-shirt and jeans. They looked like the low tier at this event, but he looked like a guy that even they would avoid.

Widow tried not to linger in one spot for too long and moved inward, back to the train tracks and closer to the livestock train. He walked the length of it, glancing at the car he had ridden in. Then he followed a long, thick line of wranglers and herding dogs as they led animals away from the train. They led them to a large area with various-sized steel pens, just north of the main crowd of ranchers, livestock traders, and farmers.

As Widow neared the main pens, a big wrangler with a cattle prod walked by, glancing at him. Widow nodded like he had to the previous big guy, and this time he put a friendly smile on it. He tried his best to appear like he was one of them, like he belonged there. The big wrangler with the cattle prod stared at him longer than any of the others had, but the man moved on, satisfied that Widow was just another worker—dressed out of the ordinary, but still one of them. At least, he seemed satisfied for now.

At around seven in the morning, a couple of men set up and adjusted a podium on stage. One of them called out to the wrangler teams to arrange the livestock into lines for the buyers to inspect. Widow stayed on the periphery, slipping into a group of farmers clustered at the back. They were grumbling about the cost of feed and the condition of the agricultural economy. Widow stayed quiet and listened, then moved on, making his way through the crowd and maneuvering through different clusters of men. Finally he reached the large stage. A small group of men who blended in with the ranchers more than the workers stepped up onto the stage. One of them picked up a microphone, his voice booming through large speakers positioned at the edges of the stage. He did a quick mic check, then called for the first round of bidding to begin. Widow realized what this was—a livestock auction. These men were all here to bid on animals: cattle, horses, goats, and more.

There was nothing nefarious about it. It was just not something Widow had ever witnessed firsthand. The auction began, and it became rather chaotic with the bidders arguing among themselves at one point. The auctioneers had to ask them to keep order.

After the first block of bidding, a guy on the struggling-farm tier approached Widow and struck up a conversation. The guy wore overalls and a green trucker hat. He was clean but ragged at the same time. He looked Widow up and down, and said, "Friend, I do believe you're lost. 'Cause you definitely don't belong here."

"How do you mean?" Widow asked.

"I've been to hundreds of these auctions, and I know who's supposed to be here and who's not. And you're not."

"Maybe I'm new to it."

Responding in a friendly way, the farmer said, "Whatever, man. Don't worry, I'm not gonna rat you out. But you better not get caught."

"Why? What happens if I get caught?"

"If the switchmen see you, you'll get more than you bargained for. They don't like intruders."

"What will they do?"

"They'll escort you out. And they've been known to be rough with trespassers. Real rough."

Widow shrugged, unbothered by the threat. He asked, "What's a switchman?"

The farmer looked over Widow's shoulder, like he was making sure no one was listening. The auctioneer announced a new lot of cattle. His voice boomed over the speakers. The farmer said, "That's just what they're called. Something to do with old switch turns—where train routes intersect, like a crossroads. They're the big guys walking around here. They work for the Brocks. And you don't want to mess with them. If you see a big ugly son-of-a-bitch carrying a cattle prod, you better go the other way."

Widow stayed quiet. With that, the farmer tipped his trucker hat to Widow, and left him standing alone.

Widow stayed where he was and watched more of the auction. Eventually he got bored with the whole thing and walked away, pushing through the crowd of bidders, merging with the wranglers and railroad workers on the sidelines.

Widow came to the end of the crowds of people. He stared opposite way of the crowd. They watched the auction, which was the natural thing to do. But Widow studied the complex. He counted the structures. Black River Rail was a large compound surrounded by the open fields. In the distance, he saw a group of low buildings—mostly brick, mostly quiet. Next to them, there was a field of old, out-of-commission train cars, like a graveyard of trains. It looked like a maze to navigate through.

The weird thing was that beyond that, there was a hill with some kind of underground structure. Widow had been on a lot of bases in his military career, including missile silos and underground installations, so he could see there was something built into the ground under this hill. It was probably some kind of bunker. It was no bomb shelter. It was too big. It must serve some other purpose.

It looked odd, because it was nowhere near the tracks. It wasn't near the roads either. Except for a service drive leading up to it, it was disconnected from everything else, like an afterthought, an addition. The hill was off on its own. It was newer than the rest of the compound. The structure was more than just whatever was underground. Around the hill, there was a security fence with barbwire on top. Metal signs were wired to the fence in twenty-five-foot increments. Widow was too far away to read them, but he got the gist of what they said because he'd seen similar signs many times before. They were warning signs—*DO NOT ENTER, NO TRESPASSING, STAY OUT*, or some other variation. There was a reinforced, locked gate, which was probably the only way to enter. The hill, and the possible bunker complex, looked more like a place to keep military secrets than something to do with livestock or trains.

Those weren't the only anomalies. On the top of the hill, Widow saw a low building that resembled a naval radar station. The building was all concrete. A cluster of satellite dishes sat on top. Two of them were large and a third was huge. He couldn't see them from where he stood, but he imagined thick cables running down the building from the satellite dishes to their power source and, probably, to large servers inside the station. The setup looked quite expensive. It looked like the operators could send signals to Mars from there.

A truck's exhaust blew loudly behind Widow. It sounded like a shotgun and drew his attention away from the hill. He turned back to the main buildings and spotted more trucks—heavy-duty big rigs lined up in a row, with trailers hitched and ready for long hauls. Widow clocked their logos—all farming companies and major food conglomerates, some he'd heard of and some he hadn't. Everything seemed legit, except for the radar station and the fenced-off hill. Otherwise, nothing about Black River Rail signaled to him that Alex Hopper, or the supposed others who'd vanished, were snatched up by mysterious phantoms.

Just then, Widow got a tap on his shoulder. He spun around and came face-to-face with the same big wrangler he'd passed earlier. This time, the guy wasn't alone. Three other guys stood behind him. Each as big as the next. And they all had angry expressions on their faces and cattle prods in their hands. They held them like weapons. They stood in a classic pyramid formation.

In a gravelly, demanding voice, the one who bumped into Widow said, "Sir, this is private property. I don't think you're supposed to be here. You got a pass? Show it to me!"

Widow stayed quiet, hands at ease by his sides. He stared at the one who had tapped his shoulder. He realized that everyone there who wasn't employed by Black River Rail must've been issued passes, like they'd paid a fee to be there. Now he understood. That's what the farmer had warned him about. These were the so-called switchmen.

Impatiently, the big guy barked, "Right now!"

Widow asked, "What're you guys supposed to be? The local bouncers?"

"He asked for your pass." one of the switchmen added from the back. He did it with a quick zap from his cattle prod, like an overdramatic threat: *Comply, or get zapped!*

Widow nearly rolled his eyes at the gesture, but he didn't want to piss them off any more than they already were. He glanced at each of them individually, just a quick flick of his eyes. Like a deadly robot from the future, his eyes scrolled over each of the three rear switchmen until they landed back on the one in front of him. The cattle prods were fat, black, wicked-looking things with metal prongs on the end. They were heavy and thick. They were designed to double as clubbing weapons. Widow figured they weren't just for controlling herds of cattle, but also meant for crowd control, although he couldn't figure out where they'd be applicable. *A prison in some third-world country, maybe?*

Widow searched his pockets—making a big show of it, like the pass was actually on him. He took his sweet time doing it too, acting befuddled that he couldn't find it. Really he was just buying more time to figure out his next play. But he couldn't put on the show forever. So eventually, his hands came out of his pockets with no results. He said, "Sorry, guys. I must've left it in my other pants."

The first switchman asked, "Where's your post?" Widow stared back at the guy, a questioning look on his face.

"What brand are you with? Show us. The head of your brand can vouch for you."

Widow paused a beat, glanced behind him, back at the auction. The cattle auctioneer's voice blared over the speakers —fast-paced, rhythmic, and persuasive. He announced the next bid, "Folks, folks, we got a fine steer up next. Take a look at this one. The whole herd is like this—strong back, good legs, look at that coat! Remember, you can get the one, or the lot! Who'll start me off? We're at a thousand to open, lookin' for twelve-fifty, twelve-fifty, do I hear it? Yes, got twelve-fifty in the back—now fifteen, now fifteen—got it, now seventeen-fifty. Folks, she's got a prime bloodline, don't miss out! Eighteen hundred, got it! Now nineteen, nineteen, who'll make it nineteen? Anyone?

"There we go, nineteen to the Whiskey River Ranch! Now two thousand, do I hear two? Look at her stance, built like a tank! Two thousand, got it right here! Now twenty-two hundred, twenty-two—got it, now twenty-four, twenty-four, who's got twenty-four? Yes sir, I see twenty-four hundred from Buffalo Gap Ranch! Don't slow down now, she's worth every cent!"

Widow saw the bidders. They had signs with numbers on them. He glanced at the crowd and saw that the bidder's numbers coincided with numbers on signs posted on poles at different stalls. The numbers must've referred to the group standing in the area around the stall. The ranchers went by their ranch name, which matched the number of their stall.

Suddenly, the first switchman jabbed the cattle prod into Widow's chest. The prongs poked into him. The switchman could flip the switch on the cattle prod, shocking Widow right there. He didn't know how many volts were in the thing, but he bet it was a lot. What's the point of having a crowd control tool that had low voltage? The switchman said, "Hey! I'm asking you a question! Identify your brand, or we'll have to take action."

Widow stared into the guy's eyes, tried to stay calm. He said, "What action are you going to take?" But he didn't let the guy answer. Before Widow finished the sentence, he exploded at the waist and rotated violently to the left, like a pitcher throwing a runner out at first base. He grabbed the cattle prod halfway through his rotation and ripped it from the switchman's hand. Before the guy could react, Widow stepped into him, grabbed him by the collar of his flannel shirt, bunched it up tight in his giant fist and pulled it, choking the guy. Then Widow reversed the cattle prod and shoved the prod's electric end into the guy's neck, up under his chin, hard. Widow dragged the guy closer to him. stared into the guy's eyes, and said, "Threaten me again, and I'll shock you with this thing till the charge runs out!"

The guy's eyes went from blindly believing he was invincible to fearing for his life.

The other three switchmen stood there dumbfounded. They were taken by surprise and slow to react. They would've failed BUD/S, Basic Underwater Demolition/SEAL, the rigorous training program Widow and every other Navy SEAL candidate had to endure just to qualify for the job. It's one of the most demanding physical and mental experiences on the planet. These three wouldn't have made it past Hell Week. Actually, Widow doubted any of them would've made it past finding the Navy's website online just to read about the whole process.

The other three finally woke up and stepped in closer, holding their cattle prods out like swords. They circled Widow, but he stopped them at a half-circle, keeping them fanned out in front of him like they were between the ten and the two on a clock face. Widow adjusted his stance to keep the three in front of him while he stayed behind the first switchman, his human shield. They stared at him, perplexed about what to do next. Clearly he'd created a situation that wasn't a part of their standard operating procedure. It probably wasn't in their training, if they even got any.

Widow could've taken them all out with his fists. He knew that. He could tell they knew it too. But he didn't want this to escalate needlessly. After all, technically he was in the wrong. He was trespassing. And they were just doing their jobs. So Widow released the big switchman's collar and shoved him back at the others, hard enough to make the point, but not hard enough to knock him to the ground. The guy stumbled backwards, farther than Widow had predicted. It was probably because of his weight. When a big guy with more blubber than muscle loses his balance, it can be a whole dramatic thing.

The one at the twelve o'clock position caught the guy and kept him from falling over. He pushed him to his feet. The big switchman stepped forward, back in Widow's direction. He brushed himself off and said, "Sir, you just made this a whole lot worse for yourself. You went from trespassing to committing assault."

Widow said, "Lose the tough act. If I wanted to assault you, you wouldn't be talking right now."

"I could call the police," the guy threatened.

"You could, but you won't. I could tell them you assaulted me. You did shove this weapon into my chest," Widow said, and stared at the guy.

After a long pause, Widow tossed it back to the guy. The guy caught it and looked back, blankly.

Widow didn't wait for the four of them to collectively have a thought. Instead he spoke first. He said, "Okay, you caught me. I'm trespassing. Don't get your knickers in a twist. I made a mistake. I took a wrong turn somewhere, saw all these people, and just came to your auction looking for a ride."

Three of the switchmen looked at each other. The one Widow had shoved rubbed his neck for a long moment, like he just got freed from a hangman's noose. He made a big show of it. Once he finally finished, he balled up one fist in anger and clenched the cattle prod tight with the other. Clearly, he wanted retribution, like he was contemplating charging at Widow. In the end, he didn't attack. He did nothing. Which was the smart decision. The switchman said, "You gotta leave. Now!"

"Point me in the right direction, and I will," Widow said.

The switchman grimaced, and ordered one of the others to escort Widow off the property. But then he paused a beat, like he was reassessing. He added, "Two of you better go. Take him to the road and leave him." The switchman turned to Widow, pointed the cattle prod at him, and zapped it once. But then he retracted it, like the memory of how Widow swiped it from him was just now hitting him. He said, "Don't ever come back. Next time, you'll be leaving in the back of a cop car on your way to the hospital."

Widow smirked, but did nothing else. He stayed quiet. The twelve and two o'clock switchmen stepped to him, but stayed out of reach. They were dumb, but not that dumb. They hadn't forgotten what they had seen him do.

The twelve o'clock guy pointed his cattle prod southeast, past the parked livestock train and rows of tractor trucks, whose engines idled, humming out of sync. He said, "Head that way, sir. We'll be right behind you."

Widow kept staring at the main switchman. He could see that fear lingered in the switchman's eyes. Widow broke off eye contact, looked at the twelve and two o'clock switchmen. He said, "You fellas lead the way. I'll follow. I'm not putting my back to you."

The two switchmen glanced at each other, took simultaneous deep breaths, and looked to the main guy. He nodded approval, and they shrugged. The twelve o'clock guy walked first, and then the two o'clock guy. They led the way, and Widow followed.

A minute later, after passing the train and some parked trucks, Widow stepped onto the mouth of the service drive that led to the road. His escorts pointed the way with their cattle prods. The twelve o'clock guy said, "Just head that way, sir."

"And then what?"

"When you get to the road, turn right or left. It makes no difference to us. Just don't come back," the twelve o'clock guy said.

Just then, one of the tractor-trailers they'd passed, with the name Greengate Hauling plastered on the side, pulled out of a stall and backed up into a dead end built for the trucks to reverse and face the exit. The truck eased forward, coming right up to Widow and the two switchmen. The driver stopped and the passenger window buzzed down. The driver leaned forward, like they could see him. But they couldn't. He was too high up. He called out, "Hey, mister, you need a ride?"

The switchmen stared at Widow with resentment in their eyes. Which was a little weird, since Widow was a total stranger. *You guys really don't like strangers,* he thought. But he said nothing to them and kept the observation to himself.

Widow turned to the truck, clutched a grab bar, and climbed onto a step beneath the door. He looked at the driver and said, "I'd be grateful for a ride out of here."

The driver looked familiar. He wore the same type of flannel shirt, jeans, and trucker hat as half the people at the auction, but his face was familiar. He had a gray beard, but brown hair. He smiled a warm, friendly smile and said, "Okay, climb in."

Widow nodded, but came back down. He stepped closer to the switchmen. Both of them flinched back, stepping one foot behind them, like they were preparing to defend themselves for an all-out brawl. Widow asked, "Either of you guys ever heard the name Alex Hopper?" He watched their reactions. There was no sign of recognition to the name.

The switchmen glanced at each other, confused, like they wondered if they were supposed to know the name. But they didn't know it. They both gave Widow a *no*, with no added words.

The truck driver blew his horn once, just a quick honk to signal to Widow he was ready to roll. Widow said nothing to the switchmen. He turned away and left them there. He climbed back up and into the cab of the truck. The driver smiled, and drove up the service drive and turned left, to the south.

It turned out the driver seemed familiar because the man Widow spoke with back at the auction was his older brother. The driver was headed out and had noticed that Widow was tangling with the switchmen.

They drove down the same old four-lane highway that cut through the woods; the one Widow crossed earlier when he followed Route 67. Widow wasn't too sure how it worked that way, but it did. The truck driver asked him about himself, but Widow only wanted to know more about Black River Rail and what the driver knew about it. The driver knew very little, just that the switchmen didn't like outsiders on their turf. Which was understandable. Their main job was to keep order on the premises. The cattle prods and bad attitudes seemed excessive to Widow, but then again, he didn't own a railyard.

At one point, Widow asked if the driver had ever heard of Alex Hopper, which he hadn't. Widow asked him about people taking Route 67 and vanishing. The guy knew nothing of that either.

After about thirty minutes, Widow had learned more of about the town called Iron Crossing. The driver said, "Maybe the people in town will know more about your missing friend?" Alex Hopper wasn't Widow's friend and he was asking the guy about more than one missing person, so he knew the driver wasn't listening, not totally. Widow got very thirsty too. He realized he hadn't had any water in hours, not since he'd left St. Louis. Looking around the cab, he saw no beverages. He asked the driver for water, thinking maybe he had a stash somewhere on board, but the driver had nothing. Widow asked when they might stop for gas, thinking that's where he could buy a bottled water. The driver casually looked at his gauge cluster, and replied, "Don't need gas. I got a full tank."

Widow turned and looked out the window. He saw farmlands and lush woods. He stared for several more minutes, then turned back to gazing out the windshield. There was a crossroads up ahead. A big sign warned of an intersection coming up. The driver slowed the truck, preparing for the stop. Big trucks like his didn't stop on a dime; it took time to brake and come to a full stop. He calculated the probable distance to the intersection from the warning sign, and started the braking process early. He stared through the windshield, looking for the stop sign. But there wasn't one. There was a pole where a stop sign used to be, but the sign was gone.

"This is dangerous," the driver said, like Widow was part of the conversation he'd been having in his head. The driver stopped the truck at a faded white line in the road even though the stop sign was missing and the other road had no vehicles on it, like a good driver would.

Widow noticed the same things the truck driver had. The warning sign, the white lines, the crossroads, and the missing stop signs. He knew why the driver stopped and didn't question it.

At the stop, a trucker who apparently didn't see the crossroads or warning signs blasted through the intersection in the lane right next to Widow's door. The truck flew past, blasting its horn, and shaking the cab's interior. "Whoa! This is a dangerous spot," the driver said.

Widow didn't respond. He looked left, down the rural road that crossed over the highway. He caught a glimpse of a little farm right there off the crossroads. And he saw something of great interest. It looked like two little girls with a lemonade stand. There was a whole setup, including a sign.

Thirst hit Widow like a punch to the gut. The closest way he could describe it was like being hungry without realizing it—until you're around food. The truck driver took his foot off the brake and the vehicle started rolling forward. Widow said, "Hold up," and the driver hit the brake again. "I'm getting out here," Widow said, unbuckled his seatbelt, and opened the passenger door. "Thanks for the ride." Widow got out and closed the door. The truck driver was confused because they hadn't even left the town limits yet. But he shrugged and drove off, leaving Widow standing at the crossroads.

Widow looked both ways. Aware of the missing stop signs, he waited for another speeding tractor-trailer to blast through the intersection. It flew through and the slipstream behind it blew Widow's hair around. He crossed through the intersection and approached the lemonade stand, the girls, and Nora's farm.

CHAPTER 4

The questions that Nora asked the giant stranger were: *So, who are you? What're you doing talking to my girls?* But those weren't the only questions on her mind. Those were the questions she spoke out loud. But there was another, similar question that she also asked—only she asked it with her rifle. With the Marlin 336 in hand and without speaking it, she asked if the giant stranger meant her and her girls any harm. She asked him two questions, and her rifle asked one. She wanted answers to all three.

The giant stranger answered the last question by opening his hands to show his two massive but empty palms. He had no weapons. She could see that. Opening his palms and showing them to strangers who pointed guns at him was something he'd done countless times in the past. It's how he showed that he was unarmed and surrendering. Of course, many of those times it had been a trick. It was a tactic he'd used many times before. In the past, the giant stranger opened his hands to show the enemy in front of him that he was not a threat, which lowered their guard. That's when he would strike. This was a different scenario. He had no intention of stripping the rifle from Nora and turning it against her. If he had wanted to, he would have done it already.

Nora and her daughters stared, and traced the lines on the giant stranger's hands, up to his huge forearms and biceps. The giant stranger's forearms alone were like bowling pins. Nora didn't want to get too close to the man for fear that he could easily rocket her into the next life with a single punch from one of those colossal fists.

Meanwhile, her daughters only wanted to give the man lemonade so they could talk him into adopting some of their puppies. Whereas the family protector and mother of the free puppies, their Cane Corso, Joan of Bark—Joanie for short— sat at the giant stranger's feet, giving him enormous puppy eyes as if she wanted to go home with him.

But the giant stranger had no home. He liked dogs though. If he ever decided to settle down somewhere, he could see himself owning a home and having a couple of big dogs.

The half-naked woman repeated her questions. With a dry, thirsty voice, the giant stranger said, "The name's Widow, ma'am. And I only wanted some lemonade. It's very hot out and I've not had any water or anything else to drink since last night. I apologize. I didn't mean to scare you or your daughters."

Nora didn't introduce herself. But Poppy said, "My name's Poppy. I'm five years old. That's the same age as Joanie." And she glanced at the Cane Corso at Widow's feet. Widow smiled at her and said, "It's nice to make your acquaintance, Poppy." Then he looked at the dog, and said, "Nice to meet you, Joanie."

Joanie barked back at him, like it was the way she said hello. Poppy pointed at her sister, and added, "This is my older sister, Violet."

"Nice to meet you too, Violet," Widow said, "Violet and Poppy. Huh. Aren't those flowers?"

"Our māmā named us after flowers," Violet added.

Poppy said, "She used to arrange flowers, before our dad left."

Nora stepped in and said, "That's enough. Mr. Widow, I think you're better off heading to town. There are plenty of places in town to get a drink. And a job, if that's what you're looking for. We don't have any work here." Nora gestured at the worn sign posted in the grass, which claimed that very thing.

Widow glanced at it and realized she must have taken him for a transient, looking for work on her farm. Then he glanced back at the crossroads. It made sense. She must've gotten plenty of such men passing through, looking for work. Being that they're in the Ozarks, Widow could guess what the majority of those men looked like. They were probably low-educated roughneck types—hard men. Many of them may have been dangerous, too dangerous for her to allow them onto her farm. Especially with two little girls, and no man around.

The problem was if the wrong type of roughneck transients heard that she was all alone on this farm with her two girls, those types of men might get bad ideas. Those types of men might have bad intentions. Especially if this was how she normally dressed around the farm. He thought that part rather unusual, but said nothing about it.

Widow glanced at the lemonade stand, and at the glass pitcher of lemonade. It called to him in the way coffee normally did. This thirst was about the most powerful urge he'd felt in a long time. The day was blisteringly hot and that lemonade looked so refreshing. Against his better judgment, he asked, "Mind if I get just one glass of that lemonade?"

Violet looked at her mother, and asked, "Can we give him some lemonade, Māmā? Then talk him into taking the puppies?"

Nora didn't return her daughter's look. She kept her eyes on Widow.

Poppy glanced at Joanie, who still sat on the ground, wagging her tail and smiling at Widow. She pointed at Joanie, and said, "See Māmā, Joanie likes him."

Widow tried his best to give Nora a look like he was no threat to her. At the same time, he tried not to stare at her because his eyes were drawn to look down from her face. But it was very difficult. Not only was most of her body out on display, an immaculate display at that, but also she held the rifle competently enough to tell him that she knew how to use it. In Widow's experience, whenever someone points a rifle at you, you should keep eyes on that person. Especially this momma bear, who was only protecting her cubs. Right then, she might've been the most dangerous person on the planet.

Widow didn't want to be on the receiving end of that demonstration. A beautiful woman with an amazing body and a scared mother who's deadly with a rifle was the dual reality standing right there in front of him. Impasse. These two realities made it hard for him to do anything but stare at her. Still, he figured his staring at her probably didn't help ease her fears of him.

Nora heard what her daughters were telling her. They were at their lemonade stand, trying to give away free puppies. And this Widow guy came up to the stand, asking for lemonade. It seemed like a reasonable exchange, but she didn't like the look of him. He was a stranger who was undeniably dangerous. Nora had survived out here this long by trusting her gut. She'd protected her girls for a whole year without help from

THE GHOST LINE 59

any man by trusting her gut. And her gut told her this guy was too dangerous to trust.

She couldn't take the chance on being kind. So she raised the rifle, but didn't point it directly at him. She raised it to a thirty-five degree angle, just enough to hit the dirt at his feet if she shot it.

Nora said, "Mr. Widow, I think it's time for you to leave my farm."

Widow slow-nodded, and backed away from Nora's driveway. He didn't want to turn his back on her, not just yet. So, he backpedaled until he was at the road, then asked, "Which way is town?"

Nora pointed the business end of the rifle in the direction of town, and said, "Go down that road. It's faster than taking the highway."

Widow thanked her, and walked away from them.

Joanie barked at him as he went. Not an aggressive bark. It was more like: *Wait! Come back!*

The girls stayed quiet.

CHAPTER 5

Several minutes later and a mile down the road from Nora's farm, Widow walked the right side of the road, with his back to oncoming traffic. Normally he walked against the flow of traffic, for fear of having his back to oncoming vehicles. But this road had very little traffic to worry about. And he thought that if he walked with traffic, maybe a driver would know he was headed the same direction they were going and would give him a ride. So far, no such luck.

There were no sidewalks. If he walked off the road's shoulder, then he risked falling into a ditch. Even though it was hot out, the ditches were filled with what had started as rainwater but now resembled what could only be described as a swampy sludge. Widow really didn't want to be near it. Not only did he not want to slip, step in it, and get it all over his boots, but he could only imagine what lived in it. There could be snakes and snapping turtles.

The morning sun beamed down on the Ozarks with a humid summer heat. It was unavoidable. The saving grace for Widow was the terrain had plenty of tall trees with thick canopies of leaves overhead, which provided him with a lot of shade. He stuck to the shady areas as best he could.

Widow passed several more farms and saw a few vehicles pass him. Some went toward the crossroads, Nora's farm, and Violet and Poppy's lemonade stand. Others went the direction Widow walked, which was supposed to be toward Iron Crossing. No one stopped to offer him a ride.

As Widow passed another farm on the right with bright yellow shutters and a large American flag flying high on a pole, he glanced at a guy on a tractor, who was cutting grass in the field near the road. The guy stopped the tractor and stared at Widow like he was looking at an escaped gorilla roaming through his neighborhood. The look only lasted a moment, and then the guy went back to cutting his grass.

The thought of approaching the guy to see if he could ask for some water crossed Widow's mind. But after the rifle-hospitality Widow had gotten earlier, he realized the locals weren't keen on strangers. He could understand the sentiment. He was intimidating to most people, and this area was rural. Rural homeowners tended to be suspicious of strangers walking through their lands, especially when there wasn't much foot traffic to begin with. Hulking men such as Widow walking stuck out in a place like this.

Just then, over a hill and down the road, Widow heard a loud bass noise. It was a sound normally heard in neighborhoods in major cities every day, all across America. It wasn't something he expected to hear out here.

The noise grew louder and the bass got stronger, as if the sound were mobile and headed in Widow's direction. The bass thumped and echoed off the houses and trees.

The source of the sound came into view. A supercharged, lifted truck appeared from the other direction. Black paint and chrome everything shined and glimmered in the sunlight. The Ford name was embedded in a black grille on the front in huge letters. A rack of lights lined the roof of the truck. It was a Ford Raptor on huge tires. The windows were all tinted a dark black. The door windows were all buzzed down and smoke drifted out. Music thumped from the truck's interior.

The Raptor barreled toward him. Widow watched it. The only thing he saw of the driver was a sleeve-tattooed arm that hung out the window. The other windows had similar-looking arms hanging out. The music blasted and the truck came on fast. Widow sidestepped onto the dirt, just before the drop-off into a ditch. He stood on the opposite side of the road, opposite lane. He felt it wise to give these local boys a wide berth. He didn't want to catch their attention. The big arms, loud music, speeding down a residential road, and the flashy $200,000 truck all warned him not to engage with these guys.

The guy on the lawnmower stopped and watched, like he too was concerned about these boys.

The Raptor raced past Widow as he'd hoped. He breathed deeply and got back to walking. The truck's loud music thumped away for a minute. But then it grew louder again, like the truck was coming up on Widow's rear. He stopped and glanced back. He was right. The Raptor had U-turned and was heading back toward him. Only this time, the truck drove the speed limit. Widow glanced at the guy on the lawn-mower, who was watching the truck too. He made eye contact with Widow. Then he did something weird. He shut off the mower, halfway through his cutting job. He hopped off it and left the mower in the middle of the field. He didn't run, but he high-stepped it back to his front porch. A woman, who Widow guessed was the man's wife, came out their front door and said something that was inaudible to Widow. The husband pointed to the truck and then to Widow. He ushered the woman back into their house and followed behind her. Widow couldn't hear it, but he assumed they deadbolted the door behind them.

Someone in the house moved to a large front picture window, eyes on Widow and the truck, like they knew something was about to go down. They wanted to witness it but wanted no part of it. The curtains flapped slightly, just enough to show they were watching, waiting for a show to begin.

Widow turned and faced the oncoming truck. He stepped off the road again and back onto the grass. He waited. He had no idea what they intended to do. But he got a feeling in the pit of his stomach that they were going to do something to antagonize him.

The Raptor slowed as it approached him. The music thumped. The truck slowed to a crawl just yards from Widow. There were four guys inside the truck. At least three of them looked like big, strong, steroid-enhanced boys. Widow couldn't see the fourth one.

The truck eased forward. The music quieted to a low thump from the bass. A marijuana smell filled the air around the truck, like someone had exploded a smoke grenade inside the vehicle. Widow heard mumbling, like they were arguing over what to do. One of them asked, "What's the plan, Junior?" But those were the only words Widow could make out. The rest were murmurs and mutters. All with some kind of thick Missouri accent, only with broken words and backwoods IQs.

Widow stayed quiet and waited, thinking these clowns were about to jump out and mess with him somehow. Maybe they were drunk, high, and hated outsiders. Widow knew the type. He'd had his fair share of dealings with guys like these.

Instead of jumping out and starting something with him, they cranked the music up again. The bass thumped as loud as before. And the truck's engine revved up. The driver kept the brake and gas pedal engaged at the same time. The back tires smoked under the action. Then he released the brake and the Raptor tore off back the way it had come. Widow turned and watched the truck vanish over the same hill from earlier. He waited. The music thumped on. He guessed they were gone. He glanced at the lawnmower guy's house, expecting them to stop watching because the show was over. But they didn't.

Whatever, Widow thought. He returned to the road and continued toward Iron Crossing, toward the direction the Raptor had gone. Suddenly, the music thumped louder again, and the truck bounced up over the hill. It sped toward Widow. He sidestepped back onto the grass. He half-expected these boys to slam on the brakes in his lane this time and hop out with whatever their plan was. But they didn't. The Raptor stayed in the other lane, driving fast, until it got close to him. Then the truck slowed. The occupants yelled profanities at Widow, but they didn't stop. He watched them as they passed him by.

Widow kept facing the direction of Iron Crossing. But they weren't done with him. The truck U-turned and made another pass and this time one of the boys leaned out the window and threw a beer bottle at Widow.

The bottle smashed against Widow's upper back. It hit right between his shoulder blades, then bounced to the road. The bottle shattered into pieces, dousing his boots with beer.

Widow turned and watched the Raptor speed away. He could hear the boys laughing, filling the truck with inebriated cackling.

If there was a meter that measured Widow's anger on a scale of one to ten, this immature event only raised it to a two. He wasn't hurt. It was rude more than anything else. But the thing that stuck in Widow's mind wasn't that those clowns taunted him and threw a beer bottle at him; what bothered him was the direction they were headed. These clowns were heading towards the crossroads, towards the lemonade stand, towards that woman and her two little girls.

CHAPTER 6

Nora was still wearing the black string bikini, but that would come off once she was working. At least she hoped so. And not because she was proud of her side job, or that she liked it. She hoped she'd end up naked in front of her webcam. Most days when she livestreamed, she just sat around in her bikini, underwear, or lingerie, because normally she only had a couple of guys logged into her stream. If they wanted to see her naked, they had to pay for a private session. That was when she made the most money, which was good because of her situation, with two girls to feed and a farm to keep afloat. It was about ten months ago that she had gotten so desperate she decided to get a job. That was two months after her husband vanished.

At first, she applied for local jobs. But there wasn't much around Iron Crossing. Most jobs were already filled by locals who'd worked them for years. The jobs that became available were often temporary jobs. She did get an interview at a local diner for a waitress job, even got hired on the spot. That was because the manager took one look at her and hired her based on how attractive she was. She knew that because he ogled her during the whole interview. Plus, he kept licking his lips and staring at her, like he was a starving cannibal stranded on a desert island and she was the only person around.

That job didn't last long. She worked two shifts on a weekend. One was training. And the next she got a two-table section. But she dropped an entire tray of drinks on a table of regulars. The manager fired her on the spot so he'd look big and tough. Working around Iron Crossing was out.

She could grow enough food and harvest enough eggs from her chickens to feed her girls, but chickens and vegetables all require money to maintain. Plus, little girls aren't good with only having a limited diet. They want cereal in the morning and snacks throughout the day. On top of all that, Violet was supposed to start her first year of school in a couple of weeks. Nora still had to get school supplies and work out all the logistics.

She had tried to take advantage of welfare programs, like food cards to at least buy groceries. But Missouri's red tape made it very difficult. They considered her husband's income even though he was no longer around. The lady on the phone at the Missouri Department of Social Services told her they needed proof that he ran off or that he was dead before they could issue her food assistance. Nora hung up on her, frustrated, and sad because she didn't want to think about her husband maybe being dead.

One day, she thought about the one thing they did have out in her area that was good. That was the internet. Ever since Nora hit fourteen, boys had lusted after her. When she became a woman, those boys had turned into men. And it never stopped. Every day of her life, they looked at her like she was a piece of meat. It was just the way it was. She didn't complain about it. But she also never embraced it. She didn't want to use her looks or her sexuality to make money. Never in a million years did she think she would make money this way. But when her husband vanished—taking his income with him and leaving her to fend for their daughters and keep the farm afloat—what choice did she have?

Nora was already late to the livestream she had announced would happen today. Before she could do any of that she had to make sure her daughters were safe. So she went back to the house, keeping the rifle with her, and got the walkie-talkie that Violet and Poppy were supposed to keep with them. Joanie followed her to the house, and then back down to the girls.

Nora gave them the walkie and told them to radio her if that man came back. She also told them to radio her if any strangers came around. Violet argued back that the Widow-guy seemed genuinely interested in their puppies. Nora gave her a look, and Violet replied with a *Yes, Māmā.*

Nora returned to the house, glancing at the goats playing in their pen. Even they stopped to stare at her, like they judged her life decisions. She muttered to them, "What're you staring at?"

Joanie stayed with the girls and the box of puppies.

CHAPTER 7

Violet and Poppy brainstormed about changing their business tactics because nobody was showing up for either free lemonade or free puppies. Poppy held one of the puppies in her hands. The little thing wobbled around like today was its first day on earth. She said, "I bet that Mr. Widow would've taken them all."

"Yeah, maybe," Violet said.

"Why do you think Māmā scared him off?"

"Maybe because he was a stranger? We're not supposed to talk to strangers."

Poppy said, "He was a tall boy." The puppy licked her face and she giggled.

Violet said, "Mr. Widow's not a boy. He's a man."

"What's the difference?" Poppy asked, scrunching her face up to avoid the licks from the puppy. Joanie came close to her and sniffed the puppy. Then she grabbed it by the scruff, lifted it, and transported it back to the box with the others.

She stared into the box like she was head-counting to make sure they were all there.

Violet first gave her sister a look, like she was saying: *How do you not know what the difference is between a man and a boy?* But then she changed her expression to one of confusion. She cocked her head up and stared at the sky. Suddenly, she realized that she didn't understand the difference either. Not entirely. So she said, "That's an adult question. It's better if Māmā explains it."

Before Poppy could respond, they both heard bass thumping in the distance. They looked down the country road, but saw nothing.

Suddenly, another eighteen-wheeler tore through the crossroads on the highway from the opposite direction. They turned their heads in shock. The semi drowned out the thumping bass for a long moment. The girls went back to chatting. But then, Joanie's ears and tail perked up. She rushed around the lemonade stand and put herself between the girls and the country road, then sniffed the air.

Poppy said, "What's she doing?"

"I don't know," Violet responded.

This time, Joanie had heard the sound before they did. And a moment later, they heard it too. Heavy bass thumped from down the country road, and this time they could hear loud music. The music blasted from a big, scary truck. The truck hopped the hill.

Joanie barked, violently, like her protection system had activated suddenly, whereas it hadn't with that Widow-guy. Joanie barked deeply and ferociously at the oncoming truck, like she knew the occupants were no good.

It was the Raptor with the guys who had harassed Widow. Of course, Violet and Poppy didn't know that. But what they did know was their māmā had warned them about the guys in the truck. Nora pointed out the truck every time they saw it in town. She told them never to talk to those guys. This was the first time the girls had seen them outside of town.

The Raptor tore up the road and skidded to a stop out in front of their farm driveway, nearly missing it altogether and bursting through the crossroads. Violet reached for the walkie to call their māmā, but just then another eighteen-wheeler rushed through the crossroads, kicking up the usual dust cloud and thunderous road sound. It startled the girls and Joanie, who barked even louder. All things converged in such a way that Violet froze for a moment.

Then, just as she reached for the walkie again, the occupants of the Raptor jumped out of the truck. Four guys came out, including the driver. They left the truck so that it blocked anyone from entering or exiting the Sutton Farm driveway. In police training, it's called tactical parking.

All four men left their doors open as they hopped out of the truck. The driver had left the music on and the volume down, but the bass remained up. It thumped, vibrating the Raptor's exterior shell.

Three of the men were huge in muscle and bulk. To Violet and Poppy, they were larger than life; it was like walking onto an NFL practice field and seeing the players. They weren't as big as Mr. Widow, but there were more of them.

The fourth guy wasn't big at all. He stood at least a foot shorter than the shortest of the others, but he walked like a boss. He immediately pushed his way out in front of the others and barked orders at them.

All four men wore expensive sunglasses and expensive clothing. They had sleeve tattoos. One of them had face tattoos, as did the shortest guy. The girls recognized him. They'd seen him in town. They'd heard his name mentioned between their father and mother, back when their father was still around, only Poppy was too young to remember it, but Violet did. The short one's name was Collin Brock, Jr., but people around him called him *Junior* because his father was better-respected.

Joanie growled at the men. She could've charged them, but she didn't. She stood her ground between them and her girls and the puppies. She barked a warning.

The three larger men fanned out across the mouth of the driveway, like Secret Service agents might while guarding an important protectee. Two of them kept their eyes forward on the dog, the girls, and Junior. One of them stood outer perimeter and watched the crossroads, which was the most likely place danger might come from, outside of the farm. They weren't worried about the country road because they had just driven it, and it was used less than the highway.

Junior approached the girls. Gravel crunched under his shoes. Joanie growled. Two of the guards stood by. One of them rested his hand on a gun tucked into the waistband of his jeans. The others were also carrying guns. However, they kept theirs concealed.

Joanie barked viciously at Junior, as he was the closest to her and the girls.

Junior stopped walking, staying several feet away from Joanie. He slid his sunglasses off, folded them closed, and stuffed them into the pocket of his shirt. He looked over the girls, the stand, and the sign the girls had posted. He read it aloud, "Free Lemonade."

Junior licked his lips. Joanie growled continuously. Junior said, "This is a hot damn day, girls. I sure could use some lemonade." He glanced around at his boys and asked, "What about you boys? You want some lemonade?"

They boys each grunted a yes. But added nothing on top of it, like they knew when to say more and when to shut up.

Poppy said, "The lemonade is for customers only!"

Violet squeezed her sister's hand, quieting her.

Junior asked, "Customers? That's what I am. I'm here asking for some lemonade."

Ignoring the hand squeeze, Poppy said, "Customers who want to take our puppies."

Junior glanced behind them to the box full of puppies. His eyes lit up. He asked, "Puppies?" And he slow-nodded, like now he understood. He said, "So, the lemonade is to get people to stop by? But really you girls are giving away puppies?" He chuckled, and added, "Oh, that's a clever sales tactic. Which one of you came up with that?"

The girls stayed quiet. Junior stepped closer. Joanie snapped at him, but stayed back. She glanced at the other men, like she didn't want to attack Junior for fear of the other men getting past her to her girls.

"Let me tell you something, girls," Junior said, "If this dog attacks me, my boy here will shoot it." Junior glanced at the guy with the gun showing in his waistband.

The guy nodded, stared at the girls, and tapped the grip of the handgun in his waistband. The girls stared at him. Neither of them knew the make and model of the gun, but Violet knew enough to know it had a magazine and wasn't what her māmā called a *revolver*.

Poppy started to speak, but Violet squeezed her hand hard. Poppy knew her sister's signals. This time Poppy kept her mouth shut. Violet called to Joanie to stand down. Joanie growled at Junior again, but stayed put.

Violet reached for the walkie, slowly. She grabbed it and clicked the talk button. Junior saw her, and said, "What're you doing, little girl?" The guard with the gun stepped closer to the girls. Joanie jumped to her feet. The hairs on her back stood straight up. She twisted away from Junior and barked violently at the guard. He froze, grabbed his gun, and jerked it out of his waistband. He aimed it at Joanie but didn't shoot. He glanced at Junior for permission.

Violet held the talk button down, raised it to her lips, and started to call her māmā. Junior snapped, "PUT THAT DOWN!" at Violet. And she froze, walkie to her lips.

Junior had overstepped, and he knew it. He exhaled a breath to lower his temper, and said, "Put that down and my boy will put his gun away. Deal, little girl?"

Violet stared at him, unsure of what to do. Joanie barked. Eventually, Violet set the walkie down, releasing the talk button.

CHAPTER 8

The guy on the other side of her private show stared at Nora intensely, like he'd never seen a woman topless before. They'd only been in the private show for a couple minutes before he'd shelled out an extra two hundred dollars to see her lose the undersized crop top she wore. This was going faster than she liked. Most guys she got into a private show liked to chat for the first five to ten minutes. She liked it when they did that. She'd met some nice guys that way. She even thought she could be friends with them in real life. Some of them more than that, if she weren't married.

This guy wasn't one of them. He was straight to the point. Nora liked it better when they got to know her a little. But she was under no delusions. She had grown used to it by now—jaded by the whole experience, like it was just another day on the job for her. The guy already paid a hundred for fifteen minutes with her in a private show. He would pay more as she moved from her top to her panties. However, that part never came about because just then, Nora's walkie crackled. She heard sounds on it. She froze in the middle of talking to the guy in a sultry voice and looked past the camera, staring at the walkie on her dresser.

The guy paused a beat. An awkward silence fell between them. He noticed that she had stopped the show. Her behavior had changed, like she was suddenly someone else. She stared off in the distance with concern on her face. He said, "Hey babe! What gives?"

"Quiet!" she barked. She stared at the walkie on the dresser, and listened. It stood upright behind a ring light setup and a camera on a tripod. The walkie crackled again. She heard a man's voice on it. It was faint, but she knew she'd heard it. She couldn't tell what he said. But she didn't need to hear any more. The sound of a man's voice, and not her daughter's, was enough for her to switch gears back to momma-bear mode. She leaped up from her bed, standing tall.

The guy stared at his screen, because now he got a whole body view. He said, "Oh, baby! I like! It's time to get that underwear off!"

Nora scrambled to the walkie, leaving the camera on. Now she was out of view. The guy in the private show said, "Hey! Where'd you go?"

Nora grabbed the walkie-talkie and listened. The man's voice was gone. She was left with nothing but static. She clicked the talk button, and asked, "Violet?!"

No response.

"Violet?!"

Nothing.

Nora could hear Joanie barking up a storm. *That Widow guy came back*, she thought. *I knew he was dangerous!* She scrambled out of the room, snatching up her crop top and slipping it back on. She ran through the house to the front door. Nora didn't even bother to check out the situation from her kitchen window. She shoved her feet into a pair of tennis shoes that were already tied.

Nora left the walkie on a table near the front door and scooped up her rifle. She ripped open the door, let it swing closed behind her, and ran down the porch steps. She hauled butt down the driveway, just like she had done before. This time, she might give him more than a warning. This time, she might have to demonstrate how the rifle worked.

Nora ran hard and fast, same as before. This time, however, she slowed to a walk about two-thirds of the way down her driveway. The bass from the Raptor boomed, alerting her that this wasn't Widow. But she saw who it was a moment later. The adrenaline left her almost immediately. Her demeanor changed.

Nora had expected to see Widow back in her driveway, harassing her girls. For that, she was pumped full of determination and the need to protect her daughters at all costs. But that feeling left like smoke on the wind.

Nora was deflated. The reason was because she knew the man standing over her girls. She didn't know his guys, but she knew exactly who he was. Suddenly, she wished it were Widow instead. She could scare him off with a warning shot. She could call the sheriff and have a deputy come out and deal with him. The local sheriff might send a deputy out for this guy and his goons. But they wouldn't do anything to him. The guy and his goons were a known quantity.

Junior was bent over her girls. Joanie barked viciously, but she didn't attack. Nora wondered why? As she closed the distance, she saw why: A rope leash restrained her. One end was around Joanie's neck and the other was tied tight around Nora's mailbox post. Joanie pulled and jerked against her restraint, trying to get at Junior. She foamed at the mouth. Joanie looked as terrifying as a rabid dog.

Nora walked to the end of her driveway like a woman walking the last mile on death row. She knew her fate just from a single glimpse of Junior and his men.

Junior's boys saw her before he did. One of them stood several feet from Joanie. A gun's grip peeked out from the waistband of his pants. He made eye contact with Nora. Unlike most men, he didn't ogle her half-naked body. He glanced at her rifle, and then back to her eyes. He rested his hand on the grip of the gun, ready to draw it. Nora knew she was good with the rifle, but not good enough to get him first. This guy would quick-draw and take her out before she got a shot off. She knew that. Even if she did put him down first, no way would she get the other two. And the other two were also carrying guns. They always were. Junior was probably the only one unarmed. He didn't need to be; that's what his boys were paid for.

Nora made it down the driveway. Junior spoke to her girls, but Nora was still out of earshot. It looked like he was negotiating with them for the puppies. They weren't having it. Junior spotted her and looked up, made eye contact with her. He stood up and gestured for her to come to him. He said, "Nora. You look fine, girl." He stepped away from the girls and met Nora halfway in the driveway's mouth.

Junior circled her—slowly and menacingly. He looked her up and down, like a rancher inspecting a horse before buying it. He took strands of her hair, raised them to his face and sniffed. Nora winced.

Junior released the strands, and asked, "Where're your clothes? What's the occasion?" He circled around to the front of her, paused a beat, and stopped. He faced her and leered down at her crop top. Tauntingly, he asked, "You dress like this for me? How did you know I was coming by?" His boys chuckled appreciatively, as if they were expected to laugh at all his remarks.

Nora stayed quiet. She didn't tremble, but she felt afraid. She feared Junior and his guys. And Junior knew it because everyone feared him. In fact, his whole life, people either feared or respected him. At least, they were paid to do so. Never had he ever experienced fear himself, only the power of being feared.

Junior said, "I bet you've been dressing like this every day, hoping I'd come by. If I'd known, I woulda come by sooner, darling."

His boys laughed again, right on cue. Junior looked directly into Nora's eyes, and reached for her rifle. He grabbed it and slowly pulled it from her grip. Nora didn't struggle, didn't resist. She was scared of the repercussions to her girls if she resisted.

Junior took the rifle, stepped away from her. He inspected it. Joanie snarled and barked. Junior aimed down the rifle's sights over her daughters. He didn't point it at them, but that moment was the longest of Nora's life. She trembled the whole time. Joanie's growls grew more vicious. She pulled at the rope so hard the mailbox post—which was cemented into the ground—budged a little. The wood cracked audibly. It was merely a fraction of a second and a small *crack*, but the guy closest to it heard it.

He grabbed his gun and drew it, but pointed it at the ground. He kept it ready, in case Joanie got free.

Junior went a threatening step further. He aimed the rifle at Joanie, slowly, like he was posing for the camera on a movie set. Nora trembled more, scared that Junior would shoot her dog in front of her girls. Joanie lunged, but the rope stopped her from getting free. She growled and snarled.

Junior put his finger on the trigger and aimed at the angry dog. Suddenly, he pointed the rifle at the sky and pulled the trigger. The rifle boomed, leaving them no idea where the bullet would land once it came back down. Junior and his guys didn't care about that, but Nora worried it might come down on a passing car on the highway.

Violet and Poppy stared in horror. Violet held her tongue, but her sister didn't. Poppy shouted, "Stop it!"

Junior stared at the girls dumbfounded, like no one had ever dared give him orders. But he said nothing. He lowered the rifle and reached behind him, toward the guy closest to Joanie. The guy came forward, shoved his gun back into the waistband of his pants, and took the rifle. He levered the action, ejecting the spent casing and inserting a new round into the gun.

"We'll hold that for safekeeping. I'd hate for it to go off," Junior said, and glanced at the girls. "You know accidents happen all the time and people get hurt. Sometimes it's the people you love." Junior looked back at Nora, stepped over to her. He got uncomfortably close. She could feel his breath on her face. It smelled like whisky. "Sometimes the people you love, well, they're here one minute and gone the next."

Nora stared up at him—suddenly suspicious of him. *What does he mean by that?*

"Not to worry. You don't need that 336. My guys will protect you. We got plenty of firepower," Junior said, and glanced at his guys. Every one of them grinned back in response.

Nora stayed quiet.

Junior stepped even closer to her, nearly pressing his body to hers.

Bravely, Nora asked, "Why're you here, Junior?"

Junior backed away and said, "Truthfully, it's a little business, a little pleasure. You see, one thing you may not know about me is I'm a dog lover. I heard you had some puppies to give away." Junior glanced at the box of squeaking puppies, then Joanie, and then at the girls. He locked eyes with Violet and said, "I'll take them all. And I'll take that one off your hands too. Is she a purebred? She looks it. Good enough I guess. I like her spirit."

Joanie barked as if to refuse his offer.

"Yeah, she'll make a good dog for me," Junior said.

Poppy couldn't hold back anymore. It didn't matter how much Violet squeezed her hand. She shouted, "YOU CAN'T HAVE ANY OF THEM!"

Junior laughed at her, mockingly.

Nora wanted to take his attention off her girls, so she asked, "What's the other thing you came here for?" She said it as nicely as she could, which wasn't believable, but Junior didn't seem to care.

He turned his attention back to her, stepped in close again, and put his lips close to her ear. He half-whispered, "I think you know what I want." His whisky breath wafted out of his mouth. Nora nearly gagged from it. But she dared not break eye contact with him. Making him angry or insulting him would only make things worse for her. She knew it. Everyone knew it. The whole town knew never to cross the Brocks.

"What do you say we go in the house? My guys'll watch your girls and their lemonade stand," Junior said.

Nora trembled. And this time she couldn't hide it. She glanced over his shoulder at her girls. Even Poppy looked scared for her, for what was going to happen.

Junior said, "We can negotiate terms for your dogs."

Nora muttered, "They're not for sale. Not to you."

"What's that?" Junior asked, on the verge of anger. No one told him no. Not ever.

Nora said, "And we're not going into the house. I'm married."

Junior laughed. Rhetorically and mockingly, he asked, "You're married?" He backed off just a step. "Where's he at? Your husband? Where is he? I don't see him."

His guys chuckled, like they were enjoying the show. But there was something else there. Some kind of undertone, like a hidden meaning. Nora noticed it. It was like they knew something.

Anger washed away from his face. A kind of insanity replaced it. It was a certain look in his eyes, like he could snap at any moment and hurt her, hurt the girls. She knew Junior was capable of it, and that his guys would do nothing to stop him. Not that any of them were the heroic kind anyway.

"Your husband's been missing for nearly a year now. Face facts, baby. He left you. He abandoned you. He left you here with your girls to fend for yourself. The whole town knows it," He stepped forward and pulled her close, pushing his body into hers again. He whispered, "Your old man ain't coming back. Why not let me protect you? You know I can take care of you and your girls. My dad's a powerful man. You know? We can make a deal. I'll come by from time to time, and you take care of me. In exchange, I'll make sure you and this farm are taken care of. I hear you're on the verge of foreclosure. It'd be a shame for something to happen. My family literally owns the bank. You know?"

Nora swallowed hard at the proposition. She tried to be nice, to pretend, like she did with the guys on the other side of her computer screen, but she just couldn't take it anymore.

Without a second thought, she pushed Junior away and snapped, "GET OFF ME!"

Joanie barked louder and louder, nearly uncontrollably. She jerked and pulled at her rope, mouth foaming like a wild dog that had been starved for days, and there, right in front of it, was a meal.

The puppies in the box, hearing their mother, squeaked furiously.

Stunned, Junior stepped back several paces from Nora's push, staring at her in disbelief. The only other time he'd felt this way was at twelve, when a nanny slapped him for groping her. His father had fired her on the spot. What happened to her after that, he never found out—though rumors swirled. Supposedly, someone punched her so hard they dislocated her eyeball, leaving her partially blind in one eye.

Junior's guys were stunned as well. They'd never seen anyone shove him before.

Junior's face flushed with rage. He hollered at his men, "Shut that bitch up!"

Joanie barked and growled. The man nearest her slammed the butt of Nora's rifle into Joanie's face. She yelped and reeled a little from the attack, but it didn't stop her. Cane Corsos have skulls that are thick like concrete. She recovered quickly and rage-barked at the guy who had Nora's rifle. He raised the rifle to deliver another blow.

Before the guy could attack again, Poppy shook free from Violet's hand and ran at him full force. She slammed into him and kicked him in the shin. Violet decided it didn't matter that she had intended to restrain her younger sister to keep her from getting hurt; she threw that intention out the window the second Poppy attacked the guy. She ran at him too, and stomped on his toes. Both attacks caused the guy mild pain. None of it was enough to piss the guy off, not until Poppy's second attack. She lunged at the guy's trigger hand and bit into his wrist.

The guy shrieked because a five-year-old can bite hard, even with baby teeth, and it hurt bad. He reacted by backhanding Poppy right across the face. She tumbled away like she weighed nothing at all.

Violet proceeded to kick the guy in the same shin that her sister had kicked. This time it hurt. The guy shoved her away, only he did it harder than he intended. Violet fell back, stumbled, and slammed into the lemonade stand, breaking much of the structure apart. The table toppled over, and her mother's good glass pitcher, the one filled with homemade lemonade, flew through the air and shattered on the ground into hundreds of shards. Lemonade flooded across the driveway, seeping in between the rocks, dirt, and gravel, leaving behind a lemonade puddle.

Joanie raged harder than she ever had in her life. She jerked the rope, lunging forward. The post didn't break, but it tilted to one side. The rope was a different story. It ripped at a weak spot in its strands, and Joanie ran free. She lunged at the guy with the rifle. She clamped a powerful jaw down on his wrist, and he cried out in pain.

One of Junior's other guys, the closest to the struggle, scrambled over to help his friend. Joanie pulled the guy's wrist so hard he tumbled to the ground. She stayed on top of him, wrestling with his arm like she intended to rip it off his body. The second guy reached them and kicked Joanie in the neck. The blow hit hard. It forced her to choke and she let go of the rifle guy's wrist.

The guy stationed on the road, thirty meters from the crossroads, took one last look at the highway. It was mostly empty of traffic, and what vehicles did pass sped by, the drivers unaware of what was happening in Nora's driveway. He glanced back at the country road and saw nothing but a lone figure in the distance. The guy heard the commotion behind him and turned to watch. He didn't want to miss the show.

The rifle guy winced in agony. Blood seeped out of a pair of bite holes in his wrist. Joanie whimpered and retreated. She backed away toward the girls, the lemonade stand, and her puppies in the box. She stood between them and Junior's boys.

The second guy drew his gun, aimed it at Joanie. Nora shouted at them to stop. She tried to run to her girls, but Junior grabbed her by the arms. Nora pulled and jerked, trying to get away from him, but he bear-hugged her to keep her restrained.

Joanie regained her strength and barked furiously at the second guy. He aimed at her but didn't shoot. He glanced over his shoulder at Junior, for permission.

The girls were on their feet. They came together several feet behind Joanie, near the lemonade stand, the lemonade puddle, and the broken glass. Violet squeezed Poppy with all her strength, trying to both comfort her and keep her from running at the guys with the guns.

Junior grinned and nodded, giving the kill order. But the rifle guy intervened. He said, "Wait!" He grabbed at his bloody arm, trying to stop the bleeding from his wrist. Blood dribbled between his fingers. He stumbled to his feet. "Hold up. Don't shoot her yet," he said, and scooped up the rifle. He walked over to the second guy, and said, "Let me do it. Payback!"

The second guy nodded and lowered his gun, but kept it in hand, ready to use. The rifle guy lumbered over to Joanie. He raised the rifle, bearing most of the weight with his good hand. He aimed it at the dog.

"No! Please! Don't!" Nora begged. "Don't shoot my dog in front of my girls!"

Junior said, "Your dog attacked my boy. In this state, we don't tolerate that. We put down dogs that attack people."

"Please don't shoot her!" Nora repeated. She nearly gave in, nearly told Junior they could go into her house. She was on the brink of begging him to go with her, just to stop them.

Junior waited, like he wanted to hear it. The guy stationed on the road scanned the highway, and saw light traffic and more unaware drivers. No threats there. He glanced at the country road again and saw the same lone figure walking in the right lane, towards the crossroads, towards them. He squinted and watched the lone figure.

Tears streamed down Nora's face. She twisted in Junior's grip and faced him. Junior wasn't a big man, maybe a hundred and fifty pounds at the most. And since he stood at five feet, ten inches tall, he looked scrawny for his height. Even though Nora was substantially smaller than him, she probably could've gotten out of his grip. But she was tired. Her morning had been filled with running up and down her long driveway, her work, and all the other daily chores she had to do every morning with her girls. She couldn't fight. There was no more gas in the tank to resist Junior and his guys.

So, she played the only card she had left. She begged, "Please, Junior, don't shoot my dog." She paused a beat, swallowed her pride and disgust, and said, "What can I do to make it right?"

Junior looked at her, smiled, and said, "You know what I want. You know the price."

Nora shuddered and glanced at her girls. Violet held Poppy tight, but they both stared up at her. Their eyes were huge and glassy, like they knew she'd have to do something bad to save Joanie. But what choice did she have?

Joanie barked again. The rifle guy felt dizzy from losing blood from his wrist. But he kept the rifle aimed at Joanie. He called out, "Boss?"

"Don't shoot! I'll give the order when I'm ready!" Junior snapped. He looked at Nora, and said, "What will you do for me? If I let your dog live."

Nora pulled away from Junior and he let her go. Slowly, she backed away. She glanced at Junior's boys. Two of them watched her eagerly, like they knew what she was going to do. The guy stationed on the road looked away at first, down the country road. But then he too joined in watching. Once he saw her, he couldn't look away. They all watched her as if they knew she was about to show them something they wanted to see.

Nora looked at Junior. He watched her with a look resembling a hungry dog's. She glanced at her terrified girls one more time and squeezed her eyes shut. She thought, *Do it! Get it over with!*

Reluctantly, Nora grabbed her crop top and raised it up. She revealed her breasts to Junior and his guys. The men all stared. Junior watered at the mouth. The guy stationed on the road audibly gasped, like he'd never seen anything better in his life. The second guy leered, his mouth hanging open. The rifle guy stared so hard, he released the pressure from his wrist. Blood gushed out from where Joanie had bit him like water from an open pipe. He quickly put pressure back on the wounds, nearly dropping the rifle. He readjusted and aimed it back at Joanie.

Nora squeezed her eyes tightly in shame. Junior stepped closer to her. She opened her eyes, afraid of what he planned to do. And with good reason, because he did just what she'd feared he'd do. Junior reached out a hand and groped her breasts, and hard too. Her husband had been the last man to ever touch her breasts. Only he had never grabbed them like this. He was a gentle, kind man. Junior was rough, like he was trying to hurt her.

Nora flinched, and not just from the thought of his disgusting hands on her body. She flinched because it hurt. She tried to bear it. She tried to stay where she was for him to get his twisted kicks, because maybe he'd spare her dog. Maybe he'd get his jollies right there, and then leave them in peace. She knew her daughters were confused by what was happening. But they loved that dog. She had to put up with it.

Junior groped her for a long, long moment. It felt like an eternity, like the first circle of hell. It was the prelude before the devil brought her to the torture room. Junior salivated as he groped her. His eyes rolled back in his head, like this was the most exciting sexual encounter he'd ever had.

Nora fought to stay put, to stay quiet, to stay submissive. She took it until she couldn't stomach it anymore. Appalled, Nora ripped away from his grip. She took several steps back, lowered her top, and grabbed her girls. Junior's eyes rolled back to their normal position and he stared at her.

Violet released Poppy. The two girls grabbed their mother and hugged her tight. With tears in her eyes, Nora begged, "I let you have your fun. Now, please let my dog live?"

Junior stared at her hard. He said nothing for a long moment, like he was thinking about the whole proposition. Then he grinned. Nora saw the evil in his face. Junior said, "Kill the dog."

Nora protested, "Wait!"

Junior said, "Sorry, baby. The price is much higher than that."
He paused, waiting for her to respond, waiting for her to offer
more. But she didn't. She couldn't. She already felt like she
had betrayed herself.

"You know? I would spare her. In fact, I came here to take her
off your hands. The puppies too. But now, I think different,"
Junior said, and glanced at each of his guys, except for the
guy stationed on the road. He couldn't see him anymore,
figured the guy had stepped out of view behind the truck. But
the other two watched intently—like they were cult members,
true believers, and he was their leader. "Ever wonder why
people in this town let me behave the way I do? Ever wonder
how my boys and I run around doing whatever the hell we
want without consequences? Hell, even the cops leave us
alone. You know why?" Junior looked back at Nora and the
girls.

They trembled in fear. Tears streamed down their faces. Nora
grabbed both girls' heads and covered their eyes.

Heatedly, like a dictator giving a speech, Junior said, "It's
because I run this town! I call the shots! Me!" He pounded on
his chest with one fist. "And I think you need to learn that
lesson. You need to fall in line."

Junior glanced at the rifle guy and said, "Do it!"

Dazed from blood loss, the rifle guy nodded, aimed at Joanie,
and squeezed the trigger. The rifle blasted and Joanie stopped
barking.

CHAPTER 9

The bullet meant for Joanie rocketed out. The gunshot echoed through the trees, across the farm, and over the crossroads. Highway vehicles drove by like nothing happened. The rural country road stood empty of cars, and the lone figure the guy stationed on the road had seen was no longer there.

The rifle fired correctly. The bullet meant for Joanie shot out the barrel, as expected. The whole event started as it was meant to. The rifle guy aimed at Joanie and squeezed the trigger the second Junior gave the kill order. But something went wrong. In fact, the moment the rifle guy went to shoot her, she stopped barking for some strange reason, like she knew something they didn't.

Joanie stopped barking, stopped raging, and sat. She looked up at the man with the rifle, her entire demeanor shifting. She went from a berserk, terrifying protector of her family to a playful, happy dog. When he squeezed the trigger, she looked at him as if she were glad to see him.

Did her sudden friendly demeanor cause him to hesitate,

which caused him to miss? Did it stop him from shooting her? No, it didn't. That's not what happened.

The rifle guy aimed, squeezed the trigger, and waited for her head to explode. Only it didn't happen. The rifle fired as it was designed to do. The bullet zoomed out of the barrel as it was meant to do. Only the bullet didn't hit Joanie.

The bullet fired haphazardly into the sky because a massive hand had clamped down on the rifle's barrel and jerked the weapon up. The rifle guy fired it and the bullet went into the heavens, lost forever.

The rifle guy stared dumbfounded at the man behind the massive hand. The guy stood huge in the sunlight. How did they miss him? The rifle guy couldn't make out his face. The morning sun beamed past the stranger and into the rifle guy's eyes, as if the stranger had planned it that way. It was like the guy used the morning sunlight to mask his movements. Which, if true, would've been a nearly inhuman feat because the guy was huge. He wasn't exactly easy to hide. But no one saw him, not until he made his presence known.

The rifle guy tried to get a look at him. The stranger was a beast of a man. He hulked over the rifle guy. Like two strangers in a crowd, everything seemed somewhat friendly at first. But then beast of a man smiled tauntingly at the rifle guy and jerked the rifle out of his hands.

The beast of a man was Widow. When he smiled at the guy, it wasn't out of friendship. It was out of a deep need to correct guys like him, guys who needed to be punished.

Widow jerked the rifle away with one hand. With his free hand, he clamped down on the guy's bloody wrist, forcing him to turn towards Widow. Then, like a kicker punting on fourth down, Widow straight-kicked the rifle guy full-on in the nuts..

The rifle guy pulled away from Widow, fought the immense pain, stumbled several feet away, and went for the gun in his waistband. Widow waited for the guy to clear his gun, then, holding the rifle by the barrel, came around like a Major League Baseball batter swinging for the fences. He slammed the rifle butt into the rifle guy's face. The rifle guy came straight up off his feet, flew back, and spit out a couple of bloody teeth—roots and all—on his way to the ground. He thudded onto the dirt. Blood gushed out of the dog bite wounds and out of his mouth. The kick to the nuts burned in his groin. It hit him slower than it normally might, probably because of adrenaline, but that was gone now. All the pain scorched throughout his nervous system. The rifle guy landed hard and didn't get back up. His eyes stayed open. If Widow's rifle blow to the guy's face hadn't knocked him out cold, then he would've been staring across the mouth of the driveway, under Junior's Raptor, and straight at the guy who had been stationed on the road, who would've stared back him with near-lifeless eyes. He too was knocked out cold.

A couple of minutes earlier, Widow had walked over a hill on the rural country road and saw Nora's farm. He saw a Raptor like the one with the guys who threw the beer bottle at him. And he saw the lone guy stationed on the road. The guy was standing there like a guard, like a sentry watching for incoming danger. That's when Widow knew it was bigger trouble than he wanted to face. But that had never stopped him before, and it wasn't going to now. Widow was cursed with an unrelenting need to protect the innocent, to right wrongs.

Widow heard yelling from near the lemonade stand. The moment the guy stationed on the road turned away to watch whatever was happening in Nora's driveway, Widow took advantage of the distraction and hightailed it down to Nora's farm. He entered the guard's supposed security perimeter rather easily because the guy stationed on the road was looking at Nora.

Of course, Widow caught the tail end of the grotesque show. It infuriated him. A truck full of drunken bullies was one thing. They had thrown a beer bottle at him. So what? All he would've done was give them a warning, maybe smack them around a little to show them the error of their ways. But treating a struggling mother like this was unacceptable. And in front of her children? Two little girls who're still learning what's acceptable from men and what's not? On top of that, they were going to shoot the family dog in front of the girls?

This was too much. A line had been crossed. Widow wasn't going to let it go unpunished.

Junior stared at Widow in horror as the rifle man went down. He glanced at the other guy, then looked for the guy who had been stationed on the road. He didn't know that Widow had snuck up behind that guy, tapped him on the shoulder, and, when he turned around, punched him once in the stomach, then straight in the throat. He hit the guy hard enough to stop him from calling out to the others, but not hard enough to kill him. Then Widow had slammed the guy's face into the driver-side door of the Raptor, leaving a head-sized dent in the metal and knocking the guy out cold.

The second guy went for his gun, got it out, and pointed it at Widow. This was a variable that Widow had underestimated, because the guy was fast. He quick-drew his gun like Clint Eastwood from one of those old spaghetti westerns—steadfast and unwavering. In Widow's experience, a man who could draw that fast was usually a good marksman too. There's no sense in practicing to draw quick and not shoot straight. It'd be like practicing a good fighting stance and never throwing a punch. So it was best to presume the guy could shoot. And Widow wasn't a long distance away. He was right there in the driveway, big as day. He might've been the easiest target the guy had ever shot at in his life. Widow could've died in that moment. It could've been lights out right there, right then, except for one thing.

Widow wasn't the only danger standing against these clowns. Joanie roared to life like she'd been waiting for the perfect moment to strike. She charged the second guy, lunged at him, and clamped her powerful jaws down on the guy's groin—hard. She did more damage than she had done to the rifle guy's wrist. The second guy dropped his gun and cried out in extreme agony. He fell to the ground. Joanie shook her head like she wanted to rip off everything that was in her mouth. But the guy desperately, frantically, fought to keep everything intact.

Widow reversed Nora's rifle and aimed it at Junior. Nora and the girls no longer trembled in fear of Junior and his guys. There was something much worse to be afraid of—Widow.

Widow barked at Junior, "Get your hands up!"

Junior didn't utter a word. No protesting. No attempts to negotiate. He couldn't because he was frozen in fear and realizing it would be pointless. Instantly, he shot his hands up to the sky in surrender.

Joanie shook the second guy violently. He screamed and writhed in pain. Widow stayed focused on Junior, and asked, "You armed?"

Dumbstruck, Junior muttered, "What?"

"You got a gun on you?" Widow asked.

"No," Junior said. Terrified, he stared at Widow.

Widow said, "Show me! Pull up your shirt and spin around!"

Junior slow-reached for his shirt and hauled it up. He spun around slowly, showing Widow there were no gun bulges in his waistband. Then he stopped, faced front again, and dropped his shirt, keeping his hands out and visible.

Joanie kept biting and tearing at the second guy's groin. Widow glanced at the guy. He had stopped moving. Widow kept the rifle trained on Junior, looked at Nora and said, "Better recall her before she kills him."

Still rattled by everything, Nora slowly stood up, released her tight grip on her girls, and called out to Joanie. Joanie's cropped ears perked up. The dog was well-trained. Joanie stopped and listened. Nora called to her again, and she released him. She ran back to Nora and the girls. Both girls hugged her tight.

Widow glanced at Junior's guys again and then back to Nora and the girls. He said, "Better call 9-1-1 and get the cops out here. Ambulance too. Tell them to send three of them. And step on it. These guys don't look so good."

Shaken to her core, Nora said nothing. She thought for a long moment. Calling the cops presented her with a real problem. And if she called for an ambulance, the emergency operator would alert the police due to emergency center policies. The cops would be called before an ambulance was even dispatched. Nora's dilemma was that if the cops were called, they might search her farm. The melee that had occurred on her property was more than enough to give them probable cause. And they'd discover her business, which might be illegal in the state of Missouri, or a violation of the county code. Being that she lived in a southern state—or a Midwestern state, depending on who you asked—there might be strict laws in place regarding adult businesses. She wasn't sure. She wasn't a lawyer.

The second reason to keep the cops out of it was more important to her. Nora didn't want police to get involved because that'd just make everything worse for her. This Widow guy wasn't from here. That was for sure. He was some kind of transient. He didn't care about the repercussions of calling the police. He wasn't going stick around and live with the consequences of crossing the Brocks. She had to. So she muttered, "The ambulance will take an hour. They're on the other side of town. And slow."

"Better get them on the phone then," Widow reiterated.

But Nora wasn't the only one who had a problem with getting the cops involved. Junior didn't want them called either. Not that he feared them. Hell, some of them were on his father's payroll. That wasn't the problem. The problem was that since some of them were on his father's payroll, they'd report this whole thing back to him. Junior's absentee father would go from ignoring his son to suddenly showing a great bit of interest. So Junior said, "No ambulance!"

Widow shot him a look, surprised that Junior felt he could give input into the decision.

Junior trembled and said, "I mean no ambulance, please. Or cops. Let me take them to the hospital. There's no reason to make a federal case out of this."

Widow stayed quiet.

Junior said, "The cops won't do anything anyway."

Nora said, "He's right. They'll all walk free."

Widow glanced at her, and then stared at Junior. The puppies squeaked in the background. Joanie sauntered over to them and stuck her head in the box. She licked them.

"Why?" asked Widow. But Nora didn't answer.

Junior did. He said, "Because I'm important around here. My father's a very important man in this state. He's powerful."

"Oh yeah, who is he?" Widow asked.

"Collin Brock?" Junior said, and waited for Widow's expression to change to one of amazement, as if he were holding the governor's son at gunpoint. But Widow's expression didn't change. He stayed quiet. His face remained stoic.

Junior repeated, "Collin Brock?"

Junior spoke as if he hoped Widow would recognize the name. Still, Widow stayed quiet. The name Brock was vaguely familiar, but it wasn't registering with him. So, he shrugged.

"I'm his son? Collin Brock, Jr.? People around here call me Junior?"

"Is that supposed to mean something to me?" Widow asked, blankly.

Nora looked at him with an awkward expression, like she was shocked he'd never heard the name. Widow glanced back at her and saw it in her face.

Junior asked, "So, what now?"

Junior's hands came down, slowly, bravely, like he had some newfound insight.

Widow noticed, and realized something. The rifle wasn't chambered with a new round. Which gave him the opportunity to terrorize Junior, reminding him who was in charge of the situation. Widow levered the action, the spent casing ejected, and a new bullet chambered, ready to fire. Widow stayed quiet, and aimed the rifle at Junior. He stepped closer.

Junior froze, but said, "Come on, bro. You're not going to shoot me. I know that."

"What makes you think that?"

"Because you were talking about ambulances and cops. You got me at gunpoint, and I'm unarmed."

Widow glanced down and saw one of Junior's guys' pistols in the dirt. He kicked it at Junior. It skidded across the gravel and stopped at Junior's feet. Junior looked down at it.

Widow said, "Pick it up."

Junior looked at Widow, confused and panicky, because Widow was pointing the rifle at him. He knew if he picked up the gun, Widow would shoot him.

Widow said, "Go on. Pick it up!"

Junior glanced at Nora and the girls. Widow barked, "Why're you looking at them? They're not going to help you. Pick it up!"

Junior looked at the gun on the ground, and then back to Widow. He said, "No! You'll shoot me!"

Widow lowered the rifle, giving Junior the opportunity to go for the pistol, but he knew Junior wouldn't. Widow walked to Junior, stopped in front of him, and stepped a heavy boot down on the pistol, dashing all of Junior's hopes of getting to it.

Widow stared down at the guy. Junior trembled in Widow's shadow. Widow grinned at Junior, the same way Junior had grinned at Nora when he ordered his guy to shoot their dog.

Junior stared at Widow's eyes, which looked menacingly back at him. Junior knew this look, but only because he'd seen it in his father's eyes before. But never had he ever seen it directed at him. A moment ago he was certain Widow wasn't going to shoot him. But now, he wasn't so sure. Junior asked, "What?"

Widow said, "You shouldn't have thrown that beer bottle at me. That was stupid. If you'd just passed me by, I wouldn't be here. And you all wouldn't be going to the hospital."

"It wasn't me! It was him!" Junior said and pointed at the second guy, who was still on the ground. Widow didn't look. But whether it was the second guy or Junior, it didn't matter. The second guy had problems of his own.

"I don't care which one of you threw it. You're the one who gives the orders. That's clear. Therefore, you're responsible. Besides, this isn't about a beer bottle. It's about what you're trying to do to this woman and these kids."

Suddenly, Junior's confidence that Widow wasn't going to kill him went right out the window. He begged, "Don't kill me!"

Widow smirked, and said, "Kill you? You're the one driving to the hospital." He glanced at Nora, then back at Junior ominously, and asked, "Say, was that your right hand you groped her with?"

"What? Ah, yeah. Probably. I'm right-handed."

Widow glanced at the Raptor, and said, "That's a nice truck. It yours?"

"Of course it's mine. Why? Do you want it? Take it, man! Just don't hurt me!"

Widow asked, "Is it a stick?"

Junior stared at him, confused. *Today's generation*, Widow thought. He asked, "Is it a manual? Do have to shift gears to drive it?"

"No," Junior said, but then fear of why Widow asked the question crept into his mind. He shuddered.

"Good. You a good driver, can drive with either hand?"

"Yeah. Of course," Junior said, and read the look on Widow's face, suddenly realizing what it said about Widow's intentions. "Wait?! No! No, man! Don't!"

Widow glanced at Nora, and said, "Catch!" He tossed the rifle back to her. She caught it. Widow spun back around to face Junior. He reached his hand out and grabbed at Junior's right hand. But Junior jumped back, pulling away, and begged, "No, man! Please! Don't!"

Widow jabbed Junior square in the face, rocking the guy to the core. Widow followed up and kicked Junior's foot out from under him. Junior tumbled forward, nearly falling flat on his face. Widow caught Junior's right arm on the way down. Widow glanced at Violet and Poppy, and said, "Cover your ears and look away."

Nora was horrified but didn't protest. She didn't try to stop Widow. Instead, she turned to her girls and said, "Ear muffs and look away." The girls obeyed. But Nora knew ear muffs wouldn't block everything—especially the sound of bone snapping. So, she had taught them to sing the ABCs out loud to themselves. They did, their small voices trembling but determined.

Junior was on his knees, but tried to squirm away. Widow jerked his right arm, extending it all the way out. Then Widow lunged his own leg forward, right-angled his knee, and broke Junior's arm over it. It cracked so loudly, every living creature on the farm heard it, except the girls. Even the goats, chickens, and horses heard it. The horses neighed from the stables.

Junior fell back, clutched his broken arm, and screamed in agony. The forearm hung off the elbow, like the broken limb of a tree that still hung on by a shred. Junior fought back tears, but lost that battle once the pain set in. He sniffled to himself, but said nothing to Widow. He refused to look at him.

The three guys on the ground stirred. The guy on the road stood upright. Though probably concussed, he stood to be in the best shape of all of them. Next, the rifle guy clambered and fumbled his way back to his feet. He was dazed and confused. He tried to speak, but his jaw hinged open. Blood seeped out from his mouth and from the dog bites on his wrist. He just wobbled around. The second guy woke up, but he was in the most pain. He grabbed at his groin desperately. Joanie saw him moving about and growled at him. The growls made the guy shudder, like he was afraid she was coming back for more carnage.

Widow picked the pistol up out of the dirt and checked it. It was in good working order. He held it by his side, ready to use it if he needed to. He barked at Junior's guys, "Listen up! From now on, this farm is off limits! Don't come here again! This woman and her kids are off limits! If you see her in town, then you go the other direction! If I see you here again, or even looking in her direction..."

Widow paused a beat, making sure Junior was paying attention. He was. Junior glanced at Widow, but didn't look at his face. He just looked in his direction. Widow said, "... the next time will be your last time!"

The road guy and the rifle guy helped the second guy to his feet, although most of the effort came from the road guy. They couldn't get the second guy back into the Raptor, so they dropped the tailgate and helped him lie down in the truck's bed.

Widow turned to Junior, and said, "Get back in your truck and get to the hospital." He paused, and repeated to Junior, to make sure the guy understood: "Don't let me catch you back here again."

Junior sniveled the whole time and walked back to the truck, deflated. Widow watched each of them carefully. They had left their weapons where they lay, but Widow watched them to make sure they didn't come out of the Raptor with whatever guns they might have stashed inside. Junior didn't drive after all. The road guy drove. They peeled away, kicking up dust. They got on the highway and headed back to Iron Crossing.

CHAPTER 10

A nother tractor-trailer blasted through the crossroads, kicking up more plumes of dust. Suddenly, Widow realized Nora's farm, in proximity to the crossroads and the busy highway, reminded him of Stephen King's *Pet Sematary*. That was the first King book Widow ever read. In the novel, there's a busy road with large trucks barreling down it, right in front of a family's new home. He read it when he was eight years old, and it scared him.

After Widow was certain that Junior and his guys were gone and not doubling back around, he put the Glock 19 in the waistband of his pants, concealing it from the girls. He then picked up another pistol, the one dropped by the second guy when Joanie attacked him, and pocketed it.

Nora stood there frozen, holding her girls for a long moment. Widow stayed quiet, thinking it best to let her come to grips with what had just happened. If she needed time, he'd give her the time. Not everyone had his training, his battle experience. She was doing well compared to a lot of people. People often act tough, think they're tough. But when exposed to violence, many overestimate their durability. They think they can handle it, but in reality, they don't have the stomach for it.

Finally, Nora stood up. She kept a girl under each arm, like a mother eagle protecting her hatchlings under each wing. Anger colored her face red. She turned to Widow and said, "Why did you do that? Why did you interfere?"

Her words blindsided him. Widow didn't expect her to throw him a party, but some gratitude would've been nice. Instead, Nora seemed angry with him, even resentful. Widow stared at her, completely dumbfounded. He asked, "Are you serious?"

Nora opened her mouth to speak, or maybe to yell at him. But Poppy pulled at her legs. A big red mark stretched across her cheek where the one guy had backhanded her. And Violet had taken a big spill into the lemonade stand, which broke her fall. She was shaken up, but physically unharmed.

Nora said nothing more to Widow. Ignoring him as if he weren't even there, she gathered up the girls and escorted them back to the house. She left Widow standing there alone with Joanie, the box of puppies, and the pile of shattered glass. He walked over to the lemonade puddle and stared down at it.

Joanie sauntered over to Widow, seeking affection, like nothing violent had happened. She nuzzled his hand with her head. She wanted petted. She liked his big hands because he could palm her brick-hard head. Widow petted her and said, "At least, you're grateful." Joanie hung her tongue out and kept picking his hand up with her head. Her tail wagged. Widow petted her for a while longer after he picked up the lemonade stand and the knocked-over table and milk crate. The lemonade stand had broken apart when Violet crashed into it. The damage was minor, but structural. It needed some reconstruction.

Widow lifted the skeleton of the lemonade stand and set everything back up as well as it would stand. Then he shuffled the broken glass into a pile with his boot. There was blood all over the rocks from the two guys Joanie had bit, so Widow kicked dirt and gravel over the blood, hoping the girls wouldn't have to look at it every day.

Widow spent several minutes out there straightening things up as best he could. After he finished, he started to wonder if he should just leave. He didn't want to be there if Nora wasn't coming back out. He also didn't want to leave Joanie and the puppies out there alone. But at the end of the day, this wasn't his responsibility. He had stepped in and stopped something bad from happening to Nora and her girls. His responsibility stopped there.

Nearly a half-hour had passed when the front door to the house opened and Nora appeared. She had put on a tank top and jean shorts. The girls came out behind her, and she escorted them to a ten-year-old single-cab pickup truck that was parked in the driveway. Nora pressed a button on a key fob, unlocking the doors. She stopped at the grille and stared at Widow. He stared back. Violet opened the passenger door, because Poppy couldn't even reach it. Violet helped her sister climb up and into the truck, and she followed.

Nora came down the driveway and stopped in front of Widow, but kept her distance. She stayed out of his reach. She put a hand over her face, to visor out the sun, and looked at him. She said, "I'm sorry I snapped at you. I appreciate what did."

Widow shrugged and said, "It's alright."

"I'm also sorry I pointed my gun at you earlier. Maybe if I hadn't overreacted, you'd have been here when they came by. Maybe it would've deterred them."

Widow stayed quiet.

Nora kept her distance from him, and said, "I'm Nora Sutton."

"Jack Widow."

"You told me, Jack. Can I call you Jack?"

"Widow."

"Oh, sorry. Mr. Widow."

"Just call me Widow. That's what I go by. No *Mister* required."

Curious, Nora asked, "Why don't you go by Jack?"

"My whole life, people just called me Widow. In the Navy, it was commonplace."

Nora looked him up and down, and then sideways.

"What?" Widow asked.

"You were a sailor?"

Widow said, "Yes, ma'am."

She blinked in disbelief, and said, "Sorry, I guess I always think of my dad."

"He was in the Navy?"

"Yeah, but he was more…," she paused and went silent.

"What?"

"He was more *Officer and a Gentleman*," she said, and fell silent again.

"And what?" Widow asked, "I'm nothing like that?"

"You're wearing a shirt that says: *I'm weth Stoopid*."

Widow shrugged, and said, "I can clean up when I want to."

"Uh huh," Nora said, doubtfully. "Okay, just call me Nora, if you like." She frowned and her face flushed, like the anger was gone, but worry had set in.

Widow asked, "What?"

"Don't get me wrong. I'm appreciative that you showed up when you did. I would've been forced to do something I didn't want to do to get them to leave us alone."

"But?" Widow asked.

"You kicked a hornet's nest."

"How so?"

Nora thought for a long moment, like she wanted to explain, but then she didn't, like there was some unwritten rule about talking to outsiders. She said, "They'll be back, and want more next time. It could be much, much worse."

"What was I supposed to do? Let them harass you? Let them kill your dog? Or worse?"

Nora stared at the ground in shame. Then she said, "Yeah. I think it's best that you're gone in case they do come back."

"You should call the cops."

"Yeah, I will," Nora lied. "But first, let me give you a ride to town. It's the least I can do."

He thought about insisting that she call the police. But in the end, Widow decided not to. Nora asked if he'd pick up the box of puppies, so he did. She led him back to her pickup truck. Joanie followed behind Widow. He climbed into the truck on the passenger side. Violet and Poppy squeezed into the middle of the bench. Widow held the box of puppies on his lap. Joanie jumped into the truck bed, and Nora drove them to Iron Crossing.

Not much was said between Nora and Widow on the ride. Violet and Poppy talked Widow's ear off, but he didn't mind. Poppy asked Widow if he knew the difference between boys and men, but Violet hushed her up, claiming it was *rude*. Nora zoned out during most of the drive, like worrying was all she could do. Widow wanted to know more about it, but from her cold reception, he figured it best to mind his own business.

They drove into town, getting looks from the locals. Nora dropped Widow off at the bus depot. She offered him money so he could get a ticket out of town, but he refused it. He told her he had money. So she left him there, hoping he would take the next bus out.

CHAPTER 11

ron Crossing's town founders had built a hospital on land donated by the railroad, intending it to service the town's growing role as a central hub for travelers and workers. The town's location made it ideal for shipping and for passenger travel to the southern states. On the back of the railroad, a budding community grew around this slice of the Ozarks. Workers came in from all over the country. The vast railroad system was where the town got its name. Originally, Iron Crossing was the ultimate place where major Midwestern rail lines crisscrossed. Iron crossed here. Thus, Iron Crossing became the town's name.

In the early 1900s, the hospital was nothing more than one building, which quickly needed to expand as the town grew. It went through multiple renovations and transformations over the decades. Iron Crossing's hospital originally catered to railroad workers and locals, but offered services to the barrage of railroad passengers who traveled through as well. For decades, the hospital acted as a lifeline, especially during the town's heyday when railroad work led to massive injuries. New railroad construction required a lot of iron and timber. Therefore, the timber industry also boomed in the area. However, US railroad expansion fell into decline in the 1950s, and as Iron Crossing lost residents, the hospital lost patients.

People stopped passing through by rail. Workers stopped moving to Iron Crossing because there was no work for them. With the ever-growing interstate system, the need for railways declined, causing the town to become forgotten. Iron Crossing joined the wave of towns lost to the public lexicon. It was a town forgotten. But some families had already staked their claims here. Family seeds had been planted. Roots grew. Foundations were built and generations lived and died. Some families uprooted and left. But some stayed behind.

The power structure changed. Iron Crossing became lawless for a time. A power vacuum was left in the railroad industry's wake. And the thing about power vacuums was that something always had to fill the void. Something had to come in and take up the reins. Something needed to take control. This was how criminal empires rose. At first, various factions tried to seize control over the town. Some good, some bad. A power struggle ensued. Eventually the good was pushed out and the bad fought among themselves, leaving one family to rise. One family reigned supreme—the Brocks.

Collin Brock, Jr., better known as Junior, ordered the hospital staff to give him *the good shit*, as he put it, referring to painkillers to deal with the excruciating pain from his broken forearm. His guys were all piled into one hospital room, as the supply of rooms was limited. But not Junior; he got his own room, the nicest one in the house. He was given preferential treatment as if he were the President's son, which, in the eyes of the hospital administration, wasn't far from the truth. After all, Brock's name was on the building. The hospital, renamed Brock's General Hospital, bore the name of Collin Brock Sr., who had financed and spearheaded its expansion.

The hospital's best staff catered to Junior: the best doctors, the best nurses—and of course, the best-looking nurses—as per his requirement. His guys got taken care of too, but for them, there was a limit, a dollar line that couldn't be crossed. For Junior, there was no line; top dollar would be spent on caring for his injuries—period, end of story.

The Brock name was the reason. Who his dad was made all the difference. In the state of Missouri, Junior's last name carried a lot of influence because of his father. Brock, Sr. had taken their family's power and influence from Iron Crossing and expanded it across the state. It took him twenty years, but he managed to become the man behind the scenes. He grew his criminal empire to a status so high in Missouri that it became legitimate. It became respected. Brock, Sr. hardly visited Iron Crossing anymore. In fact, the last time he was there was so long ago; it was the day Junior graduated high school. Now, most of his communication with his dad was done through an emissary.

At that moment, the emissary—who was also an enforcer for Junior's father—strode into the hospital. Despite the scorching Missouri heat, he dressed like a professional, wearing an expensive black suit and tie. The tie was a clip-on, in case he had to do the enforcing part of his job and the guy on the receiving end tried to choke him with it. Clip-ons rip off easily, whereas regular ties do not. It was one of the many tradecraft secrets Franklin had picked up from his time in the Secret Service.

That was ancient history now. Franklin only went by his last name, and that too was a product of ancient history—military history. He had served in the Army first, where everyone called everyone else by their last name. His first name was Wyatt, but few in the Brock organization knew it.

Junior knew it, but he had never called him by his first name, and never would, as a sign of respect. Junior respected very few people, and Franklin was top of the list.

Franklin walked into the hospital in his black suit, with a gun in a holster on his hip. No one batted an eye at him. Those who'd seen him before knew better. And those who had never seen him before just assumed he was some kind of law enforcement professional. Although he was on the opposite side of the law now, he retained that federal-agent look about him. Hospital security said nothing to him about the gun because it was concealed under the flap of his suit coat. And even if it hadn't been, they probably wouldn't have given him any trouble about it anyway. For one thing, this was Missouri, an open-carry state. Lots of residents carried firearms in public. That wasn't new. Hospitals have policies against carrying on campus, whether concealed or open, but those rules didn't apply to Franklin at Brock's General.

So Franklin didn't bother himself worrying about any of that. He walked into the hospital, took the elevator, and went to Junior's room. A young nurse, who appeared uncomfortable, stood close to Junior's bed. She giggled in a kind of fake, plastic way, like there was a gun to her head making her pretend to like the guy who pointed the gun. Junior grinned and whispered things to the nurse—the kinds of things that Franklin could only presume were of a pornographic nature. He knew Junior better than anyone else did.

This was the problem with children: As badly as they might behave, at the end of the day, they're *your* children. Junior was no different. He had a father, and that father happened to be the most well-respected criminal in the state. Junior had won the genetic lottery by being born into a rich, respected, and feared family like the Brocks. However, like many spoiled rich children, Junior didn't appreciate it. He was ungrateful. Humility was as foreign to Junior as being poor.

Franklin hated this about him. But he tried to rear it out of the kid. Even though it wasn't Franklin's job to proclaim his judgments, he did anyway. Franklin had known Junior for twenty years. For more than half that time, he'd acted as the father Brock, Sr. never cared to be. Junior had been his life at times. He hated seeing him turn out this way. But that's the way it went sometimes.

Franklin specialized in many things, the kinds of things that made for great Black Ops commandos. That's why he was so good at being a Secret Service agent. When they forced him out, he resented it.

Like everything else under the umbrella of his profession, Franklin was good at protection. That's not why they forced him out. It wasn't that he failed to guard his protectee. It was that the other agents on the same assignment failed to guard the protectee against Franklin.

The protectee was a senator who was famous for being caught having illicit affairs with barely legal women. The last of those women wasn't even barely legal. As it turned out she was only fifteen. She had been trafficked. The mob that worked her used girls from Eastern Europe. The senator knew she was underage and knew about the trafficking. He had his most-trusted agents stand outside his hotel room door while he enjoyed his girls. One time it went too far. The girl didn't want to have sex with him, so he slapped her around. She got a letter opener off a desk and tried to defend herself. The senator got it away from her and slashed her across the face.

The commotion brought the agents into the room. Franklin had been one of those agents. Now, he was no saint, no guardian angel, no hero. But one thing about him was he had a teenage daughter from back when he pretended to like women. His daughter no longer talked to him, but that was a different story. She still existed. She was still his daughter. He saw what the senator had done, and snapped.

By the time the other agents got him off the senator, the man's face had been beaten to a bloody pulp. He had to have facial reconstructive surgery to fix his busted nose and shattered cheekbones. To this day, Franklin sees the guy on TV from time to time. His physical wounds are healed now, but his smile is crooked. That happens when you have to wear an upper denture for the rest of your life. Franklin prayed the senator's mental wounds never healed. He hoped the guy would remember Franklin for the rest of his life, and that the fifteen-year-old trafficked girl would forget the senator for the rest of hers.

Nothing happened to the senator. He wanted to avoid criminal charges. And the mob didn't want the exposure. So strings were pulled. Favors were called in. And the government covered the whole thing up. Of course, Franklin was terminated with his pension intact—payment for his silence. He could've faced criminal charges himself, but that would've implicated the senator as well, which wasn't on the table. The whole thing went away like it had never happened. But the senator still carried that crooked smile.

Franklin had changed since then. Those were the days when he had morals, when many thought of him as one of the good guys. He wasn't like that anymore. If he could go back in time, as the man he was now, he'd let the whole thing go. It was a moment of weakness, of humanity. But he wasn't that person anymore. Since then, he had discovered working for the Brocks paid a whole hell of a lot better than the Secret Service did. Plus, he'd done things for the Brocks, bad things, things he never thought he'd do. He was no pedophile. He still didn't like to think about minors used as sex slaves. But he'd done worse to people for the Brocks. He'd tortured people for the Brocks. And he'd killed people for the Brocks.

If he ever saw something again like what the senator had done, he'd turn the other cheek.

The Brocks weren't involved in child sex trafficking anyway, and Franklin would know because he'd worked for the family for twenty years. He knew everything they were involved in, and never saw a shred of evidence implicating them in such things. He'd never heard a rumor or even a whisper about it.

Franklin's experience in protection had gotten him this job. Collin Brock, Sr., his boss, hired him to protect two things—his son, and this region of his business. However, for Franklin, it was more than just a job. Junior was like a son to him. Since Brock, Sr. paid Junior no attention during his teenage years, Franklin had stepped in. He acted as a substitute father figure behind the scenes.

Oftentimes, protecting Junior meant protecting Junior from himself. And he was sure Junior being in the hospital was one of those times.

Junior saw Franklin enter the room, and dropped the grin from his face. Whatever mischief mood the kid was in drained from him completely. Seeing Franklin meant it was time to talk business and probably get scolded. Junior only really feared two men—Franklin and his father. Of course, now a third had joined the list—Widow. But there was an added layer with Franklin and his father. These were two men he also hated disappointing.

Franklin firmly grabbed the nurse by the arm, removed her from standing near Junior's bed, and escorted her to the hospital room door. He shoved her towards it and said, "Beat it."

The nurse said nothing, but seemed grateful to be relieved from her post. Junior called after her, "You come back later, now." The nurse hurried out of the room, saying nothing.

Franklin closed the door behind her and turned back to Junior.

Before Franklin could speak, Junior shot profanities at Franklin about his broken arm. "Look what he did to me!" he shouted, holding up his arm, which was in a fresh cast that started at his right hand, trailed up his arm, and stopped a few inches above his elbow. "He broke my arm!" Junior shouted, and followed the statement up with more profanities. He played the victim card extra thick with Franklin, even though he knew it wouldn't work. It never did. It barely worked on his father, and never on Franklin. Junior suspected this was part of Franklin's duties anyway. Franklin acted as an emissary between Junior and his father.

Franklin held a hand up, and said, "Cool it with the cursing. You know I hate it. I taught you better than that."

Junior quieted. He knew that one of Franklin's few policies was that he didn't tolerate vulgarity. Franklin liked to portray himself as a gentleman, which he was to a certain point. Push him past that point, and the man was as violent as they came. Junior knew that too. He'd heard the stories. Franklin was a violent gentleman.

Franklin grabbed Junior's arm, gently, and tilted it under the hospital's bright lights. He inspected it and released it. He looked at Junior with judgment in his eyes, and then gave him a *tsk tsk* like a concerned father might.

Franklin removed his suit jacket. Sweat stains shone through his dress shirt, under his arms. He stepped to a visitor's chair, hung the coat on the back, and removed his gun from its holster. He set it on a side table and took a seat. He said, "Okay, tell me. Who did this to you? What happened?"

Junior told him the story, only he recited the version of the story he wanted to be known, and left out some important details. The version he told made him sound like the victim in the whole affair: Junior and his boys were there to inquire about the free puppies, as dogs, especially breeds like Joanie, were critical to Junior's business. He added that they stopped for the lemonade, then wanted to talk Nora into giving up Joanie and her puppies.

Franklin interrupted with, "What did you want the puppies for?"

"We gotta think about the future. We need a backup for Bruiser."

"Why? What happened to him?"

"Nothing, but he's a little sick is all."

Franklin asked, "Nobody watches for the dogs anyway."

"Are you kidding? They absolutely watch for the dogs. In the UFC, people might come for the title cards, but they need the prelims. Without those, there's no show. You know how short the main events are."

"Prelims?"

"The preliminary cards. The amateur fights. Without those, there's no showmanship. Plus, people like to bet on the whole thing, on Bruiser. Without the lower dogs, there's less show, which means less bets…"

"Which means less revenue for us. Got it," Franklin said. "So, Bruiser's sick? What difference does that make? Can he still perform?"

"It makes a difference. It undermines the sport, if he's seen as sick. It undermines the legitimacy of the whole operation."

"It's to the death anyway. So, how does it hurt anything if the dog's sick?"

Junior glanced past Franklin at the door, like he was worried someone was listening. He said, "We can't fight a sick dog. It's an unfair disadvantage. If one of our bettors on the internet notices he's sick. They'll post about it on message boards, tell their friends, and word will get around that our games are rigged. It'll blow the whole operation up."

"How're they going to know the animal's really sick? Aren't they just watching on screens?"

"He's got a canine cold."

"Is that bad?"

"There're symptoms. It's noticeable. He's sluggish, coughs a lot, and his nose was running all last night. He can't go in tonight."

Franklin looked at him sideways, and asked, "You're not going on with the games tonight?"

"Of course I am. The show must go on! We've never missed a scheduled event, and we're not missing this one. Or the one coming up in a few nights. Nothing can stop the games from airing!"

"Okay, can't the doc give him some steroids or something?"

"He's already on steroids. It's a bad cough," Junior said, paused a beat, and got visibly upset. "You know what? Why not leave the animals to me. What the hell do you know about them anyway? Remember, your part is to keep it from my father. I'll run the business side. It's mine. Your job is to help with dad's business. My side business is mine."

Franklin knew Junior's father would disagree. In Collin Brock's eyes, all of the businesses that happened under the Brock name belonged to him. Even his son's internet gambling business, or however Junior categorized it. Franklin said, "First off, we're partners, remember?"

"Yeah, I know. That's what I meant."

"Leave your father to me."

Junior nodded and stared at his broken arm and the new cast.

Getting back on topic, Franklin said, "Tell me what happened again. Don't leave anything out."

Junior recapped the morning's events as he saw it. This time he embellished the story even more, but didn't change the part about him being the victim in the whole affair.

Franklin knew Junior lied about much of the story. But he got the gist. He had known Junior long enough to piece it together for himself.

At the end of Junior's dramatization, Franklin stayed calm, cool, and collected, which he had done for twenty years straight. The only time he had lost it was on that senator, but that was long ago. Even though he stayed calm, Franklin was shocked by one part of Junior's embellished story. In fact, it was the only part he wasn't sure of, if it was a lie or if it was the truth. So he asked about it: "One guy did this to you? Just one?"

"Yes!" Junior retorted, "That's what I've been telling you! Aren't you listening?"

"Calm down," Franklin said, "Being upset solves nothing." Except for his dad, Franklin was the only man that got away with ordering Junior to *calm down*. If it'd been one of Junior's own boys who told him that, he'd be going home with a severance package that included broken bones.

Junior held his tongue and said nothing.

Franklin asked, "This woman, who is she?"

"You know who she is. It's Nora Sutton. Her husband vanished a year ago. Remember, he was that veterinarian in

Old Town? South of us? She lives out on the edge of town, near the highway. She's still waiting for her old man to return. It's pathetic."

Franklin nodded. He remembered. She was the woman who stayed even though her husband had disappeared. The rumor mill around town said that he got sick of her and the kids and took off. Maybe he ran away with another woman? At least, that was one of the rumors Franklin had heard. He didn't spread rumors, but he needed to be up on the town's gossip. It helped his job, which was to protect Mr. Brock's assets and his ungrateful, spoiled son. But also he had to put himself in a position to protect his own interests. Was it a bad idea to partner with Junior in his gambling business? Probably. However, it had paid Franklin a lot of money so far. And he was in too deep to back out now. He'd have to keep Junior's secret. If Collin Brock, Sr. ever found out, it would be bad. Brock didn't like having secrets kept from him. He especially hated being lied to.

Franklin asked, "So what? This guy's her new boyfriend or something?"

"I don't know. I never seen the guy before."

"Did he look like her boyfriend?"

"I don't think so. He could be, I guess. All I know is the guy was walking down the road, away from Nora's farm. We saw him when we were driving there. I was talking to Nora when this maniac came out of nowhere and," Junior said, paused a beat. "I done told you the rest. Look at my arm! Look at my guys!"

Franklin said nothing. He watched Junior closely. Junior had about a dozen tells when he was lying that gave him away. Franklin was trained in spotting lies and liars. But no one needed training to see Junior's lies. He knew Junior had embellished and lied about much of the story. The problem was that when Junior spoke about the one guy who beat him and his crew up, it didn't seem like a lie. The way Junior told it, the way he shuddered when speaking about the lone man, told Franklin the guy was real. That's what he was having a problem with. So he watched and listened to Junior repeat the whole thing again.

After Junior retold the story, he said, "This dude put two of my guys in the hospital. I want retribution!"

"Do you think he's still on Nora's farm?"

"I don't know. He could be staying there. Like I said, I have no clue. But we'll take care of it."

Occasionally, Franklin liked to show aggression and anger with Junior. The kid was stubborn. Sometimes it took Franklin showing his own anger to get Junior to pay attention. So he did just that. Franklin mustered up angry emotions and said, "One of your guys got a concussion. Another has his jaw wired shut. And one of your boys might not ever have another orgasm for the rest of his life due to trauma from dog bites." Franklin stood up from the chair, pressed his fists into Junior's bed, and leaned over him. "So, how the hell do you intend to deal with this guy?"

Intimidated, Junior swallowed. He said, "I got more guys."

"You mean *your father* has more guys. You might've started this little business of ours. And it's grown into something very impressive. But you didn't do it alone."

"Impressive? We've made millions from it so far. Have you forgotten?"

Franklin put his hands up defensively, and said, "I know that. But don't you forget something. Those guys." Franklin pointed to the hospital door, like he was pointing directly at

Junior's incapacitated boys. "Technically, they work for your father. He pays them. Not us."

"They're loyal to me."

"That's fine. But let's not forget your father's running an operation a dozen times the size of our little venture. His business is worth billions, with a *b*. He runs the organized crime in this state. And he pays me to make sure this corner of Missouri runs smoothly. Our side business only exists because your father doesn't know about it."

"I get that. I'm not going to tell him."

"I know. But he's not stupid. When you and your boys go around harassing people like this Nora woman, you're begging for trouble—trouble that we don't need. Your behavior's tolerated because your father is who he is. I don't care that you went too far. That you stepped out of line. I care that this sort of thing brings unwanted attention to us. You keep stepping out of line and eventually you're gonna piss off the wrong man. It sounds like that's what you did."

Junior muttered under his breath. Franklin asked, "What's that?"

"I said okay. I get it."

Franklin stood back up, leaned against the bed, and tousled Junior's hair. Junior recoiled, like he was afraid someone would see. Franklin said, "Relax. It's just us."

"I know. I'm not a kid anymore."

"I know you aren't. I'm proud of what we've built. Someday your father will be too. We'll tell him together, when the time's right. But for now, this is even more reason for you to keep a lower profile. It's one thing to have an occasional spat with the locals. They're a known quantity. They're sheep. But outsiders are unknown quantities. They require more caution, a more professional touch. Get it?"

Junior nodded, and said, "Maybe this guy should visit the Iron Ring?"

"I don't think that's a good idea. We got people already lined up for that. Too many people go missing and eventually the cops will get wind of it."

"So what? We only take nobodies. No one's even gonna notice they're gone."

"Not true. Did you forget about Mr. Camp?"

"Who?"

Franklin shot him a sideways glance, like he was disappointed Junior forgot the name so quickly. He said, "The state auditor. The one who came around asking about our books. He's locked up, waiting his turn to go into the Iron Ring."

"That guy? Who cares? He's a nobody, a peon. No one's missing him either."

Franklin shook his head in disappointment. He said, "Camp may be nobody to you, but he's a government employee. He's somebody's husband, somebody's son, and somebody's father. They'll check up on him. There's going to be an investigation."

"He's been missing since when?" Junior asked, and counted in his head. "Like five days. No one's turned up asking about him yet. And even if the cops ask us about him, you can pay them off, like always."

"All I'm saying is you gotta be more careful. If they come asking for him, I'll handle it. But this won't always work. The whole reason we took Camp was..."

"He was asking too many questions. I know," Junior interrupted. "I'm not stupid. It's his own fault anyway. I tried to bribe him, like the others."

Franklin said, "He could've been intimidated, if you'd told me sooner."

"It's too late for that. You weren't around. He was asking too many questions. So I had my guys grab him. He'd seen too much anyway."

"Anyway, in the future you gotta be more prudent. I can make our Camp problem go away, but this other guy doesn't sound like a nobody to me. Even if you think he is. A man like that needs to be handled with precision."

"So what? He gets to break my arm? Hurt my guys? Embarrass me? And we do nothing? He's gonna get away with it?"

"I didn't say that," Franklin said. "I'm telling you to be more careful in the future. And I'm asking you nicely to let me handle it. Your father won't be so nice if he finds out. He might just come back here and punish us both for keeping our business from him. Understand?"

Junior nodded. He understood.

Franklin said, "Let me handle this stranger. You stay away from him. Got it?"

Junior nodded again.

"I need to hear you say it."

"Yeah, I got it," Junior said.

"Good. Now, on to other business. When's Camp going into the Iron Ring?"

"Tonight. He's one of the ones on schedule for the main event."

"Good," Franklin said, and picked up his gun, holstered it, and put his coat back on. He turned, walked to the door, and stopped. He looked back and said, "You know, Junior, you're more than just my job. You're like a son to me. Don't forget that. Take care of that arm."

Junior stared at him. He wanted to tell him that he felt the same way. It was written on his face. The smallest tear formed in his eye. He blinked it off, toughened up, and said nothing.

"Don't worry about this stranger. I'll pay him a visit," Franklin said, and walked out.

CHAPTER 12

Widow watched as the only three people he knew in a two-hundred-mile radius drove away, leaving him at a bus depot in downtown Iron Crossing. The old pickup drove down a busy street, stopped at an intersection, and stayed there for a long moment. Nora glanced back at Widow through a side mirror. She waited at the stop sign, watching him, hoping he would get on a bus.

Joanie stared at Widow from over the top of the truck bed. She barked once at him, and he looked back at her. The old pickup was too far away for Widow to see that Nora was looking back at him. Nora kept the truck at the stop sign too long. Cars waited for her to go. Finally, a couple of them honked at her.

Widow stopped watching the truck. He stepped onto a sidewalk and headed east, into the center of town. Nora saw he wasn't getting a ticket, wasn't leaving town. She cursed under her breath and drove off, away from him and back to her farm.

Widow walked on, taking in the old town—never expecting to see Nora and her girls again. He headed toward a place he knew would have cafés, diners, and restaurants—the town's center. All towns and cities had a main hub, like Times Square in New York City or Main Street in Widow's old hometown.

It didn't take long for Widow to reach the downtown area. It butted up against a river, with more of the town on the other side. The downtown was a mix of weathered storefronts, some still open for business, and others boarded up or with cracked windows. There was a general store, a few dive bars, and a small branch of a major bank chain. As he walked, Widow heard nature sounds—rustling leaves and the distant call of a whippoorwill—which made him realize how isolated this place was.

As the wind rustled through the trees, Widow threaded past cars parked at a row of meters and approached a quaint diner, the kind that usually served the best breakfast in town. A delicious smell wafted from the place. It was a combination of bacon, eggs, and toast. The diner wasn't packed, but the place was busy. Large tables had been pushed together for big families, while couples young and old sat at tables for two. The patio stood empty. Widow stepped inside, hoping to grab a table. A hamster-like man spotted him right away—it was the diner's manager, a guy called Ronnie, according to his nametag. Before Widow could ask the young hostess at the lectern for a table for one, Ronnie intercepted him.

Ronnie studied Widow up and down, expressing a judgmental frown, which the hostess recognized, as she'd seen it before. A cue was given. And the hostess shuffled away because she knew this routine. Ronnie commandeered the lectern and said, "Sir, I'm afraid we're not seating any more this morning."

Widow looked around. The place was crowded. But that's not how this exchange normally went. Usually, places told him that there was a long wait. They didn't send him away. So, he said, "I can wait."

"I mean we're not seating anyone else."

Suspicious, Widow asked, "You mean breakfast is over?" He glanced at the time, which displayed on the back of a register behind Ronnie. "This is kind of early to stop serving breakfast."

Ronnie's frown grew even larger. He said, "Sir, I'm sorry. We're not seating anyone right now."

You said that already, Widow thought. He said, "I can sit on the patio."

Nervously, Ronnie glanced at the empty patio. He said, "It's too hot outside."

Negotiations began. Widow said, "I don't mind the heat. I'm thirsty, and very hungry." He paused to sniff the air. "And your food smells delicious."

Ronnie sighed and glanced around, like he was seeing if anyone was listening. They weren't. No one was paying attention to them. He leaned across the lectern, like he had a secret to tell Widow. He said, "I'm sorry, sir. But we have a dress code here."

Frustrated, Widow asked, "What's wrong with the way I'm dressed?"

Ronnie said nothing. He just stared at Widow, like it should be obvious.

Widow glanced behind him. "Dress codes have to be clearly posted on a sign for patrons to see in the state of Missouri," He said and rattled off a long statute designation. He made it up, but it sounded real. The hunger and thirst were making him desperate, and a little irritable. Widow didn't know if what he claimed was true or not, but it sounded legit. He'd seen signs in other establishments in other cities. He figured that Ronnie didn't have a law degree and probably wouldn't be certain of such a claim in the first place. Plus, Widow said it with confidence. And he used to lie for a living, while under cover with Unit Ten of the NCIS. The key to good lying was having confidence in the lie.

But Ronnie was stubborn. He shifted his weight from one foot to the other, which made him look even more hamster-like. He pointed over his shoulder to a sign in the corner. It didn't mention a dress code. But it was also a sign that Widow had seen before. Ronnie summarized it. "I have the right to refuse service for any reason."

Widow stared daggers at him for a brief moment, and thought, *If I smashed his head into the lectern, would the staff still serve me?* It was an impulsive thought. Back in reality, Widow took a deep breath and said, "Listen, I've had a rough morning. I just want some water and a hot breakfast. I'm not looking for a handout. I have cash."

Doubtful, Ronnie said, "I'm sorry. You can't eat here. Not looking like that."

Widow stepped closer to the lectern. He put a massive hand on the top, rested it there. He leaned in, menacingly. He narrowed his eyes, stared at the nametag again, and said, "Ronnie Bass. I'll make sure to remember that name. Maybe for the rest of my life."

"What for?" Ronnie asked, and gulped.

"In case I ever run into you again. You know," Widow said, paused a beat, and made a fist, "outside of here. Away from all these witnesses."

Ronnie gulped again. He tried to speak, probably to say something authoritative, only nothing came out because he stared at Widow's huge fist and saw the look on his face. He was frozen in terror. He glanced around, like he hoped there was someone around to help him. But there wasn't. No one had witnessed a thing.

Widow didn't linger. He left the guy standing there, quaking in a pair of cheap loafers.

Widow moved on. He passed a tractor and feed store. Local farmers loaded and unloaded feed, grain, and farming equipment. He passed a public library with an empty parking lot. Widow stopped and looked at it. Surprise slapped him in the face, because of a sign in front of the library. It didn't make his jaw drop, but it did make his eyebrows arch. The sign read: *Iron Crossing Public Library.* That's not the part that shocked him. It was the extra bit after the name of the library. Under the name, it read: *Donated by Collin Brock.* Standing in front of two large glass entrance doors was a statue of a man in a suit. A plaque at the base of the statue read: *Collin Brock.* There was more to it than that. There was a whole paragraph engraved in the plaque about how great Brock was and all he did for the town. Widow didn't read it. He just rolled his eyes. Now he knew who Junior's father was and why that name was familiar. He thought back to the train yard and the auction. The sign there had read: *Black River Rail & Stockyard,* and underneath that, *A Brock Industries Company.*

A Brock Industries Company, Widow thought. Whatever.

That was all behind him now, or so he thought. Thirst was more important to Widow at the moment.

So he glanced around, searching for another diner, or a convenience store. But all he saw were passing trucks on the street and non-food businesses. Just about all of the locals glanced at him long enough to mark him as an outsider, but not long enough to be considered staring. He looked up and down the street. There wasn't a food place in sight. Widow's thirst really irritated him. He felt desperate, like a man on his last leg in the desert. A thought occurred to him. Libraries are publicly funded buildings, like courthouses and the mayor's office. Generally, public buildings have restrooms open to the public. And they also usually have water fountains.

So Widow turned and entered the library. He immediately felt cool gusts of air from an overhead vent. The library was kept at a cool seventy degrees. It was both to keep patrons cool, and to stop people from sleeping. It probably was also recommended for keeping the books in prime condition.

Widow stood under the air vent a long beat, and let the cold air blow across his face. Then he entered the lobby and made eye contact with a blonde librarian, a woman younger than him. She might've been just out of college. She weighed about a hundred pounds less than he did.

The librarian smiled and welcomed him in, but Widow recognized a certain kind of look on her face. It was a look of fear, well-hidden by her sense of civility, but it was there. It's a look murder victims get when they meet their killer at random in public, unaware until that moment that the killer was about to snap and take their life. It's like when an unmasked armed robber walks into a bank and demands money, but doesn't leave it at that. Instead, he leaves no witnesses behind.

Widow sensed her fear, and said, "Hello. Do you guys have a public restroom?"

She smiled and pointed at the restroom around a corner from the librarian desk, a long circular counter that gave her a 360-degree view of the library floor. Widow thanked her, and went to the restrooms. There was a public water fountain. However, it was busted, so he shrugged and went to the men's room, used it, washed his hands, and drank water from the tap. Not the best thing to do, but after the morning he'd had, it was as good as drinking spring water straight from some exotic mountain source.

Widow stared at himself in the mirror. He had to admit that he didn't look like the most auspicious man to walk into a library with only a tiny, young female coed running the ship. He washed his face and hands again. Then he wiped sweat off his body using recycled paper towels from an old metal dispenser. He made himself as presentable as he could, and left the restroom.

When he opened the restroom door he realized he had underestimated just how much the young librarian had feared him, because they were no longer alone in the library. Standing outside the men's room, ten feet in front of him, were two Iron Crossing sheriff's deputies—in full uniforms with black shirts and dark gray pants. Each had a Glock 9mm gun shoved into a holster on his belt. One stood at a clock face's eleven o'clock position. The other stood at the one o'clock position. They were either jarhead wannabes, or had been jarheads in a past life, because they both sported the Marine haircut. The eleven o'clock deputy was an older white guy, maybe in his mid-fifties. The one o'clock was a younger Hispanic guy. The white guy demonstrated the higher rank, as he set the stage. The Hispanic guy looked so young this had to be only his first or second year on the force.

They stared at Widow, each with a hand resting on a department-issued Taser as a precaution. However, their planned tactic changed from precaution to potential use of deadly force as soon as they saw Widow up close. He didn't strike them as the type of assailant that'd be taken down by a Taser. Both deputies sized him up and shifted their resting hand positions from their Tasers to their holstered guns.

Widow stepped away from the men's room door, which hissed shut behind him. He stared back at the two deputies eyeballing him. He knew they were there for him. That was obvious. There was no one else in the men's room, and it had seemed like there was no one else in the library but him and the librarian.

Widow's first thought was these deputies were there because the librarian called them. He came in off the street, looking the way he looked—maybe she got scared by his appearance and called her deputy friends. No doubt that she was on a first-name basis with them. In small towns, the cops usually knew all the public servants by name.

Widow's second thought was they were here because of what happened at Nora's farm this morning. *Maybe that's why she pushed me so hard to get a bus ticket out of town?* he wondered. If that was the case, then he might be in real trouble here.

Then Widow thought about everyone he'd encountered in this inhospitable town so far. There were the switchmen, but they wouldn't call the cops on him. They didn't know he stopped at that crossroads, got out, and stayed in the area. Ronnie Bass, the diner manager, was as good a suspect as anyone else. Maybe he called the cops the moment Widow walked away from the diner. He might've called them and reported Widow for threatening him. Which might be a criminal offense in Missouri—assault perhaps? In many states, there exist assault and battery laws: The battery part was the actual physical contact, and the assault was the threat. So were they looking for him for assault? Maybe.

Widow didn't think he had threatened Ronnie, not a real threat anyway. But Ronnie took it that way, which was sort of the point. Hamster was the wrong animal to compare Ronnie to. It was an insult to hamsters. He was more like a weasel.

Suddenly, a real fear invaded Widow's thoughts. What if they had cameras in the diner? Tons of businesses that handle money have security cameras. There was a cash register right there at the entrance. It was feasible that they had a camera on it. It could've recorded sound. Maybe it caught Widow speaking? Maybe it recorded the whole thing? This would be bad for Widow.

When it came to dealing with police, rule number one was to treat them on a need-to-know basis. Whether he was at Nora Sutton's farm that morning or not, it wasn't something they needed to know. If the cops asked questions, his policy was never volunteer information, especially when he was their number-one suspect for whatever crime they were investigating. You never give the cops too much information. That's how you end up charged with the crime they're investigating.

Widow's first instinct was to use the most useful tactic in war —diplomacy. He said, "Good morning, officers."

They responded to it, but not with pleasantries. The eleven o'clock deputy said, "Sir, you got some identification?"

Widow glanced between the deputies, locking eyes, but keeping a friendly smile on his face. Quickly, he glanced at their nameplates. The eleven o'clock deputy was Dillard. And the one o'clock deputy was Torres.

Widow kept his hands at his sides, loose, with palms open. He didn't want either of them to get the wrong idea. He didn't want either of them to say he went for a weapon after they wrongly shot him to death.

Widow'd had more than his fair share of run-ins with the law. He'd never been shot by a cop, but they'd drawn guns on him many times. He wasn't a gambling man, but he wondered how good were the odds that streak would continue. You get guns pointed at you enough times, how long will it be before a trigger gets pulled?

Then Widow noticed something else, something that gave him a little sigh of a relief. Both deputies wore bodycams.

He'd seen bodycams before, but they used to only be a requirement in major cities. Now they were getting implemented by law enforcement agencies across the US. He figured it lowered the odds these guys would shoot him because of the accountability factor. Gone are days of rampant unlawful police violence, because of bodycams and the fact that nearly everyone had powerful cameras on their phones. Even so, unnecessary and criminal police violence was far from gone. It just wasn't as easy anymore.

Widow maintained a friendly demeanor and asked, "What for?"

"Because we're asking, sir!" spouted Torres.

Widow could've just given over his passport and been done with it. But without knowing why they were asking, Widow didn't want to be identified. So he said, "I don't mean to be difficult, but there's no law requiring me to identify myself."

"Yes! There is! If a police officer asks for your driver's license, you must provide it!" Torres snorted.

Widow said, "You're thinking of probable cause. If you got probable cause you can demand my identification. I don't have a driver's license anyway. I don't own a car."

Before the one o'clock deputy could argue with Widow. Dillard said, "We have probable cause."

Widow swallowed, fearing this was about what happened this morning. He asked, "What's your probable cause?"

"Sir, I don't think you came in here with any intent to check out a book," Dillard said.

Widow looked at him dumbfounded, wondering what law required him to do that just because he entered a library?

Both deputies looked him up and down. "I'm not sure he's even read a book before," Torres snickered.

Not sure what to say, Widow stayed quiet. Need to know. And they didn't need to know his reading habits.

Dillard repeated, "Sir, can I see some identification?"

"What for? I've committed no crime," Widow said, but thought, *That you know of.* "If you're getting my ID, you'll need to give me a reason."

Torres said, "Freda texted me and said you came in giving her the creeps. That's good enough reason for me."

Widow glanced at the young librarian. She shied away, a quick rejection of his glance. She was too far away for him to read her name tag. But he was pretty sure the first letter was an *F*, and he counted five letters total. The last letter could've been an *A*. She must've been Freda. He looked at her, and said, "My apologies, miss. I didn't mean to give you the creeps."

Freda made eye contact with Widow. She could tell he was genuine by his facial expression. She nodded, smiled, and said, "I didn't say he gave me the creeps. I just said there's a big, scary stranger here and I'm all alone." She glanced at Widow. "Sorry, I meant no offense."

Widow shook it off, and stayed quiet.

Torres ignored Freda, and repeated, "I gave you a reason. Now show us some ID."

Dillard said nothing. He didn't correct his junior officer. He waited for Widow to respond. Widow recognized the tactic instantly. Dillard didn't correct Torres because law enforcement officers are free to ask as many questions as they want. Most people answer without a second thought, feeling compelled to comply. But they shouldn't. There is no law in the United States requiring citizens to answer police questions, unless under specific legal circumstances. The Fifth Amendment to the Constitution explicitly protects against self-incrimination, affirming every citizen's right to remain silent.

The one o'clock deputy repeated, "Well? I gave you a reason. Now cough up that ID."

Widow was a little irritable because he came into town on a hot summer day and couldn't get water for hours. He got pegged with a beer bottle. Then he got no gratitude for saving Nora and her children. Then he couldn't get breakfast. And now he couldn't even use a public restroom without cops rolling up on him. Widow said, "A legal reason. So unless you got probable cause, am I free to go?"

Suddenly, Dillard came up with something that might've been pulled out of his ass, as far as Widow knew. He said, "Sir, we got a vagrant law inside of town lines. And I believe you're a vagrant."

Widow took a deep, deep breath. Kept his cool. "Okay. Okay. Relax, guys. I'm not a vagrant," Widow lied. Both deputies glared at him again. Freda looked at his clothes with serious doubt on her face. Widow noticed. He glanced down at how he looked.

Torres stepped closer. He glared at Widow's t-shirt, like he was reading it. He asked, "Is that blood on your shirt?"

Widow didn't look down. His shirt was red, so he figured if there was blood on it, the color would camouflage it for him. He didn't think any of those guys from Nora's driveway had bled on him. But maybe? He said, "Listen, I'm not a vagrant. Sure, I used the restroom. But I'm here to look at some books too."

The deputies glanced at each other in doubt. "Really?" Dillard asked.

"Yeah," Widow said.

Torres asked, "Books on what?"

Widow glanced past them at the various signs marking the different section of the library. He said, "I'm interested in learning about the town. I figured the library's the place to start."

"You came here to learn about the town?" Dillard asked.

Torres asked, "Why would you come in here to do that?"

Widow glanced at both cops—and at both holstered Glocks, making sure they stayed that way. He nodded, and said, "That's right. I'm a historian."

The deputies looked at each other and frowned, like there wasn't much more they could do.

Widow glanced at Freda, asked, "Miss, what section do I start in?"

Freda moved from behind the circular counter and stepped behind Torres. He put a hand up to stop her, but she brushed if off. He muttered something to her and she shot him a glance that stopped his objection dead in its tracks. They knew each other. Perhaps they were friends, perhaps more than that. But she must've texted him when Widow came in, and that's why the deputies were here.

Freda said, "Follow me. I'll show you." Widow followed her, passing between both deputies.

Later, Widow glanced up at the giant wall clock above the table where he'd been skimming a book about Iron Crossing. Forty-five minutes had passed. Widow's stomach growled. He was so hungry that he daydreamed about the breakfast at the diner where Ronnie, the manager, worked. But he couldn't think about eating right now. He couldn't think about the time either. Watching the time pass was like watching paint dry. It never happened while you paid attention to it. So, he buried the hunger pains down and concentrated on looking like he was legitimately studying about Iron Crossing. The best way to do that was to actually do it.

Against his will, Widow became somewhat familiar with its history. His current situation reminded him of grade school. More than a few times, he'd had to cram information into his noggin in order to ace a final exam. Sometimes it was he could pass the class. Widow didn't really have good marks until college. In high school, he just did enough to get by. And it always worked. Perhaps he had undiagnosed ADHD, or maybe he just didn't care until it really mattered. Either way, this situation was like that, except this was cramming at gunpoint. In the former scenario, he'd get quizzed by a teacher and it was pass or fail. Here, he might get quizzed by a small-town deputy and get tased. Freedom, or jail time.

Nestled deep in the rugged hills of the Ozarks, Iron Crossing once thrived back in the golden age of railroad. Named for the iron tracks that crisscross through it, the town was now a relic of its former glory, with rusted railcars and abandoned locomotives dotting an old train graveyard—a haunting reminder of its industrial past. Decades ago, the town's bustling train station connected it to the rest of the Midwest, but that had all changed.

The only railroad company still operating in Iron Crossing was the Black River Rail Company, named after a local river, Widow figured. There are lots of rivers and water systems in the Ozarks. After all the fighting and power struggles, Black River was the rail company to survive. All that read like ancient history now. Iron Crossing lost most of its relevance in the railroad business. Black River was now used mainly for livestock and farming transport. At least, that was its sole function in Iron Crossing.

Without the lakes that draw tourists to nearby towns like Branson, Iron Crossing had clung to life in quieter ways. The land was carved by winding rivers and fast-moving creeks, where old wooden bridges and forgotten footpaths served as reminders of a time when the town saw more traffic than just the occasional drifters like Widow. The rivers ran clear, reflecting the dense forest that encroached on the town like a memory slowly reclaiming what was once built there.

At one point, Freda stopped by Widow's table, to the dismay of the two deputies, who had stuck around and were watching Widow from afar. There aren't many things more annoying than bored small-town cops. However, Widow preferred they stay where they were rather than stop by the local hospital and discover Junior and the other guys.

Freda dropped off a magazine that highlighted Iron Crossing's history and culture. She came around the table, stood over Widow's shoulder, and whispered, "I'm sorry for causing you trouble. I didn't mean for them to harass you."

"No need to apologize. I understand why you felt hesitant being alone here with me. I'm not the most presentable customer. I get that," Widow said.

"Still, I feel guilty. I didn't know they would be so annoying about it."

Widow glanced at the cop called Torres. He stared back, like a jealous lover. Widow asked, "Is that one your boyfriend?"

"Oh gosh, no! I mean, we text, but that's it…Well, sometimes I let him take me to dinner. But nothing happens. I don't have a boyfriend. Got no interest in one either. I mean, it does get lonely here, but no way."

"Does he know that?"

"He's nice to me," Freda said, but added nothing else.

Widow's stomach rumbled, which sounded loud in the library. Freda looked at him, and even more guilt came over her face. She asked, "Are you hungry?"

"Yeah."

"You should eat," she paused a beat, and said, "Do you need money for food?"

Widow smiled at her and said, "That's kind of you, but no thanks. I've got money. I just can't seem to get served in this town. I tried that diner down the street, and got turned away by the manager."

"Let me guess, Ronnie Bass told you they wouldn't serve you?"

"That's the one. You know him?"

"Everyone knows him. He's one of the fixtures here," she said, paused, and smirked. "Some people around here call him Ronnie Ass, behind his back, because he's an asshole."

Widow nodded but gave no opinion on the subject, although he totally agreed.

"He turn you away because of how you look?" she asked.

"He said they had a dress code."

"When you leave here, go right on Polk Street, and head up two more blocks to Cattleman Road. There's clothing stores and a YMCA. You can get a shower. There's a barber too. If you clean up and go back to the diner, they'll have to serve you. Ronnie probably won't even remember you."

He'll remember me, Widow thought. "Screw Ronnie. I could

just go to another restaurant. That diner can't be the only place?"

"They're all going to send you away, looking like that. Most people here are a certain kind of way. They're not keen on outsiders, especially when they look rough like you. They all think you're here looking for handouts or taking away jobs from locals. But you really should eat there. It's worth it. Trust me."

"I'll think about it."

"You should get a haircut too."

Widow didn't respond to that. It dawned on him that Freda and those sisters from the train were about the same age. So, he asked, "How long you lived here?"

"I've been here my whole life."

"You ever heard of a young click-clocker who calls himself TrackHopper? His real name is Alex?"

She looked at him sideways and asked, "Click-clocker?"

"Yeah, it's this app with videos? It's real popular with people your age. I've seen them filming themselves on their phones all across the country."

"You mean *TikTok*? He's a TikToker?"

"I guess that's it. *TikTok*. Ever heard of him? Supposedly, he came here and hasn't been seen or heard from again."

"I've never heard of him."

"Never mind, then," Widow said. His stomach growled again.

Freda said, "You don't really have to sit here and pretend anymore. I think you've done enough convincing."

"Will they let me walk out?"

"Don't worry about them. I'll make sure they don't follow you."

Widow thanked her, and glanced through the magazine. It described the town as a real crossroads, saying: *Iron Crossing sits at a crossroads, both literally and figuratively. It's a place where the old and the new collide.* The magazine went on to talk about how younger generations left for bigger cities, leaving behind an aging population too stubborn or too proud to abandon the town's fading history. The few who remained kept Iron Crossing running, not because there was money to be made, but out of a deep-rooted connection to the place.

The magazine claimed that Iron Crossing had its charm, but there was also a creeping sense of unease—the kind of place where the past never quite let go, and rumors spread about what still moved along those abandoned tracks after dark. And while it didn't boast the flashy tourist attractions of Branson, the town had its own quiet pull for those who could hear the faint echoes of its railroad past. Of course, the magazine never mentioned the Brocks.

Closer to the hour mark, Dillard leaned against a wall and scrolled through his phone. Torres stayed near the librarian counter, and near Freda. Occasionally, he spoke to her and she pretended to be interested. Then she shifted to another side of the circular counter, like she had work to do that required her to step away from him.

Widow flipped the magazine closed. Ready to get on with it, he planted his palms on the table and pushed himself up. He made a big show of getting up so the deputies knew he was leaving. Both deputies noticed and got ready again, like robots on standby powering up.

This time, Freda stepped in before there was an issue. She talked with Torres, distracting him. The guy was locked into their conversation.

Widow left the magazine on the table, skirted through some tables with book displays, and around some book shelves. He passed the librarian counter, Freda, and the cops. Dillard watched him leave.

After he exited, he wasn't out of the woods yet. Widow froze outside the library's entrance. The parking lot had been empty when he first walked into the library. Now, it wasn't. Five Iron Crossing sheriff's patrol cars were parked in the lot. Three of them were parked close with their noses facing the library's entrance.

Two of the cars must've belonged to Dillard and Torres. But the other three belonged to three more deputies. Widow knew that for sure, because they were in the lot. Each of the three outside deputies sat in their respective parked cars. The windows were all the way up so they could run their a/c units—keeping cool, and out of the heat.

Their cars faced the library entrance. They were parked side by side. Dillard's and Torres' cars were parked farther out in the lot.

Two of outside deputies were distracted. They stared at their phone screens. One of them wasn't. He stared right at Widow. They locked eyes. The deputy opened his door, stepped out, reached over and knocked on one of the other deputy's car windows. The second deputy looked up, saw Widow, and also got out of his car. The third deputy saw them do it, and joined them. They closed their car doors and sauntered out to the front of their cars. Their eyes stayed locked on Widow.

Widow stayed quiet and returned the stares for a long moment. Then, he shook it off and walked through the lot to

Polk Street. He turned right on the sidewalk, and headed to Cattleman Road to clean himself up.

CHAPTER 13

By eleven o'clock in the morning, the sun was beaming down on the crossroads in front of the Sutton farm, piercing the canopies of a couple of large sugar maples at the end of the driveway. Nora and her girls were perched there, in the shade, sitting in two lawn chairs. Nora sat in one, fully dressed in shorts, a t-shirt, and flip-flops this time. Violet and Poppy sat side by side in the other one. Their milk crate was between the two chairs. A brand new batch of lemonade—mixed in a rush with Nora's help—rested in an old plastic pitcher on top of the crate.

Since the lemonade stand was damaged, all three of them wore big straw sunhats. All three hats belonged to Nora. Violet struggled to keep hers from swallowing her head, but at least she could see out from under the brim. Poppy was a different story. She had to hold her hat up just to see out from under it. She tipped it back, but then it just fell right off.

To go with their straw hats, both girls wore big sunglasses. The glasses also belonged to Nora. She wore big sunglasses too, but they didn't look as big on her. Sunglasses weren't her only accessory. Nora's rifle was rolled up inside a blanket under her chair. After what happened this morning, she wasn't going to chance letting her girls out of her sight, and she wouldn't be going outside without her 336 rifle either. If trouble came their way, she was ready for it this time.

They had cleared up the rest of the devastation to the girls' lemonade stand and made more lemonade after they got back from town. They came back out and set up shop to try and give away those puppies. Nora didn't know what else to do. The girls were shaken up by the early morning violence in their driveway, which made them a little anxious. Nora decided to spend the rest of the day helping them.

So far, they'd been pretty successful. Just in the last couple of hours, they'd given out several puppies. At one point they had a small crowd on their hands. A convoy of churchgoers was out on a Sunday drive after church. They cruised the town and the surrounding areas. Officially, they were on a mission to offer help to local families with no strings attached. *No strings attached* wasn't entirely true though, because really they were trying to recruit non-churchgoers over to their beliefs.

They stopped at Nora and the girls' lemonade stand to recruit them into the fold, but got out-negotiated by the little girls, and left with puppies. The first vehicle in the church convoy was a van filled with women and children. They got turned to the dark side, and left with puppies—and with their bellies filled with lemonade. They texted their friends, and so on. Nora had to send Violet back into the house to refill the pitcher from a large batch of lemonade they'd hoped to keep for themselves.

They had almost given away all the puppies when the convoy stopped coming. They sat out there for another thirty minutes, hoping and waiting for more people to come by. Much to Joanie's chagrin, there were only two puppies left in the box. Joanie didn't cry about it, but she seemed sad to see her puppies go. So much so that she gave Nora the cold shoulder when Nora tried to pet her. Still, she stayed friendly with the girls.

The last thing Nora wanted to see pull into her driveway was Junior's Ford Raptor. And she didn't. But another hundred-thousand-dollar truck eased into her driveway. It was all black, sleek and expensive-looking, like a Mercedes. It wasn't the same as Junior's truck, which was big and loud, with chrome everything. This was more like the truck of a gentle-man-type of guy, not a bunch of hooligans.

That didn't ease Nora's fears. She sat up in the lawn chair and nervously gripped the armrests tight. She remembered the rifle, under her the chair. She watched the truck.

Poppy asked, "Māmā, is that those bad boys?"

"Men," Violet corrected her. "We talked about this. Those weren't boys; they were men."

"Is this the bad men?" Poppy asked.

"No sweetheart. I don't know who this is," Nora said, hiding her fear. Which worked on her girls, but not on Joanie. She stood up from her spot near her last two puppies, and joined Nora. She sat at Nora's feet, stared at the truck, and growled. It wasn't a vicious-protector-growl, like she'd given Junior. It was more like an alert to her family to be wary.

The driver-side door opened and a man in a black suit and tie stepped out. He left the engine running, but closed the door behind him. He traced the nose of the truck. The man in the suit moved toward Nora and her girls, stopping at the edge of the shade from the sugar maples. He stayed there. It seemed to be as close as Joanie would let him get.

The man in the suit said, "Good morning, ladies. What have you got going on here?"

"Are you a boy or a man, Mister?" Poppy asked.

The man in the suit smiled at her with a charming grin, yet there was something sinister behind it. The only ones to see behind the smile were Nora and Joanie. Joanie growled a low, threatening growl.

"He's a man. We've been over this!" Violet said.

Nora ignored her daughters, rested her hand near the blanket covering her rifle, and said, "We're giving away puppies to good homes."

"Yeah, can't you read the sign, Mister?" Poppy asked, and pointed at a cardboard sign with two words scribbled on it in barely legible child writing. It read: *FWEE PUPPEES.*

The man in the suit glared at it sideways, smiled, and said, "Free puppies. That's nice. How's that going?"

Violet said, "We've given most of them away. There's two left."

Poppy asked, "Do you want them, Mister?"

"No thanks, honey. I'm not in the market for a dog. I just need to talk with your mom for a moment," the man in the suit said.

Nora felt uneasy and yet safe at the same time, which told her to be on her guard. The man in the suit gestured for her to come to him. She slow-nodded and scooted forward in the chair. She reached for the rifle, about to bring it out, but the man in the suit said, "Leave the rifle."

Nora looked up at him. He had one hand inside his coat, and the second she looked at him, he flapped his coat open enough for her to see his hand touching the grip of a gun. He said, "If you're wondering, I can draw faster than you can. There's no question about that."

Nora released the blanket and rifle. The man in the suit withdrew his hand, letting both fall to his sides. Nora stood and began walking to him, but Violet grabbed her shirt, stopping her. She whispered, "Māmā. Is he a detective? You know they dress like that."

"I don't know, sweetie," Nora whispered back, and continued to the man in the suit. She patted Joanie on the head as she passed the dog. The animal grunted and kept a close eye on the man in the suit, but she stayed back in the shade of the trees. Nora stopped in front of his truck's grille, staying out of his reach.

The man in the suit said, "Do you recognize me? Cause this will be easier if you do."

Nora shook her head.

"My name's Franklin," the man in the suit said, and looked for a hint of recognition on her face. But there was none. Which was okay. Not everyone knew his name. The good, everyday people of Iron Crossing didn't know his name. The citizens with lesser morals, the ones who crossed the line over to more criminal activities were a different story. They knew his name. And he wasn't a person they wanted to meet. When they did, it usually ended badly for them.

Nora stared at him blankly. Which was a good sign as far as Franklin was concerned. So, he added a name that everyone knew. He said, "I work for Mr. Brock. I'm what you call a fixer. I've worked for Mr. Brock a long time. Do you understand?"

Her expression dimmed. She felt deflated by the very mention of the name. But she'd never seen Franklin before. He didn't look like the kind of guy who would work for

Junior. Which could only mean that he didn't work for Junior. He worked for Collin Brock, Sr. A man with a sweeping reputation. Collin Brock was a name everyone in Missouri and the neighboring states feared. It wasn't the same with Junior. He was a low-level gangster-wannabe who happened to have a powerful father. Senior was on a different level. He was one of the untouchables, like a gangster elevated to a position in the President's cabinet.

Nora muttered, "I see."

"Step closer," Franklin demanded. Nora froze, unsure what to do. Sensing Nora's unease, Joanie low-growled again. "Don't worry. I'm not here to hurt anyone. I just want to talk."

Nora nodded and moved closer. Franklin gestured for her to come closer still. She edged a little closer, staying about six feet from him.

He nodded and asked, "Do you know why I'm here?"

"I can guess. It's because of what happened this morning?"

"And what was that?" Franklin asked. Nora stiffened, unsure of how to answer the question. So he added, "Just tell me the truth. I just need to hear your side of things. I'm not here to cause you more problems."

Nora slow-nodded, terrified, but she explained to him what had happened. Only her side was the truth. It had no embellishments, like Junior's version had. She told him about the giant stranger and chasing him away, and about Junior showing up with his guys, harassing her and her girls. She told him about Junior getting up close and personal with her, about his suggesting sex for protection, etc. But this didn't satisfy Franklin. She saw it on his face. He wanted to hear something else from her.

Franklin asked, "Tell me about this giant stranger, as you call him."

"I told you all I know about him," she lied.

Franklin shook his head, frustrated, and said, "Junior told me this one guy took out his whole crew by himself. Is that what you're saying too?"

"It's true. I saw him."

"One man," Franklin said, raising his voice, "took out four armed men by himself?"

Joanie barked and moved closer, stopping only because Nora put a hand up. Joanie saw it as a command and stopped inches from Nora's foot. Nora said, "I'm telling the truth. He came in like out of nowhere and he was alone. He had no help from anyone." She saw disbelief on Franklin's face, so she added, "Maybe he was on PCP? You know? He looked like a hobo. You know some of them are drug addicts. I've heard of guys on PCP who take down cops barehanded. And some of them get shot while doing it and keep on going."

Franklin didn't buy it. It couldn't be true. He couldn't imagine how it was possible. Junior was a loser, but his crew was well-trained and they were capable killers. They were more than able to protect Junior from any trouble they might come across. Junior's father insisted on paying top dollar for premium men to protect his son and his business.

Franklin asked, "What's his name?"

Nora trembled, just a slight shudder. It was quick—slower than the flap of a hummingbird's wings, but fast enough that if Franklin had blinked, he'd have missed it. She hoped he missed it. She said, "How would I know? I told you, he's a stranger."

"And he just came out of nowhere, beat up Mr. Brock's guys, and then vanished again?" Franklin asked, leaning over the hood of his truck. He stared her down. There was evil in his eyes. She'd seen men with that look before. She'd seen more than her fair share of it just in one morning.

"I dropped him off in town."

"You gave him a ride?"

"I had to. I didn't want him sticking around here, around my children. Not after what I saw him do to Junior and his crew."

Franklin wasn't sure she was telling the truth about not knowing the man's name. But she wasn't lying about this. She had wanted him gone. He asked, "If he saved you from Junior's shenanigans, then why would you want him gone? He had just helped you out, right?"

Nora shuddered, but didn't hide it. She said, "He scared me."

"The stranger scared you?"

"Yes. I've never seen anything like him before in my life."

Franklin studied her face again. She was telling the truth. She was visibly afraid of the stranger. He asked, "So, what's his name? I'll make sure he never bothers you again."

"I told you. I don't know his name."

Franklin looked up at the kids. Then he glanced around the farm to the house. He asked, "You're sure he's not shacking up with you? Is he inside the house right now?"

"I told you! I dropped him off in town!" she said. "He's not here. He's gone. And I'm married."

"Right," Franklin said, pushed off the truck, eased his coat flap open, and adjusted his gun in its holster. He made it look like he was just making it more comfortable under his arm, but really it was to remind Nora it was there. "So, what's his name?"

Terrified, Nora said, "I don't know."

Franklin looked at the girls, who stared back at him intensely. He asked, "Would they tell me his name?"

Nora looked back at her girls. Poppy waved. Nora's eyes watered over. She feared Widow, but he wasn't this man standing in front of her. This man had subtly threatened her children. Without saying it, he was threatening to shoot them all unless she gave up Widow's name. She knew it. So she said, "Wait! He did mention his name…on the ride into town. I just didn't want to know it. It was Widow. Jack Widow."

"Widow?"

"Yeah."

"You're not making that up?"

"No! I mean, he might be lying. But that's what he called himself."

Franklin slow-nodded, looked over the farm once more, and back at Nora's girls. He stepped closer to her. This time he stood within reaching distance. He went into his pocket and pulled out a thick, expensive wallet. He flipped it open to reveal a wad of folded money. It was all hundreds. He peeled off a grand and offered it to her. He said, "For your troubles. Mr. Brock knows his son can be…difficult."

Nora stared at the money. She didn't want to take it. But she thought that if she didn't, Franklin might take it as a sign of her being a problem for him. The quicker he left, the better her life would be. She took it and said nothing about it. No thank-you. Nothing.

Franklin folded up the rest of the money, returned the wallet to his pocket, and turned back to his truck. He said, "Okay. Well, you ladies have a good rest of your day." Nora backed away, the money still folded in her hand. Franklin opened his truck door and climbed in. Before he shut the door, he added one last menacing statement. He said, "I'll be seeing you."

He shut the door, put the truck in reverse, and backed out of the driveway. A moment later, he drove away. Nora stayed there, frozen, watching the truck until it was gone from sight.

CHAPTER 14

Widow felt like a new man after showering at the local YMCA, swapping out his clothes for a new set, and sitting for a haircut and shave at a barber shop. As he passed through an empty alley, he dismantled the pistol and tossed the parts in various dumpsters. But not the magazine and the chambered bullet. He thumbed the bullets out of the magazine, dumping them into a storm drain, and threw the empty magazine into one of the dumpsters. Widow kept the Glock 19 and its fifteen rounds.

Shortly after, he sat on the patio of the diner Ronnie had sent him away from earlier. The first thing he did was gulp down a large glass of water, followed by two mugs of coffee. Then he ate bacon from a large pile on his plate, followed it with a forkful of egg, and ended it with a large bite of buttered toast. He devoured the breakfast so fast it didn't hit him until the last bite that he was probably full.

After his breakfast, his waitress—another young local girl—took his empty plate, making a joke about him licking it clean. Only Widow had in fact practically licked the plate clean. He was starving when he sat down. He wasn't starving anymore.

In fact, he was so full, a wave of sleepiness came over him. He thought about finding a motel and grabbing a nap for an hour.

The waitress came back to refill his coffee. She poured him a fresh cup from a steaming coffee pot and giggled. He asked, "Something funny?"

"Oh, I was just thinking of something."

"Is it something about me?"

"Kind of."

"What is it? Is it my haircut?" he asked, looking into a blurred reflection of himself in the outside window.

"No, you look great! Much better than before."

"You saw me?"

"Oh yes. We all saw you. It may have looked like we didn't. But we did. The staff, I mean. We saw everything."

"Did you hear what I said to your manager?"

"We couldn't hear it. But we got the gist of it."

"And you're not afraid of me?"

"No. Why would I be?"

"Because of what I said to your boss?"

The waitress glanced around to make sure her boss wasn't listening. She whispered, "I hate Ronnie. We all do. He's an asshole!"

"Does he know I'm here? Did he call the cops?" Widow asked, thinking about those two deputies from the library. Ronnie could call them, make a formal accusation against him. It'd be enough reason for those deputies to arrest him. Which they'd be thrilled to do, Widow figured.

"Are you kidding? He looked right at you and didn't even recognize you. You look totally different."

"He didn't recognize me?" Widow asked. He thought that was weird. He had put the scare into the guy so bad that he probably wouldn't forget Widow for the rest of his life.

"I think he would recognize you if you stood up. But he only glimpsed you seated. And he didn't give you a second look."

Widow nodded. He figured she was young enough to be up on social media. So he asked, "You ever heard of a TikToker named Alex?"

The waitress paused a long beat, like she was thinking. She said, "I don't watch TikTok videos."

"He went missing somewhere around here about a year ago?"

"Are you a private investigator or something?"

"No, I'm just a curious man. I heard a story about him. He was a trainhopper who wanted to disprove this rumor about people going missing along Route 67."

"Trainhopper? Is that a thing?"

"Apparently."

"I don't know anything about this Alex guy, but we're famous for trains here. At least, we used to be, like a century ago."

"Okay. Thanks anyway."

The waitress asked if he wanted anything else. He told her to bring the check, but that he would like to have another coffee in fifteen minutes. She thanked him and left him there.

Widow drank his coffee and watched people going about their day, walking the sidewalks, going back to work from their lunch breaks, and just generally living their lives. Most people were dressed for the hot weather—summer dresses, shorts, t-shirts, sneakers or flip-flops. Cars drove slowly up and down the street. Work trucks passed, carrying various farm-related items. He saw two different trucks pulling livestock trailers and wondered if they were from the train he'd had to leap from, back on Route 67.

A breeze blew in from the street. An outdoor ceiling fan above Widow's head, set to high, spun around and picked up the breeze, pushing it over his face. It felt good. The first breeze with a hint of chill in it before the fall season kicked off. Widow thought about Nora and her girls, and how the girls talked him into a glass of their *World Famous Lemonade*, as Violet described it.

He had actually had an intelligent conversation with them about lemonade in respect to the economy. Actually, it was more like the one called Violet was instructing him on the economy and that they had something better to offer him than lemonade.

That was when Nora mad-dashed out to interrupt their transaction with a rifle and little-to-no clothes on.

Widow thought about Nora. She was a sexy woman. No doubt about it. A blind man could see it. He wondered what she was doing before she came running out at him. Maybe they had a pool in the backyard? But she wasn't wet. Maybe she'd been lounging by it, sunbathing? That would make sense. Whatever she'd been doing right before didn't matter. One thing was clear: Widow wasn't going to forget her anytime soon.

Right then, as if on cue, Nora's pickup truck swung around a street corner. It stuck out immediately. Unlike the rest of the late-morning traffic, she drove a little fast and a little frantically. She was maybe upset, but definitely looking for something.

She drove by, passing Widow on the patio. Presumably, the girls were on the front bench with the box of puppies. He couldn't be certain because he couldn't see them. From his point of view, he couldn't see the top of the girls' heads through the truck's windows. Joanie was in the truck bed, like earlier. She saw him, and barked at him and wagged her tail. And the old pickup drove on, vanishing around another corner.

Widow thought nothing of it and finished his coffee. The waitress returned as promised with his last cup. She left it with the check. But she stopped and froze there for a long second. She said, "You know, I never heard of this Alex guy, but I've heard about people going missing before. It's just a rumor though."

"Who've you heard about?"

"Oh, did you see that lady that drove by here just now?"

"You're talking about Nora?"

"I'm not sure of her name. Do you know her?"

"I met her briefly this morning. I don't know her."

The waitress leaned in, shifting the coffee pot from one hand to the other, she said, "Supposedly, her husband went missing about a year ago. Like he just up and vanished without a trace."

"You sound like you don't believe it?"

The waitress shrugged and said, "These men around here are good for nothing. I didn't know him, but I wouldn't put it past any of them to take off on their wives and just leave them behind."

"Do you think that's what he did?"

"Again, I didn't know him. And I could be wrong. Probably am. I just think what's more plausible, he was abducted by aliens or he left his family?"

"Who says he was abducted by aliens?"

"Who else would've taken him?"

Widow said nothing to that.

The waitress said, "Then again, I think if he did leave her like that, he's real stupid. I mean, you saw her. She's a gorgeous woman!"

Widow nodded, and thought, *Yes she is.*

Widow thanked her for the information and the service. She thanked him back and left his table to go about her other duties. Nora's husband went missing a year ago? *Interesting,* Widow thought. That's potentially two missing men—two apparently unrelated missing men. By all accounts, Alex Hopper and Nora's husband didn't know each other. Not as far as Widow could see. He needed more information. And the thing about Widow was he had nowhere to go, and all the time in the world to get there.

Widow took out a wad of cash, peeled off some bills for the check, and a five for the tip. He folded them under the check, laying a saucer on top to weight it all down. Then he finished his last coffee before venturing out and seeing where the day would take him.

CHAPTER 15

Deputy Eddie Torres sat in his patrol car off the shoulder of Old Black River Road, a cracking highway that paralleled the river. He clocked traffic on the highway with a radar gun. Except for the mysterious giant stranger at the library and seeing Freda, his day had been pretty uneventful. Eastern meadowlarks were nesting in a tree about ten meters away, singing. Their songs sounded honeyed, almost flute-like, echoing across the open field between his cruiser and the tree line.

Alone and bored, Torres let his mind wander. He checked his phone again. No response from Freda about his last text message. He thought about her when he was bored. The pool of singles their age wasn't huge in a place like Iron Crossing. He hoped she'd see that and give him a chance, but for now he would settle for being friends. Better to be friends than not. At least this way he stood a chance of growing on her. She was always talking about leaving Iron Crossing and going off to college in Europe. But she'd been saying that for two years and had yet to make any moves.

Torres wanted to stay in the town he grew up in and start a family. But Freda dreamed of a faraway land, a place of *excitement and adventure,* as she put it. He didn't understand. They had everything they needed here. The Ozarks had lots to offer. On the weekends they could go fishing in Black River, or hiking through the thick forests and mountains. Plus, it was a quiet, safe, and cheap place to raise kids.

Suddenly, Torres' phone dinged—a text message. At the same instant, his radar gun buzzed. A car sped by, going ten miles over the speed limit. He saw the car, but paused a beat. *Go after the speeder, or check my phone?* This was the question he asked himself. Catching speeders was part of his job, but courting Freda could be his future. Ten miles over the limit wasn't that bad anyway. So he ignored it, set the radar gun on the dash, and checked his phone. Freda had texted him to ask if he'd checked into the stranger's inquiry about an allegedly missing TikToker named Alex Hopper.

Torres rolled his eyes, but instantly regretted it. It was an automatic response. Freda had criticized him a few times for *not listening to her* and *not taking her seriously.* His mother had told him he needed to make a conscious effort to listen more attentively to Freda, and to try and take her seriously. Which was hard for him because he didn't always understand her. When he rebutted his mother with this claim, she corrected him with some valuable information. Freda worked in a library. She read a lot of books. She would want a man who was smart and understanding. Not one who brushed off her curiosity about things.

Torres told his mother that sometimes Freda seemed ridiculous to him because she talked about things that didn't matter in real life. "Like, who cares about ancient philosophers, old love poems, and what happens in outer space?" he said, exasperated.

His mother raised an eyebrow. "You care about Freda, sí?"

"Of course!"

"She cares about those things," his mother replied, her voice tinged with her Latina accent.

"But Mamá, those things don't apply to life here. Why does she want to know about all that stuff? We got everything we need right here."

She shook her head gently. "Son, the world is full of people different than you. Freda's a nice girl, but she's like..." She hesitated, searching for the right word. "*Aves*?"

"Birds," he corrected softly.

"Freda is like a caged bird. She wants to fly free. If you want her, you must either fly with her or let her go."

Torres' mother had died last year, but the memory of that conversation haunted him. Ever since, he'd tried to be more like the man Freda wanted. He stared out the open driver-side window of his cruiser at the Eastern meadowlarks in the tree. *A caged bird?* he thought.

Torres read Freda's text again. He had asked her when was the next time he could take her to dinner, and she was talking about some great mystery told to her by the stranger, a guy that she was so scared of she texted him to come to her rescue.

The Eastern meadowlarks warbled from the tree. They were birds that flew and nested together. So, why couldn't he and Freda do the same? Maybe there was a chance?

A TikToker named Alex Hopper a year ago? Torres had never heard the name before Freda mentioned it. *What could it hurt to look into it?* Reluctantly, he got out of the text message and went to the *TikTok* app, which he had only looked at once before. He searched the name and it came up under some videos of various creators telling the mystery of Alex's disappearance. And then he found Alex's handle, which was Track-Hopper. He watched the last videos, and the videos explaining the mystery. Slowly, he became mildly interested.

Alex's *TikTok* videos appeared credible, and were probably true. Alex was a trainhopper who filmed his adventures and uploaded them to *TikTok*. He supposedly came to Iron Crossing to investigate the rumor that other trainhoppers went missing when going down a line called Route 67, dubbed The Ghost Line by other hoppers.

There was more than one missing trainhopper and they all went missing down Route 67? Torres asked himself. Now he was much more interested. If this were true, it could be a big case.

He studied it for another twenty minutes and texted Freda that he was looking into it. She texted him back immediately. She was very interested. He liked the attention. It was worth investigating just to have Freda so excited to talk to him. Plus, maybe there really was something to it.

Torres put his phone down and got on his department-issued laptop, which was strapped between the center console and the dash. He typed in the various bits of information he had and came up with nothing. No cases on a missing Alex Hopper, or any other trainhoppers. Not in the town, the county, or the state.

Torres paused a beat, then read Freda's messages again. He was looking for a time frame. He found that she'd said it happened a year ago, according to the stranger. Torres went back to his phone, to the *TikTok* app, and checked the dates of Alex's last videos. It was about a year ago. Torres had just started the force back then and didn't remember ever hearing about Alex Hopper. But he vaguely recalled another case of a missing local man. *What was his name?* Torres asked himself.

He couldn't remember the name, but he remembered the guy left his wife and kids behind. He couldn't remember her name, but he remembered where she lived. It stuck out because of its proximity to a busy crossroads. So he went into the computer and looked at maps of the area. He figured out her address, and looked up her name. It was Nora Sutton.

He typed her name into the police computer. It kicked back the information he needed. Her husband, a man named Wade Sutton, had been a local veterinarian. He vanished a year ago, nearly the same day, and definitely in the same week as Alex Hopper's last video.

Now, this is interesting, he thought. *Freda will love it.* He pulled up the case file on Wade Sutton and read it. But he was surprised to find it pretty flimsy. There was a police report, of course. There were notes on Nora Sutton's claims and about her being persistent. The word *hysterical* was used a few times.

The strange thing was that there was no signature from any one deputy. So he wasn't sure who investigated it or created the case file. Which wasn't totally abnormal for their department, because they had no detectives. And there was no sheriff, not at the moment and not then either. There were just the five deputies, including him. If anyone was sheriff, it'd be Dillard. Technically, he was the acting sheriff.

Someone had written notes on the investigation. Torres read them. Basically, the story went like this: One day, Sutton left for work early in the morning, only he never arrived there. A bare-bones investigation was done. The cops asked questions and searched for his vehicle. They never found it. There was no evidence of foul play.

They did pull phone records, which shed light on some of the story. On the morning that Sutton went to work, he received several phone calls. The timing suggested he was on his way to work. He took the calls but never showed up for work.

This was where the investigation was the most egregious. There was never any follow-up on the phone calls. Whoever was working this case either never checked the incoming number or didn't put it in the report.

Torres rubbed his chin stubble and stared out the windshield. Cars barreled along the highway, braking as soon as they noticed him parked on the side of the road. He paid them no attention. He typed into his computer and swiped across the mousepad until he found answers to the question that burned in his mind. *Who owned the number of the incoming calls to Sutton's phone?*

Torres sat back in his seat and stared at the screen. The answer raised a lot of questions. It struck him as shocking and yet not—not because of the name, but because of the name that owned the name.

The number belonged to Black River Rail and Stockyard. Collin Brock's company.

CHAPTER 16

Widow's day didn't take him far. After he finished his coffee, he waved goodbye to Ronnie—who couldn't place him until he saw Widow stand up. Then he left the diner and turned left on the street. He had no idea where he was going. So, he figured he'd canvass the town and get an idea of the layout. That's where everything went off the rails. He only made it a couple of blocks when he saw Nora's old pickup again. This time she was backtracking the way she'd traveled earlier, when she had passed Widow. She looked right at him standing on the sidewalk on the opposite side of the street but didn't recognize him. There was a frantic look on her face, like she was desperately looking for something or someone. As before, Widow couldn't see Violet and Poppy because they weren't tall enough to be seen over the truck's dash. But he assumed they were next to her on the front bench.

Widow knew Joanie was still with her because she was in the truck's bed, barking at him happily—more so than before, as if she had missed him. The funny part was, she'd only seen him a few hours ago. Widow had heard once that dogs don't have a real sense of time. For them, three hours or three days

169 THE GHOST LINE

didn't make much difference. That's why they're always so happy to see their owners again.

Nora passed Widow after staring right at him. He traced her truck, watching it to see if he could figure out what she was doing. Halfway back down the street, towards the diner, she braked hard. Her tires smoked and squealed. The truck came to a complete stop. The driver in the car behind her honked the horn at her, then pumped a fist out the window and followed it with cursing.

Widow stayed where he was, curious as to what she was doing.

Nora didn't apologize to the other car behind her. She U-turned right in the middle of the road, cutting off a vehicle that was going the other way. She sped up, then hit the brakes again. She stopped her truck right in front of Widow. He stayed where he was in the middle of the sidewalk. He leaned down to look in through the passenger side at her. Violet stared at him and Poppy smiled and waved.

Nora said something to him, or more like at him. He couldn't hear her because their windows were up. The old pickup truck didn't have automatic windows. It was the old roll-up system. It looked like Nora realized Widow couldn't hear her, and now she was explaining to Violet how to put the window down, a lesson that should've taken place months ago, in Widow's opinion. Violet was old enough and strong enough to roll down a truck window. However, it was obvious that they'd never had this talk because Violet stared at the window, confused.

Nora threw her hands up in frustration, but she didn't yell at the girls. She shouted to Widow, but still he could barely hear her. He shrugged at her. She rolled her eyes and put the truck in Park. The gear whined. She stomped the parking brake and opened the truck door. She climbed out and leaned over the truck bed. Angrily, she asked, "Why're you still here?"

Widow stared at her, and said, "It's a free country."

Nora closed her eyes, took a deep breath, and leaned over the truck bed. Joanie stared at Widow and barked. Nora opened her eyes and said, "I thought you were going to take a bus out of here? I dropped you off at the bus depot."

Widow stepped to the truck, leaned against the opposite side of the bed, and said, "I never said I was leaving."

Inside the truck, Violet and Poppy pressed their faces against the rear glass. They smiled at Widow. They spoke to each other. He couldn't hear them. If he could, then he'd have heard Violet say, "Mr. Widow is definitely a man and not a boy."

Poppy asked, "So what's a boy?" And so it went.

Joanie rushed to Widow's side of the truck bed, put her paws up, stood on her hind legs, and licked his face. "Okay. Okay," Widow said, pushing her aside, but petting her.

"Jack, I thought I told you it was best if you left?" Nora said.

"Widow."

"What?"

"Just Widow. Nobody calls me Jack," Widow told her for the second time that day.

"What does your mother call you?"

Widow breathed deeply, like a flood of buried memories suddenly rushed over him. He choked up just a little, and said, "Nothing, she's gone."

Nora's facial expression changed. It lightened up, She pushed herself off the truck and walked around. Widow met her at the tailgate, but he stayed on the curb, giving her space. She stood nearly two feet shorter than him because he was boosted by the curb and she was near the gutter. So, he stepped off the curb, dropping several inches of the difference between them. He met her at the center of the tailgate.

Then she did something he didn't expect. It took him completely off guard. Nora reached her arms up around his neck and hugged him. She said, "I'm sorry, Widow. I didn't mean to bring up painful memories. I'm just shaken up."

Widow bent over a bit to hug her back. Her breasts poked his gut. They felt firm, but soft, and big for her small frame. Of course, he already knew that from seeing her in the tiny string bikini earlier. He had tried not to look at her, but it was hard because she had been pointing a rifle at him.

They stayed in that hug for a long moment, longer than Widow had expected. Nora was trembling, and he could feel it. She was running on fear; that much was clear. Sometimes, a person needed a good hug to steady themselves, to find their footing again. Widow didn't mind. He liked it and didn't pull away. He let her hold on as long as she needed. Why would he complain? Nora was a beautiful woman, her curves fitting against him perfectly. Widow hadn't been touched by a woman in a long time. Human connection wasn't something he experienced often—he'd had his fair share of women, but never for long, and never like this. This felt different, raw, and unguarded. Finally, she pulled back, her eyes searching his face. She took a long look at him, her voice trembling as she asked, "It's really you?"

"It's me."

"You look… so different."

"I cleaned up," Widow said. Nora nodded and smiled, like

she approved of his new look. Which she did. She told him so. He thanked her.

Nora's smile faded and she said, "I was searching for you. I must've driven right by you. I didn't even recognize you."

"You did. I saw you once."

She stayed quiet.

Widow could see something was bothering her. Even though she was calm now, there was a lingering thing on her mind. It was like she held a dark secret that gnawed at her from within. And she had to tell someone. So, he asked, "So, why do you want me to leave so bad? Is it because of those guys from earlier?"

Nora glanced over her shoulder, followed by a look up and down the street, like she was making sure they weren't being watched. Widow noticed and asked, "Is someone watching us?"

"Sorry. I'm just being paranoid. It's been a day."

"Are you afraid of those guys from this morning? I wouldn't worry about them. They're just a bunch of hooligans. I doubt they'll mess with you again."

"But see, you're dead wrong. Those weren't just a few thugs who got out of line. The one whose arm you broke, that was Junior."

Widow shrugged.

"His name is Collin Brock, Jr. Everyone calls him Junior," Nora said, and stared at Widow like he should recognize the name, but he didn't.

"Okay. Am I supposed to know who that is?"

"You should've heard it before unless you're not from here. Did you come from somewhere else and fall off a turnip truck or something?"

She wasn't far from the truth. He did come in from somewhere else. And you could say he fell off a train. Widow said, "I'm not from Missouri. I literally just arrived this morning."

"Oh, I'm sorry. I'm just on edge. I don't mean to be sarcastic or snappy with you."

Widow shrugged, and said, "Don't worry about it." Joanie barked again, like she wanted attention. Violet and Poppy mashed up against rear window, making faces on the glass.

"So, when are you planning to leave town?"

"Soon."

"Today?"

"I'll leave when I'm done here."

"Done with what?" she asked.

"I don't know yet. I'm feeling the place out," Widow said. The waitress at the diner had told him about Nora's missing husband. He presumed it was true. Therefore, he didn't want to mention Alex Hopper to her, not yet. Widow wasn't even sure if Alex Hopper was really missing or not. There were a lot of rumors and speculation, but nothing to indicate that it was all true. Until he could verify some of it, he thought it best to keep it from her. Why bring up her missing husband if it were true? Besides, maybe the guy really did run out on her, like the waitress suggested.

Nora said, "Collin Brock, Sr. owns a lot of the land here and some of the local industry. He owns Brock Industries. It's a huge transportation company; trucks and planes."

"And railroad?"

"Oh sure, it started as a railroad company. That's what Iron Crossing was founded on."

"Yeah, I read about it at the library."

Nora looked at Widow sideways. It was instinctive, like when someone tells an obvious lie, and everyone just stares at them, fully aware of it. For a split second, she didn't believe Widow could read, much less would be caught dead inside a library. Widow noticed it, but he said nothing. Often people misjudged him—a book by its cover and all. Besides, could he blame her? When she'd first met him, he was dirty and unkempt, and he brutally beat up four guys in her driveway. He didn't give a first impression as that of a man who reads a lot of books.

Nora continued, "Most of Missouri knows Brock as a politician of sorts."

"He holds office?"

"Not like that. More like he's the man behind the scenes. He's a big donor to the current governor. And he's constantly at public events and ceremonies, like ribbon cuttings and charity things. Many just see him as some kind of rich philanthropist, but he's something else entirely."

"He sounds like a kingmaker."

"Yes, that's what he is. He has this public image of a good Missourian who only cares about the environment and such."

"But you know better?" Widow asked.

"Everyone here knows better."

"Is he a criminal?"

"Not the normal kind. He's not like a murderer. He's never robbed a bank or anything that black and white. I think he's more like one of those…" Nora paused, seeking the right word. "Oh, what do you call them?"

Widow stared at her, blankly, and stayed quiet.

Nora said, "Oh, you know like a tax evader, or someone who bribes politicians?"

"White-collar criminal?"

"Yes, That's it. I doubt he's ever hurt anyone personally. Junior's a different story. He's more like a mobster. Or at least, he wants to be."

Widow said nothing.

Nora said, "But that's not why I was looking for you. I had a visitor after you left. This guy came to see me. We had set up for giving away lemonade again…"

Just then the sliding glass in the middle of her pickup truck's rear window hissed open. Both Violet's and Poppy's little hands smudged their handprints on it just pushing it open. They fought to stick their heads through the window. Violet said, "And we gave away more puppies. Don't forget to tell him about that."

Poppy said, "Hi, Mr. Widow." And she waved her tiny fingers through the opening at him. Widow waved back at the girls.

Nora said, "Girls, close that window. I need to finish talking to Mr. Widow."

"We're hungry, Māmā," Violet said.

"Okay, we'll eat soon, honey. Now, give us some space for a minute," Nora ordered the girls, and both girls pushed the little window closed again.

Widow said, "You should take them to eat."

"Did you eat yet?"

"I had brunch at this diner," Widow said, pointing back at it.

"That place is good, but expensive."

"Do you want to go back in? It's my treat."

"Oh, no. Thanks for the offer, but I couldn't."

"It's not a problem."

"But you just ate there?" Nora asked.

"I don't mind. I could get more coffee. Really, it's okay. You have more to say and they're hungry. Let me treat you."

Nora stayed quiet. She glanced back at her girls and then back up at Widow. There was a real struggle going on behind her eyes. "Or we could go somewhere else. Is there someplace where people might not recognize you?" Widow said, in case her dilemma was about being seen with an outsider, a man who wasn't her missing husband.

"I'm not worried about being seen with you. I just don't like this place. Maybe that's partially because it's overpriced, but also because it's where everyone goes."

"And you prefer a lower-profile place?"

"I like to support other restaurants. There's a Hawaiian place on the other side of town. Well, it's part Hawaiian, part Japanese. I know the owners. They've got good Poke. And desserts for the kids. Poppy's favorite ice cream is there," Nora said, excitedly, like she'd not been out of the house for a meal in ages. "But you just ate?"

"They got coffee at this Hawaiian-Japanese place?"

"I think so. I'm sure they do."

"Okay, I'm game. Let's go there. My treat. You can tell me more about what's worrying you," Widow said, and instantly regretted it because Nora had forgotten all about it for a brief moment. And once he mentioned it, that look of worry splashed across her expression again. It was like someone had thrown paint across her face.

Reluctantly, Nora agreed, and Widow walked her to the driver-side door, opened it for her, and she slid in. He closed the door, squirted around the nose, and squeezed in next to the girls and put the box of puppies on his lap. Both girls stared at Widow. Nora ordered them to put their seatbelt back on, which was one seatbelt they shared. Technically, the girls were supposed to ride in a booster seat on the backseat. It was a Missouri state law, like most states. Only Nora's truck didn't have a backseat, and the booster seats were in the back of a closet somewhere. And law or no law, nobody in the rural areas of Missouri cared about car seats.

Widow remembered riding in the truck bed of his mom's pickup truck when he was a kid. He glanced back over his shoulder to look at Nora's truck bed. It gave him a memory of riding in his mother's truck. He thought it was a single memory, but really his mind simply montaged a bunch of childhood memories together. He smiled, thinking about it. Those were good times. Joanie leaped up, pawing the window, interrupting his reminiscing. She barked once, and smiled at Widow. He smiled back.

Nora reversed the truck and U-turned again, and drove to the other side of town.

Just a block over, Franklin sat in his truck. It was parked on the street. His engine idled, a low rumble. Country music played on the radio, turned down low.

Franklin's gun rested in a plastic holster set into the console. It was an aftermarket addition to the truck. And in his line of work, it came in handy. He chewed on a toothpick, clamping down on it at the sight of Widow and Nora riding off together. *That's gotta be the guy*, he thought. Junior's description was off in one regard. Widow didn't look like a scruffy hobo. He was no distinguished gentleman or anything, but he looked pretty normal. However, Junior was right in general. This Widow guy was big and tall. There was another element about him. Even though the guy dressed civil, he had a dangerous quality to him. He looked like the kind of guy who could take out four armed men, maybe. Franklin had never personally seen such a feat, but he'd seen plenty of deadly men in his life.

Dangerous men like that carry themselves in a certain kind of way—with a certain kind of confidence. This Widow guy had that feature in spades. And Franklin was only looking at him from a distance.

Better to be careful in approaching Widow, and to keep his gun nearby. He brushed his fingers over his holstered gun as the thought of shooting Widow crossed his mind.

Franklin put the truck into Drive, slowly came out of his parking spot, and followed behind Nora, the girls, and Widow.

CHAPTER 17

Iron Crossing was bigger than it appeared from the farmland where Nora lived. The Black River snaked through the town, dividing it into two uneven slices. Both lush and green. Both populated with local families. However, the families had distinct differences. There were the old families who'd lived in Iron Crossing for generations, and there were the new families who had only been there for a generation or two.

The west side of Black River was the old side, steeped in history and tradition. The east side, known as New Town, was developed by ambitious builders fifty years ago. This newer part of Iron Crossing carved out its own identity, distinct from the west. New Town had become more diverse over time, driven by a variety of factors. By contrast, Old Town was rooted in the railroad boom that once defined the area. Even after Iron Crossing's role in the rail industry faded, families stayed put. Generations adapted to the changing times, transitioning from rail work to farming, keeping the legacy of the town alive in their own way.

New Town simply provided the newest available land; therefore, providing new opportunities for newer families. The state offered big tax incentives for developers to offer affordable housing and land to residents willing to relocate there. It happened back in the 1990s, when Collin Brock was still up and coming in the political world. It was one of the many deals Brock helped to facilitate—his way of growing the economy of the town he was born in. But really it was an opportunity to make himself look good while gaining political favor in the state.

Families living in Branson and Memphis were encouraged to give up the busy city life and move to Iron Crossing. It helped to expand the community. And it worked too—for a time. Throughout the 1990s and early 2000s, New Town prospered. But by the mid-2000s it had started to crumble. After the 2008 housing crash, it all fell apart. Everyone felt the pain. People lost their homes, businesses, and life savings. Some families left and some families stayed. New Town was hit the hardest as the families that lived there had mortgages and jobs and small businesses with debt. Old Town was mostly long-established families who owned their own farms and homes and businesses with little to no debt. Maintaining the status quo was easier for them.

Things became more stable for both sides of town. A lot of people left New Town after the 2008 collapse, but then everyone settled down and the community got by pretty well. In Old Town the diner, fast food joints, and a handful of bars were all good places to eat, but there was not much variety. If you wanted Japanese, Mexican, or Chinese food, then you came to New Town. The same was true for traditional Hawaiian food. There was one place to get it in Iron Crossing and that was where Nora headed.

Nora drove, winding through the town streets. She checked her mirrors more than consistently. She checked them obsessively, like she was worried about someone following them. Widow said nothing about it. He had his own drama going on. Violet and Poppy couldn't take their eyes off him. They sat in silence staring at him. And that wasn't the only thing happening on his side of the truck. He also held the box of puppies. There were only two left, and they were wiggling all over the place. They were young, but old enough to see, stand, and play. They just had terrible balance and the truck ride made it hard for them to stay still.

At one point on the ride, Poppy tapped Widow on the forearm. He looked down at her and she stared up at him. Matter-of-factly, she said, "You're the biggest person I've ever seen."

"Thank you," Widow said. That was all she said, and all, it seemed, she wanted to say.

They turned onto a road that ran along the river's edge. Widow glanced down and saw the Black River. The water streamed and ran at a consistent pace. There were fishing boats parked along the river. Several fishermen stood on the banks and fished.

A train extension bridge crossed the Black River, along with a car bridge. Three hundred feet separated the bridges. They drove over train tracks twice: once on the west side of the river, and again on the east side. Widow saw why this place was called Iron Crossing. There was a section near the river where there were some old train tracks and some current tracks, and they crossed several times.

Nora crossed over to New Town, made a few more turns, and finally stopped at the Hawaiian restaurant, which was a small place inside a shopping mall. They left Joanie inside the truck with her puppies, with the engine on and the a/c blasting, because it was too hot to leave her outside. The passenger-side window was cracked enough for her to stick her face out and that was it.

The restaurant was box-shaped on the inside with plain, hard, wooden tables and chairs to match. The floors were big off-white tiles. The place had a beachy Hawaiian vibe to it. A long counter ran along the wall, creating a barrier between the kitchen and the front of the house. The walls were painted in various Hawaiian scenes. Beaches with clear blue water and sunsets faced Widow. Pristine Hawaiian landscapes grabbed the imagination, while making customers forget they were still in Iron Crossing. At least, that was the goal. And it worked on Poppy. At one point, she had ice cream on her face, pointed to one of the wall murals, and said, "Mr. Widow, check out the volcano." Widow looked at it. Poppy asked, "Have you ever seen a volcano?"

Widow thought for a moment, sipped his coffee, and answered, "I have."

Nora drank some kind of bubble-tea thing that Widow wasn't familiar with. She stared at him over the rim of the plastic cup as she drank. A surprised and skeptical look washed over her face, like she wasn't sure whether he was telling the truth or was just making it up for her girls' sake.

But it was Violet who questioned him first. She asked, "Where did you see a volcano?"

"Mount Cleveland erupted back in 2006," Widow said.

"You were there?" Poppy asked, a big expression of amazement and wonder filling her face.

"I was there."

Nora asked, "Where's that?"

"It's on one of the Aleutian Islands of Alaska," Widow said, taking a pull from his coffee.

"You've been to Alaska?" Violet asked.

Widow looked at her, and said, "Sure, plenty of times."

"What were you doing on an island in Alaska? You a fisherman?" Nora asked.

"Navy," Widow said, finishing the coffee off. He held the mug upside down over his lips, desperately trying to get the last drop out of it.

"You were in the Navy?"

Widow gave up on trying to get coffee out of the empty mug. He set the cup down on the table and nodded a response to Nora's question.

Nora asked, "So, what? You were stationed on the islands at the time? Where?"

Both Violet and Poppy leaned forward over their ice creams and stared at Widow, like they wanted a story. Violet said, "Tell us, Mr. Widow."

"Naval Air Station Adak used to be on one of the islands, but it was decommissioned in '97, which was long before my time," Widow said, and leaned back in his chair, sliding the empty mug aside so the waitress might see it and refill it for him. "I was out in the Bering Sea. The north seas are like you imagine—freezing winds and choppy waves. At the time, I was stationed on the USS *Makin Island*, an amphibious assault ship. We were running exercises."

Poppy asked, "What's an exercise?"

"It's like we were practicing our war capabilities," Widow said, seeing a blank expression on her face.

Poppy asked, "War?"

Widow said, "We were pretending, like make-believe. Don't you do make-believe?"

"Yes. We pretend with our animals at home," Poppy said.

Nora looked at Widow, and said, "She means their stuffed animals."

Widow said, "It's just like that, only I was on a big Navy ship."

"Was it cold?" Violet asked, "Daddy told us Alaska was north and up north it's very cold."

"It was cold, even though this was in May. We were doing cold-weather amphibious drills, prepping for potential Arctic operations. It was all routine."

He paused, smiling faintly at the distant memory. It was another time—another life. "We weren't far from the Aleutian Islands when it happened. I remember seeing the sky get dark, thought it was just another storm. But it wasn't. A few of the guys and I stepped out to the deck to get a better look, and that's when we saw it—Mount Cleveland, the most active volcano in America. It blew massive ash plumes up into the sky. And the sound! Nothing prepares you for the sound. It's loud and explosive in the way you think of a nuclear bomb. The volcano erupted and the sky cracked, like someone had torn a hole in the world."

Widow's eyes narrowed as he recalled the scene. "A giant ash cloud shot up, must've been 20,000 feet high, or more. Once the ash reached its apex, it fell back to earth, drifting toward us."

Poppy spooned more ice cream into her mouth and asked, "Did you escape?"

Violet sideways-looked at her sister, and said, "Of course he escaped. He's sitting right here."

"But were you scared?" Poppy asked. Nora reached over to Poppy and wiped ice cream off her cheek with a napkin.

Widow said, "Of course. I was terrified."

"Really?" asked Violet.

"Oh, sure. I'm not as brave as you girls."

Violet said, "We're not that brave."

Poppy said, "But you're much bigger than us."

"I am, but size doesn't matter. What matters is how much courage you have on the inside," Widow said, and he tapped his chest.

Violet asked, "What's cartridge?"

"Not cartridge. Mr. Widow said *courage*," Nora explained. "Remember, you learned that word from *The Wizard of Oz*?"

Violet looked at Poppy, like she was looking for her sister to remember it too. Poppy said, "That's what the Cowardly Lion wanted." And Violet nodded.

Poppy looked at Widow, and asked, "Have you seen *The Wizard of Oz*?"

"Oh, yeah. I've seen it many times. But that was a long time ago," Widow answered.

"I like the Scarecrow," Poppy said.

"I do too," Widow said. They said nothing for a long minute. Widow waited for one of them to speak. Nora looked happy, and it was the first time Widow had seen that expression on her face. She looked like she'd forgotten all of her morning woes for a brief moment.

That changed after a while and Nora's worried expression returned, like the elephant in the room that she'd been ignoring suddenly slapped her across her face with its trunk. She wrecking-balled the silent ambience with a question. She asked, "Widow, was there more to your volcano story?"

"Yeah, tell us more. What was it like?" Violet asked. "Did you get hit with the fire rain?"

"I think you mean the ash from the sky?"

Violet nodded, like she understood the difference.

"We weren't close enough to get hit with anything. Not directly," Widow said, and noticed that she wanted more. She sat on the edge of her seat. Both of the girls did. Their eyes opened wide, like it was a story that rivaled *The Wizard of Oz*.

Widow glanced at Nora. She mouthed to him, "Please, go on." And he realized that there was more going on in their lives than just giving away puppies and dealing with Junior and his thugs. Nora mouthed it like she needed this. She needed the distraction. It was as much for her as it was her girls. So, Widow said, "But, I remember the whole horizon turned black, the kind of black you only see on a starless night. The ocean looked darker, too, like the ash was seeping into the water. There was this strange silence, like the sea itself was waiting for something."

"Were you scared?" Violet asked.

Widow said, "Oh yes. Very much!"

"You were?" Violet asked.

Widow nodded, and Poppy asked, "Did you lose your courage? Like the Cowardly Lion?"

Widow slow-nodded and smiled at her. He said, "I did. Just like that."

"What happened next? How did you escape?" Violet asked.

Widow said, "The ship's radar picked up ash particles at a distance. It messed with some of the sensors for a bit, but nothing serious. The air was thick with the smell of sulfur, even that far out. The captain came over the PA, told us to keep our eyes peeled in case it affected our exercises. We ended up continuing. But I'll tell you what—seeing the raw power of that thing… no war exercise compares to what Mother Nature can throw at you."

Violet and Poppy stared at him, still wanting more. So, Widow leaned in, lowering his voice to a dramatic whisper, and said, "You don't forget something like that. The volcano belched fire and ash." Exactly after he said it, he belched on purpose, and smiled at the girls with a big grin. Both girls made faces and laughed at him.

Widow sat back and drank more of his coffee. Nora grinned from ear to ear, like she'd not felt this happy in a long time. At least, she'd not felt this distracted from whatever troubled her.

CHAPTER 18

Franklin sat in his idling truck on a curb across the street, his gun at the ready in the aftermarket gun holster tucked into his console. A phone mount magnet held his phone to a spot just right of his steering wheel on the dash, near the closest air vent, which blasted cold air against his face. The temperatures outside had risen with the hours of the day. It got so hot out that Franklin had to take his coat off and drape it across the passenger seat. That helped for the first half-hour that Nora Sutton, her girls, and Widow sat inside the Hawaiian food joint.

Brock's influence stretched across the entire state of Missouri, and with it, so did Franklin's authority. Iron Crossing was the area most under the family influence since it was the place of Brock's birth. The Brock name was baked into the fibers of Iron Crossing, but more so in Old Town than in New Town. Everyone in Old Town knew the Brock name. Most feared it. New Town was less influenced by the Brock name. The name still carried weight, but not as much as in Old Town. The residents of New Town were more idealistic than the families of Old Town.

Collin Brock, Sr. didn't concern himself with trivial matters around Iron Crossing. That's what his son was for. He left his son to rule over the town of his birth. For the most part, Junior did his own thing. Brock had enough loyalists in place to ensure that the family business ran smoothly enough, regardless of what Junior did. The strategy worked because Franklin was there. He kept Junior in check, but also he ran most of the business. And the Feds stayed out of it because Iron Crossing, a place most people had never heard of, had a low crime rate. Crime statistics for Iron Crossing were low overall, although they were higher on the east side of Black River than on the west. But the thing about statistics was that they weren't always true. Stats and polls don't always reflect reality. Sometimes reality and truth are completely different.

Since Junior ran his own operation back in Old Town, crime was technically higher there. But another thing about crime stats was that the results are based on *reported* crimes. *Reported* was the keyword.

Lots of people knew of Junior's operation, but these were all the right kinds of people. Many of them were people in positions of power, the kind with fat pockets, all of which Brock, Sr. greased up with regular payments to keep them looking the other way. The next rung down the ladder of people who were in the know were the customers themselves. A smaller portion of people who knew the exact nature of Junior's business worked for Brock, Sr. And they weren't going to say anything to anyone. There was another group of people who knew of Junior's business. It was an even smaller number of people. They knew because they were his victims.

Sometimes the victims were chosen randomly, and sometimes Junior targeted people for a specific reason. The reasons varied. Some were chosen because they were photogenic, because they looked good on camera. Others were picked because they had crossed Junior. He was known for being petty. The everyday people of Iron Crossing didn't know about Junior's secret business, but they knew not to cross him. Rumors swirled through the town, and no one was stupid enough to ask questions. Asking questions was what got people on the victim list. It made them targets. A certain face came to Franklin's mind, the face of a current victim. It was a guy who had asked too many questions. He got too nosy. He should've just stayed in his lane, minded his own business, or, better yet, picked a different profession. But he didn't. He was someone who crossed over into two of the victim buckets. He was in the wrong place at the wrong time, and he had crossed Junior by asking too many questions about the business. One question he asked, the one that got him into the victim column, was *What're you hiding?*

He shouldn't have asked that. If he'd not asked that, or if he'd taken the bribe money they offered him, then he'd be in the friend column. But he was a goody two-shoes, a boy scout. Now he faced the consequences of that choice.

Franklin thought about the man. He pictured the guy's face in his mind. In a way, he felt sorry for him. Being in the wrong place at the wrong time was just bad luck. No way around it. Sometimes we get what we get, no matter what we choose. Call it fate. Call it karma. Either way, this victim was going to get what he got. And he'd get it tonight. The face of the victim belonged to a state auditor. He was slated to be thrown into the Iron Ring tonight. Franklin wasn't a sadist. He didn't love watching extreme violence, like some kind of sicko. But thousands of people were like that.

At first, Franklin had wanted the state auditor dead already. The guy was a nobody, but still a loose end. But all in good time, as he knew. The extra time keeping him alive, ultimately didn't matter. Junior's business had a need. There was a schedule to keep. Junior had a secret business to run and there was a show to put on. So why not let the state auditor fill the role Junior had planned for him? Why not let the state auditor stand center stage for the role of his life?

Mr. Brock didn't need to know about the state auditor. Why tell him? It was such a small-scale problem, and Mr. Brock didn't like to be bothered with trivial things. So, into the Iron Ring the auditor would go.

Still, Franklin kept thinking about it because the guy's credentials were questionable. Not that he wasn't who he said he was. It was just that the state outsourced some of its workload, like auditors. Which might be a stroke of luck for Franklin and Junior, because after the guy was torn to bits, they could just deny he was ever there. Who would even question it? Not the state government. It's not like they were tracking every freelancer's whereabouts.

This state auditor had shown up a few days ago, asking too many questions. He'd shown that he couldn't be bought. He was a man with character—an idealist. But government work was no place to show character. It was not the place for idealists. Being the high-moral good type got plenty of men in politics killed. That had been Franklin's experience.

The guy had to go. But there was no rush. He wasn't going to say anything to anyone. Not ever. So putting the state auditor's death off a few days made no difference. Dead was dead. And tonight, the guy would be dead, in the most gruesome fashion. The viewers would get their money's worth. That was for damn sure. They always did. Franklin had to hand it to Junior; he knew what he was doing when he created the Iron Ring.

Back to his surveillance, Franklin shook off his thoughts of the state auditor. That guy wasn't Franklin's main concern. He wasn't their biggest problem. Not anymore. Not today. Not this morning. Franklin had a bigger threat to worry about —this new outsider. Widow was a dangerous question mark;

he had broken Junior's arm and beat up three of his guys, putting them all in the hospital.

Franklin's number one priority was protecting Mr. Brock's business, and his son. But his secret priority was to protect his and Junior's side business. Brock couldn't know. Not yet. The problem was, they were growing. It was only supposed to have been a small-scale kind of business. But that was changing. It made Franklin think of cryptocurrency. It was something that started small but grew exponentially, despite all the doubters. Franklin didn't get it. He was born of an older generation. There were a lot of things that were extremely profitable, that, like a lot of those in his age bracket, he just didn't get. He never would.

Country music played low over the truck's radio. Franklin lip-synced along with the music while he watched the Hawaiian joint. Suddenly, he got a phone call, which showed up on a touchscreen built into the middle of the dash because his phone was bluetoothed to the truck. When it rang, the music paused and an AI voice from his phone asked if he wanted to take the call.

Franklin glanced at the name identified by his phone. It was a name from his contact list. *Shit*, he thought. Worry formed in the pit of his stomach. This wasn't a call he wanted to take. Not today. He had way too much on his plate already. It was also a call he couldn't ignore.

Franklin didn't respond to the AI voice. Instead, he clicked a green *talk* button on the dashboard's touchscreen.

A man's voice said, "Franklin, are you alone?"

"Yeah. I'm in the truck."

"Junior not answering my calls. Every time I call it goes to voicemail. What the hell's going on?" the voice asked.

He's not answering because Franklin told him not to. They can't afford for his father to find out about this situation. It would bring too many eyes on them.

The voice belonged to Garret Rourke, Brock's number one and Franklin's superior. Technically, he and Franklin had the same title. However, Rourke outranked Franklin in the hierarchy of Brock's organization. And that made total sense. Rourke was older, more experienced, and had been with Brock for twenty-one years, one year more than Franklin. Rourke knew all of Brock's dirty secrets. He knew where the bodies were buried—literally. But he didn't know about Franklin and Junior's side business.

Franklin didn't answer Rourke's question at first. He started with pleasantries, and not because it was protocol. He was stalling on purpose, trying to come up with an angle. He had to tell Rourke some of the truth because Rourke would relay it directly to Brock. He had to tell him about Junior being in the hospital. He probably should tell him about Widow. You never want to lie and then have Brock find out. That's how you get stuffed into the trunk of a car and smashed to bits in one of those giant car crushers. Franklin knew this because he had stuffed a few guys into trunks of cars and sent them into the car crusher himself—all on Brock's orders.

Brock had spies everywhere. Lots of the people who worked for him made good money. That money buys loyalty, and the most loyal of Brock's stable were the switchmen. They were more dangerous because they also served as his local muscle, not just part of his spy network.

Maybe Franklin could lessen the blow with some niceties first. He asked, "Where're you guys now?"

Rourke cleared his throat. From Rourke's side of the phone, wind rustled and blew static over the phone. The connection wasn't great. Rourke said, "We're in a place called Kalahari."

"Where's that?"

"It's in the Northern Cape. We're like 300 kilometers from Upington."

"And where's that?"

"It's in South Africa. We're 600 kilometers from Johannesburg," Rourke said, his voice growing frustrated. Franklin had spoken to him enough times to know where Rourke's red line for patience was. And he had just come right up to it. He knew not to cross it. Franklin had worked with Rourke for a long time, and never, not once, had he ever been on the bad side of a conversation with Rourke. That was about to change.

"What time's it there?"

Rourke paused and silence came over the phone. He was checking the time on his phone, Franklin figured. Rourke said, "It's nearly seven o'clock at night."

"How's the hunt going?"

"It's cold as shit. It's wintertime here. But we're heading out soon."

"A night hunt? What's he shooting this time?"

"Franklin, quit stalling and tell me what's going on. How come Junior's not answering me?"

Franklin took a deep breath, and told Rourke a safe version of the story, one that left out the Iron Ring. He told Rourke that Junior and his guys went out for a drunken morning joyride. They stopped at Nora's farm, harassed her, and then this big Good Samaritan guy intervened, beating them all up and breaking bones, including Junior's arm.

At the end of the conversation, Franklin took another deep breath, waiting for Rourke's response. But he didn't respond, not for a long minute. Franklin couldn't see him, but he heard him breathing. He assumed Rourke was either facepalming or waiting around for a punchline to follow, like this was just a twisted joke.

Finally, Franklin asked, "Rourke?"

"Yeah," Rourke answered. "I'm here. I'm just trying to wrap my head around this. Did you say one guy did this?"

"Yes. I didn't believe it either, when Junior told me. But he's real. Not sure he did all that by himself, like Junior claimed. But why would he lie?"

Rourke said, "He wouldn't. I guess. He lies about lots of things, but you're right. He wouldn't lie about that. It makes no sense. Either way, this isn't good."

"I know it sounds bad. But you know how Junior is."

"I know. And lucky for you, Mr. Brock also knows. But he ain't going to be happy. Is Junior an asshole? Sure. But he's still Mr. Brock's kid. And nobody messes with the Brocks. Period. So, what've you done about his guy? Is he in the back of a car trunk by now?"

"Not yet."

"And why not?"

"It's not that simple. There's other elements to worry about."

"Like what? Who is this guy?"

"That's what I mean. I don't know who he is. Since he took out Junior and three armed men, I think it's best to figure that out. Right now, I'm gathering intel on him."

"You don't even know who he is yet?"

"I got his name, but I don't know anything about him, is what I mean. Like, how dangerous is he?"

Silence. Franklin could hear Rourke breathing, and imagine his rage building.

Franklin said, "I know. I'm sorry. He's not easy to get a read on. But I'm working on it."

"Didn't you ask this woman about him?"

"I confronted her about him. That's how I got the name. But she swore she didn't know him. She said she'd never seen him before."

"What's the name?"

"Jack Widow. Does it ring a bell?"

"Never heard it before," Rourke said. "You're sure this woman doesn't know more? Maybe Jack Widow is her boyfriend?"

"I'm sure. He wasn't on her property. I don't think he's staying there. And Junior and the boys claim he came from the road. They said he looked like a nobody, a hobo. But…"

Rourke asked, "But what?"

"When I first saw him, he was mostly as they described. But when I saw him again, he looked cleaned up, like a different man. I just want to be cautious with him."

There was a pause, a defeated sigh, and Rourke said, "Get with it then." He clicked off the call, leaving Franklin relieved that Rourke hadn't seemed to know anything about it, and eager to get rid of this Widow guy by any means possible.

CHAPTER 19

Across the world, Rourke clicked off the call with Franklin. He paused and watched his breath as he exhaled in the cold night. Then he stuffed the phone into his coat pocket and fumbled with his rifle. Not that he would need it. Brock would kill him if he took the kill shot and stole Brock's glory. Still, it was best that Rourke be armed with a rifle that could kill a five-hundred-pound beast, in case it attacked them.

Rourke pulled a pair of hunting gloves over his hands to keep them warm. Night had fallen an hour earlier. The temperature had dropped down to the low thirties. He shivered. Cold was not his thing. He was born in the American South, in Florida. Now he spent most of his time with Brock in the state of Missouri. Missouri got cold in the winter, but Rourke spent his time indoors, where there was heat. Still, he didn't complain.

Rourke, Brock, another guy who worked for Brock, and a hunting guide—an expert tracker—were the entire crew. Brock had paid a small fortune to be able to hunt this particular animal. It came with a lot of risk, because the beast they hunted had a reputation for being evasive and particularly violent. It was Africa's most-feared predator. And this one had killed humans. It killed a man who tried to hunt it a year earlier, and it killed at least two poachers a few months ago.

Right then, Brock was huddled in front of the headlights of a Land Rover Defender with the other three guys in the hunting party. Like his son, Brock stood at 5'9" but he claimed to be 5'11" on all his IDs. He wore shoes with lifts to feed the illusion. He had the same cropped-blond hair and blue eyes as his son. But that's where the similarities stopped. Whereas Junior was scrawny at 150 pounds, Brock had more meat on him. He wasn't fat, but had more weight hanging off his frame, a product of time and age. Unlike Junior, Brock didn't inflate his sense of authority to compensate for anything. He was the real deal. He'd built his empire from nothing. And also unlike Junior, who stood to inherit everything by blood, Brock had earned it all by spilling blood.

Brock saw Rourke get off the call, and called out to him, "Hey, what's going on?"

Rourke was older than Franklin, but the same age as Brock. He wasn't the same height. He stood just a hair over six feet, so he was taller than Brock. But he never looked down at Brock. He learned to never look down at Brock a long time ago, so he always stared at Brock's forehead when speaking to him, and not his eyes. Rourke said, "That was Franklin. There's a situation."

"Something wrong with our shipments?"

"No."

"Our supply line?"

"No, it's Junior."

"Is he dead?"

No, but he's in the hospital, Rourke thought, but said, "No."

"Okay, let me guess. He's in some kind of trouble again?"

"You can say that. He's…" Rourke said, but Brock put up a hand to stop him. Rourke stopped mid-sentence. He knew better than to interrupt Brock. Never look down at Brock, and never interrupt him. These were rules to live by, or infringements to die by—dealer's choice.

"He's not in jail, is he?" Brock asked, but doubted it since he had a few guys on the payroll in the sheriff's department in Iron Crossing. Unless Junior had left the town and taken his guys with him to party down in New Orleans again, which was out of Brock's scope of power and influence.

"No. That's not it."

"Good, then whatever it is can wait. Right?"

Rourke thought for a second. Junior wasn't dead. He just had a broken arm and probably a bruised ego. The other guys got the same and worse. But it wasn't a critical issue that Franklin wasn't already handling. Besides never looking down at Brock, never interrupting him, and never lying to him, there was another rule: Never ruin his vacations. Which might fall under the *never interrupt him* category. There was nothing pressing. Nothing that he needed to know right then. They were already geared up for the night hunt. So Rourke said, "No. Franklin's handling it now. It can wait."

"Good," Brock said, clapping a hand against Rourke's shoulder and giving a slow, sinister grin. "Then let's get to it,."

With that, all four men climbed into the Land Rover. The tracker drove and the others took the passenger seats. They drove down a sand dune and off into the darkness.

Less than an hour later, and a mile from where they had parked the Land Rover, the four men walked through a thick grove of trees, rifles in hand. Brock carried a Holland & Holland Royal Double Rifle, chambered with .470 Nitro Express cartridges, a classic weapon so powerful that it could take down any king of the jungle, anywhere in the world. Which was good, because that was the stature of animal they were hunting. Brock had fired it before, many times, killing other big game animals. He knew the power behind the rifle. It was the classic choice for big game hunters. It was all polished wood and steel with a solid weight that made lesser men tremble, but Brock considered himself among the great white hunters of history. The rifle's stock was dark walnut, oiled to a high gloss that caught the faintest sliver of moonlight, casting it in a ghostly glow. The other two men opted for the Ruger RSM, chambered with .458 Lott Bolt-Action cartridges, a more modern choice. All four rifle barrels gleamed in the night as the men made their way through the trees. The tracker led the group, but Brock led the charge.

Brock revered the whole experience. He'd better too, because it wasn't cheap. He had shelled out a few hundred grand to hunt this creature. He revered the hunt, the adrenaline, the fear, and the kill. He even revered the rifle. He thumbed over the engraving on the side, an intricate weave of vines and beasts, as if the rifle itself was etched with the ghosts of every creature it had killed. And there were plenty—cape buffalo, rhinos, even a bull elephant. This was no beginner's gun. The Holland & Holland Royal Double Rifle was a beast all its own, built to bring down animals so big they could crush a man without a thought.

The real power of the Holland & Holland Royal Double Rifle was in the huge .0470 cartridges. They were all power and no mercy, making the gun optimal for hunting big game. The heavy brass rounds, each the size of Brock's largest fingers, packed enough power to send a 500-grain bullet screaming at a rate of more than 2,000 feet per second. That's enough force to punch through muscle, bone, and anything else that stood in its path. Enough to stop a charging lion dead in its tracks, which was good because that was their quarry.

As the four men stalked through the cold wind and blowing brush, the Kalahari night stayed eerily silent. They felt the night's faint whispers of peril, like sirens warning them to turn back. Under a moon barely piercing through the tree canopy, Brock, all swagger and dressed in tailored winter khaki, squinted into the darkness. The night winds gusted cold breezes at them, slapping their faces. The other men were cold, but Brock liked it this way. The combination of elements and danger was one of his favorite parts. It made him feel alive. As a man of his stature, he rarely felt fear. In fact, the last time he was afraid of something was over forty years ago. It was his abusive father. The man had been a tyrant, much like Brock was to his own son, although he didn't see it that way. The difference between Brock and his father was that he had money, and lots of it. His son may have been neglected, but he also got all his wants.

Most people would call Brock a thrill-seeker, but that wasn't quite true. For Brock, the thrill came from the risk. It was the closest he got to fear. Tonight he hoped to feel the rush of fear. Truth be told, that's what he searched for. Fear was the thing he chased, not adventure. Hunting a man-eating lion gave him great hope, great anticipation. The anticipation of fear was the next best thing to fear itself. So he savored that feeling.

Rourke walked at Brook's three o'clock. Normally, Rourke stood as a guard, like a Secret Service agent with his protectee. But this time, Rourke paid little attention to Brock's safety. He was worried about his own. Rourke didn't have a death wish, as he thought of it, like Brock did. He didn't chase death, or chase fear. Rourke was fine in urban settings, dealing with lowlifes, but not chasing lions out in the jungles of Africa.

Rourke, like the others, watched the dark, shadowy brush for the lion. Not because he was protecting Brock, but because he was afraid. If the creature lunged at him, he didn't care about interrupting Brock's moment of glory, he'd shoot the damn thing. He didn't want to get mauled to death.

Rourke cradled his Holland & Holland Royal Double Rifle, keeping his eyes sharp. He listened and watched, scanning the dunes beyond the trees. Suddenly, he saw something. It darted just over tall, windblown grass. He turned towards it, aimed his rifle, and paused. Whatever it was, it was gone now.

Brock noticed Rourke's sudden jerk to the right, and whispered, "Rourke, what is it?"

"I saw something. That way. In the brush," Rourke said, and pointed in the direction of the movement he had witnessed. His hand trembled, just slightly. He'd hunted other big game animals with Brock in the past, but never a beast of a lion and never at night. The lions they'd hunted before were already prepped for the hunt and the kill. In other words, they were drugged to the point of being dazed, a common practice among big-game-hunting companies. Usually, the hunted lions were old, sick, and drugged to boot. It's one of big game hunting's dirty little secrets. Rich tourists came from all over the world, paid a country a huge sum of money for the privilege of hunting lions. But what they weren't told was that the sanctioned lions were often drugged, making them weak and not much of a threat. But the clients didn't know that. They paid for the experience of hunting one of nature's most fierce killing machines, thinking they were some kind of big bad hunter just because they got the king of the jungle. The reality was they got a lion that was on its way out anyway.

Not this time. This time, Brock made sure to pay for the real deal. That's why they were out at night. He'd paid for this privilege, but it was still kept a secret. No reason for the South African officials he'd paid to broadcast it to the world.

All four men looked in the direction of Rourke's sighting. The tracker raised a hand for quiet, halting them. He was a local man, tough and grizzled, with skin as dark as the night around them. He knew the terrain as well as any other man, but that wasn't the only reason they hired him: None of the other trackers would take this job. That's how bad the lion they hunted was; it had a reputation and was on the verge of becoming legend.

Suddenly, they all heard it. In the distance, a lion roared. They were facing the direction of the tall grass, but the roar came from the opposite direction. It was hard to pinpoint because the roar echoed faintly around them.

"No, man!" the tracker said, his accent thick and unmistakable. "Don't look away, hey! If you saw the lion that side, then that's where it is, *bru*. Out here on the plains, their roars can mess with you, make you think they're somewhere else."

Brock said, "So, it's this way? Let me out in front. I will shoot it."

The tracker was unsure, but he didn't argue. He pointed the way. The others stayed at the rear, except for Rourke. He followed closely behind Brock.

The four men stepped forward toward the tall grass, coming out of the trees and into the clearing. Brock slowly stalked into the grass, pointing the Holland & Holland Royal's double barrels in front of him, ready to fire. They continued for a good ways, then Rourke said, "This is where I saw it."

"There's nothing here," Brock said.

The tracker stepped forward, passed Brock, and knelt. He studied the ground. With his rifle, he brushed aside tall grass, and stared at something. "Here," he said.

Brock looked over his shoulder. There on the ground was a huge paw print. The tracker reached a hand out and fanned it over the print. Rourke came up behind them, followed by the other guy. Brock said, "That's massive."

Putting his usual scripted pitch on it, the tracker said, "This lion's a beast, *bru*, a proper monster—pure muscle and rage, made by the harsh Kalahari. This isn't some lazy lion you see on safari, hey. No, this one's different. He doesn't lounge around under a tree in the midday sun. This one's as big as they come, a shadow of the night." The thing was, even though this was his usual script, this time it was true. He meant every word of it.

The tracker released the brush and stood up. He said, "From these tracks, looks like he's lean, but pushing 500 pounds. And don't underestimate him, man. This guy's been out here living on buffalo and poachers."

Rourke trembled at the description. The other guy took up the rear, keeping his eyes trained on the trees.

The tracker said, "Come on. He's headed this way." He led them through the tall grass, over sand dunes, and back to another cluster of trees.

On their way, they heard another heart-stopping roar. They heard it before they saw the lion—the low rumble of a growl, vibrating through the ground, seeping into their bones. It wasn't close, but it wasn't far either. Rourke and the other guy exchanged wary glances, visibly scared. Brock envied their reactions. He wished he could feel fear like that again, just to feel alive. But he didn't. He felt the rush of the hunt, but no fear. He felt invincible. He tilted his head, his lips curling into a grin as he met Rourke's eyes. Rourke knew Brock well enough to know he was a bit demented. But so was Junior: like father, like son.

"That's him," Brock whispered excitedly.

The tracker paused, halting them, and said, "Stay sharp, hey. Sounds like he's hungry."

Rourke looked behind them, and said, "That sounds like it's behind us?"

"Nah, he's straight ahead, *bru*. Don't let the roars fool you," the tracker replied. He moved forward into the trees and signaled for them to spread out, but not too far. They fanned out, slipping into the trees, moving in sync, footsteps as light as feathers on the dry soil, creeping deeper into the darkness. Brock's heart pounded in his chest, the thrill and excitement beating like a relentless drum against the quiet night. He felt alive—more alive than ever before—and wondered if this was fear. He glanced at Rourke and knew it wasn't. Rourke trembled, gripping his rifle tightly. Brock looked at the others. They all trembled a little. But not him.

Suddenly, the wind shifted, carrying a scent—something musky and primal. The lion. It was close now, prowling just beyond the trees. Brock could almost feel the lion's golden eyes sizing them up, targeting them as intruders in its territory.

The tracker led them further into the grove. All four men's hearts pounded—three out of fear, one out of excitement, all fueled by adrenaline. The tracker looked down at the sand, spotted the beast's tracks, and said, "This way. Further in."

The other three men stayed fanned out, but followed. The tracker took the lead, Brock at his three o'clock, Rourke to his ten, and the other guy at his six. The tracker followed the tracks, until something went wrong. Something was very different about this predator. The tracks stayed straight, but then suddenly veered to the right and circled back behind the men.

Then, like a flash of lightning, a streak of tawny fur ran at them from out of the blackness. Only it didn't come from the front. It came from the back. It was almost surreal in size, a ghostly shape gliding through the night. Brock's heart leapt, shock and awe mingling into a heady rush. The beast snarled, low and guttural, a sound man has feared from the dawn of time.

The other three men were terrified. The lion swooped through their fanned positions and snatched up the six o'clock guy in its massive jaws. Its fangs clamped down on the guy's neck, crunching it with an immense bite force. The guy's neck snapped right there in front of the frozen men. Blood pooled around the lion's enormous fangs.

The lion dashed out of their sight, dragging the six o'clock guy's body with it. It all happened in seconds. The three of them, even the tracker, stood there dumbfounded. Blood streaked across the sand and vanished into the tall grass, leaving behind a crimson trail.

"Come on!" Brock said, leaping into action. He followed the trail. The tracker shook off his stunned reaction and followed Brock. Rourke pulled up the rear, mostly because he didn't want to be left alone. Brock ran, chasing the lion's trail. The creature raced ahead of him. Brock stopped at the edge of the trees and peered into the grove. He saw the lion's tail vanish into the darkness, but not the other guy's legs; they were lying in a pool of moonlight. The lion had stopped dragging him. Brock put a hand up to keep the others from running past him. They stopped behind him.

All three men stood in horror, not at what they saw, because they couldn't see much—they stopped because of the terrifying sounds they heard. The lion had stopped dragging the body, laid down on its haunches, head down, and started eating it. They heard the horrible chewing sounds.

Brock started to whisper, but then he realized the lion wasn't aware of their presence. So Brock readied his rifle, aiming in the direction of the macabre chewing, and said, "Rourke, get your light out and light him up."

Rourke lowered his rifle and fished his flashlight out. He found it and aimed it at the lion's position, but didn't flip the switch immediately. He asked, "Ready?"

Brock said, "Light him up." And Rourke turned on the flashlight. The beam fell across the sandy ground. Wind blew puffs of sand across the ground. Rourke flicked the beam around until it was on the beast.

The tracker gasped in horror as the lion ate from the dead guy's torso. Then, like a nightmare come to life, the lion stopped, and stared at the men who were interrupting his meal. Its eyes gleamed, an unholy fire burning in its gaze. It was beautiful—a creature of power and rage, a king by the laws of nature. The animal stared at them and roared. Its roar shook them to the core, a deep, bone-rattling sound that echoed through the night.

Brock aimed, his hands steady, every muscle in his body taut with anticipation. Then he squeezed the trigger, killing the beast.

They posed it for pictures after moving the remains of their dead companion out of the frame. Before they left, Rourke took the other guy's passport and phone from his pocket.

They considered burying him, but the tracker said not to worry about it because scavengers would come by and take care of the rest.

An hour later, the tracker dragged the lion's severed head to the Land Rover. Rourke paid him the other guy's portion for the trip to compensate him for his silence.

On the way back to their hotel, Brock turned in the passenger seat, looked back at Rourke and asked a question about the story Rourke told him earlier, the one straight from Franklin. It was about Junior, and the stranger who broke his arm.

The question that Brock asked was, "Is he dead yet?"

CHAPTER 20

The sun beamed down from its 1:00 pm position in the sky. Nora's truck was still parked outside the Hawaiian restaurant. When Nora came out to check on Joanie and the puppies, Kailea—one of the restaurant's owners—went with her so she could get a look at them too. Nora and Kailea had been standing by the truck for about half an hour, talking.

Franklin watched from his truck, parked across the street. He was far enough away that Nora didn't notice him. He was more concerned about the chance of Widow seeing him, but Widow didn't come out with them.

Instead, Widow sat inside with the girls. They'd finished their meals and ice cream a long time ago, but they were having so much fun talking that they ended up staying in the booth for over an hour. Nora had seemed relaxed for the first time since she pointed a rifle at him a few hours earlier. In fact, she'd smiled more than once during the sit-down.

The girls were happy and laughing, and Widow enjoyed talking to them. How often did he get to be around young children? The answer was not very much. He didn't mind being Nora's relief.

Nora and Kailea talked outside and then returned as Poppy was showing Widow a scar she got on her hand from a bee sting. "I guess you're not supposed to pick them up," she told him.

The girls' faces lit up because Nora and Kailea brought Joanie and the box of puppies in with them. Kailea had decided to forgo state health codes and allow the dogs inside. Joanie ran to the table and popped a squat next to Widow's feet. Kailea was carrying the box of puppies, and Nora said, "Guess what?"

The girls stared at her, and nearly in unison, they asked, "What?"

Nora told them that Kailea had agreed to take the last two puppies. The girls cheered and thanked her. She told them they had to help her name the animals. Widow spent the rest of the hour listening to name suggestions from the girls.

After they settled on some name ideas, but no definitive answer, Kailea said she'd take the puppies home and her husband could weigh in. She invited the girls to come and visit them any time.

Nora led the way as the girls, Widow, and Joanie took up the rear. The girls walked in front of him, skipping, occasionally turning back to ask him more questions. Joanie trotted along-side Widow, tongue hanging out of her mouth.

They stopped on the curb, near the truck. Nora said, "So, where to? The bus stop?"

Widow said, "You didn't tell me more about this guy that scared you so much."

Nora said, "I guess I got so wrapped up in the moment, I forgot." Then she asked the girls to get in the truck. They protested at first, but she told them to start it and play with the radio, which they liked doing. So, they obeyed. Joanie stayed out on the curb, standing next to Widow, as if she was his dog now.

Nora went into more detail about Franklin visiting her. She told Widow she'd heard rumors that Franklin was more than just one of Junior's goons, that he was some kind of enforcer. But one thing she specifically said was, "He's not just a switchman."

Widow said, "Switchman?"

"Yeah, they're these locals that work for the Brocks. They work at the railyard, but they're also like thugs for the family."

"Yeah, I ran into them this morning. How do you know they're thugs?"

"It's rumors, mostly. Iron Crossing is small enough that everyone knows something about everything."

"How many are there?"

"I don't know. Locally, not many. Maybe a dozen, maybe less. They ride the rails and work at protecting the trains, mostly."

Widow said, "Okay. What about this Franklin guy?"

"What about him?"

"What else can you tell me about him?"

"He's clean-cut, professional, like a seasoned detective from a movie."

"What did you tell him?"

"I told him what happened," she said, and paused a nervous beat. "I'm sorry. I told him your name. I didn't know I'd see you again. I just wanted to get rid of him."

Widow smiled, which was the opposite of what she had expected from him. She asked, "What? You're not mad?"

He shrugged, and said, "Why? I don't care if they all know my name."

"You're not afraid?"

"Should I be? Look, I know the Brocks seem to have an iron grip on this town. But I'm not one of you. I'm something else completely."

"Okay, so what now?"

Widow said, "I will leave—eventually. Right now, I got no plans to leave. I came here looking for an answer to a question, one that I thought was just a bullshit story, but now I'm not so sure."

"What question? What story?"

Widow caught a flicker from the corner of his eye. He glanced up and saw trucks parked along the street, pedestrians walking, and nothing else out of the ordinariness of daily life. He said, "I'll tell you later. But I'm not leaving right this second. Not yet."

"But you're leaving today?"

"Probably not," Widow said, and glanced up at the parked vehicles again. He felt eyes watching him. "Maybe you should go. It could be risky for you, us being seen together. I don't want to cause you and the girls any more trouble."

"What about you? It's not safe for you here."

"Why did you come and find me? Why warn me?"

Nora paused, looked away, and then up at him. She said, "Because as long as you're here, then it's not safe for me either. They think we know each other. Shit, Franklin thinks I'm with you. At least, he asked about it."

"Where is he? I can go have a chat with him. I can straighten it out."

"No! No. That's not possible. Just leave town. Please?"

"I can't. I told you. Not yet. But I'll be gone soon enough. Then I'll be out of your hair. Don't worry about it."

"Where're you going to stay?"

Just then Violet and Poppy popped the passenger door open and stuck their heads out. Like she'd been listening to everything they said, Violet said, "He can live with us, Māmā!"

Nora shushed the girls and stayed quiet for a moment. Then she did something surprising. Widow didn't know her, but he'd guess it was out of character for her, especially in her situation. She said, "Well, Franklin already thinks I'm hiding you. And if you're going to stay in town anyway, it'll be safer for both of us together instead of him thinking that and you being somewhere else."

"You think so?" Widow asked.

"If they can't find you, they'll come back to my farm. It could get dangerous for us."

"Yeah, but if I'm there, they'll find me."

Nora smirked, and said, "Exactly, then I can hand you over and they'll forgive me. Hell, they'll probably reward me. You know he gave me money already."

"He did? For what, to locate me? Is this a trap?"

"It was to buy my silence. That's what they do. They buy people's silence," Nora said, but she thought, *Or kill them.* She knew it was risky to ask Widow, a dangerous man himself, to stay at her farm. But she figured he'd proven himself more than capable of protecting them. And maybe they were better off with him in their sight, rather than wandering Iron Crossing and causing more trouble. *Maybe the Brocks will give up on him after a time?* she wondered.

Widow looked around the street, glancing over Franklin in his truck as he did. Only he didn't know it was Franklin because Franklin sat behind tinted windows, parked far enough away not to be spotted. Widow looked at the sky. Joanie barked at him. The girls slid out of the truck and pulled at his fingers, one kid hanging off each hand. They shouted, "Please, Mr. Widow! Please!"

Widow looked at Nora, and said, "Are you sure you want me to stay there? It could be worse if they find me there."

Nora looked at Joanie, and said, "I'm not worried about that. Not really. I got guns, this dog, and you're not too bad on your feet."

Widow nodded.

She added, "Plus, I need a bunch of stuff done around the farm. You can help us. I'll pay you."

"I thought you weren't hiring? You know, the sign?"

She smiled, a big hearty grin. Widow said, "I guess I can stay there. You can afford to pay me now anyway. Since you got that Franklin money."

"Oh, no! I'm keeping that. I'm paying you with room and board," Nora said, and ushered the girls back into the truck. Widow put the tailgate down, pointed at it, and Joanie hopped in, like she understood him better than she did her own family. Widow shut the tailgate, glanced around the street once last time, and got into the truck.

Seconds later, they were on the road, heading back to Nora's farm.

Franklin watched them leave together.

CHAPTER 21

The day went by quickly, like good days usually do. The late afternoon sun dipped low over Nora's farm, casting a warm, amber glow over the careworn fields, a toolshed with a rusted roof, and the rundown old barn behind her house. Her farm wasn't dilapidated, but it was a far cry from King Ranch.

The farmhouse was in pretty good shape, but the rest of the place needed a little to a lot of work. Some upgrades wouldn't hurt the place, that was for sure. The house was painted white with black shutters and a big front porch, decorated with too many pots of plants and flowers to count. There were bolts in the porch ceiling from which a porch swing had once hung. Big picture windows at the front of the house faced west to pick up the sun setting grandly over the green trees and rolling hills. It was picturesque, if you could ignore the trucks blasting through the crossroads.

With a hammer in hand and nails stuffed into the pocket of a too-small work apron draped awkwardly around his neck, Widow stood on a shaky ladder, feeling uncertain about his center of gravity. After the girls had pulled him around the farm, introducing him to their animals, Nora handed him a list of chores. She hadn't been kidding when she said he'd be put to work. He quickly realized it wasn't just about taking advantage of his help. She was keeping him busy, giving him a reason to stay on the farm and out of town, where he might catch the attention of the wrong local and end up being ratted out to Franklin or to one of Brock's switchmen.

Besides, the farm needed these chores done—tasks that Nora didn't have time to handle. And there were plenty of them. Widow didn't mind. It felt good to do something out of the ordinary, to step out of his comfort zone.

Hammer in hand, Widow patched a large hole in the roof of Nora's weather-beaten old barn. A pair of horses neighed at him like they were laughing as he worked. He couldn't remember their names. But he remembered Violet and Poppy told him one of them was the mother and the other the son. He could only tell the difference by their sexes, because the mare looked too young to be the colt's mother. Plus, the colt looked too big to have come from her. Widow could relate. His mother had been a tiny woman. People commented in disbelief that a tiny, beautiful woman like her could birth a big scary guy like him.

Widow patched up the rest of the holes in the barn's roof. Thudding hammer sounds echoed through the quiet building. The horses neighed more and shuffled around in their stalls. They stared up at him quietly a few times. After he pounded the last nail he realized that their stall doors were wide open, meaning they had chosen to stay in there. It dawned on him that they had been watching him for entertainment.

Violet and Poppy stuck with him most of the day. Widow and the girls horseplayed around at the beginning, but once Nora put Widow to work, the girls became his little helpers, asking more questions about everything than actually helping him. He didn't mind. As the afternoon rolled on, they grew bored of chores, as little kids do. They opted to leave him to do the rest on his own.

After they left him, his progress sped up. Joanie stuck around for a little longer, but eventually she followed the girls' example and sauntered off. Widow continued burning through the chores. So far, he'd replaced a broken section of outer fence, fixed the latch on the goat pen, replaced several burnt-out light bulbs, and cleaned some gutters. He was heading off to put the ladder away when he noticed something covered up in the corner of the barn. It was big. Cobwebs covered sections of the large object. He thought it could be an old tractor.

Out of curiosity, Widow leaned the ladder against a wall, and uncovered part of the object. It was a motorcycle—an old one too. Widow used to know nothing about motorcycles, although he knew some basics of vehicle maintenance. But a few years ago he had to disguise himself as a biker in order to infiltrate a motorcycle club and rescue a mother and her son. Ever since then, he'd found himself more interested in bikes.

Seeing the motorcycle reminded him of Kara and Christopher Sabo. The last time he saw them was on a Mexican beach. Widow wondered how they were?

He shook off the memories, pulled back the canvas, and saw a beautiful, fully restored old motorcycle, a ghost from another time. It sat low, squat, and mean, with a quiet power, in a *walk tall, but carry a big stick* kind of way. The bike was vintage, probably holding a significant monetary value.

Widow wasn't a bike enthusiast or a collector, but he had an appreciation for things that were vintage. He was looking at a classic—a valuable machine that only got better with age, like a well-worn leather jacket.

Ever since his run-in with the Phantom Sons, Widow had felt the pull of what motorcycles signified—a raw, relentless freedom that went beyond the open road. It was the promise of shedding everything, of not living by society's rules, of moving without limits, untamed and unbound. It was a life stripped down to the nuts and bolts, where the only thing that mattered was the road ahead. It wasn't unlike his own life.

"My husband bought that bike," a voice said behind him. Widow turned to see Nora standing in the old barn's door-way. She had taken a shower and changed her clothes. She wore a short sundress, bright pink with a hibiscus flower print, and a pair of bohemian flat sandals. She looked comfortable, casual, and yet stunning all at the same time. Her blonde hair waved behind her in the low sunlight. It looked like she had not only showered, but had blown her hair out and styled it.

Nora's eyes sparkled. There wasn't much to the top and bottom of her dress, and both areas mesmerized Widow for obvious reasons. Her breasts pressed gently against the fabric, hinting at hard-to-ignore curves, while the hem of her dress flirted a few inches above her knees, revealing smooth, tanned legs. Widow tried not to stare, but the dress demanded his attention as much as her rifle had that morning. Nora was a stunning woman. But there was a strength in her, too—something real and untamed. She was both beautiful and formidable, a force of nature.

This morning she'd been nearly naked, aiming a rifle at him. And he'd seen much more of her then. But now, he was just as intimidated. He didn't know where to look. He tried staring at her eyes, but even her baby-blue eyes drew him in. At this moment, he felt more unsure about his center of gravity then he had when standing on the rickety ladder.

She carried two glasses with her. A familiar liquid swished around inside each glass. The ice cubes made a clinking sound. Nora showed them to Widow and said, "I brought you some lemonade. I made a fresh batch just for us."

Widow stood tall, slipped the hammer into a pocket on the apron, and smiled. Nodding at the bike, he said, "Sorry, I didn't mean to pry."

"Nonsense! Don't be sorry," she said, and approached him. The closer she got, the smaller she seemed compared to him, like she shrank under the shadow of the Incredible Hulk. She handed him the lemonade. Widow reached down and took it. Her fingertips slightly grazed his, like a bullet across his skin.

Widow thanked her for the lemonade with a head-nod, because he was too overwhelmed by her presence to speak. He drank the first third of the lemonade in one giant gulp.

Nora stepped back, and said, "Wow! You really were thirsty!"

"It's a hot day," Widow said, still struggling to speak, look at her, and not stare too hard. "This lemonade is delicious. Thank you."

Nora sipped hers, and said, "Thanks for all this work you've done for us. I wanted to…" She stopped.

"What is it?"

"I'm sorry again, for this morning. You know, I thought about it all day. If I'd just not overreacted like that when you first got here, none of this would've happened."

"What do you mean?" Widow asked and took another pull from the lemonade, reducing it to half a glass.

"I was just thinking that if I'd not run you off earlier, then you would've stuck around. Probably, you'd have been here when Junior showed up. Maybe things wouldn't have gotten so out of hand. You know? Because you were here as a witness. They might've just moved on."

"Doubt it. Those boys were out looking for trouble. You can't blame yourself for that."

Nora nodded, sipped some of her lemonade, and asked, "You into motorcycles?"

"I was in a motorcycle club once. But only for a couple of days."

"Really? How'd that happen? Or do I not want to know?"

"It's a long story."

"Motorcycle clubs normally are for life. How'd you get out so fast? Was it a trial and error thing, and they decided you made too many errors?"

Widow said, "I was undercover."

"Undercover? You're a cop?"

He shook his head, and said, "It was a lifetime ago. Now I'm just a guy passing through."

"I got that part when I saw you this morning. Your clothes. That shirt," she said, and giggled.

Widow shrugged.

Nora said, "You know, I was in a biker gang once too. Not undercover though."

"Really?"

"Back in Honolulu. That's where I'm from. I ran with them. I wasn't really like a rider or anything. I was just a biker chick."

"What happened?"

"I met Wade, and he was just so different. He was nothing like the guys I'd been dating. Eventually, I realized they'd been a bunch of losers masquerading as gangsters. I only really ran with them to piss off my parents. Mainly, my dad," Nora said, taking a big pull from her lemonade. She swallowed, smiled, and continued, "I was a teenager at the time. I'm so glad I grew out of it."

"Is Wade your husband?"

Nora's smile shrank away, like ashes on the wind. She looked down, stared at the ground, and said, "He was."

"Where is he?"

"That's the million-dollar question. No one knows. He disappeared a year ago," she moved away from him, back to the open barn door, and leaned against the frame. She stared out at the farmhouse and the driveway beyond. Widow followed her, stopped beside her, and looked out over the same vista.

In the distance, two tractor-trailers actually stopped at the intersection where Widow had gotten out of the Greengate Hauling truck eight hours earlier. Both truckers pulled their horn pull-cords, activating the loud, distinct sound from the trucks' air horn systems.

"I'm sorry to hear that," Widow said, thinking about Alex Hopper. He nearly asked her about him, but decided not to. Call it his first instincts or not wanting to disrupt her train of thought in the moment, but he thought it best to wait until he had more information about her husband. He wanted to allow her to just share it with him naturally, and not pry too much. Bringing up Hopper might ignite a firestorm of questions from her, for which he had no answers. Hopper and her husband disappearing at the same time might be something, or it might not. No need in firing her up over it just yet.

"Anyway, he bought the bike. But it's not his. It's mine."

Widow looked at her, surprise on his face.

"What? I told you. I'm the biker chick. Although the men back in Hawaii didn't want me riding in their club, I still knew how to ride. I dated enough bad biker boys to pick up all the tricks," Nora said, and turned back to the motorcycle. She walked towards it and brushed the fuel tank with her hand. The bike was painted the same blue as her eyes. "Wade knew how much I loved riding and he got it for me."

Widow mentioned it. "The color matches your eyes."

"That's what Wade used to say. He claimed that's why he bought this one in particular. But really he got it because the guy was selling it for like five grand, much less than it was worth."

Widow stayed quiet.

Nora asked, "Do you know about bikes?"

"I know where the gas goes."

She smiled, and said, "This is a 1969 Honda CB750. This is the world's first superbike, built back when Honda decided to change the game. They built it with a four-cylinder engine, and even now, after a whole year sitting idle, it looks ready to go."

Widow looked at the bike, studied it. Four chrome pipes snaked out from the engine block, each one waiting to roar back to life. He reached past Nora's small frame and ran his hand over the handlebars, feeling the grit and the cold steel beneath his fingers. The seat was low-slung, wrapped in cracked black leather that had seen thousands of miles and bore the scars to prove it. Yet the whole machine felt solid. Honda had built it to take damage and keep rolling, designed it to out-ride the years.

Widow tried not to crowd her, but he stood close to her. He asked, "Does it run?"

"It runs, but I've not ridden it since he left. Probably needs gas, maybe a new battery, and it should roar back to life, as loud and unstoppable as the day it rolled off the line. I put a lot of work into it."

She slow-turned and stared into Widow's eyes. Sensing he was too close to her, he backed away a step. She didn't budge. Ice clinked softly in her glass. She stared at him with those blue eyes. Her chest rose and dropped, slowly, with each breath.

Widow nervously cleared his throat, and said, "I finished all of the things you needed done. Next I was thinking I should put that lemonade stand back together for the girls."

"Widow, you've done a lot for us already."

"I don't mind."

"Are you sure?"

"Sure, it won't take long. What else am I gonna do?"

Nora smirked like something had crossed her mind. She didn't tell him what she was thinking about. But he got the feeling it was about him. She said, "Okay, let's get them to help. And while you're doing that, I'll make dinner for all of us." She beamed with joy. Something she'd not felt in a year. Even if it was imaginary, she wanted to live in the moment, forget about her financial troubles, about the potential danger from the Brocks.

They finished their lemonades out in the sun, in front of the barn. Then they walked close to each other, walking the yard, searching for the girls.

They found the girls running around the yard with Joanie, giggling as they chased one another through patches of long grass halfway between the farmhouse and the road. Nora called to them and they came over. Widow told them repairing the lemonade stand was the next project on his list. They cheered, mentioning that it was one of their favorite memories with their father. Minutes later, Widow was on his knees in the driveway, behind Nora's truck. The lemonade stand's remains lay in broken pieces between him and the girls. They sat on their haunches across from him, rubbing their chins, like the three of them were figuring out the next steps. Joanie circled them slowly, like she was standing guard.

Widow rebuilt the lemonade stand using tools which he had learned were Nora's and not Wade's. He used old boards from the fence he had replaced earlier to patch up the broken pieces of the lemonade stand. The whole thing took forty minutes. He stood it up and the girls rejoiced at its reconstruction. They hugged Widow's legs, one each. Satisfied, he glanced over his shoulder, catching Nora watching from the open front doorway to the house, staring out at them from behind the screen door. She wore a cooking apron over her sundress. A soft smile stretched across her face.

As the sun sank lower, Nora called them all in for dinner. Widow returned the tool apron to the shed, went inside the house, washed up, and sat with them at a big family dinner table, round and all wood. The place settings were set up like Widow was the king of England or something. All of the décor and fanciness was unnecessary, but he stayed quiet about it. He could see how happy the whole presentation made Nora. It was like she was imagining he was her husband and this was special family dinner. The kind she used to make for them, before Wade Sutton vanished. Who was Widow to take that away from her by asking needless questions?

Nora had cooked a big dinner to for the occasion. It was Huli Huli Chicken, a classic Hawaiian recipe taught to her by her mother. It was chicken thighs and drumsticks that had been marinated in soy sauce, brown sugar, pineapple juice, garlic, and ginger. Widow ate his portion so fast he went for seconds before the girls even got through half of theirs.

Poppy said, "You eat a lot, Mr. Widow."

He said, "I got a bigger fuel tank than you."

Poppy laughed and retorted, "I don't have a fool tank." No one corrected her, including Violet, which surprised Nora. She waited for it, but Violet seemed to miss the mistake.

There was a lot of warmth around the dinner table. It felt like a real family in a real family gathering, something Widow hadn't known for a long time and might never know again. Suddenly, Joanie pawed at Widow's leg. Nora shooed her away. After Widow ate his second helping he thought about going in for thirds, but talked himself out of it. They might need to save the leftovers for the next night.

After dinner, Nora ordered the girls to feed Joanie while she and Widow sat on the steps of the front porch, watching the sun set over the hills and trees. Tractor-trailers buzzed through the crossroads. Widow drank coffee, and Nora drank Mamaki tea.

At bedtime, Widow and Nora tucked the girls in. This was an experience out of his wheelhouse. He'd never done something like this, and yet it felt natural. The girls asked if Widow could tell them another story, like the one about the volcano eruption. So, he embellished a story about being caught in a storm at sea. It started with: "Fifty-foot waves crashed over the bow…" and ended with goodnights.

On his way out, Poppy yawned and asked him what's the

difference between boys and men, but Nora told her, "No more questions. It's time to go to sleep."

Nora left their door ajar so Joanie could roam in and out, as she did every night. Nora yawned, thanked Widow, and went to the kitchen to clean up. Widow helped with the dishes and took the trash out. Joanie ran through a doggie door in the kitchen and walked Widow out to the trash cans.

Later, Nora showed Widow to a spare bedroom; a simple, small space, with the bed neatly made. It was a queen, which was a little tight for him. But not a big deal. Widow had slept in cramped quarters on nuclear submarines submerged in water in tidal zones. A bed was a bed, and this one was much better than those in most combat zones.

Widow thanked her for letting him stay, and for the meal. Nora expressed her gratitude again for what he had done for them. But she didn't leave, not yet. She lingered in the doorway, her gaze holding his. Widow swallowed hard. She seemed to hesitate, like a question weighed on her.

"I haven't been with a man in a year," she murmured, almost to herself, "not since... well, since Wade disappeared." She stared at Widow, vulnerably, and yet something intense flickered in her eyes. Then she corrected herself, "I meant I've not had a man in the house since then. Not what I said."

Widow met her eyes. He was stoic on the outside, but nervous inside. "You don't have to explain," he said.

Nora smiled, a little sad, a little grateful. "Maybe I do. Maybe it's time I let someone in again. Maybe it's time I let go of him. Moved on." Her hand lingered on the doorframe, fingers tracing the grain of the wood, as if reaching for something— or someone.

Widow shifted slightly, feeling the weight of her words, the invitation hidden beneath them. But he stayed still, knowing this moment was hers to decide. She could choose to close the door to it, or leave it open.

Widow stayed quiet, waiting, sensing she had more to say.

"Am I stupid for waiting for my husband to return?" she asked, her voice nearly a whisper.

"I don't think you're stupid," he replied, steady and reassuring.

She looked down, her shoulders tense, like she needed a minute to finish a deep, lingering thought. Then she asked, "Would you do something for me?"

"Sure."

She opened her mouth to ask a question, but she froze, then finally said, "Never mind. I can't. It's too weird."

"Ask me," Widow said.

A pause. Heavy silence. Then Nora took a step closer, her voice soft. "Would you... would you lay with me for a while? Not for... anything, just... I thought we could watch a movie."

Widow nodded, and he followed her back to the primary bedroom. It was lively and vibrant, reflecting Nora's tastes. The walls were painted a soft teal, and a colorful quilt covered the bed, woven with deep blues, greens, and warm reds. The cozy ambiance was disrupted by heavy lighting— softboxes and ring lights were strewn about the room. She flipped a switch on the wall and the lights went dark, leaving only the faint glow from a couple of corner lamps.

A camera stood on a tripod in one corner, facing the bed, its lens capped, with coiled wires and a neatly folded blanket nearby. Widow stared at it, puzzled.

Nora said, "Sorry about that. Just ignore it. It's only for extra money. I don't make sex videos with strangers or anything. It's just me. I had to do something to keep the farm going."

Widow stayed quiet.

She said, "Please don't judge me."

"No judgments here. It doesn't bother me. I think any reasonable person would understand a mother on her own trying to provide for her kids."

Nora's dresser held more than just her personal mementos; alongside a framed photo of her daughters and a carved wooden bowl of seashells, there was a small microphone and a set of neatly stacked storage drives.

Nora moved quickly to one side of her bed, grabbed an open shoebox, and smacked the lid back down on it. Then she bent over and stuffed the box under her bed. She returned upright and sat on the edge. She looked up at Widow and smiled. Her face went flush with embarrassment, like he'd just caught her doing something she wasn't supposed to be doing.

"What's that?" he asked. An involuntary reflex.

"Nothing. Sorry. I forgot I left it out. It's just a box of my... work tools," she said, and smiled playfully.

Widow smiled and nodded. He didn't ask anything else about it.

"Come on," she said, patting the bed next to her. "Watch a movie with me."

Widow did as ordered, surreptitiously slipping the Glock onto the floor beside the bed first. They laid there for a few minutes in silence, as she scrolled through streaming services on a TV in the corner. She clicked the remote, looking for something to watch. She settled on an old movie, but one of Widow's favorites— *Casablanca.*

A few minutes into the movie, Nora asked hesitantly, "Can I cuddle with you?"

"Sure."

She smiled and snuggled up on him, her head resting against his chest as he wrapped his arm around her. They heard thunder roll outside and rain started plinking against the roof and exterior of the house. It pattered softly against the window, creating a soothing rhythm, a quiet lullaby.

They watched *Casablanca.* The TV screen cast soft flickers of light across their faces. Widow glanced down at Nora. Somewhere between Humphrey Bogart saying: *Of all the gin joints in all the towns in all the world, she walks into mine,* and *Here's looking at you, kid,* Nora drifted off to sleep, breathing deeply and steadily, enveloped in his arms. Widow stayed awake, watching the movie credits roll across the TV screen, listening to the rain, feeling the weight of her head on his chest.

Widow faded into sleep too.

In the quiet of the night, Nora stirred, her voice barely a whisper, like she wasn't sure if she was awake or dreaming. It woke Widow up. He flicked his eyes open and looked at her. She raised her head and asked, "That volcano story... did you really see it?"

Widow hesitated, then smiled faintly and said, "I made it up."

She chuckled softly, her breath warm against his neck. She said, "I thought so. But I liked the story." She dropped her head and fell right back into a deep sleep.

The rain continued, soft and steady, and slowly Widow drifted back off, with a rare feeling of peace, of being home.

Nora rested against him. The weight of the world, if only for a night, was pushed back, held at bay.

CHAPTER 22

The same rain pattered outside, only the man didn't know it because he was underground. What he did know was that his real name was Camp—Tim Camp. They thought he was Michael Walters, but he wasn't. That was part of his cover. His employer had given him the Walters name and set him up as an auditor working freelance with the State of Missouri. He had come to see this company's books and inspect its files, like a normal auditor would do. He did have a Masters in Accounting degree. That part was true. He knew what he was looking for.

Camp was no tough-guy. He wasn't a cop, and had no experience in Special Forces or anything, but he was no novice with a gun or in hand-to-hand combat. None of that mattered when they came for him though. He met Junior first, and then Franklin. They didn't know who he really was. The switchmen didn't know who he was either. In order to achieve the goals his employer had set out for him, he needed complete anonymity. No one could know who he was, not until the job was complete.

The name Michael Walters was fake. So was the cover story of being a state auditor coming to check the books of Black River Rail. But the auditing part was real. The purpose of the audit was to find the truth. There's always a certain level of danger in auditing criminal organizations. There's danger in dealing with criminals to begin with. That part was common sense. But in a decade of auditing criminals, Camp never had things go this wrong.

If auditing was about finding truth, then Camp was a truth-seeker. His success rate was top in his field. That's why he had found consistent work across the northern hemisphere, working for criminal organizations, finding the gaps in their books for them. It was lucrative too. There were not a lot of people in his field, probably because it was both little-known and dangerous.

Most of his work had been with drug cartels. When cartel leaders in Mexico figured out they were losing money some-where along the chain from the plants being cared for in Colombia to the dealers on the streets of American cities, they knew someone was stealing from them. Naturally, they had expected this. It was the cost of doing business. Especially when all along the pipeline they dealt with criminals. When everyone in your criminal empire was a criminal by defini-tion, theft was inevitable. They factored it in.

The problem was that someone was taking dollar amounts higher than what was factored in. The infraction was fine for a while, but the thief got greedy. The amount of money vanishing got too high. It ate into their profit margins. And this was unacceptable. So they hired Camp to find the source of the theft. He came in as a government agent, as an auditor with the Mexican government's Unidad de Inteligencia Financiera, its financial intelligence unit. The UIF's main responsibility was investigating money-laundering and other financial crimes. Camp posed as an agent and used his cover to walk into various points along the cartel's chain to look at their records. This way he could analyze financial transactions to help pinpoint the thief they were after. He even had a real federal agent with him, to help sell it. Getting real Mexican agents to pretend he was who he claimed to be was a lot easier in Mexico. The cartels had lots of corrupt police and federal agents on their payroll.

In the US, things were a lot trickier because there wasn't a huge supply of corrupt agents. That doesn't mean there were zero. No country was free from corruption. But it was easier to fool people along the chain in the US than it was in Mexico.

In Mexico, if he didn't come in with real *Federales*, the targets of the audit wouldn't believe him. They would pull a gun on him, take him out behind their shop and shoot him in the back of the head. In the US he could show up with no credentials, but as long as he looked the part, a scary number of businesses would take him at his word.

Black River Rail was above average because of Franklin. When Camp showed up at their railyard, the switchmen didn't run him off. They called Junior to deal with it. Junior and his guys took Camp in with friendly smiles and accommodating words and led him into a back office to show him their records. They handed him off to their accounting team, which had been told to stonewall him. Junior called Franklin, who showed up within the hour. Camp had been told Franklin would be the roadblock that'd be hard to get past. Franklin inspected Camp's certifications and paperwork. He researched Camp online, made some phone calls—all to people who'd already been paid off to back up Camp's fake cover.

Camp spent several hours going through the paperwork and records of Black River Rail. He made the whole dog and pony show look real. He performed an actual audit and could tell some things weren't adding up, but his employer had already told him to expect to find certain discrepancies.

However, Camp got far more than he bargained for when he asked for a tour. He wanted to confirm some of the major purchases on their books by laying eyes on them. He told Junior he needed to see things for himself. Junior and his guys showed Camp around the premises, trying to avoid the hill. It didn't work. Camp saw it and asked about it. *Why was there an odd hill with a security fence around it and a building with satellite dishes on top?* That's where things went south for him.

As Junior and his guys took Camp to see the building, he noticed the same things Widow would see a few days later. The hill was odd—a mound of piled dirt with grass growing over it, clearly constructed, not natural. The security for no obvious reason, the building with satellite dishes perched on top—all of it made the hill stand out to Camp like a beacon in the dark.

That's when Junior's guys pulled guns on him. He didn't panic because he knew something they didn't know. His employer would save him if anything went sideways. At least, the employer would if he knew things had gone sideways.

Junior said, "Mr. Walters, you're damn good at your job. No wonder the state hired you. Unfortunately for you, you're too good at your job. You've stumbled onto something, but it's something you shouldn't have stumbled upon. Truly, this is a case of wrong place, wrong time."

Camp pretended to be scared, but he had that ace up his sleeve, so he kept his cover. Junior showed him the inside of the satellite building, which turned out to house computer servers, thick cables snaking along the floor like tangled vines, and heavy-duty cooling units humming against the walls. The servers, stacked in metal racks, blinked with tiny lights, a forest of green and red indicators pulsing like a heartbeat. Overhead, thick fiber-optic cables looped down to connect routers and switches, all feeding into a set of sleek black satellite routers. The air was cool, almost frigid, from the industrial a/c units keeping the machines from overheating. A diesel generator was in one corner, a silent guardian against power failures. Camp noticed a line of monitors displaying encrypted feeds, with scenes too brutal for most eyes. This wasn't just a tech setup; it was a fortress built to hide dark and terrible things.

That's when he realized he'd made a huge mistake. One where the ace up his sleeve might just be completely worthless, like a bullet without a gun. They took him down several flights of concrete stairs buried in the hill. It led them into the depths of lowly lit concrete halls and down a long corridor of near darkness. That was when he realized how bad it was for him.

The next few days and nights passed. Because bunkers are underground, Camp had no sunlight, no moonlight, nothing to gauge the passage of time. He had no idea how long he'd been held captive. He assumed it'd been at least three nights.

Camp slumped against the cold tile wall of a large concrete bathroom. It was like the inside of a cell, only without bars. There was a heavy door, locked from the outside. The floor was concrete. Next to the toilet, there was a heavy, metal sink, which only had cold water. The toilet tank had no lid on it, so there was no chance of using it as any kind of weapon.

Camp's voice went hoarse after yelling into the emptiness. A heavy camera perched high in the bathroom's corner stared down at him, unblinking. It had audio, he was certain, because the camera looked expensive. But no one answered him the first few hours that he screamed at it, begged, demanded answers. Even though no one responded to him, he couldn't help but feel like there were a thousand eyes on him. He remembered the camera feeds he had seen on the monitors in the satellite building. And he knew he was being watched by someone, somewhere.

He finally got a response to his begging. A voice crackled over a speaker. saying, "Stop yelling. It's useless."

Desperate, Camp tried to bargain with the voice. He told the truth. He told them he was not Michael Walters, but Tim Camp. He told them he wasn't a state auditor. He even revealed his employer. It didn't help.

Time stretched into a blur, each moment filled with a gnawing sense of dread. Usually it was quiet, except one time. In the silence, he heard something, and it sounded non-human. He heard its low, guttural growls near his cell. It sounded violent and unrestrained. The source of the growls had to be an animal. He had no idea what, but it sounded big. The thing growled and snarled for what seemed like hours, like a starving beast.

Then they came for him.

Two men entered his cell. They were dressed all in black, and wore black devil-masks. They were terrifying. He couldn't see their faces; the masks completely hid their features. Each of them held a weapon. The weapons looked like clubs. But they weren't just clubs. They were cattle prods.

The men tried to grab him, but he fought back, kicking one in the shin, and pulling back from the other one. The one he shin-kicked rammed the club into his midsection and clicked a button. Twelve thousand volts shot out the end and into Camp's gut. He jumped back into the wall and squirmed around, involuntarily, dancing up against it. The men laughed and yanked him up by the arms, dragging him out of the cell and down a large corridor. They were Junior's guys. Cameras lined the hallway, like they were shooting a film from every angle. Another of Junior's men, also in all black with a black devil-mask, stood at an opening at the end of the hall. He held an expensive video camera. He filmed Camp the whole way down the corridor, then followed him into the next area.

The corridor opened up into a huge room. The cameraman followed Camp into the room. Camp tried to speak, tried to protest, but his voice was gone. They dragged him farther into the chamber. It was enormous. It looked to be a fifty feet underground. Starlight twinkled above, through a huge circular opening in the ceiling that was like a giant skylight without glass. Rain trickled into the chamber, the sound of the drops echoing throughout the room.

The chamber was a big octagon-shaped space with dust on the ground. Everything was brick, iron, and concrete. Long iron rails traced the walls.

Loose bricks stuck out of the walls. Above the iron, loose bricks, and concrete was another floor. There were no handrails, just ledges about ten feet up. A catwalk stretched from one side of the upper area to the other. Iron rails were laid out as beams to hold it up. Wooden planks were placed along the rails, as with railroad tracks, to be used as a bridge.

More cameras were scattered around the chamber. Cameras were pointed at Camp from various corners and other strategic placements. He struggled with Junior's guys but they were too strong. They threw him forward and he stumbled, landing hard on the dirty concrete. His impact kicked up dust. The cameras followed him, like he was the latest contestant on a reality game show.

Big square chunks were cut out along the chamber walls. Candles stuffed into these cut-outs dimly lit up the chamber. It was like they were mainly there for ambience, and not practical to use as a light source for the massive open air-chamber. Wall sconces lit up the floor, but left plenty of shadows. Above him on the bottom of the catwalk, he saw a spotlight. It was off. He wondered why all the cameras and lights? They must be filming something here, he just didn't know what. Not yet, anyway.

The chamber smelled of rot. He assumed it was from whatever beast he had heard.

Suddenly, the cameraman jumped in front of Camp, and aimed the camera at him. The spotlight above switched on and lit up the chamber, showing the dusty concrete floor—and more than Camp wanted to see.

He had been wrong about the source of the odor. The rot smell came from scattered human bones. They littered the ground, their surfaces gnawed clean except for scraps of sinewy meat here and there.

Camp tried to scream, but nothing came out of his mouth but air. He tried to run but two of the devil-mask men cattle-prodded him again. He buckled to his knees, and they released him. They backed away from him, leaving the cameraman. He stayed and zoomed in on Camp's face, like he was filming for some unseen audience.

Above Camp, the spotlight swiveled back and forth, casting light over the chamber. The beam caught something in the shadows—a tiger, or some kind of big cat. But it was no longer a tiger. It was what was left of one. The creature's carcass was twisted, torn, its limbs scattered like gruesome puzzle pieces. Something had ripped it apart and left it half-eaten. The meat had rotted to black. It'd been there for at least a couple of weeks.

Camp's heart raced as his gaze shifted to a human skull lying nearby, its eye sockets staring back at him—black and empty, like a silent warning of things to come.

From above, he noticed the glint of more cameras, all focused on him. Suddenly, he saw a figure leaning over the edge of the catwalk. At first, the face was covered in shadow. It slowly emerged. It was a man dressed in a black suit and tie. There was a cast on one of his arms. A wireless microphone was clipped to his lapel. The most terrifying thing about the man was the mask. He wore a gold devil-mask. Camp figured it was Junior .

Camp stared up at him, and forced words out of his mouth. They came out all hoarse. "Please," he whimpered, his voice cracking. "Don't do this. Let me go. I'm not what you think."

The cameraman came in close and clicked a button on his camera. A bright light emitted from the camera and across Camp's face.

Camp stared into the camera, hoping Junior could hear him. He pleaded, "Don't do this. Your father hired me. He thinks you're up to something, like a side business. He wanted me to spy on you and find out what it is. Please."

The begging made no difference because the moment he started speaking, loud heavy-metal music blasted over speakers somewhere above the chamber. Camp looked up and saw that another masked cameraman had joined Junior on the catwalk. The camera light was on him now. Junior waited for the music to end, like it was the intro to some kind of macabre TV show.

Junior said something that was inaudible to Camp. Judging by his gestures and stance, he was introducing an audience to something, like a pay-per-view announcer at a boxing match.

Suddenly, Camp heard the sound of some kind of machine and then the clanking of chains, like a rusty old elevator coming to life. But it wasn't an elevator. The sounds came from a large automatic door in the far corner of the chamber. He turned to watch as the door screeched open. Behind it was utter darkness. The opening led to a cavernous hole of some kind.

The cameraman zoomed in to Camp's face, like he was waiting to catch some kind of big response from him. It was Camp's close-up. The cameraman got the big response. It came in the form of pure terror.

A deep growl resonated from the darkness of the cavernous hole. It was loud and bone-clattering. The cameraman stayed focused on Camp, but he slowly backed away several feet, then darted away, joining the other devil-mask men back at the corridor they'd dragged Camp through. They slammed a heavy door shut behind them, locking Camp into the chamber with whatever monster was growling.

Camp froze, his eyes darting to the cavernous hole. Suddenly, a massive shadow shifted. The growl grew louder, a sound so primal it rattled his teeth. The spotlight swept around the chamber, then focused on the cavernous hole, lighting up a creature from Camp's nightmares. The beast stepped into the light, then, stepping out on all fours, came farther into the chamber.

It looked at the tiger carcass first. Recognition flashed across its eyes. It knew the dead beast was an adversary that it had mauled to death. Then the beast turned its attention to Camp. He stood there frozen in terror.

The beast stepped forward. The cameras stayed locked on the two. The creature stood up on its hind legs, stretching up ten feet tall. The creature was a monstrous grizzly bear, its fur blood-matted and its eyes gleaming with hunger and rage.

The grizzly opened its massive jaws and roared at Camp. He was on the ground groveling in fear and didn't even know it. The grizzly's teeth glinted in the spotlight. This bear looked different than other bears. Camp stared at it in horror. He saw the difference. This bear's teeth were razor-sharp and steel-plated, something that a madman had done to it. That madman was Junior.

The grizzly stared at Camp, nostrils flaring, as it prepared to charge. Camp barely had time to scream before the creature was on him, claws raking through flesh and bone, tearing him apart in a horrifying frenzy. Camp's agonized cries were drowned out by the unnerving sounds of the bear chewing on him. It wasn't until his torso was torn open that Camp's world blurred into darkness.

The viewers watched their device screens as the disturbing event unfolded. They watched like they were sport spectators, sitting in dark places all over the world. They first had to boot up their security measures—VPNs and secure routers. Then they had to go to the dark web, find the site for The Iron Ring, log in, and begin placing their bets on the lower tiers of entertainment, which were everything from dog fights to wild animals battling it out in the Iron Ring.

Some of them lost money betting on dog fights. Some of them won money. In the latest episode, a portion of them had lost money betting on the tiger to win. Most regular viewers knew better.

But win or lose, everyone paid the price to watch Junior's champion, the prize animal of the Iron Ring, the huge grizzly bear called Bearzerker.

As Camp stopped moving, Junior's voice crackled over the audio that accompanied the livestream. Calm and detached, Junior said, "I think Bearzerker's still hungry. Maybe we should find him someone else to eat."

CHAPTER 23

Midnight brought an end to the rain. The ground around Nora's farm remained wet and glistening under the faint moonlight, with puddles pooling in dips along the gravel driveway. The fields beyond the house lay quiet, damp and softened, as if holding their breath. In the stillness, every sound carried—the soft drip of water off the eaves, the faint rustle of leaves settling after the steady rain.

Tractor-trailers blasted starkly through the crossroads, passing each other in a constant swoosh. The wet highway did nothing to slow down the supply chain that ran through the route. Birds huddled close to each other to keep warm.

Inside Nora's house, a similar scene took place. Two people huddled together, staying warm, sleeping peacefully. Widow lay in his new clothes, stretched out on top of the covers on Nora's bed. She slept next to him, nestled against his chest, her head rising and falling in time with his breathing. Sleep overtook her in a way it hadn't in a year. It was deep and peaceful—worry-free, as if all the unrest in the world had washed away with the rain.

Nora was still in her sundress, but the skirt had slipped all the way up her legs, exposing more than she had planned to. One spaghetti strap had slipped down her arm earlier, exposing most of her breast. Soft and smooth, both breasts pushed against Widow's chest.

At one in the morning, Widow's eyes drifted open to the sound of Nora's soft breaths. For a moment, he forgot where he was. He woke drowsily and realized there was a beautiful stranger sleeping on his chest. A split-second later, he recognized it was Nora, the woman who'd pointed a rifle at him eighteen hours earlier. He smiled to himself, thinking about how crazy his life was. Twenty-two years ago, he graduated from the Naval Academy. Less than ten years ago, he'd left it all behind. Now he wandered without a home, without a master, like the *rōnin* of feudal Japan. Widow went everywhere without belonging anywhere.

For him, the road was endless, stretching out into an uncertain horizon. He had no ties, no roots, nothing holding him back. Just the path in front of him and the people he crossed along the way—people like Nora, with her free spirit and fierce loyalty to her girls, making him feel, even if just for a moment, like this might be the place for him to stay.

That feeling was dangerous. Widow glanced down at Nora's sleeping form, feeling a rare sense of calm but reminding himself it couldn't last. He didn't want to feel too comfortable. He didn't want to get too attached. Attachments were like anchors on a ship. They held you down from setting sail. Widow wanted to keep moving, to stay gone forever. But this didn't mean he couldn't stick around and enjoy his time here. Besides, he had come to Iron Crossing out of curiosity about the Ghost Line and the story about Alex Hopper, and potentially other missing trainhoppers. Then there was Nora's husband, Wade Sutton. What happened to him? Were the Brocks involved somehow? There were questions that still needed answers.

Widow glanced up at a bedroom window. Outside, the night was black, thick, and silent. Everything appeared still. Then suddenly, Joanie barked ferociously in the distance, breaking through the quiet. Widow stayed still, watching the window, listening. He didn't live here, so he had no idea if this was her usual way of barking at night or not. But he'd heard her barking at Junior and his guys earlier, and he knew the difference between a dog's casual bark and one laced with distress and warnings. This sounded like the latter. Joanie's bark, sharp and piercing, carried an edge that set off alarm bells in his head. He watched the window, and listened.

Nora stirred against him, barely awake. "Joanie's scaring off coyotes," she murmured, already drifting back to sleep. Widow nodded, but stared at the window. He felt something was off. Still, Nora knew her dog better than he did. So he closed his eyes and tried to go back to sleep.

Minutes later, Joanie's bark stopped. Just like that—suddenly, unnaturally. Widow's eyes snapped open. He didn't like it. The silence felt wrong. He thought about nudging Nora awake, but she was sleeping so peacefully. He decided it was probably nothing. Joanie must've chased them off, he thought. He tried to sleep, but it nagged at him.

Before he could reconcile the feeling, a vehicle horn shattered the silence, blasting into the night. Several horn bursts rang out, like someone beckoning him to come outside. The horn bursts came from the direction of the crossroads, but they were too loud to be that far away. Widow jumped to his feet, crossed the bedroom, and walked down the hall. Passing the girls' bedroom, he glanced in the open doorway and saw them sleeping, dead to the world. A breeze gusted in through their window. It was open a few inches.

Widow walked to the front of the house, crossed over to a window. He half-lifted a curtain and peered out the window. The horn stopped, but there was something else. The driveway was lit up with headlights—a truck, sleek and black, idling out front, at the end of the driveway, where Widow had broken Junior's arm.

Nora stumbled out of bed and down the hall, pulling her falling spaghetti strap up on her sundress. It was crinkled up from her sleeping in it. She came over to Widow and leaned into him, looked out the window with him.

A figure got out of the truck, leaving the headlights on. The beams sprayed out over the gravel. The figure closed the driver-side door and walked out into the headlight beams. It was a man, but they couldn't see any details beyond that. The headlights washed over him. He stood out in front of his truck's grille, like he was waiting for someone to come out and join him.

Sleepily, Nora asked, "Who's that?"

"I don't know," Widow said. "It looks like he's wanting us to come out there. Think I'll go see what he wants."

Nora's sleepiness fell away. She snapped, "No! Not with nothing. Hang on." Now she was wide awake—something sudden danger does to a person. Her brain snapped from zero to a hundred, adrenaline spiked, and her heart raced. She stepped away from Widow and the window, disappearing into a hall closet. She came back out with the Marlin 336 rifle in hand. She offered it to Widow, and said, "Take this."

He shook his head. "You keep it. You might need it."

"I have more guns," she said, handed him the rifle, and went back to the same closet. She reached in and pulled out a pump shotgun with a box of shells. She showed it to him.

Widow handed her the rifle one-handed, and reached for the shotgun and the box of shells with the other hand. He palmed the shotgun and the box of shells. He said, "Let me take the shotgun."

"Why?"

He looked her up and down, assessing. "Are you even a hundred pounds?"

She narrowed her eyes. "What's that supposed to mean?"

"No offense, but I think the kick from this shotgun will knock you on your ass."

Nora took the shotgun back, left the box of shells in his hand, and the rifle in the other. She pumped the shotgun's action, slow and deliberate, and said, "Shotguns are deadly close-quarter weapons. That's a long gun. I'm in the house. This is more practical inside than that rifle. And before you ask, yes, I've practiced with it too. Think of me as a modern-day Annie Oakley."

Widow's lips curved into a grin. "Alright. You convinced me." He gave her back the box of shells. She loaded the shotgun. Widow checked the rifle. It was still loaded from earlier, minus the bullet that had been meant for Joanie. After he checked the gun, Widow stuffed his feet back into his boots, grabbed the rifle, and went outside.

A sleepy Violet and Poppy stuck their heads out of their room, curious as to what was going on. Both girls rubbed their eyes. Nora ushered them back to bed and back to sleep.

Widow stepped out onto the front porch. The boards under his boots were wet. The air was damp, thick with the lingering scent of rain, and the night was dark enough to disappear into. He stayed low as he made his way down the drive. The idling truck's headlights stayed on, casting a shadow around the stranger standing in front of them. The lights were bright, illuminating a path for Widow to follow.

Widow chose a different way. He walked down the porch steps, and stepped out of the light path and into the darkness alongside the driveway. The stranger stayed where he was. When Widow reached him, the stranger turned and became fully visible in the headlights' glare. The stranger was a professional-looking man in his fifties. Graying hair mixed with black was slicked back on the guy's head. He wore a black suit and tie.

Widow kept his distance, rifle chambered with a bullet and held steady at his side. The man stared up into Widow's eyes, cool as sniper before making a kill shot. Widow asked, "Who're you?"

The man adjusted his collar, fast and sudden, a test to see if Widow would react. It was a trick the man had used many times before. It tested to see if his subject was just a normal man, someone inexperienced and not combat-ready. Ninety-nine percent of people jumped out of their skin because they were already on edge. They lacked the combat experience and training to stay calm. The moment they thought that he was about to attack them, they jumped. They always jumped.

But Widow didn't react. He stayed still, eyes locked on the stranger's. The man was intrigued. He said, "People around here call me Franklin. And who are you?"

Widow didn't bother answering. "Okay, Franklin. Why're you out here, honking your horn at one in the morning?"

Franklin smiled, not amused, but faintly thrilled to encounter a man like Widow. He repeated, "What's your name?"

Widow ignored the question again, and asked, "Are you the one who came by here earlier, looking for me?"

Franklin matched Widow, and didn't answer. Instead, he asked, "Are you the new boyfriend?"

Widow's patience was thinning. "Not important."

"Well," Franklin continued, unfazed, "I know you're not Wade Sutton."

That was Nora's missing husband's name. Widow's eyes narrowed, his grip on the rifle tightening. But he stayed quiet.

"She didn't even tell you?" Franklin pressed.

"Tell me what?"

"Wade Sutton's her husband. That's his wife in that house you're sleeping in."

Widow's face was stone, unreadable. "What're you? His lawyer or something?"

Franklin's smile slipped, his expression hardening. "That's funny. You're a funny guy," he said, testing Widow again—this time by antagonizing him, seeing if he'd crack under pressure.

But Widow stayed quiet. Even the rifle didn't move. It stayed in his hands, ready to rock and roll. Widow stood about ten feet from Franklin. Franklin's gun was under his open jacket in a shoulder holster. He could draw it and fire. Nothing wrong with the distance. In fact, he figured he had the advantage there. Not that the rifle wasn't deadly from that distance. It was deadly from nearly any shooting distance. His handgun was better for such close quarters. But would he draw it fast enough? Could he get the drop on Widow? The answer to that question was no, and he knew it.

Franklin showed Widow his hands, slowly, reached into his jacket, and froze in that position. In a way, this was another test. And this time, Widow reacted. He raised the rifle fast and pointed it at Franklin's center mass. By the time Franklin registered it, he could've been dead if Widow had pulled the trigger. He knew it too.

"Relax," Franklin said, "I have something for you." He pulled out an envelope, and extended it to Widow.

Widow eyeballed it and asked, "What's this?"

"See for yourself."

Hesitantly, Widow took it one-handed, keeping the rifle trained on Franklin. He brushed his fingers across the edge of the paper, forced the flap open, and saw cash, lots of it—hundreds, neatly stacked. He asked, "What's this for?"

"It's from me to you. You look like you could use some money. Don't worry about this woman. Just take this money, and go," Franklin said with a hearty grin on his face. He looked sinister, like a devil on someone's shoulder might.

Widow handed the money back, no expression, no hesitation. He said, "I'm not going anywhere. Not for money."

Franklin watched him, eyes narrowed, and the grin melted away. "You sure about that?"

Widow's response was cold and flat. "I'm sure."

A flicker of something crossed Franklin's face—respect maybe, or recognition, like two battle-hardened warriors coming face-to-face before a fight to the death. "I thought so. I offered you the carrot. Now here's the stick."

Widow levered the action on the rifle, expending an unfired bullet, but it created the dramatic effect he was looking for to emphasize his rejection of the money. "I think you should leave."

"Sure," Franklin said, unruffled. He adjusted his coat, preparing to turn back to the truck. He paused, hesitantly, and said, "But this is the only warning you'll get. Think about yourself. Think about the girls sleeping in that house."

Widow didn't blink. Franklin held his gaze for a beat longer, then went back to his truck, opened the door, and country music wafted out. He climbed in, but before shutting the door, he leaned out with one parting shot. "Tuck those girls in good. Make sure they're snug, safe and sound."

Franklin closed the door and the truck backed out, headlights fading as it pulled away into the night. Widow stood there with the rifle still ready. He watched until the taillights were gone from sight.

Widow waited there a long moment. Two more trucks blasted through the intersection. The night fell silent again, as if nothing had happened. Nora opened the front door and popped her head out. When she saw the coast was clear, she walked out onto the porch, barefoot. She called out to Widow. "Was that Franklin?"

Widow turned, headed back up the driveway to her, and said, "That's what he said."

"He's the guy I told you about. The one looking for you."

"Yeah, I figured that."

Widow and Nora returned to the house and checked the girls' room. They were safe, tucked in under the covers. They'd fallen back to sleep, completely oblivious to the visitor who'd lingered outside. Widow let out sigh of relief. He and Nora went back to bed. Widow offered to go into the guest bedroom, but Nora pulled him back into her bedroom.

This time, she took her clothes off in front of him. Modesty wasn't one of her characteristics. That was for damn sure. But with a body like hers, Widow could understand why. She had nothing to be modest about.

Nora stood there, naked. Moonlight streamed in through the window and caressed her body. She got under the covers and said, "I usually sleep naked. I hope that's okay?"

"It's your bed," Widow said.

She said, "You can still sleep next to me. And you don't need those." She pointed at his clothes—first his shirt, and then down at his jeans.

Widow thought for a brief moment, just a flicker of hesitation. Not because he didn't want to, but because he didn't want her to regret it.

Like she could read his mind, she said, "Don't make me beg."

Widow smiled, kicked his boots off, and stripped down, laying his clothes over a chair, covering an extra camera. He slid into bed behind her. She scooted back into him, grabbed his arm, and draped it over her like a warm bear paw.

They lay in bed, listening to the quiet, till they fell back asleep. It wouldn't be until the next day that anyone realized Joanie was no longer barking.

CHAPTER 24

Widow woke early the next morning to an empty bed. He sat up, hung his legs off the bed's edge, feet on the floor, and rubbed his eyes—letting them adjust to his surroundings. Sunlight crept in through the curtains, casting dull cones of light across the room, the camera tripod and the light stands forming long fingerlike shadows along the floor.

Nora was already up and gone from the room. Widow got out of bed and stretched, tall and mighty, like Hercules reaching to the old gods in the sky. He went into Nora's bathroom, fishing out his toothbrush from the pocket of his jeans on the way. Widow brushed his teeth, used the toilet, and washed up. Then he dressed and stepped out into the hall.

Hushed, anxious voices rumbled from the kitchen. Widow walked the hall, passing the girls' room. They were already up and out of bed too. He had thought he was an early morning person, but farm life was a whole different ball game than the US Navy. Nora and the kids were up every day before dawn. They got up early, fed the animals, and tended to the various chores of running a farm. And all before sailors, like him, were even brushing their teeth. Widow figured that was obvious, but he just hadn't connected it. He entered the kitchen to find Nora and the girls bunched together, agitated about something but staying quiet, like they were arguing but didn't want to wake him up.

Violet and Poppy saw him first. Their faces were stretched tight with worry and fear, like the world stood on the precipice of annihilation. They looked like they had just been told enemy forces had launched their entire nuclear arsenal, leaving only seconds to live.

"She's gone, Māmā! She's gone!" Poppy said, her voice shrill and desperate. Her little hands clung tight to the bottom of Nora's skirt. Nora wore another sundress, this one white with yellow flowers dotted across it. It had the same style as yesterday's; low-cut top and above-the-knees skirt.

Poppy released Nora's skirt. Nora knelt down, held Poppy's hands in one of hers, and brushed her fingers through Poppy's hair, like it was something she did to calm her daughter. Violet pulled close behind them and hugged them. Both girls' eyes were filled with tears. Nora said, "We'll find her, honey."

Something was going on, and it appeared to be the kind of thing families go through. Widow had little experience with family emergencies and situations. The last family he'd had was his mother. The last time he saw her, and held her hand, she was on her death bed. He regretted it that the last time he spoke to her before that was at the end of the last century.

Unsure of social protocol for this kind of thing, Widow cleared his throat and stepped into the kitchen. Violet saw him first. She let go of her mom and charged Widow. She wrapped her arms around his leg. Widow let out a gasp of surprise. He hadn't expected her reaction. He patted her back.

His hand was bigger than the space between her shoulders. He said, "Hey. What's going on here?"

Nora scooped Poppy up into her arms, turned to Widow, and said, "Joanie's gone. She went out last night and didn't come back." Then she mouthed *Help me*, out of her daughters' sight.

Widow knelt down to eye level with Violet. Nora set Poppy down and they joined Widow and Violet. Widow grabbed both girls, stared them in the eyes, his voice calm and solid, he said, "Dogs have a great sense of direction. Joanie's no different. She's probably just off on an adventure somewhere. We'll find her."

Poppy's lips quivered, and she asked, "Promise?"

Widow gave a short nod, and said, "I promise." Then he turned to Nora. "Have you already looked for her?"

Nora shook her head, and said, "We just realized it. We went out to feed the animals, called out for her, but she didn't come to us. That's it so far."

"We'll start by checking the farm. Okay?" he asked the girls, flicking his gaze from one little face to the other. The girls agreed, renewed by Widow's confidence that they'd find her. "Good. In the SEALs we'd regroup and form a search party."

Violet asked, "Search party?"

Poppy and Nora asked, "SEALs?" Only their inflections were completely different. Both questions. Both curious. Poppy questioned what a SEAL was. But Nora asked it like it was a surprise to her. Kind of like, *Why didn't you mention that before?*

Widow explained what a SEAL was to Poppy, in simplistic terms, basically saying it's a special kind of sailor. Nora didn't question him any further. Widow reassured all of them that he knew how to track down Joanie. He told Violet what a search party was, also explaining it in simple terms.

Together, the four of them combed through every inch of Nora's farm. They checked the pens, stalls, and sheds, calling Joanie's name. But they found no sign of her anywhere. They accounted for all the other animals. They were all calm and unfazed, like nothing had happened. There were no signs of coyote activity or of any other kind of predator.

Widow said, "Let's walk the fence line. Maybe there's a gap or hole somewhere she slipped through." Which he doubted because he patched the fence's holes the day before. But Widow was only human. Maybe he missed one.

They walked the length of the fence. Widow scanned for clues. Nora and the girls called out Joanie's name, over and over. There was nothing wrong with the fence, not a gap, a hole, or loose post anywhere. Nora mentioned that coyotes can leap over a fence easily. So, Widow scanned both sides of the fencing for coyote tracks. He saw none. No tracks, no disturbance, not anywhere. And no Joanie. Just empty fields stretching from the farthest point on the farm all the way to the road and the crossroads.

For the girls' sake, Nora and Widow took them along the fence line twice. When they reached one corner of the property, Widow led them back to another. He found plenty of Joanie's muddy pawprints from last night's rain. But they led nowhere. Joanie was nowhere to be found.

At the end of their search, they stood in front of the house. Widow stared at the crossroads. Nora reached up and grabbed Widow's shoulder, pulled herself up to him on her tippytoes, and whispered, "What now?"

Widow kept staring at the crossroads. More tractor-trailers blasted through. Some stopped at the intersection and some didn't. A horrible thought clawed away at his mind. He muttered, "Oh no."

Nora started to ask, but then she looked at the crossroads and thought the same thing. But it was Violet who asked the question Nora and Widow were thinking. She asked, "What if she ran onto the highway?"

As if on cue, another rumble of an eighteen-wheeler growled over the morning silence. Its brake lights swept the road behind it as the truck barreled through the crossroads, the driver only realizing he slammed through the intersection after passing it. He released the brakes and kept on going.

Poppy picked up on her sister's fears. Tearfully, she said. "Maybe she got hit."

Nora dragged both girls close to her and said, "No way! Joanie's too smart to do that."

Widow said, "Hey, I've got an idea. In the Navy, we'd split up into teams. We called it a search and rescue mission. Let's do the same. I'll check the highway, and you girls can take your mom and check with the neighbors."

Nora nodded, a hint of relief softening her worried expression. The girls said, "Okay."

They split up. Nora took the girls down their road, calling Joanie's name with every new yard they passed. Widow started at the crossroads, at the same spot he'd gotten out of the Greengate Hauling truck, and turned north. He walked along the shoulder of the highway, scanning for any sign of Joanie. He looked for her fur on the ground and her tracks in the dirt. He found nothing. There was no sign of her, just empty road stretching into the distance. He walked a mile out and then turned around and walked back through the crossroads, searching another mile of highway. He found nothing and turned back around. Maybe Nora and the girls had better luck?

Widow found them back at the farm. Nora put on a brave face, but underneath, she was more than worried. It was obvious to Widow. Although he'd only known her for twenty-four hours, he could see it. It was like two people taking a long plane ride next to each other. At the beginning, they're complete strangers, but by the time they arrive at their destination, they're friends.

The girls weren't as good at hiding their emotions. Their faces looked defeated.

"No sign of her along the road," Widow said, and shrugged. "What about y'all?"

Nora shook her head and said, "We knocked on every door within a mile. And no one's seen her."

Violet said, "We didn't ask the Graces."

Poppy added, "That old man is mean. What if he did something to Joanie?" The girls exchanged looks and shuddered at the thought.

Widow raised an eyebrow and asked, "Why not them?"

Nora sighed and said, "They live several houses down. It's an old married couple."

Poppy scowled, "They're mean."

"They've never been friendly. They've just kept to themselves. They've acted like they have some kind of grudge against me, ever since…," Nora paused, and mouthed to Widow. "Wade disappeared."

"Which house is theirs?" Widow asked.

"The one with the flag out front."

"The one with the bright yellow shutters?"

"That's it," Nora said.

Widow recalled the house—the old guy on the lawnmower, cutting grass, and how the couple had watched as Junior and his guys harassed him. He said, "I know the one."

Poppy tugged on Nora's skirt and said, "I bet they took Joanie."

Nora shook her head and said, "No one took her, honey."

Widow said, "I'll go ask them. They might be willing to talk to me."

Violet asked, "Are you gonna beat them up?"

"Why would I do that?"

"You know, like on those cop shows? You gonna beat the information out of them?"

Poppy added, "You can make them spill the beans." And she made a pair of fists and took a fighter's stance.

Widow was glad to see the girls in better spirits, but he didn't like the image they had of him as some guy who beats up people. Widow knelt down to their eye level and said, "I'm not going to hurt them. Hurting people is what bullies do. You don't think I'm a bully, do you?"

"Nope," Violet said.

Poppy said, "But what about beating up Junior and the other guys?"

"That was different."

"Why?" Poppy asked.

Widow glanced up at Nora, a little out of his element, and a little worried he was stepping over her toes into territory that was out of bounds. She locked eyes with him, and said, "Mr. Widow's not a bully. Junior and his friends are bullies. They bullied us. They went too far. And Mr. Widow stepped in to save us."

Violet stared at her sister, and added, "Mr. Widow is a hero. Heroes stop bullies."

Poppy nodded like she understood. Then she asked, "Am I a bully?"

Widow said, "You're a hero too. Both of you are heroes."

Violet asked, "Mr. Widow, then what's a bully?"

Widow said "A bully is a bad guy who tries to hurt other people just to feel big and strong. They might say mean things, push others around, or terrorize them."

Poppy asked, "Terrorize?"

Nora said, "It just means to scare someone."

Poppy asked, "Why would they do that?"

Widow paused a beat, picking his words carefully, and said, "Sometimes, bullies feel small or sad inside, so they think being mean'll make them feel better. But it doesn't—it just makes them mean. It makes them feel more sad on the inside. And they become bad guys."

Violet asked, "If a bully hurts us, are we supposed to fight back?"

Widow grabbed one of each of the girls' feet and lightly tugged them. Poppy giggled. Widow said, "If you ever get picked on by a bully, your first line of defense is your feet. You walk away. Ninety-nine percent of the time, this is all you need to do. Don't give them your energy or the time of day."

Poppy asked, "What if they push me down?"

"Yeah, what if they don't let us go? Like those bullies from yesterday, when Māmā told Junior no?" Violet asked.

Widow made a fist, glanced at Nora, and showed it to her, silently seeking her approval. She nodded, like she understood exactly what he wanted to convey to the girls. Widow turned and held up his fist for them to see. They stared at it in awe, their wide eyes fixed on its sheer size, like it was the biggest fist they'd ever seen.

Widow's fists were hard like stones. Balled up, they were the size of heavy carpenter's mallets—built to break, built to decimate, designed not for rocks but for bones. He said, "Only as a last resort, you make a fist. Go ahead and make one now."

Both girls made a fist. Poppy made two. Seeing this, Violet also made two, because she couldn't be outdone by her younger sister. Widow said, "Good. Now, ONLY as a last resort, that means if you got no chance to escape or just walk away, then you take your fist and punch them right in the nose." Widow showed them how to throw a quick jab to the nose. Both girls repeated his movement. They were adorably clumsy.

Nora smiled at watching Widow with her girls. For the first time in a year, she felt a ray of hope that her daughters might have a good man in their life again. They might gain a male role model for them to learn from, to look up to. Then she remembered what Widow was. He was a nomad, a wild animal, not meant to be caged, not meant to be tied down to a life like the one she'd chosen for her girls.

Nora shook off the thoughts, the fantasy, the hope, and said, "I guess it couldn't hurt for you to talk to the Graces. Maybe they know something."

Widow stood up and asked, "What will you do?"

"I'll take them and the truck. We can drive around and check the roads around the back of the farm, just in case Joanie somehow slipped through back there. We could've missed a hole somewhere."

Widow nodded. The girls loaded up in the truck. Nora hugged Widow tight before she got in. It was spontaneous. He didn't see it coming until her arms were already around him. She stretched herself and still couldn't get her hands anywhere near touching at his back. He didn't argue. He returned her hug.

Nora climbed into the truck, started it up, and buckled the girls into a single seatbelt. Widow watched them drive off, then walked down the road to the house with the bright yellow shutters, the big flag on a pole, and the freshly mowed lawn. He walked up their driveway, which was paved black. Their farm seemed a lot more prosperous than Nora's. Widow saw no one in the yard. There was a *No Trespassing* sign on the gate, but Widow walked right past it. He figured this wasn't the kind of situation where he'd obey their signs.

They had no dogs on the premises. None came out to bark at him. But he did see security cameras. There was one on the corner of the farmhouse, trained on the driveway and the road beyond. Another was installed above the front door. It pointed down at the porch, to record anyone standing there.

Widow peeked up at the sun, checked the shadows it cast, and guessed the time was somewhere around eight in the morning. He figured the Graces, like Nora, had already gotten up and fed their animals and farmed whatever needed farming, and now they were done for the morning.

The farmhouse was quiet and still, but a dull glow from a TV somewhere inside cast a faint light. It seeped through the same large picture window where they had watched Widow's first encounter with Junior and his crew. Widow stepped onto the front porch, boards squeaking under his bulk. The camera stared down at him blankly. There was no verbal message, and no light indicating it was on. Usually, the cheaper ones clicked when recording was activated. But not this one. Which didn't mean anything. Maybe it simply didn't work anymore. Or maybe the clicking problem had been solved. He heard what sounded like cowboys firing guns; the couple was probably watching an old western on the TV. He stood on the welcome mat, knocked, and waited. The American flag flapped in the wind. Somewhere behind the farmhouse, he heard cows mooing and horses neighing.

The TV glow stayed, but the sound muted. Muffled voices groaned and whispered. After a moment, footsteps came toward the door, accompanied by more old-person groaning, and then the door creaked open. An older woman peered out, eyeing him with suspicion.

"Can I help you?" she asked, before she saw Widow. Her voice was clipped and wary. She gazed out at him, staring directly into his massive chest. She craned her head back and raised her eyes up to his face.

Widow kept his voice calm and respectful. He said, "Ma'am, my name's Widow. I'm friends with one of your neighbors. Their dog ran away, and I was wondering if you or your husband saw her?"

"Who?"

"Widow, ma'am. I'm only looking for a dog."

"Which neighbor?"

"Nora Sutton, ma'am. Joanie, their dog, is missing. She's a Cane Corso," Widow said, and proceeded to describe Joanie.

"I've not seen her," the old lady said, and started to close the door. Widow didn't shove a foot into the doorway to stop her. He just put his hands up, desperately, and said, "I see you got cameras."

The old lady opened the door all the way back up and asked, "What about them?"

"I'm wondering if your cameras might've picked her up last night. You know, if she ran away, she might've wandered down the street and in front of your camera over there," Widow said, and pointed at the corner of the house.

The old lady studied him up and down, and sneered at him, curling her lip. She asked, "You're staying at that woman's place, aren't you?" She nearly added, *the floozy*, or something like it. She said nothing, but Widow could read it on her face. There was an Old Testament kind of judgment there. Sadly, it was a common trait among older people in rural places.

Widow kept a friendly smile on his face, and said, "I'm staying at the Sutton farm. That's right."

The old lady stiffened and glanced over her shoulder. She called back into the house, "Frank, come here."

An older man shuffled into view. He wore a t-shirt, and shorts that showed skinny, pale legs. He wore house shoes.

It was the same old man from the lawnmower the day before. The one who had done nothing to warn Widow about Junior. He saw Widow standing in his doorway, blocking out the sunlight, and his gaze was a mix of disdain and fear. He asked, "What do you want?"

Widow kept his tone friendly, and said, "I'm looking for a missing dog."

"I done told him we've not seen him," the old lady said.

Widow said, "She. The dog's a she, ma'am."

Martha said, "That woman's married, you know?"

Widow said, "She mentioned it."

"Martha, I'll handle this," Frank Grace said. His wife lingered behind him, like a pit bull ready to strike. Frank looked at Widow, waited for Widow to say more.

Widow said, "I'm wondering if you could check your cameras, see if she passed by last night. She went missing around one a.m.—if that helps narrow it down for you?"

Frank eyes narrowed and his mouth pulled into a tight line. He said, "We don't meddle in that farm's business."

"Why's that?"

Martha crossed her arms, behind Frank, and gave a defiant expression. She retorted, "Because that farm's been marked."

"Marked? What's that mean?"

Frank's face tightened. His voice dropping, he said, "If you care about that woman, you'll leave her alone and never come back."

Widow held his ground. He said, "Listen, I don't care about your opinion. You want to be bad neighbors, that's your choice. It's a free country. All I'm asking is to check your cameras from last night."

Nothing. Not an answer or a reaction from the Graces.

Widow asked, "Aren't those things motion-sensored? They only record when there's a reason to record?"

"So what?" Frank asked.

"So, that means you'd only have to take a second, check some app on your phone for notifications from last night. How much trouble is that really gonna cause you?" Widow asked.

Silence. Neither of the Graces checked with the other, like they were unified on this topic.

Widow asked, "You got grandchildren?"

Nothing.

Widow looked over Frank's shoulder and into Martha's eyes. She broke a little. Shame streaked across her face, like it was a sore subject. Widow said, "Nora's got two little girls—five and six. Their dog, Joanie, means the world to them. Please, I'm asking nicely. Could you at least check the footage?"

Silence, but they both were thinking, contemplating, calculating. Widow saw it in their eyes. He said again, "It would mean the world to them."

The man exchanged a look with his wife. Teary-eyed, she nodded. Frank sighed and said, "Fine. But you wait outside. I'll go get my phone."

Widow stepped back from the welcome mat, letting the door close as he waited in the warm morning air. The flag flapped and fluttered in the wind. Several minutes passed before the door creaked open and Frank returned, holding a phone. This time he was wearing shoes. He had also put on a hat. The hat was a US Navy hat, cotton twill. It was Navy blue, with the USN symbol stitched into the center. "Retired" was stitched on the edge of the bill.

Widow asked, "That hat for real?"

Frank reached up and touched the bill. He said, "It's real. I'm not stealing valor."

"Okay."

Frank walked to Widow and led him down the porch steps like he was ushering him back to the road. He stared at his phone like a caveman seeing fire for the first time. Finally, he tapped the screen and searched, finding the right app. He pulled up the record for the night before and said, "There's only one video from last night." He watched it, and shook his head slowly. "Sorry, there's no dog, just a truck passing by."

"Are you sure?"

"Son, I told you what it was. Now I think it's time for you to go."

Widow paused a beat, then asked. "What did your wife mean by *marked*?"

Frank stopped walking and shifted, glancing nervously at the house. He said, "You're putting us on their radar by coming here."

"What're you talking about?"

"The Brocks. They don't like people asking questions."

Widow nodded, and said, "I keep hearing that name. Tell me about it."

"Junior is the son. Collin Brock is the father. He don't come around here no more. Who can blame him, having a loser son like that," Frank said, and glanced around, like he was afraid someone would hear him. "He's the one who threw that bottle at you yesterday."

It wasn't Junior, but Widow didn't correct him.

Frank continued, "People around here know better than to cross them. They're bad news—the kind you're better off staying away from."

"Explain the marked thing?"

"It's nothing. A rumor is all."

"What kind of rumor?"

"Wade Sutton. He seemed like a good man. I talked to him a few times. He was a veterinarian. He came here, to the house, and helped my cows. A couple of times. The thing is, he'd never up and leave like that."

"He didn't leave?"

Frank shook his head, he said, "When people go missing around here, everyone assumes one thing. The Brocks had something to do with it."

Widow stayed quiet.

Frank added, "I grew up in a house five miles from here on Old Maple Road. Except when I was deployed, I've lived here most of my life. So I know a thing or two. Let's just say over the years some people have vanished. The kind of people who asked too many questions. When Collin left, we stopped hearing about it. People stopped vanishing. But as soon as Junior was growed up, he took over the Black River Rail, their company, and things got worse. We started hearing about more people disappearing."

"What about the cops?"

"They never do anything about it. Nowadays, they wouldn't believe it if we told them. Most of the people who've disappeared are normally…" Frank paused a beat.

"What?"

"Well, transients, like you."

"So, people who won't be missed," Widow said. "What about Wade? You think Collin Brock had something to do with Wade's disappearance?"

Frank shook his head, and corrected Widow, "Not Collin, but Junior. He's been running the show here for years now. Collin's off playing politician, running his drug empire."

"He's into drugs?"

"Or whatever. Anyway, if Junior killed Wade Sutton, that means Nora's marked. That's just what people say. I'm not sure exactly what for. Maybe Junior has his eye on her, or maybe it just means steer clear of them unless you want trouble, like that letter in that Hawthorne book."

"The Scarlet Letter?"

"That's the one."

Widow asked, "Ever heard of Alex Hopper?"

Frank gazed at him with a blank expression, and said, "No." Frank began ushering Widow back down the driveway, past the flapping flag, to the road.

Widow stayed quiet, turned to leave him, but stopped and asked, "Hey, let me see that video. You said a truck passed? Show it to me."

Frank shook his head slowly, like Widow was wasting his time. But he tapped his phone again, and pulled up the security video. He handed it to Widow. Widow watched it, and realization hit him like a ton of bricks. He gave the phone back to Frank, turned and walked back down the road to Nora's house.

In the video, a black Chevy Silverado drove past the Graces, coming from Nora's farm.

Widow thought about what happened last night. They heard Joanie barking like crazy and dismissed it. Then Widow woke to Franklin honking his horn. Franklin had taken Joanie. It had to be.

Franklin's warning to Widow echoed through his mind: Think about yourself. Think about the girls sleeping in that house. Right before he got into his truck, Franklin had said, "Tuck those girls in good."

CHAPTER 25

Widow strode back to Nora's farm, his mind racing. Franklin's last words to him tormented him, like the low growl of wolves circling in the dark. Think about yourself. Think about the girls sleeping in that house. The message was loud and clear. The threat was real. And he missed it. That's the part that ate at him. No sense in beating himself up over it. He knew the girls were safe and sound before he went back to bed. He didn't fail in protecting them. He just failed in receiving the message.

There must be more to the message than just what Franklin said.

Nora and the girls sat on the porch steps, waiting. Violet sat one side of her and Poppy on the other. Each girl had dried tears on her face. Nora sat, hugging them, telling them it'd be okay. She reassured them that they would find Joanie. Widow stopped in front of them. She met eyes with him, and asked, "What did they say?"

He held up a hand, and said, "Hang on a second. I need to see something first. Keep the girls out here."

Nora nodded, curious, but stayed put as Widow entered the house. He went straight to the girls' room. It was just as they'd left it earlier: Small beds neatly made, bright drawings taped to the walls, and stuffed animals arranged just so along the top of a dresser. Hot wind breezed in from the window, like it had the night before.

Widow's eyes locked on to the window. The window was behind a chest of drawers that was lined with more stuffed animals. Widow didn't want to disturb the arrangement. But he needed to move it so he lifted the whole thing, careful not to drop any of the stuffed animals on top. He lifted the chest of drawers away from the window and set it down several feet from the sill. Then he went to the window, crouched beside it, and studied the frame. A corner of the insect screen was peeled slightly out, just as it had been the night before. He checked the brackets and found one bent outward. He leaned into it and looked outside.

Dried mud was sprinkled across the outer sill. Widow gazed at it through the insect screen. A smudge of dirt looked like it might have a fingerprint in it. He jolted back, scanned the girls' bedroom again, but saw no sign that Franklin had entered past the sill.

Then he noticed something else. There was an object set upright on the outer sill. It was tucked into the corner, like whoever put it there didn't want the wind to knock it over. Widow knew what it was instantly. Anger boiled his blood.

"Widow, what's going on?" Nora asked. Her voice came from the doorway, sharper now.

But Widow didn't respond. He stormed out of the house, past Nora and the girls. He leaped off the porch in one big step, bypassing the girls altogether. His weight dropped him down into the dirt, leaving a deep, huge shoe print behind. Widow circled around the farmhouse to just outside the girls' bedroom window. Nora followed, pulling the girls with her. But she stayed back far enough to let him do whatever he was doing.

Widow inspected the outside of the girl's bedroom windowsill. It did look like a dirty fingerprint was left behind. But that wasn't the part he was the most interested in. The thing he really wanted was the object on the sill. He picked up the object, small and metallic: a bullet, unfired. He held it up and stared at it.

Nora shooed the girls back to the front of the house and walked up behind Widow. She tried to see what was in his hands.

"What is that?" she asked, her voice shaky.

Widow glanced at her, his face filled with rage. He showed it to her and said, "A message,"

Nora's jaw dropped. She stared at the object and said, "That's a bullet. Where did you find it?"

Widow pointed at the windowsill. Nora asked, "What does it mean?" But Widow didn't answer. Instead, he pocketed the bullet, crouched, and examined the ground beneath the window. The soil was still damp from last night's rain, but there were clear boot prints in the dirt—deep impressions filled with muddy water. Widow reached down, not caring about getting dirty. He dug a deeper hole with his bare hands and then dug a trench from one boot print to the new hole. The shallow trench drained the water from the boot print. Widow brushed the water along to help move it. After, he stared at the word embossed in the mud. It was a word stamped on the soles of a particular boot, an expensive one. The word was BOSS.

Nora stared at the boot print and the sole mark left behind. She said, "Hugo Boss."

"Māmā, what's taking so long?" Poppy asked.

Violet asked, "Can we make fliers now?"

"Hold on, honey," she said to both of them. They started to walk closer. Nora put a hand up. "Stay there!" She turned to Widow. "What does it mean?"

Widow stood slowly, looking back at the window, then at the ground. He said, "Let's talk inside." And they moved indoors, sending the girls to their room to make missing dog fliers with their computer and printer. After the girls shut their bedroom door, Nora turned to Widow in the kitchen. "You're hiding something from me. What is it?" she demanded.

Widow pulled a wooden chair out from a round kitchen table, dumped himself down in it, and set the bullet on the tabletop between them. He said, "Sit with me." Nora sat. "It's them. They're warning me. They want me to know they could've done much worse."

Nora brushed her hands across the tabletop. She said, "Franklin left that?"

"Yes, but it's on orders from Junior, surely. Those're Franklin's boot prints, no doubt."

"He went to my daughters' bedroom window? Stood out there. And left this bullet. To what? Scare us?"

Widow tapped the bullet, and said, "I think he wants to scare me away."

"But why? Why didn't he just do something?"

"What do you mean?"

"Why didn't he attack us? Why the terror tactics? Why warn you at all?"

"I don't follow?"

Nora said, "Franklin could've killed us in our sleep. He could've set the house on fire. He could've come with more guys."

Widow stayed quiet, thinking about it.

Nora said, "Hell, he could've brought the switchmen. The rumor for years is they do all kinds of dirty work for Brock."

"You know Franklin offered me money to leave?"

"Money?"

"Yeah, he tried to give me an envelope with cash. A lot of cash."

"Why didn't you take it?"

Widow shot her a look, and said, "You know why."

"I know. I'm sorry. But I don't understand, why all the scare tactics?"

"That's a good question. You know, he said something else too. He referred to himself as the carrot."

"The carrot?"

"As in the carrot and the stick. It can refer to politics. A nation might try to persuade an enemy nation to do something they want them to do with money or gifts or something of value for them to do it; that's the carrot. If the enemy refuses, then they revert to the stick, or the threat of armed conflict."

"I know what it means," she said. "But why offer a carrot at all?"

Widow thought for a moment, and said, "The only possible answer was he can't send the switchmen."

"Why not?"

"Maybe the right hand doesn't know what the left hand is doing?"

"How so?"

"Maybe the switchmen's loyalty is to Collin Brock, and whatever criminal empire he's running? Maybe Junior's guys are separate? Maybe it's him?"

"Because you beat up Junior and his guys?"

Widow nodded, and then thought about how really, it was Joanie that took out one of them. Then he realized something. What if Franklin took Joanie? He nearly said it, but then he thought maybe he should keep it to himself for now. Nora was dealing with a lot already and he didn't want the girls to know. Maybe he could find a way to get Joanie back. If it was true.

Widow said, "Right. Let's say Brock is into something typical —drugs, gun-running, money-laundering, whatever. Maybe Junior and Franklin are up to something else entirely."

Nora said, "And they don't want Brock to find out, because if he does, he might be angry about them keeping a secret from him. But Franklin told me he was Brock's fixer. Wouldn't that imply that he doesn't keep secrets from Brock?"

"How did he say it? Can you remember his exact words?"

Nora searched her memory, tried to remember. She said, "He said he worked for Mr. Brock, for a long time, and that he was a fixer."

"Sounds to me he wants me gone and having me killed isn't an option. Maybe because Junior's out of guys."

"Or they're afraid to mess with you after what you did to the others."

Widow nodded, and said, "It's a theory. Sounds like Franklin and Junior are running something on the side, and don't want daddy to find out about it."

"It must be something lucrative, for Franklin to risk getting caught."

"That, or maybe there's more to it."

"Like what?"

"I don't know," Widow said, stared at the bullet. "You should take the girls and leave."

Nora shook her head emphatically. "No. This is our home. It's Wade's home. My girls think their daddy's coming home someday. I'm not taking that away from them. We're not running."

Widow rolled the bullet, a stark reminder of what she was risking. He stopped and caressed her hand, said, "Wade's gone, Nora. I think it's time to face that fact."

Her eyes teared up, but her face turned flush with anger. She blinked the tears away and jerked her hand away from his. She asked, "What do you know about it? You think he's dead? Why would you think that?"

It was time to tell the truth. So Widow told her about the young sailor, the trainhopping, and the sisters. He told her their story about Alex Hopper, the rumors of missing train-hoppers, and the Ghost Line.

She sat there, quiet and overwhelmed for a long moment. Then she looked at him and said, "Oh my God, Wade's dead. You're right. He must be."

"Yes," Widow said, realizing she needed to face the truth. "A whole year's gone by. He's not coming back. You can't just sit here risking your life, and the girls' lives, waiting for a ghost."

Nora balled up her fists and pounded them on the table. She shouted, "You don't know that! You don't know that!" Tears streamed out of her eyes.

Widow stayed where he was. He let her cry it out. Then he stood up, got close to her, knelt down to her level, and reached for her. She rejected him at first, but then she grabbed onto him and sobbed. She buried her face into his chest and cried. It was a long-overdue crying jag, like she'd held it in for a whole year. The truth had been staring her in the face but she had ignored it, holding out hope that Wade would return to her. Now she realized he was never coming back.

After she finished, Widow glanced at the girls' door. It was still closed. He could hear music playing. They were listening to pop music while making the fliers.

Widow said, "You and the girls still have a chance. You mentioned family in Hawaii. Go to them. Leave this place. Go start a new life." And he thought he'd gotten through to her, that she'd actually see the light, and leave.

Instead, she shouted, "No! I can't!" Her voice rose, then softened and she glanced toward the girls' door. They still didn't come out. "I can't. This farm's all we have left of him. I won't let them scare me away."

"What if they come for you? What if they come for the girls?"

"You'll protect us," she said. Her voice was quieter now. "I know you will."

Widow crossed his arms, and said, "What happens when I leave?"

"You're leaving?"

"I'm not sticking around forever. Come on. This is insane. Don't you see that? You have to let him go."

Nora opened her mouth to respond but stopped when Violet opened her door, holding a stack of fliers. "Māmā, can we go to town? We made these fliers so people who see Joanie can call your phone," she said, peeling one of the fliers off the pile and shoving it in Nora's face.

Nora turned away, wiping away her tears and wiping the expression off her face. Just a quick second and she was back to normal, like she'd done it a million times over the last year.

Widow could only imagine how painful and hard this year had been for her. He took the flyer from Violet and looked at it. It was printed on high-quality poster paper. There was a full-color picture of Joanie and a message describing the situation, along with Nora's number. "You did this?" he asked.

"Uh-huh," Violet said. "On my MacBook."

Widow nodded, impressed. "You're smarter than you look," he said, and poked her teasingly in her tummy.

She giggled and said, "I did the words. Poppy helped with the picture." Just then, as if on cue, Poppy came out of the bedroom and joined them.

"It's a different world," Nora said, her voice steadier now. "I swear, kids today are born knowing how to do these things."

Widow handed the flyer back to Violet. "Let's go to town," he said. He glanced at Nora, who gave him a silent nod.

She looked at Widow and smiled. "I'll think about what you said. I don't have to make a decision right now, today."

"Of course not. I'll stay for as long as you need me to," he said, not realizing he added that last part automatically. He wondered if he meant it. *Would he stay?*

CHAPTER 26

Widow, Nora, and the girls had just stepped out of the farmhouse on their way to give out fliers in Iron Crossing when an unwanted visitor showed up. An Iron Crossing sheriff's patrol car pulled into the driveway and blipped its siren. It was just a quick bleep to alert them that he was pulling in behind them.

Nora looked at Widow, who stared at the patrol car. Violet said, "Police car," while Poppy pointed at it. Nora asked, "What do they want?"

"Maybe Junior decided to report what happened yesterday after all?" Widow said. Nora said nothing, but picked Poppy up, held her on her hip, and took Violet's hand. She led them to the pickup truck and set them inside. She told them to wait there, and to behave. The girls sat in the passenger seat and Nora rolled the windows down to let air in. Nora stood by the truck and Widow approached the rear.

The cruiser rolled in, its tires crackling on the gravel. It slowed, pulled up behind Nora's truck, and stopped—nose to tailgate. The young deputy from the library—the one who'd flirted with Freda and given Widow a hard time—stepped out, his hand resting casually on his belt, where his radio chattered. The aviator sunglasses he wore reflected the sunlight.

He ignored the radio, looked at Widow, then Nora. Widow nodded at him. The deputy asked, "You guys going somewhere?" He took off the aviators and slipped them into his shirt pocket.

"We are," Widow said. "You don't seem surprised to see me here."

"I'm not. I knew you were here."

"How's that?"

"You're the reason I'm here," the deputy said, keeping his hand on his belt, but close enough to go for his gun. He stepped up to Widow, but stayed out of reach.

Widow stayed quiet.

"We got a 9-1-1 call about you. One of your neighbors called, said that you were at their house, harassing them."

The Graces, Widow thought. "I wasn't harassing anyone. I was only looking for our..."

"Missing dog," the deputy said. "Yes, I know."

Widow clenched his fist. It was automatic. This cop had given him a hard time the day before. Now he showed up claiming to have gotten a 9-1-1 call. Widow had heard several times that the cops were in Brock's pocket. Did that include Junior's pocket?

"Relax, Widow. I'm not here to arrest you," the deputy said.

Widow thought back. They asked for his ID at the library, but he refused to give it. So how did the deputy know Widow's name? Franklin?

The young deputy said, "My name's Torres. Eddie Torres. I can see you're wondering how I got your name. You told it to the neighbors that called. I'm not here to arrest you or even question you. The wife called it in. She said some orc was at her house, harassing her. As soon as I heard that, I knew it must be you. No offense."

Orc? Widow thought.

"Anyway, about ten minutes after the wife called us, the husband called to say it was a false alarm. And you were just looking for your dog. But I was already headed out here."

Widow asked, "You were? What for?"

"What kind of name is Widow, anyhow? That a last name?"

Widow nodded.

Torres asked, "You got a first name?"

"I do," Widow said, but didn't give it.

"Okay."

"If you're not here for me, then why are you here?"

Torres ignored the question, glanced at Nora, and then at the girls in the truck. They were squeezed into the open window, waving the fliers at Torres. He said, "Cute kids. They make those fliers?"

Widow stayed quiet. Torres walked past him to the passenger side of the truck. He stopped a few feet from Nora and reached a hand out to the girls. He asked, "Can I have one of the fliers? It'll help me ask around if anyone's seen your dog."

Poppy shoved a flier at him. He stared at it, and said, "She's a good-looking dog. She's a Cane Corso, right? Big dog. Shouldn't be too hard to spot."

"Her name is Joanie," Violet said.

"Or Joan of Bark," Poppy added.

Torres nodded, folded up the flier, and pocketed it. Widow moved closer, stopped behind the young deputy. Torres looked at Nora and asked, "You check the fence line? Big farms like this, there's usually a lot of spots a dog can get free."

Widow folded his arms and said, "We checked."

Nora added, "We looked everywhere."

Something was weird. Torres was acting completely different than he had the day before. *Why was he being all friendly?* Widow wondered.

"Let me talk to you for a second, Widow," Torres said. He walked away from Nora and the girls, back to the space between his car and the truck's tailgate. Widow followed him.

Torres said, "Freda mentioned that you asked about an Alex Hopper?"

Widow's attention piqued. He nodded.

Torres said, "I looked into it. You know, out of curiosity. I couldn't find any reports about an Alex Hopper, but I watched his videos. I'm not sure about him. But it got me thinking about Wade Sutton. Do you know the story?"

"I'm aware of it."

"Have you talked to Nora about him?"

Widow stayed quiet.

"Look, man. I'm not here to arrest you. I told you that. I'm really curious about Sutton and Hopper. If they both went missing a year ago and it was from here, then there should be someone looking into it."

Widow glanced at Nora, who stared back at him with a questioning look on her face. Widow said, "She knows about Hopper. And she's told me about her husband."

"Okay, so tell me everything."

Widow stared at him, unsure about going that far. Should he even trust this cop? He decided to chance it. He told Torres everything, from his lifestyle as a drifter to the trainhoppers, the sisters, their story about Alex, and how he ended up here. He left out all the stuff about the Brocks, Franklin, and breaking Junior's arm.

"Wow, you live quite a life. Strange that you ended up at Nora's doorstep, and her husband missing too," Torres said, and pinched a small object under his uniform shirt, like an automatic reaction. Widow saw the object's shape. It appeared to be a crucifix hanging around Torres' neck.

Torres confirmed it by asking, "You believe in God, Mr. Widow?"

"I went to Sunday school when I was a kid."

"That's not really an answer."

"I believe in live and let live."

Which wasn't an answer, unless Torres read between the lines. He said, "I see. Well, I'm a believer. My mother was a staunch believer, and she taught me that God does things for a reason."

Widow nodded, but stayed quiet.

Torres said, "Anyway, I believe you may have been sent here for a reason. And that's why we crossed paths. I want to help if I can. Think I can talk to Ms. Sutton about this?"

"It's a free country."

Torres nodded and motioned for Nora to join them. Nora told the girls to wait and she joined them at the tailgate. Torres explained it all to her. He told her some of what he found, also leaving out any mention of the Brocks.

After Torres was finished, Nora looked at Widow and asked, "Did you tell him?"

Widow stayed quiet.

Torres asked, "Tell me what?"

Nora started to speak, but Widow said, "Last night someone showed up here, threatening me, telling me to leave. And then this morning I found this outside the girls' window." He took the bullet out of his pocket and showed it to Torres.

"Whoa. Why didn't you report this?" he took the bullet from Widow.

"I think it's got something to do with the Brocks." Whether she could trust Torres or not, Nora blurted it out. Widow wasn't mad about it, although he thought it best to limit what they shared with this deputy. Nora had more to lose. It was her missing husband, her children, and her farm on the line.

Torres' eyes perked up. He asked, "What makes you say that?" Nora glanced at Widow. The girls called to her, asking loads of questions. They weren't going to sit there quiet for much longer. That was clear.

Widow put a hand on Nora's shoulder, and said, "Go keep them occupied. I'll tell him the rest."

Nora nodded, and joined her girls. Widow said, "Follow me." And he took Torres to the side of the farmhouse, where the ground below the girls' window still bore the boot prints. He pointed to them without a word.

Torres crouched and inspected the boot prints. "These are from your visitor?" he asked. He glanced at the bent insect screen and back to the unfired bullet in his palm.

"I'd say so."

"You should come to the station and file a report."

"No way. I've heard the cops here are in Brock's pocket. No offense."

"I'm not," Torres said.

"How about the rest?"

"Dillard's not. He's the guy you saw me with yesterday."

Widow nodded, he remembered Dillard's nameplate. He said, "You sure?"

Torres's radio crackled again. He switched it off and said, "Yes. He's a good guy."

"What about the others?"

"I've only been on the force for a year. I joined just after the Wade Sutton disappearance. The others, they've all been here longer."

"So, you can't rule it out?"

Torres stared at the boot print and said, "It's deep. The guy must've been big." He stood up and looked up at Widow. "Not as big as you though. You said he threatened you? What did he look like? Give me the details." Torres took out a pen and notepad, flipped the pad open, and waited for Widow to answer.

Widow said, "No, I don't think so."

"Seriously?"

"I'm sorry. You might be alright, but I definitely don't trust the others."

Torres flipped the notepad closed, and pocketed both it and the pen. He took his sunglasses out of his pocket, slipped them on, and said, "You're a real pain in the ass, Mr. Widow. Anyone ever tell you that?"

"Lots of times."

"I'm keeping the bullet," Torres said, dropping it into a pocket. Then he walked past Widow, back to the driveway. Widow followed. They found Nora and Violet tickling Poppy under her armpits. Violet held her down and Nora tickled her. She laughed and laughed.

Widow stepped in front of Torres, trying to usher him back to this patrol car, but Torres sidestepped him and went to Nora. He said, "Ma'am?"

Nora stepped away from her kids and over to him and Widow. Torres reached into a back pocket, pulled out his wallet, sifted through it, and handed Nora a business card. He re-pocketed his wallet and said, "I can't promise anything, but I'm gonna keep looking into Wade's case. But you call me if you think of anything or if something else happens."

She thanked him and he left her there. Widow escorted Torres back to his cruiser. Torres stopped at the driver-side door, turned to Widow, and said, "I know you don't trust me. I've heard rumors about the Brocks too. Same as everyone. But until someone reports that Junior or any of his guys have committed a crime, all I can do is ask questions."

Widow asked, "What's your interest in this anyway?"

"Justice. What else?"

Widow nodded and Torres got back into his cruiser and fired it up. Before he backed out, Widow said, "Hey Torres?"

The deputy stopped his car and looked at Widow through his open window.

Widow approached the window, clamped a hand down on the sill, and bent down so Torres could see his face. "You said Wade made a call the day he vanished?"

"He didn't make a call. He received a bunch of calls."

"Who from?"

Torres' eyebrow arched and he said, "Collin Brock's company owned the numbers that called him. It was a company line, so I can't tell exactly who dialed it."

Black River Rail, Widow thought. He nodded and released the windowsill. He stepped back and away.

Torres said, "I'll keep an eye out for their dog." But Widow already had a good idea of how to find Joanie. He nodded to Torres and watched him drive off. He watched until Torres was gone from sight.

CHAPTER 27

By the time the afternoon sun hung low in the sky, casting long shadows across Iron Crossing's streets, they'd covered a lot of ground. Nora drove while Widow rode shotgun, the girls crammed in the middle. They'd ridden from street to street, business to business, hanging up and handing out fliers. The girls asked anyone and everyone they came across about Joanie. They were fearless. The response from the locals ranged from polite shrugs to outright avoidance.

Widow took note of some of the businesspeople stiffening up the moment they saw him with Nora and her girls, like he didn't belong with them. Store owners glanced at the four of them, hesitated, then dismissed them as quickly as they could. It wasn't hard to connect the dots. Widow figured these were the kind of people who knew which way the wind blew—and that the Brocks were the ones who told them which way that was.

They crossed the river into New Town and had much better luck there. They handed out fliers and asked questions. Widow helped the whole way, knowing it wouldn't return any results. But it was really to keep the girls' hopes up that they'd see Joanie again.

Their last stop in New Town was the Hawaiian joint, where they had another lunch. The girls visited with the puppies. Nora's friend, Kailea, was very upset about Joanie being missing. She treated the girls to extra ice cream. At the end of their meal, Kailea refused payment, but Widow left enough cash to cover it under a plate on the table. Then they made their way back to Old Town.

Widow was convinced Franklin had done something to Joanie. He was surprised that Nora hadn't mentioned it to him. He knew she'd put it together on her own eventually. He figured the only reason she hadn't so far was because she had so much going on. Who could blame her for not seeing it?

The last stop was a business in a little shopping mall. They'd passed it up twice already. The girls had begged to go there to ask around and to hang fliers, but Nora had driven right past it without a word. The third time, she decided to pull in. And Widow knew immediately why she had driven past it earlier.

One of the suites was a veterinary clinic, the one where Nora's husband used to work.

Violet had been relentless about asking to stop. She said, "They got a bulletin board for missing pets." This time, Nora listened. She figured Violet was right. And it was a good place to look, though it was clear she didn't want to be there. She parked the truck and stayed there for a long moment with her foot on the brake, the truck still in drive.

She stared at the sign above the suite, but she might as well have been staring into space. The girls watched her, worried. Violet looked at Widow. He reached his arm over the back of the long bench seat and touched Nora's shoulder. He asked,

"Are you sure you want to be here? I can go in with them. You can stay out here."

Nora glanced at him. A single tear welled up in her eye. She smiled and said, "It's fine. Let's go in." She looked down at the girls. Her expression changed into one of pretend hope. "Oh, they can check their system to see if Joanie's been turned in to any of the shelters for us."

The girls smiled and Widow stepped out first, holding the truck door open for them to hop out after him. He shut the door behind them and they entered the clinic. It smelled like scented disinfectant and animals, a strange mix of sterile and natural. Honestly, it smelled better than Nora's barn, but Widow didn't say so. The staff behind the counter greeted them warmly, their faces lighting up at the sight of Nora and the girls. Two of the ladies who worked there recognized all three of them.

One of them gave Widow a sideways, judgmental look, like she didn't like seeing Nora with a new man. But she smiled at Nora and the girls. Both ladies come out from behind the counter, offering big friendly hugs to Nora and the girls. One of the ladies gave Nora a long, therapeutic hug, like she needed it more than Nora did.

Nora squeezed the woman back, like old friends reuniting at the funeral of another friend. After pleasantries and sympathies were expressed, the long-hug woman asked, "How are you? What can we do for you?"

Nora hesitated, her hands smoothing over the edges of the fliers she held. "I'm fine," she said, but her tone betrayed her. The ladies saw through it, but stayed friendly and supportive. They didn't make a big deal out of it.

While Nora was going into the whole explanation about Joanie, Widow stepped aside and found the bulletin board that Violet had mentioned. It took up half a wall. A title, made of magnetic letters, read: *Missing Fur Babies*. It was massive. There were dozens, maybe a hundred, posters and fliers about missing pets from all over the county. Some of them looked like they'd been there for months, maybe years. He scanned the rows of fliers, taking in the pet photos and desperate pleas for information. Something caught his attention about it—which might've been nothing, but it seemed like a pattern.

There were a lot of missing dogs. More than he'd expected. And a surprising number of them were similar breeds— medium-to-large dogs, all guard-dog breeds. Joanie would've fit right smack in the middle of this lineup. Widow didn't say anything about it. He just mentally noted it. No sense in adding conspiracy theories to the troubles they already had. But suspicion lodged itself in his primal brain like a splinter.

The ladies led Nora and the girls over to the bulletin board. They helped the girls thumbtack their flier onto the board. The other office workers came by and gave Nora their condolences, like Wade was dead. Which was probably true.

Widow shuffled away, melted back into the waiting room, and exited the building without anyone noticing. He waited in the truck. He had felt out of place in there. And he figured his presence was only stirring up rumors and trouble for Nora down the road.

Nearly twenty minutes later, Nora and the girls came out. Widow got out and helped the girls into the truck, and Nora drove. The sun began setting across the river. Widow stayed quiet while they drove through the rest of the town.

Violet looked disappointed. Poppy yawned a couple of times. And Nora kept it together pretty well, but Widow could sense that they all felt defeated. No answers on where Joanie was. As they turned down the last road in Iron Crossing proper,

Widow spotted the back of a hospital direction sign leading back the other way. His eyes narrowed. He knew it was now or never. A plan had been forming in his head from the moment he found that bullet on the girls' windowsill.

"Pull over," Widow said.

Nora glanced at him. "Why?"

"Just pull over for me."

A tired Nora yawned as she eased the truck to the curb in front of a bank. A couple of employees pressed themselves up against the bank's front window, hoping they didn't have new customers. They were closing in five minutes.

Widow opened his door and hopped out. He stood on the curb, squatted down a bit to see into the truck. "What are you doing?" Nora asked, confused.

"I gotta run a errand," Widow said casually, like it was no big deal.

Nora frowned and asked, "Errand? Now? Like what?"

"There's just something I gotta do."

Poppy snored in the seat. Her head fell against Nora. Violet scrunched the rest of the fliers together and reached up to Widow with them. She said, "Take these. Maybe you can hand out the rest?"

Widow smiled at her, reached in and brushed her hair back. He took the pile of fliers and said, "Of course! I'll make sure to give the rest of them out."

Violet smiled and Widow pulled back out with the fliers. He closed the door. Nora asked, "How're you going to get back to the farm?"

Widow leaned down, resting his forearm on the open window so he could see Nora's face. He said, "Don't worry about me. I'll find a ride."

Her eyes searched his face. Something was bothering her. Widow asked, "What?"

"Are you really coming back?"

Widow smiled and said, "Yes." He met her gaze, steady and reassuring. "I promise. I'll be home in a few hours."

Home? Did he really use that word? It startled him. He'd never called a place home before. At least not in over two decades.

"What're you going to do?" Nora asked.

Widow straightened up and gave her a smirk, like he had plans to do bad things. She'd seen that look before, but on bad biker boys. He said, "Don't worry about it. Just go home. I'll see you tonight."

Nora hesitated for a moment longer, kept her eyes locked with his. She hoped he would come back. She just didn't know how to say it. But she didn't have to. He saw it in her eyes. She just gave him a slight nod, and said, "Alright. Better keep that promise."

Widow tapped the roof of the truck twice. The sound reverberated from his hand. Even a light tap with a hammer still makes a sound. Poppy stirred and then fell back to sleep. Widow whispered, "Sorry. I'll see you later." He backed away and watched as Nora's truck pulled back onto the road. Violet waved goodbye to him out the window. Widow watched them until they were gone from sight. Then he turned to the direction of Iron Crossing's hospital and started walking.

CHAPTER 28

Widow walked with the setting sun at his back on the last stretch of road to the hospital. He reached it, stopped outside, and stared up at the sign for the complex: Brock's General Hospital.

Of course, he thought. What other name would it be? The name hit him like a dull punch to the gut, a constant reminder that the Brocks had their fingers in everything around here. How much of the pie did Brock have at the state level? Widow could only imagine.

Widow walked through the parking lot, hoping to see Junior's Raptor still parked in it. But it wasn't there. Which didn't necessarily mean anything, because there was a four-story parking garage too. But Widow wasn't going to search it.

Widow entered the hospital, stepping through a pair of automatic doors. They sucked shut behind him. He entered a lobby. It was pristine, clinical, and impersonal—marble floors, polished metal railings, the faint scent of bleach, and the rumblings of bureaucracy to go with it all. A brass plaque near the reception desk displayed some claim to excellence in health. It was attributed to Collin Brock. Widow didn't bother to read it.

A portrait of Collin Brock hung high on a wall, overlooking the people in the waiting room like a monarch from an ancient feudal society sneering down at his servants. Widow passed the receptionist, a young woman. She offered him help, but he responded with, "I know where I'm going." He didn't know, but he could figure it out. He wanted to minimize his interactions with people.

Widow made his way to the elevators, walking past a patrolling security guard who had a flashlight and jingling keys. He pressed the Up button and took the elevator to the top floor. He figured he'd start at the very top and work his way down, although he suspected he would hit paydirt on the top floor. Rich, powerful, and corrupt people often think of themselves as untouchable, as above everyone else. They often think common people are beneath them. Collin Brock's portrait reflected that sentiment.

Widow had a target list in mind. At the top was Junior. Finding him would be ideal. But Junior only had a broken arm, not something requiring an overnighter in the hospital. On the other hand, Junior was a spoiled rich-kid punk, and a bully, as Widow had explained to Poppy and Violet. One thing about bullies, in Widow's experience, was when bullies got hit they made a big deal out of it. That's why punching them square in the nose was so effective. They overestimated their resistance to pain, their strength. Usually a bully's size wasn't a strength, but a weakness. And bullies were overdramatic. Widow knew a thing or two about it. He'd dealt with his fair share of bullies throughout his life.

Junior only had a broken arm, but Widow was willing to bet they'd put him up in a single room. That's the least they could do for him. His old man's name was on the building. Maybe he would still be there, or maybe not. Widow gave it fifty-fifty odds.

If Junior had already been discharged, then Widow planned to go down the ladder of the guys who were still in the hospital. Widow thought back to them. There was the rifle guy, the one who'd lost a few teeth before he went unconscious from a rifle butt to the face, not to mention the vicious dog bites on his wrist. He might still be there. Then there was the road sentry, the guy Widow had slammed face-first into the Raptor's door after a one-two combo that left him crumpled like trash on the pavement. And finally, the second guy—the one Joanie had rushed, her jaws crushing the guy's groin. Widow remembered the guy screaming before he blacked out. It was brutal, yet Widow felt no remorse for the guy. *Cross me, and you get crossed out*, Widow thought.

All of those guys should still be licking their wounds. And where would they be doing that? The recovery floors of the hospital. They should be there somewhere, Widow hoped.

Though he preferred to confront Junior, if the younger Brock wasn't there, one of the others would do. Widow wasn't picky. He wanted answers, and he would get them—one way or the other.

Most likely, Junior had a room at the top. Maybe with a view of the river, or whatever was the best vista to look at from the hospital. Surely he would be the top candidate for such a thing. But Widow had only broken Junior's arm. For most people that was an in and out hospital visit, but Widow hoped Junior had decided to stay the night.

Widow got out on the top floor and looked around. The hallway was quiet, the kind of hush that called for most people to tread quietly, but not Widow. He didn't bother with civility. He walked normally, clicking his shoes against the linoleum floor, announcing his arrival to the patients and staff.

The nurses and orderlies on this floor seemed pretty busy. Widow counted maybe three nurses and three orderlies. No doctors so far. He walked from one end of the floor to the other, starting at the west end and making his way east. Some of the rooms were wide open. He peeked in and saw no sign of Junior or his guys. Then he found them at the eastern end of the hallway. The first room he passed was dark. He peeked in. It was a large single room with a nice corner view of the river. It was empty. Junior had been there. Widow knew it. He could feel it.

Widow closed the door and moved on to the next one. The next room wasn't empty. Widow peeked in and saw two hospital beds with lumps on them, probably Junior's guys. They weren't crammed into one of those small hospital rooms. Theirs was just as big as the corner-view room, which had likely been Junior's the day before. The bathroom door was wide open and the light was on, making a door-shaped path of light across the floor. Hospital machines blinked, but that was the only light in the room. The rest of the room was dim.

One of the guys snored and moaned all at the same time, like he was in tremendous pain. He was further inside the room, his bed pushed near the window. The view from here was good too. Not as good as the corner room's, but still, not too shabby. The first guy was also asleep, but he seemed dead to the world because he drooled on himself and his eyes were half open, and rolled back into his eyelids. His head was wrapped tightly in gauze, like he'd just come from brain surgery.

Widow entered the room and grabbed a chair from out of a corner. He dragged it to the door, took a quick peek out, and saw that no one was watching. He shut the door and wedged the chair up against the handle at an angle, making it hard for anyone to push the door open.

Widow moved to the foot of the first guy's bed and saw a chart hanging off the footboard. He opened it and read over it. This was the road sentry guy, the one he had throat-punched and then added a stomach punch to go with it. That would be okay, but the chart claimed the guy also suffered a concussion. Which was probably from having his face slammed into the door of Junior's Raptor. Apparently it left more than a dent in the truck. It left a hairline fracture in the guy's skull.

He wasn't going to be able to reveal much anyway. The chart said his throat was damaged. A recommendation of physical therapy to enable him to use his vocal cords again was suggested by a doctor whose signature was unreadable.

Widow looked at the guy. He didn't think he'd be able to wake him up anyway. The chart also mentioned some kind of heavy sedative Widow had never heard of.

Widow moved on to the guy by the window. This one was the second guy from yesterday morning, the one Joanie had bitten in the groin. She'd violently shaken the guy till he passed out. Widow checked his chart, expecting to find a diagnosis he never wanted to hear about himself. And he wasn't far off. They had saved the guy's groin, which was good news for him. However, it had required lots of stitches. The doctor remarked that it was a coin toss whether the guy would ever be able to use his equipment again. Those weren't his exact words, but Widow could read between the lines.

The chart also mentioned the guy had suffered severe pain and trauma. He was on antibiotics and a strong painkiller. No sedatives. Widow dropped the chart and looked at the guy.

Even though he wasn't sedated like the other guy, he was the one snoring. He must've doubled up on the painkillers.

The second guy lay motionless in the hospital bed, his face pale and slick with sweat, a sheen of discomfort etched into his expression. His midsection was swaddled in thick, sterile bandages beneath a loose hospital gown. Instead of a cast, his lower body was encased in medical supports—an elevated frame held the sheets away from his injured groin, ensuring no accidental contact aggravated the damage. Tubes snaked from an IV into his arm, delivering the painkillers and fluids to keep him stable. A faint grimace crossed his face. His posture was rigid, as if every slight movement might tear out a stitch, inducing great pain.

Widow stood in the door-shaped light just enough for the guy to be able to see most of his face. Time to wake the guy up. Widow skipped trying to call out to the guy or shaking him awake. Instead, he clamped down on the medical support frame and rocked it hard, just enough to shake things loose but not enough to tear a stitch. The guy's eyes shot open, wide with panic, like someone had stomped directly on his injuries. Then he clenched them shut, writhing as much as his condition allowed, moaning in agony from the frame's jarring motion.

Widow took note of how much damage a hard rocking could inflict. Now he knew he could dial back the pressure and still get the answers he needed. After several seconds of agonized moaning, the storm of pain subsided, and the guy's body relaxed slightly.

He slowly opened his eyes, letting them adjust to the dim light. Then he looked up, past the rig, to see Widow towering over him. His gaze lingered on Widow's face, studying the features he could make out. For a moment, he wasn't sure who he was looking at. Then it clicked. And the guy's jaw dropped open. He tried to scream out for someone to help, but Widow rocked the medical rig again. And the whole storm of pain hit the guy like a blizzard.

Desperately, the guy reached for the call button. He went to press it, to call for help from the staff. But Widow snatched it from his hand and shook the rig again. The guy screamed and moaned. Widow dropped the call button, letting it dangle off the side of the bed.

Widow glanced at the road sentry, to see if the noise woke him. But it didn't. That guy was the lucky one, because he was out cold.

After another long bout of pain flooded the guy's senses, it slowly subsided again. The guy clenched his eyes shut and started muttering to himself, like he was praying for help. Widow said, "Open your eyes!"

The guy slowly opened his eyes and stared at Widow. Then he opened them wide. He shuddered, like Widow was something out of a nightmare. Widow realized the painkillers the guy was on likely helped numb the pain, but intensified the guy's fear. Widow released the rig and grabbed the guy's call-button hand, squeezing the guy's thumb, which was what had nearly pressed the call button. He leaned down, stared into the guy's eyes, and, in an ice-cold voice, said, "Wrong move." And he broke the guy's thumb.

The guy screamed and writhed in agony. Widow glanced at the door. No one came in to check on him. The staff was numb to screams.

Widow looked at the guy, waited for him to calm down, and released the guy's thumb. Then he made sure the guy watched as he went for the index finger. He grabbed it and squeezed hard. The guy's face turned ghostly white. Widow wrenched it slowly, to as far as it was meant to bend.

The guy begged, "No! Please!"

Widow loomed over him, calm and unyielding. "I have questions," Widow said. "You answer and I'll leave. You don't and…" Widow exerted more pressure on the guy's index finger.

The guy's eyes darted toward the door, hoping someone, anyone, would rush in and save him from this maniac.

"No one's coming for you. And if you even think about lying to me…" Widow said, exerting just the slightest bit more pressure on the index finger. "I'll break this finger and then move on to the next one. Got it?"

The guy swallowed hard, his bravado cracking. He said, "Okay, man! I got it! Ask your questions!"

"Let's start with a couple of easy ones."

The guy said nothing.

Widow said, "You ever heard of a kid named Alex Hopper? He went missing here about a year ago."

The guy shook his head, big and obvious. He said, "I don't know nothing about that. Never heard of him."

Widow believed him. It was a shot in the dark, but he had to ask. Widow asked, "What about Wade Sutton?"

"No, man! I don't know him either."

Widow leaned in and said, "You sure? He was a local veterinarian. He went missing a year ago. You never heard of him?"

"I wasn't here back then. I just got hired on a few months ago. I swear!"

"Who hired you?"

The guy's eyes darted around again. Widow asked, "Are you having second thoughts? Are you thinking about lying to me?"

"I'm sorry, man! Don't break any more of my fingers! It's just the guy who hired me is scary!"

"Scarier than me?"

"No, man! But he'll kill me!"

Widow glanced at the other guy and said, "It's just us. No one will know. Your friend is out cold."

"His name is Franklin."

Which was what Widow had expected to hear. He asked, "Where can I find Franklin?"

The guy hesitated, his gaze flickering back to the door. Widow couldn't bend the guy's index finger any more without breaking it. So, he squeezed it harder and said, "I won't ask again. No more chances."

If the guy's face turned any paler, he'd look dead. The guy gave in and rattled off an address, his voice shaky. Widow listened and filed it away. He didn't know where it was, but he'd find it.

"Good," Widow said, released the guy's finger, and stepped back. He bent down, picked up the call button and ripped it from the cord. Now it was useless. He dropped it on the guy's chest. He glared at the guy. "If you warn Franklin or tell anyone I was here. I'll come back. And I'll make sure you leave here in a bucket. Got it?"

The guy nodded frantically. Widow turned and left the room, the door clicking shut behind him.

CHAPTER 29

Joanie woke to a chaotic symphony of barking, growls, and whimpers echoing through the metal walls of a kennel. The structure held several other fighting-breed dogs; some bred for it, some not.

The cages numbered a dozen, but held less than that number of dogs. There were cut-outs inside the walls of the underground structure. The builders had haphazardly cut out the holes to be turned into cells. The rugged designs made them look more like naturally formed caverns rather than intentional holding cells, but that's what they were.

Some of the cells held other breeds of animals instead of dogs. Some of the creatures made sounds and others slept away the experience, trying to escape into their minds. A few of the cells were man-sized, designed for humans, like the one Tim Camp had been in. Those were currently empty, waiting for new occupants.

Joanie's heart raced, pounding hard against her ribs. She didn't know where she was. The last thing she remembered was the soft rain, patrolling the farm, and then a truck and a stranger on her driveway. She barked at him and he pointed something at her. It was like an object the woman had, the rifle. It made a sound, but not like a boom. It was more like a quick burst of air, and then something hit Joanie, right in the chest. She felt it hit hard. Immediately there was a pinch of pain, and then darkness.

Now she was confined in a tight space, like her crate at home, only without the warmth and cleanliness. Cold steel wires surrounded her, and the floor beneath her paws felt slick and filthy. Putrid animal smells lingered in the air, worse than the goat pen on her farm. Blood streaked across it. There were shavings of other dog nails in the kennel, like other dogs had been there and tried desperately to claw their way out, to escape.

Joanie stood up and tried to turn around, but the space was tight, pressing against her sides, so she just plopped back down. She curled into a ball, the only comfortable position she could squeeze into. She tucked her tail close, trying to make herself smaller. The animal noises overwhelmed her, overloading her senses—making everything even more terrifying for her.

Joanie didn't understand what was happening. She clung to happier memories—of the farm, the girls, the woman, and the giant stranger. She wished he would open her cage and free her. But he wasn't there. She was trapped. Her nose twitched, her sense of smell seeking out anything familiar, but it found nothing.

Around her, other dogs barked. Some voices were sharp and menacing, and some were frantic, filled with terror. Others growled low, snarling like wild animals being cornered. Joanie tucked her tail, unsure if the other animals were friends or foes. The only thing she knew for sure was they were all strangers to her.

Why was she here? Why did that stranger bring her? What was she meant to do? Fear for her future filled her head. All she wanted was to be home, with the girls. She wanted to be curled up in her bed by the front door.

A distant, cavernous sound made her ears perk up. It came from deep inside the underground somewhere. It wasn't barking or growling. It was something more terrifying—a guttural roar that forced her to instinctively crouch lower to the floor. Whatever made that sound wasn't a dog, not one she'd ever heard before. It was something else. It was bigger. Stronger. Joanie's nose twitched, picking up the scent of something primal, something dark, like a wild beast that she'd never seen before. Her body shivered uncontrollably.

Above the animals' cacophony, she caught the muffled voices of men. Deep, gruff tones carried through the underground tunnels. Joanie couldn't make out any words she recognized. These were not nice men. They sounded scary. She knew that immediately too. The tone was familiar to her. They spoke with authority, like grown humans did. But these voices had a cruel edge to them. She whimpered softly, her ears flattening against her head.

The men came closer. She could smell them, but didn't recognize any of the scents. She counted three, maybe four guys. They walked from kennel to kennel, opening the cage doors where it was safe to do so. Sometimes the men had to use cattle prods to shock the dogs inside and make them back off. She noticed they did this to the more aggressive dogs. She heard one dog lunge at the man who opened the cage, but the dog was stopped by something. She knew the sound of the something; it was like a chain. She had to wear a chain choker when she was younger, to keep her from pulling. She remembered the woman had trained her on one. That was before she understood the boundaries.

The rhythm went the same. The scary men opened a cage door, an aggressive dog snapped at them, pulling on a chain and being restrained by it. Then one of the scary men would shock the dog with the cattle prod. Another man, a silent man, one she couldn't get a read on, would inspect the animal.

For most of the aggressive dogs, a quick shock from the cattle prod whipped them into submission. One dog, the most aggressive one as far as she could tell, had to be sedated by the scary men. They stuck him with a needle on the end of a stick.

One of the scary men laughed at this. He said, "Let's move on. We'll come back to this one." And the men carried on down the line. She was at the end, the last one.

The voices drew closer. Joanie stayed still, quiet. She was so scared. She just wanted to go home. She sniffed the air. Suddenly, she smelled something. She recognized the smell. It was faint, far away and yet close, like when she lost her favorite stuffed chew toy, only to find it weeks later. She'd accidentally left it out in the rain. Once the woman found it and tried to reintroduce it to her, she rejected it. At first, she didn't recognize it. How could it be her toy, when it had all those strange smells on it? But then she got to the one smell, the old familiar one, and she knew it was hers. This felt like that.

She recognized the old smell. But it was so different. She couldn't quite figure out where she knew it from. It was like a scent she'd picked up before, at the farm.

The mean men were Brock's switchmen, the same guys who'd escorted Widow off Black River Rail & Stockyard's premises two days before. They continued down the line.

"Junior's offering us extra," one switchman said.

A second switchman asked, "Above what Mr. Brock already gives us?"

The third switchman said, "Junior already pays us above that just to keep quiet about all this."

"So what's the new money for?" the second one asked.

The first switchman said, "Junior wants us to do the work his other guys did."

"You mean before some guy put them in the hospital?" the second one asked.

"That's right," the third one said. "But we won't be going to no hospital."

The first switchman said, "Ain't no stranger breaking my arms." He ignited the cattle prod, scraping the business end down the metal kennel. Sparks flew out dramatically. The dogs close to the sparks whimpered in fear.

"Shut up!" the first switchman shouted at them. "Stop, you damn mongrels!"

The second switchman asked, "So, what is it Junior wants us to do for this extra money?"

The third switchman said, "You gotta work his shows. They're fun to watch. I saw Bearzerker rip a guy to pieces the other night."

"What about the dogs?" the second switchman asked.

The third one said, "Some of them live, and some die. They're also fun to watch."

The men went quiet for a long moment, waiting for the second guy to say something. The first switchman looked at him and asked, "What? You got a problem with dog fighting?"

"I like dogs," the second switchman said, apologetically.

The third switchman said, "So do I. I got two dogs at home. But what's that got to do with it?"

The first one ignited the cattle prod again, and said, "Yeah, money is money."

The second switchman said, "So, it's easy money, right?"

"Yeah," the third switchman replied. "And he's offering even more to help run his Iron Ring fights. Says he's got a lot riding on these fights, especially since that giant stranger put his usual guys in the hospital. He's willing to give us double what they got."

The first switchman laughed bitterly and said, "Good riddance. More money for us."

They stepped closer to Joanie. She scooted her butt to the back wall of the kennel, trying to get away from them.

"Trust me, it's easy work," the third switchman said. "Say, you know how to hold a camera, right?"

"Yeah, sure," the second switchman said.

"Good, then you get the job," the first switchman said. "Just remember, only Junior and Mr. Franklin know about this. You tell Mr. Brock and it's all over. No more double-dipping."

"Mr. Brock don't know about the Iron Ring?" the second switchman asked.

"No!" the third switchman blurted out.

"And you're not to say anything. Or Junior will throw you in with Bearzerker!" the first switchman said.

The second one swallowed hard, and said, "Of course. I would never!"

Joanie couldn't make sense of their words, but their tone set her on edge. She didn't like them, not one bit. She pressed herself harder against the back of the kennel, making herself as small as possible.

The sound of a heavy chain dragging along the ground caught her attention, because it came with that same far-off smell she had recognized earlier. She stayed low and watched through the wires.

One of the switchmen prodded another creature. This one was outside with them. It walked among them. This one wasn't a dog, but they treated it like one. It stood bipedal, but hunched over like a humpbacked creature from a book. It was all bone and sinew. It was a man, a prisoner, someone who'd been imprisoned for a long time. The man on the chain was covered in dirt and grime.

The man had a long chain shackled around his neck. He dragged it around with him. The other end of the chain ran across the long corridor and locked onto a long metal bar embedded into the wall.

The dirty man's silhouette was illuminated by dim light. She stared at him, because that faintly recognizable scent came from him. Was he a friend to her? She didn't know the answer to that.

The dirty man moved slowly, his bare feet shuffling along the concrete floors, his body hunched like a beaten animal. The slack in the chain dragged behind him with every shuffle. He wasn't like the others. He smelled of despair, of dirt and fear. His eyes were hollow, his skin pale and stretched over sharp bones. He was a ghost of a man. He was clearly human, but whoever he had been was gone now.

Joanie sniffed the air, her nose twitching as the dirty man

scuffled closer to her cage. She knew there was something familiar about him, but she couldn't place it.

The man approached her cage, crouching down with difficulty. He said nothing, but his movements were gentle. One of the switchmen opened the cage door and said, "Go on! This one won't be a problem."

The dirty man's eyes were pale and lifeless. There was no soul there, only the husk of a man. He stared in at Joanie. She saw bite and claw marks all along his wrists, like he'd been attacked countless times by other dogs. Then she noticed more marks up and down his body, more claw and teeth marks. Many had scarred his skin for life. The sizes of the scars ranged from dog-attack size to something much, much larger. The guy was missing two fingers. They'd been either bitten off or torn off.

The dirty man reached in, his hands trembling as much as Joanie did when he touched her fur. Joanie stiffened, unsure of his intent. But his touch was soft, tentative, almost apologetic. For a brief moment, she felt a sliver of familiar comfort.

The dirty man examined her like a veterinarian would, checking her teeth, her paws, and her body for injuries. Joanie didn't understand his purpose, but she stayed still, sensing he was friendly. He looked in her direction the whole time, but never really looked at her. She sniffed him, still terrified and reluctant, but she licked his arm. His skin was grubby, like that familiar chew toy while it was still muddy. Also like that chew toy, there was a familiarity she couldn't place. He looked at her once, a flash of humanity washing over his eyes. And for a brief second, they seemed to know each other.

One of the switchmen poked at the dirty man with his cattle prod. He said, "Come on! We ain't got all day!"

The dirty man's eyes went cold again. He still stayed there at her cage, but that sliver of humanity was gone. The dirty man finished, and backed out of her kennel, his chain rattling softly as he moved. His shoulders slumped, and he looked down, avoiding her eyes. He bowed his head low, obediently, to his masters.

Then it came again—that loud, guttural roar. Joanie's ears shot up and her whole body froze. The sound was far away, but it echoed throughout the chamber. It was deeper and more menacing than the first time she heard it. It was followed by a snarl that echoed through the building, making her cage vibrate. The other animals in the chamber joined in. Growling and snarling mixed with barking echoed as chaotically as before. Joanie whimpered, her tail curling tight against her body. Joanie's basic instincts took over, and she couldn't stop the warm stream that soaked the floor beneath her. She peed in her kennel. Her breathing came in short, panicked bursts as the noise around her grew louder—the barking, the growling, the roaring.

She didn't know where she was or how she got here. All she knew was the overwhelming need to escape. But there was nowhere to go. She thought about the giant stranger and how he stepped in to help her girls the morning before. Where was he?

CHAPTER 30

Hours passed. The night brought on the first cool air before fall. The hot, humid summer had peaked and would soon be on its way out. Evening birds quieted down for the night, making way for the night birds to go out on the hunt.

Widow paced Iron Crossing on a similar hunt, only he wasn't hunting food. He was hunting for Franklin. He paced the edge of Old Town with Franklin's address scrawled in his memory. He realized too late that Iron Crossing at night was even more confusing than Iron Crossing in the daytime. The city sprawled out wider and deeper than he had anticipated. Widow underestimated Iron Crossing from the first moment he stepped off the tracks of Route 67. The city wasn't just a sleepy little town with a single main drag. It stretched across a web of streets split by the river, making Franklin's house a little harder to find in the dark.

Walking around looking for Franklin's street the way he had found streets in the past wasn't working. Even if he found the street, he realized that although most houses had numbers on them, they weren't lit up at night. People in Iron Crossing didn't want to be easily found at night.

Widow would've hopped in a taxi and asked to be taken to Franklin's address, only there were no taxis cruising around looking for fares. Not here. Maybe he could've done this in New York City, but Iron Crossing was no New York City. This wasn't the city that never sleeps. It was asleep now. He saw barely any pedestrians walking about the streets and side-walks. Except for a couple of people walking their dogs, Widow was alone.

Widow did see a familiar face. A patrol car passed him on one street. It was that jarhead deputy, Dillard. At first, he thought the deputy saw him, so he ducked down a side street and turned abruptly at another street. But Dillard never crossed his path again for the rest of the night.

Widow wandered the streets, scanning each house for some-thing that might stand out—like Franklin's black Chevy Silverado in the driveway—but he saw lots of trucks and it was impossible to double-check them all. Widow asked a couple of the dog walkers for directions, but no luck there.

Widow thought about Nora and the girls. He had missed dinner, and it was getting late. He gave up because he didn't want to miss tucking the girls into bed. Especially, he didn't want to miss going to bed with Nora. If that's what she wanted.

Iron Crossing turned in for the night before he did. The place seemed to fold in on itself, the streets quiet, dark shadows stretching across intersections. With no leads and no one to point him in the right direction, Widow decided to head back to the farm. Plus, he worried that if he waited too long, he might not be able to catch a ride to Nora's. How far was her farm from the middle of town? Ten miles? Maybe less. As much as he hated thinking about Joanie being scared, locked up far from her home, finding Franklin would have to wait till the next day.

Widow passed the diner, which was closing up from serving dinner. He saw Ronnie, the weaselly manager, on the patio. Ronnie was scolding a busboy over something. Ronnie saw Widow and froze, like a deer in headlights. Widow made the I-see-you gesture by pointing two fingers at his own eyes and then one finger at Ronnie. Widow couldn't help it. He passed the diner and walked on down the street, back towards Nora's farm.

Widow got lucky and caught a ride with a passerby, a lonely woman who was leaving town. She mentioned that her husband had gone to jail. "I dropped him off this morning at the county jail," she said. "He thinks I'm going to wait around for six years for him to get out. I told him I would, of course."

"But you got other plans?" Widow asked, just to humor her. She wanted conversation. He wanted a free ride. Therefore, it only made sense to go along with whatever subject she wanted to talk about. A lot of times Widow had encountered drivers who felt like they wanted to unburden themselves of guilt. They'd see Widow like some see a priest or an attorney. Only Widow didn't come with attorney-client privilege, or the oath of a priest. However, he came with something better. He was a complete stranger, someone with no connection to them.

"I sure do! I'm selling our house. I already donated all his stuff to the Goodwill," she said, and turned the wheel onto another street. "He cheated on me and thought I wouldn't find out. But don't worry. I didn't donate all his stuff. No sir. I stopped at a pawnshop. That's where I offloaded his gold jewelry. Some of it was fake, though. Stupid bastard didn't know the difference. My wedding ring had fake diamonds. Can you believe that?"

Widow stayed quiet and just nodded along.

"Anyway, I'm moving down to Louisiana. I can sell our house from there. Lawyer says I gotta put half of the profits into a bank account for my old man for when he gets out. Not sure that's good advice."

Widow pointed and said, "Drop me off there." They were coming up on the Graces' house. He wasn't sure he wanted her to see him go to Nora's farm.

She slowed the car, pulled off to the ditch, and stopped. The woman turned to Widow and said, "You know, I could use some company for the road. I can make it fun for you."

Widow already had the truck's door open. He said, "Good luck to you," hopped out and closed the door. She stayed parked as he walked on. Frank Grace was sitting out on his porch with a cold beer in hand. He just stared.

Widow waited at the end of Frank's driveway. He waved to Frank, who didn't wave back. The woman in the truck got the hint that Widow wasn't going to join her in her new life. She took a final, lingering look at him and drove away.

Widow waited till she was out of sight, waved one last time to Frank, and continued on to Nora's farm. The front windows were lit with a warm glow, and the sound of voices spilled out into the night.

Widow climbed the steps and knocked on the door. He heard Poppy and Violet's voices. There was muffled excitement. The girls rushed to the door, eager to open it. Nora called out for them to wait for her. She came to the door, peeked through the peephole, and flung the door open. The girls' faces lit up. They charged Widow and hugged his legs, with dried tears on their cheeks like they'd both been crying. He patted their backs but didn't ask about the tears. They'd been crying over Joanie, obviously. Children seemed ultra-affected by the loss of a pet. That had been Widow's observation. People love their animals, but for children of Violet and Poppy's ages, pets are their whole world.

Widow looked at Nora. There were no tears on her face, only worry and a hint of despair, which had been her whole existence for the past year. She worried about paying bills, about what happened to her husband, and about her family's future. Despair hit her for all the same reasons.

Nora smiled at Widow, relieved to see him. She said, "I worried you wouldn't come back."

"I was going to come back. There's no place else I'd rather be right now."

They went into the kitchen, where the table was covered with *Uno* cards. They'd been playing when Widow came to the door. Dishes were piled in the sink. The house smelled of pasta. He asked, "Did I miss dinner already?"

"There's leftovers. I can heat some up for you."

"I'd like that. Thank you."

Nora heated him up a plate and the girls asked if he'd found Joanie. He told them not to worry, that he was working on it.

The rest of the night passed quietly. Widow helped tuck the girls into bed, which he was getting surprisingly accustomed to. They begged for another Navy story, and he obliged, weaving a tale about the time he saw mermaids offshore. Which was all fabricated. All he did was insert mermaids in place of a pod of sperm whales. He changed it because mermaids are more interesting for kids, but also because the last thing he wanted to do was get questions from five- and six-year-old girls about what the name meant. The girls yawned and drifted off to sleep nearly as fast as Widow turned their light off. Before he left them, he checked that their window was closed and locked. Then he left their room, leaving their door cracked.

Nora waited in her bedroom doorway. Low candlelight burned behind her. She wore a kind of lacy black underwear that could only be described as showstopping. She smiled at Widow and said, "Want to sleep in my room again?"

Widow froze. He stared at her the way a starving man stares at a buffet. He asked, "Are we watching a movie?"

"No. I have other plans in mind."

Widow smiled and walked to her. Nora took his hand and pulled him into her bedroom. They didn't fall asleep until they were finished, which was long after midnight.

The next morning they woke, ate breakfast, and fed all of the animals. Widow drank the last of Nora's coffee before he helped them. The girls had him wrangling chickens before he found out it wasn't really something that needed to be done. Nora collected the eggs while the girls tricked him into doing their chores.

After the chores were done, the four of them cleaned up the kitchen, then loaded into the truck and drove back to town to look for Joanie. They checked every store and bulletin board where the girls had hung fliers, asking shopkeepers and locals if anyone had seen Joanie. They learned pretty quickly that if they let Violet and Poppy ask the questions, people were more likely to answer, whereas they avoided Widow.

Widow kept his suspicions about Franklin quiet. But he kept his head on a swivel, scanning the streets and shops for any sign of switchmen, Junior, or Franklin. If he saw them, he would confront them right there. But their paths never crossed.

By midday their search had turned up nothing, as Widow expected. At the grocery store, he added coffee to their basket. Before leaving, he also added a burner smartphone, one with a preinstalled *Maps* app and GPS, so he could key in Franklin's address and find it. When Nora wasn't looking, he paid for everything they got. She protested after, but he told her it was the least he could do because she wasn't charging him rent. She let it go.

Widow convinced Nora to stop at a nearby autobody shop. They went into the store, where Nora showed him the battery she needed for her CB750 and Widow bought it. At an ammo store next door he stocked up on more bullets for her guns, convincing her it was a necessary precaution.

When they returned to the farm, the girls seemed restless but tired of looking for Joanie. Nora told them to leave the groceries and go play. Widow helped her unload everything and took the battery out to the barn, where the girls ambushed him, convincing him to take them riding on the horses. They waited for Nora, and the four of them went riding. Violet and Widow rode on one horse and Nora and Poppy on the other.

Afterwards, Widow and Nora shot bottles and cans behind the barn. It was his idea. He wanted to make sure she was good with her rifle and shotgun. Which she was, especially the rifle. She showed great proficiency. She was precise, with steady, controlled breathing.

In the late afternoon, Nora installed the new battery. They rode her motorcycle up and down the highway, taking turns. She saw that he knew how to ride it. Widow asked her if he could borrow the bike later. When she asked why, he told her to trust him; that he had something to do.

Nora asked, "Where're you going? Why can't you tell me?"

"It's best you don't know."

"Why?"

"It's for your own safety."

"Is this about Junior?"

Widow stayed quiet. He didn't want her to be any more involved than she already was. The Brocks were dangerous. She'd had enough run-ins with them.

"Whatever you're doing, I'm not a fragile daisy. Tell me."

"Think about the girls. You're all they have," Widow put his arms around her. "I'll be back. I just gotta do something. Trust me."

Nora hugged him back. They kissed, and she said, "Be careful with my bike."

"I will," Widow said, and smiled. "Before I go, there's one more thing I could use. You must have a lot of makeup, right?"

She drew away and looked at him sideways. She asked, "What's that supposed to mean?"

Widow shrugged and said, "For your shows. You know? You wear all those sexy outfits. You must have a lot of makeup?"

"Oh, yeah. I have lots of makeup. Why, you want to see a show when you get back?"

"I do, but I actually need to borrow some."

"For what? Where the hell are you going?"

Just gonna do a little nightwork, Widow thought, and instinctively tapped the Glock 19 stuffed into his waistband. But he said, "The less you know, the better. Remember?"

"Okay, sure. Whatever," Nora said, and shrugged.

"Got blacks?"

"Let me show you what I have." Nora led Widow to her bathroom. It was large, with dual vanity sinks and a huge shower. A chair sat in front of a long counter, with makeup chaotically stored in plastic baskets. "Take what you need."

Widow glanced over the colors. He picked out two: black, and hunter green. He thanked her. She gave him the keys to her motorcycle and he kissed her goodbye. When the girls asked where he was going, Nora thought she was lying to them when she said Widow went out to look for Joanie again. Only it wasn't a lie. She just didn't know it.

On his way down the road, Widow pulled into the Graces' driveway and eased the motorcycle up to the house. The Honda's deep roar announced his arrival, the sound bouncing off the quiet countryside and echoing over the busy highway. The sun started setting behind him, casting long shadows across the Grace's yard. Their American flag snapped sharply in the wind.

Frank Grace had been reclining in a chair. He saw Widow, got up, and lumbered off his porch. The screen door creaked behind him as Martha came out, stopped on the porch and folded her arms, watching Widow. Frank stepped onto the gravel drive and headed toward Widow. His walk was deliberate, almost defensive, as if bracing for a confrontation. He wore the same Navy hat as before, its brim faded from years in the sun. Frank raised his voice over the idling rumble of the motorcycle and asked, "What the hell are you doing back here?"

Widow straddled the bike, letting it idle beneath him. He reached into his pocket and held up his burner phone, its screen dark. "I got a phone now."

"What?"

"I feel like we've gotten off on the wrong foot."

Frank scowled, his hand resting on his belt, not quite a threat, but not casual either. "Are you kidding me? Get out of here with that thing before I call the cops."

"Like your wife did yesterday?"

Frank said nothing.

"What's your rate?" Widow asked calmly, ignoring the bluster.

"What?" Frank's face tightened.

"In the Navy. What did you do?"

Frank hesitated, his eyes narrowing as he studied Widow. Slowly, he pushed his hat up with one finger, revealing more of his weathered brow. The wind tugged at his face. Finally, he said, "They called it MMC."

Widow nodded, and said, "That's Chief Machinist's Mate. That's a hard-earned title. Lot of responsibility."

Frank crossed his arms and said, "Yeah, what about it?"

Widow leaned forward slightly on the bike, his eyes steady on Frank, the burner smartphone in his hand. He said, "You can't run a ship without engineers," which was a phrase often used by engineering rates. The Navy has lots of sayings, and this one was particular to machinist's mates.

Frank shifted his weight, his stance softening though his suspicion lingered. He asked, "You Navy?"

"Once," Widow said. "A long time ago."

"What rate?"

"I was terminal at O5."

Frank stared at him with disbelief, his eyes narrowed. He asked, "Commander?"

"That's right."

"You?"

Frank looked him up and down. He stared at Widow's sleeve tattoos. He asked, "What did you do?"

"I went where they sent me. Did what they told me to do."

"That's vague. You don't strike me as a desk jockey."

Widow shrugged, his grip tightening slightly on the handlebars. He hated revealing it, because it sounded braggy. But he needed to earn Frank's trust, and fast. He said, "You could say I was a... violent nomad. Special operations."

The words hung in the air for a moment. Frank nodded slowly, as if piecing it together. "You were a SEAL?"

Widow didn't confirm or deny it. Instead, he said, "We had different jobs, but we salute the same flag. That's what matters."

"Alright, Commander. So, what do you want?"

"I'm hoping you can do me a favor?"

"What's that?"

Widow held up the burner phone again, and said, "Just wanted to exchange numbers. Good neighbors keep an eye out for each other. If you see any trouble over at Nora's place —cars, trucks, people that don't belong—call me and let me know. That's all."

Frank glanced back at Martha. She was watching the exchange intently, her lips pressed thin. He sighed, pulled a phone out of his pocket, and said, "Fine. But don't think this makes us old sailor buddies."

Widow smirked faintly. "Wouldn't dream of it."

They exchanged numbers, Frank mumbling the digits in a gruff tone, as if doing so was against his better judgment. Widow saved the number and tucked the phone back into his pocket.

Before Widow turned the bike around, Frank called out, "You better not bring any trouble to that lady and her daughters. They got enough to worry about."

With that, Widow revved the engine, turned the bike, and rode off, the Honda's roar fading into the dusk. Frank stood in the driveway, the flag snapping sharply above him, watching until Widow disappeared down the road.

CHAPTER 31

Widow couldn't find Franklin's address the night before because he was looking on the wrong side of town. Franklin didn't live in Old Town; he lived in New Town, which wasn't what Widow expected, knowing what he now knew about Iron Crossing. All the Brock action seemed to be in Old Town. Brock's businesses were there. The switchmen and Junior's guys all lived there. Brock's ancestral family home, a lavish mansion, was somewhere in Old Town. Widow hadn't seen it, but he was certain all he'd have to do to find it was look for the biggest house behind the biggest gate.

Widow found Franklin's house off a winding road on the east side of the Black River, in an exclusive neighborhood exuding post-modernism mixed with a bit of dark secrecy. Franklin's house didn't quite belong there. The surrounding homes, with their classic brick facades and wraparound porches, seemed to eye it warily, as if it were an intruder.

Franklin's house stood forlorn, like a modern fortress hidden behind a thick canopy of oak and sycamore trees. If not for the trashcans set out, the driveway, and especially the mailbox, Widow would have ridden right by it. He ran through the neighborhood once, the Honda's engine roaring and echoing among the trees and the brick houses.

At the end of the street, he turned around and waited. He looked for nosy neighbors or security measures that Franklin might have in place, such as surveillance on his house. Perhaps Widow was being overcautious, but he sensed Franklin was the overcautious type. He waited to see if there was any reaction to his driving down the street at night. But there wasn't. No one came out of their house. No porch lights switched on. The coast appeared to be clear.

The neighborhood was dark and silent. Widow tested it again. He revved the Honda's engine and roared down the street, back to where he had started. He kept an eye on Franklin's driveway and the houses across the street. He heard dogs barking, but nothing out of the ordinary. He figured out why on his way back to the beginning of the street. One of the houses had two Harley Davidsons parked inside an open garage.

Widow figured the neighbors were all used to hearing the guy's Harleys rumble through the neighborhood. Probably many complained, called the cops like Marsha Grace would have. But what can the cops do? Motorcycles are street-legal. All they can do is ask the owner to keep the noise down.

Widow was in the clear, for now. He pulled over to the side of the street, killed the engine, and turned the headlight off. He waited, studying Franklin's house from a position on a hill. He couldn't see the entire property, but he could see enough of it through the gaps between trees.

Franklin's house was all angles and glass, cold and efficient, backed up against the riverbank. It had killer views, no doubt. Which was probably why Franklin bought it. Widow could hear the soft rush of water over stones, its rhythm broken occasionally by the call of a night bird.

Widow saw no movement in Franklin's driveway. No vehicles entered or left. Some of the house lights were on, but there was no way for Widow to know if there was movement inside or not. The house was too far away and too shielded by trees to know for sure.

The street was empty, save for the trash cans lined up at the ends of the long driveways. Widow used it to his advantage. He got off the bike and eased it down the hill, parking the Honda behind a pair of oversized cans down the street from Franklin's driveway. The owners of the house had been kind enough to build it far away from the street, keeping a similar cluster of trees at the end of their driveway. And the owners appeared to be in for the night. Widow hoped they were. Dark shadows from the trees cloaked the bike completely, making it hard to tell it was parked there.

Widow left the bike, pulled the Glock 19 out and held it down by his leg, out of view. He glanced around the darkness. He scanned the street and the neighbors' houses, but saw no one. There was no sign that he had drawn unwanted attention. So he crossed the street and approached Franklin's driveway carefully, cautiously. Widow's footsteps were silent on the pavement. Quickly, he moved past the driveway and to the shadows in the front yard. The landscaping was pristine—a little too pristine, like the grass had been cut with a ruler. Then he noticed the driveway was immaculate. It appeared to have been swept clean, and recently. There wasn't a single leaf on it anywhere. Franklin must've had landscapers come by just today.

Widow walked the length of the front yard, staying behind trees where he could, and made it to the edge of the backyard. He stopped at a chain-link fence that enclosed the backyard.

So far, so good. Only it was too good, too easy. Widow figured there was no way Franklin didn't have some measure of security.

Suddenly, he met the security. Two Dobermans ran to the fence, ramming it. Jaws snapping, mouths snarling. Widow jumped back, startled. He pointed the Glock at them but didn't fire it. The fence contained them.

He should've known Franklin would have guard dogs. Big mistake on Widow's part. He froze, and glanced at the house, waiting for Franklin to come out shooting. Which he could. In a state like Missouri, you can't legally shoot trespassers just because they're trespassing; however, it's legal to shoot them if you suspect your life's in danger. Franklin could step out, shoot Widow to death, and say he thought his life was being threatened. After all, Widow was armed, and the gun was out in the open. Even if he wasn't armed, who'd question Franklin's defense? Probably no one.

Franklin never stepped out to shoot Widow. No one came out of the house. No curtains fluttered, indicating someone was peeking out. There was no sign of life from the interior of the house. Franklin must not have been home.

Widow glanced around the house. He looked up at the corners. There were cameras posted on the house. There didn't seem to be many of them, but they were there. The one he could see was focused on the gate to the backyard. Widow figured there would be more, probably aimed at all entry points. These were little wireless cameras, which was a good news, bad news thing. The good news was they were on a limited, rechargeable battery, so they didn't record constantly, meaning there was no security guard sitting behind a monitor somewhere, watching live feeds from a bunch of different cameras.

The bad news was the cameras were motion-sensored, meaning they started recording when they detected motion. So if he approached one of the entry points, the camera would come to life and record him. Worse news was that they were probably linked to an app on Franklin's phone. He'd probably get a notification telling him the cameras were recording activity at his house. Widow would have to figure out a way around these.

The Dobermans rammed into the fence over and over, until they realized they weren't going to get to Widow that way. He walked the length of the fence, towards the house as far as he could without activating the camera. The dogs paced alongside him, their sleek bodies catching the faint moonlight. The dogs growled low warnings at Widow.

Widow left them there so he could investigate the rest of the house. He walked far out into the darkness of the front yard, staying out of camera range.

The front of the house was dark. Still no sign of movement inside. Franklin's truck wasn't in the driveway. Widow bypassed another camera and made it to the garage-side of the house. He peeked through a dark window, but saw no vehicles. Instead, it looked like a boat was parked inside the garage.

Widow investigated that side of the backyard. The Dobermans met him there too. They launched at this length of fence, same as they'd done on the other side. And like before, they lunged at the fence until they realized they weren't getting at him.

Widow needed to get inside. He'd have to figure out a way. He checked the house again. There was a camera above the garage door, one above the front door, and one on each corner of the house. He avoided all of them. Then he watched the Dobermans. There were also cameras over the backyard. Each time the dogs ran in front of a camera's view, he saw the camera whir to life; it buzzed and a red light flashed at the bottom. He clocked the response time for the cameras, which was more than thirty seconds. The visual cone for each was ten meters, maybe more. Not good odds for him to get close.

Widow had an idea. First, he returned to the front of the house, getting as close to the front door as he could without setting off the camera. He studied the doorbell. It was a standard doorbell, which was good. Franklin didn't have one of those doorbell cameras, just the security camera above the door.

Widow scoured the yard till he found a plentiful stack of rocks. He grabbed a pebble off the ground, and tossed it at the door. Nothing happened. He got a bigger rock and threw it at the doorbell, setting off the ringer. The Dobermans ran from the backyard to the front door, and barked from inside the house. He ran to the backyard and called out to them. They hauled butt from the front door back to the backyard. Widow timed all of it in his head. He also clocked where their doggie door was located. It was at the back of the house, on the garage side. It was probably in the kitchen. There wasn't one in the garage. He knew that because he had been able see enough through the dark window to deduce that much.

Widow pocketed enough rocks to make his plan work. He ran to the far side of the backyard fence and threw rocks at a small boathouse attached to a dock in the back. Then he threw rocks at the doorbell, ringing it. He did this multiple times.

Every time, the Dobermans kept up with him. They ran to the boathouse, to one side of the backyard, to the other side, and then to the front door. Widow repeated this so many times that the dogs' response times slowed and slowed. Humans are bipedal, meaning they can change their number of breaths per stride while running. Dogs are quadrupedal and cannot, meaning that when they run, they're not breathing as efficiently. Therefore, they tire out fast and need longer periods of time to recover.

Widow repeated the whole thing until the dogs were tuckered out. Then he did it one last time, hitting the boathouse with a rock. The Dobermans could no longer sprint at full speed, but their nature required them to check out the noise. They lumbered to the boathouse, giving Widow time to hop the fence, skirt around to the backyard, and look for a way to enter the house through the back.

There was a security camera on him, but he didn't care about that. He figured Franklin got a notification every time his dogs were running around back there, and therefore probably ignored the backyard camera notifications. Widow figured his odds were pretty good.

The backyard was massive, with loads more trees and landscaping back there. There was no swimming pool, which surprised him. Otherwise, it was as he thought it'd be.

The dogs were at the boathouse, sniffing around. Widow didn't have much time. He scanned all the points of entrance. He saw the large doggie door where he thought it would be, only it wasn't cut out of a backdoor. It was cut right out of a wall.

The doggie door was big enough for most humans to squeeze through, but Widow wasn't going to be one of those humans. His shoulders were so massive; he'd get stuck in the door. That'd be just what he needed. He pictured getting stuck head-first in the doggie door, and how the Dobermans would react to that. They'd chomp on his groin. He pictured Junior's guy in the hospital.

The prospect didn't appeal to him. He figured he could break a window. The bad thing about that was it Franklin had cameras, then he probably had a whole security system to go with them. The windows probably had break sensors on them. He could possibly climb up onto the porch roof and go through an upstairs window. A lot of people don't place sensors up there.

While he was contemplating a way in, he heard the Dobermans barking at him. He glanced back and saw they were no longer sniffing around the boathouse. They were moving his way and not happy about it. They snarled and growled. Luckily for Widow, they were still moving slowly.

On a whim, Widow decided to just try the backdoor. Some people don't lock them. Some people simply forget. Would Franklin? Probably not, but it was worth a shot.

It turned out Franklin hadn't locked his backdoor. With two mean Dobermans, he probably didn't think he needed to.

Widow entered through the backdoor, closed and locked it. The Dobermans had picked up speed now. A stranger was in their house, and they wouldn't stand for such a thing. To them, it was an act of war.

Widow grabbed the hard plastic cover for the doggie door off a built-in shelf and slipped it into place, locking the dogs out. Both Dobermans rammed the door, one after the next. The plastic moved with each ramming. At first Widow worried it wouldn't hold, but it did. He closed off all the blinds in the kitchen so the dogs couldn't see in. They ran around frantically, barking and howling. But they never got in.

Widow searched the house. It was a big place. The inside was all midcentury modern. Expensive paintings hung on the walls. Artsy sculptures stood on stands throughout the house. A wet bar showcased top-shelf bourbons. A keypad to the security system was near the door to the garage. The system was switched off, luckily for Widow. In the garage, he found zip ties, which might come in handy, so he pocketed them.

The place was super-clean and neat. *Immaculate* was a word Widow might use to describe it. The beds were made, everything wood was dusted and polished. Every window, mirror, and glass surface was speckless, like they'd just been windexed and shined. The primary bedroom was the most pristine. It looked like Franklin was staging everything for a photoshoot in some design magazine one would find at the checkout counter of a supermarket.

The shoes in Franklin's closet were shined to a glossy perfection. His tailored suits were pressed and hung up in a neat arrangement, as if a CO might walk in and inspect them at any time. There was an expensive watch collection in a case. In the bathroom, Widow found high-priced shampoos, lotions, and colognes stored neatly on a rack. Franklin had deluxe tastes in personal grooming as well.

In the bedroom, there was a collection of music on vinyl, next to a vintage player. Widow glanced through the albums. There were lots of classics; a whole lot of singers like George Jones, Loretta Lynn, and Johnny Cash.

The furniture in the bedroom was like the rest of the house, pristine and expensive-looking wood. Widow didn't open any drawers or look through Franklin's things. He was only checking for any evidence of Joanie's whereabouts. But he did find something interesting. There were framed pictures all over Franklin's room. Some were clearly family photos. Some were of Franklin posed with famous politicians. He wore a suit in all of them, but also a gun. Widow realized Franklin was a former Secret Service agent. But a second thing of note was the collection of framed photos next to Franklin's bed.

They were of him and another man. These photos were different than all the rest. In each, Franklin appeared intimate with this man. There were photos of the two of them laughing, hugging, and holding hands, in settings like restaurants in foreign countries. One was of the two of them on a yacht. Widow glanced around the room again, and it hit him like a ton of bricks. Franklin was gay. Which meant nothing to Widow, one way or the other. Live and let live. But a thought occurred to him. What would Collin Brock think of it? Widow might be able to use this information to his advantage.

Widow left the primary bedroom and stopped checking the house. Franklin wasn't home. That was clear. The house was empty. No sign of Joanie. So, Widow did the best thing he thought he could do. He brewed a pot of Franklin's expensive Colombian coffee, poured himself a mug, and sat down on a leather armchair to wait.

CHAPTER 32

At midnight, the quiet broke. Widow was sipping his fourth cup of Franklin's coffee when he heard the dogs barking again. This time he also heard the sound of tires on the pavement. He got up from the leather armchair and looked out a front window.

Franklin's truck rumbled up the winding driveway, its headlights cutting through the thick darkness of the trees. The dogs barked furiously, like they probably did every time their master came home. The garage door didn't open. Franklin eased his truck up to the house, and parked it in the driveway. He killed the headlights and shut off the engine.

Widow went to the kitchen, slammed the rest of the coffee, and set the mug in the sink. No reason to be rude and leave it out. He moved back through the darkness to the front door, and listened. That's when he realized he had a problem. Franklin wasn't alone.

Truck doors slammed shut—three of them. Then he heard boots crunching on the gravel outside. More than one pair of them. He heard muffled voices, like Franklin was coming home with some of his buddies.

Widow glanced out the window, catching the figures of two other men following Franklin toward the front door. The other two were switchmen, he presumed. He hadn't seen them before. They weren't any of the ones he'd seen at the auction two days ago, and they didn't look like Junior's guys. That's if all of Junior's guys looked the same, and he figured they did. Widow had been around; he'd had run-ins with a lot of criminals in his life. One thing he had noticed was that gangs, or criminal organizations, were basically tribes. And tribe members often shared the same kinds of preferences— birds of a feather, and all. Usually the chief, or boss, set the tone, and the rest of the tribe followed suit. In other words, if the boss dressed in expensive Italian suits, then so did his guys. If gang leaders wore certain colors, then so did the gang members. The similar clothes, colors and styles were just uniforms.

For Junior, the big chromy truck, the attitude, and the way he treated Nora were all a part of a lifestyle, a brand. His guys wanted to display that brand. A tribe's underlings usually shared—or wanted—the same lifestyle as the man at the top. Junior was a prick with a certain kind of gangster-wannabe style: lots of tattoos, big sunglasses, and shiny watches. The two guys with Franklin had none of that, but they did resemble Brock's switchmen.

Widow didn't see any guns in their hands, which was good. They had no idea he was there. The cameras hadn't alerted Franklin to his presence. If they had, then he'd have showed up with more guys, all armed to the teeth. These were just two switchmen coming home with him. Maybe they were done with the workday, coming back to Franklin's place for some of his expensive bourbon.

Keys jingled on the other side of the door. Widow drew the stolen Glock and hid out of sight. The front door swung open. Franklin entered first and the two switchmen followed.

Franklin said, "Take your boots off and set them over there." He pointed at a bench near the door, which had shoes placed neatly underneath it.

Franklin left them there. Both switchmen clunked back on the bench, kicking their boots off. They chuckled, laughing about something Widow couldn't make out.

Franklin went toward the garage, stopped at a bathroom on the way and did his business. From the bathroom, he called out, "You guys make yourself a drink at the bar. I'll be right out."

The chuckling stopped, but Franklin could hear the switchmen talking. Their voices were muffled, but sounded boisterous, like they were having a heated discussion. Then he heard shoes scuffing on his floors. Which was weird, because he thought the switchmen already kicked off their boots? He called out, "Hey! Be careful! I just had the floors shined!"

The voices stopped and the house went silent again. The only sounds Franklin heard were the dogs barking outside and he started to wonder why they weren't charging inside. Normally, the dogs greeted him at the door when he came home.

Franklin washed his hands and headed toward the foyer. "Titan! Apollo!" he called to his dogs, his voice sharp with annoyance. "Come see Daddy!" He passed the hallway and came out into the foyer. The switchmen were gone. There was only one boot on the floor, and it was toppled over, not slid neatly under the bench, which was clearly where it was meant to go. Franklin had shoes already neatly tucked under the bench, side by side, to show visitors how he expected it to be done.

He shook his head at the boot, but was focused more on his dogs. "Titan! Apollo!" he called to them again. "Come see me! I'm home!" Nothing but barking and pawing. "Did you get locked out again?"

The Dobermans barked, and pawed at their doggie door. The barking intensified, muffled by the locked doggie door. Franklin rounded the corner into a space between his living room, foyer, and kitchen. He glanced away from the living room and at the doggie door on the wall in the kitchen. He saw that the cover was down. *Did I lock those guys out?* he asked himself.

"I gotta let the dogs in. You guys take your shoes off. Like I told ya," Franklin said, turned back to the living room, and froze. The switchmen were both on the floor, face down—out cold, their hands zip-tied behind their backs.

Franklin froze, his eyes scanning the space. He took a cautious step forward. Widow saw the gears turning in his head. It lasted only a moment, then Franklin whipped his hand up and went for his gun. He almost got it out too. Maybe in a high-noon, gunslinger quick-draw match, he'd have drawn faster than Widow. But Widow wasn't quick-drawing. He already had the Glock in hand and pointed at Franklin.

Before Franklin could clear his holster, Widow said, "Don't." Franklin froze, hand still on his gun. "Take it out slow. Pinch the grip with your thumb and index finger. And Franklin, you better move slow. You so much as sneeze, I'm gonna put a bullet right dead-center of your head."

Franklin glanced at where the voice came from. He saw Widow sitting in a big leather armchair in the corner of the living room, next to the fireplace. Only he couldn't tell it was Widow because Widow was sitting in the dark; he only saw Widow's silhouette.

The Dobermans barked outside, sounding frenzied. They pawed at the doggie door some more, desperate to get in. Franklin paused a beat, like he expected Widow to glance at the doggie door. Like he hoped it would distract Widow long enough for Franklin to drop to one knee, out of Widow's line of sight, and draw down on him.

But Widow didn't look away. He didn't budge. He stayed locked onto Franklin's position. "Franklin," Widow said, his voice low and menacing. "Keep going."

Franklin pinched his gun the way Widow had instructed and pulled it out. He held the gun out in front of him like a dead mouse he'd found but didn't want to touch. Widow said, "Toss it to my feet."

Franklin tossed the gun. It landed near Widow's feet, but he didn't go for it. He just left it. Franklin said, "I have money. Is that what you want?"

"The coffee table," Widow said. Franklin glanced at the coffee table in front of his leather sofa. There were two zip ties already looped together resting on the tabletop. "Put them on."

Franklin stared at the zip ties. He thought for a long moment. Widow said, "It's not a choice to make. Put them on, or I'll kneecap you." Widow's Glock came farther out into the light.

Franklin grabbed the zip ties, started to put them on behind his back. Widow said, "In the front."

Franklin switched positions and slipped his hands through the zip ties. They fell loose on his wrists. He offered them to Widow like he was asking Widow to pray with him. He stepped closer to Widow, but Widow said, "Use your teeth."

Franklin paused and tightened the zip ties with his teeth until they were tight on his wrists. "Sit down," Widow said.

Franklin sat on the sofa. "Put your feet up on the coffee table."

Franklin paused another beat. He asked, "Do I have to? I don't like feet on my furniture."

"Do it!"

Franklin put his feet on the coffee table. Now he was immobilized for the most part. A man who was sunk back into a big sofa, relaxing with his feet up, had his reaction time cut in half. Widow reached to his left, keeping the Glock pointed at Franklin, and clicked on a lamp that was on a side table. A dim light shone across his face.

Franklin stared at him and said, "You?"

"Me."

"Are you serious? You came here for a dog?" Franklin asked, looking flustered and angry.

Widow leaned forward, raised the Glock, and stared at Franklin through the sights. He said, "That dog means more to those girls than your life means to me."

Franklin paused a long beat. Not knowing what to say, he went for an old cliché, which Widow had heard before.

"Do you know who I work for? Do you understand how dangerous he is?"

"I've heard."

"Take whatever you've heard and multiply it by a thousand."

"Brock is that dangerous?"

Franklin hesitated, then said, "You don't want to find out."

Widow looked Franklin dead in the eyes, and asked, "How

would Brock react to finding out that one of his top lieutenants prefers the company of men?"

Franklin stared at Widow, his anger increasing. His face turned red. But it wasn't just anger; he looked like he felt violated, like Widow had crossed a line. He said, "I don't know what you're talking about."

"I'd bet money that a crime lord from Missouri, playing politician, would care a great deal. Especially if you've kept this secret from him for years," Widow said, and paused a long beat. "Does Brock know you're gay?"

"I'm not!"

"Look, I don't give a shit. But Brock will, won't he?"

Franklin said nothing.

Widow asked, "Where's the dog?"

Franklin glared at him, his eyes flickering with defiance. He said, "What dog?"

Widow jerked the Glock slightly to the right, and pulled the trigger. The gunshot boomed in the stillness. The leather cushion exploded inches from Franklin's leg. Franklin nearly jumped out of his skin. Dust particles swirled in the air.

"Whoa! Hold on! Hold on!" Franklin shouted. His feet back on the floor, he half-stood, hovering over the sofa. Instinct told him to run, but his brain told him that if he did, he'd get the next bullet. And his brain was right.

Widow pointed the Glock at him and said, "Sit back down!"

Franklin was shaken. His eyes were huge. He sat back down, waving the dust out of his face. Now, he looked terrified. "Listen. Listen." he said, panting, his heart racing. "You don't need to go showing your face around where she is. You'll get us both killed."

Widow eased the Glock forward, the barrel coming completely out of the shadow. The muzzle bore pointed at Franklin. Franklin said, "But wait! I can bring her to you."

Widow stayed quiet.

Franklin said, "Let's make a deal. Okay?"

"I'm listening."

"If the dog comes home, then no harm, no foul? I'll bring her home and in exchange you leave Iron Crossing?"

Widow stayed quiet.

Franklin couldn't read Widow's face. He asked, "Will you leave? Please?"

"You'll return the dog. And leave that family alone?"

"Yes! You have my word!"

"How do I know you'll keep it?"

"I promise. I won't trouble them. But I need you gone."

Widow asked, "Because if Brock finds out you didn't kill me…"

"He'll kill us both."

"What about Junior?"

"He got the message already. But I'll make sure. No one will bother them again. As long as you leave. Deal?"

Widow stood up, scooped up Franklin's gun, ejected the magazine and the chambered round, and pocketed the gun. He pointed the Glock at Franklin and said, "You come near them again, and I'll find you. And next time, I won't leave you breathing. Make sure everyone who needs to know that, knows that."

"So it's a deal?"

Widow stared at him, his face unreadable. He said, "If the dog's returned safe and sound, and Nora Sutton and her girls are safe, I'll leave."

Widow was half-lying, because he wasn't sure he could leave them. Usually he would be able to. But with Nora, Violet and Poppy—and Joanie—he wasn't sure what he was going to do. He wasn't sure he wanted to leave them.

Franklin didn't need to know any of that. Widow went to Franklin, showed him the Glock, and said, "Better close your eyes."

"What? No, wait!" Franklin said, scared that Widow would shoot him.

Widow reared back with the Glock and thumped Franklin over the head with it. Lights out. Franklin toppled over, landing under the coffee table. The Dobermans barked, still pawing at the doggie door.

Normally, Widow wouldn't trust a murderer like Franklin. But this man wasn't the average criminal. He had a sense of honor. He'd keep his word. Widow had no doubt about it. And if he didn't, there were always other means Widow could employ.

Widow left through the front door, slipping into the darkness.

CHAPTER 33

Morning swept over the farm like calm ocean waves. The girls refused to eat breakfast. They sat in front of their plates, staring at scrambled eggs and bacon. It all smelled good, but they had no appetites. Their spirits were down because of Joanie. Nora put on a happy face for them. She had to. It's what mothers do. Although she was happy Widow had come back, she still missed her dog. The pain was there, but she kept it hidden.

Widow was in good spirits, partially because he knew Joanie would be returned. At least she'd better be, or Franklin would have hell to pay. The other part was because he felt happy to be there.

Nora sent the girls off to play, giving them a break from doing all of the chores they normally did around the farm. As they scurried off to go on imaginary adventures, Poppy asked Violet, "Why's māmā not want us to do our jobs?" And Violet replied with, "It's called an early work-release program, duh." They left the kitchen after that.

Widow and Nora took care of all of the girls' chores themselves. Plus they did all of Nora's, which were significantly harder and more integral to the farm's survival. But with Widow's help, everything went much faster.

By midmorning, Widow and Nora were out in the barn, putting the tarp back over Nora's motorcycle. Nora carried her walkie-talkie with her. And Widow kept the Glock in his pocket, just out of caution. She asked, "Where did you go last night?"

"I told you, I just had something to take care of."

"Is it more about this TikToker you mentioned?"

Widow thought for a second. He didn't want to tell her what he did to Franklin. Not that she'd be upset by it; he was keeping her in the dark to keep her safe. The less she knew about his activities, the better for her. If the cops were in Brock's pocket, and something happened to him, then she could be culpable. Not to mention, she would be in danger from the Brocks themselves. It was also partially because he wanted to see the look on her face when Franklin returned Joanie—if Franklin did return Joanie to them. He said, "Yeah. I'm just checking up on leads."

"Any luck?"

"We'll see."

"So, are you like a private investigator or something?"

"Nothing like that."

"So what, then? Why're you searching for this guy?"

"I told you. I met these sisters on a train…"

She interrupted him and said, "I know the story. But why, though? Why're you looking for him?"

Widow paused a beat. He'd never asked himself that question

before. "I got this habit of getting involved in things that don't feel right."

"What do you mean? Like injustices?"

"Yeah. That's what I did in the Navy."

"I thought the Navy did war stuff?"

Widow paused again, and did something he'd never done before. He told her that he had worked undercover for NCIS, as a SEAL. He told her about his mother, and when he got pulled out to go and see her on her deathbed. He shared some highlights of his life with her, something he'd never done before. Not with such honesty and vulnerability.

At the end of it, Nora took Widow's hand and asked him a question no one had ever asked him before. She asked, "What about you?"

"What do you mean?"

"You do all these good things for other people. You take care of them. But what about you? Who takes care of you?"

Just then, the walkie-talkie crackled. Violet's voice broke through, high-pitched and official. "Mr. Widow. Come in. Over."

Nora smiled and handed Widow the walkie. He clicked the button and said, "Go for Widow."

The radio crackled again. Violet said, "Code red! We got a truck in the driveway! Repeat, unknown vehicle in the driveway!"

Widow and Nora shared a glance. Widow's hand instinctively brushed the Glock in his pocket. He drew it out and stuffed it into the waistband of his jeans. It would be easier to quick-draw it that way; from the pocket, it could get snagged on the lining. Nora said, "It's them. They're back."

"Let's not jump to conclusions. Let's go see who it is and what they want," Widow said, and led them both out of the barn and up to the house. The girls were hopping up and down on the back steps to the house. They rushed to Nora, asking who it was. Nora had no answers for them. Widow instructed her to put the girls inside, get her rifle, and meet him at the front. Nora nodded and took the girls into the house. She grabbed her rifle and came out onto the front porch. Violet and Poppy stayed in the foyer, and fought over which one of them could peek out the window.

Franklin's truck idled at the end of the driveway. Franklin stood beside it. The moment he saw Widow, he instinctively touched the goose egg that throbbed on his forehead. It was a stark reminder of their last meeting. He didn't want a repeat of that.

Widow walked the length of the driveway, his hands by his sides but ready to go: his left ready to lift his shirt, his right ready to draw the Glock. He glanced left, glanced right—searching the crossroads, neighboring lots, and the street for any of the switchmen. He saw no one. It appeared Franklin had come alone.

Widow stopped a few paces short of the truck's grille. Nora lingered on the porch, rifle in hand, her posture protective.

Franklin glanced in her direction, but said nothing. He nodded to Widow.

"You armed?" Widow asked.

"You know I am."

"Do I need to worry?" Widow asked, raising his shirt, revealing the Glock. He let the shirt fall behind the Glock.

Franklin raised both hands in mock surrender and said, "Relax. I'm just here to keep my word."

Widow stayed quiet.

Franklin moved to the rear passenger-side door of the truck, opened it, and ducked in. Widow's hand went to the Glock's grip, and waited. Franklin came back out, pulling on a leash. Joanie's head popped out. There was a muzzle strapped around her snout. She looked up at Widow with recognition and excitement, and started wagging her tail. She hopped out of the truck. Franklin led her to Widow and said, "Sorry about the muzzle. She bit one of my guys. Had to keep her restrained."

Widow didn't respond. He stepped forward, crouching to Joanie's level. Her tail started wagging harder. He unhooked the muzzle and the lead and tossed them back at Franklin. Joanie licked Widow's hand once before glancing in the direction of the farm, her home. Widow nodded to her, and, like she understood him, she took off, bolting toward the house, her energy returning in a flash. She felt reinvigorated.

Back on the porch, Nora could see the men but couldn't see what they were looking down at. Poppy and Violet cracked the front door open and peeked out. Nora glanced at them. Poppy asked, "What're they doing?"

"I don't know, honey," Nora said. Just then, Violet and Poppy exploded with excitement. The screen door burst open and the girls ran out, their cries of joy filling the air. Nora followed them with her eyes. She nearly yelled at them to get back, but when she saw Joanie running to them, Nora chased after the girls.

Joanie and the girls crashed into each other in a ball of limbs, tail wags, and happiness. Joanie licked each little girl's face as they hugged her. Nora dropped the rifle, fell to her knees, and hugged the girls and Joanie.

Franklin stepped closer. Widow noticed and swung back to Franklin, cursing himself for letting his guard down to watch the Joanie reunion. But Franklin did nothing. He just stood there, staring at the same event.

He said, "It's a nice thing to see. I'm sorry. Truly."

Widow stayed quiet.

Franklin looked genuinely moved, apologetic. And for a brief moment, Widow thought the guy might shed a tear about his life choices. For a moment, he was human. But just like that, the moment was gone. Franklin lied, "You know. It's a miracle. I found her at the end of my street."

"Right."

Franklin shrugged, and said, "I kept my part of the deal. It's your turn. Leave here and stay gone."

"If I don't?"

Franklin's casual demeanor slipped, replaced by the cold edge of an enforcer. He said, "Then I can't stop what happens."

Widow stepped closer, casting his shadow over Franklin. He said, "Let me ask you a question. Collin Brock's your boss. And he's supposed to be some kind of big deal around here. Therefore, Junior's a big deal too. Brock made it your job to babysit Junior. And I broke Junior's arm, embarrassed him. Which should piss Brock off. But how come you're letting me walk away?"

Franklin said nothing.

Widow asked, "Why do you want me to leave so badly? Why not just kill me?"

Franklin stared at Widow and held his tongue.

Widow said, "It sounds to me like whatever the old man's into, Junior's not a part of it. Sounds to me like Junior's off the leash. I think he's running his own show. And I think you're a part of it. That's why you want me gone, because Brock's gonna find out about what happened. And he's not gonna stand for it. You're afraid he'll come down here and ask questions. Or he'll just ask Junior, who probably can't keep the secret forever. You don't want Brock to find out that you're double-dipping."

"That's a theory. But I got one for you too. If Brock comes to Iron Crossing and finds out that you're not dead for what you did to his son, then he'll kill you, Nora, and those girls. He'll burn this farm to the ground, just to make the point that you don't mess with the Brocks."

"You threatening me?" Widow asked, his fists clenching.

"Listen, you might be some kind of badass, but I've known Collin Brock for a long time. He's got a lot of power. And I'm afraid he might get the idea of coming here. You don't want to be around if he does. If you're gone, I can say you ran away."

Widow calmed himself, and glanced at Nora and the girls. He asked, "What about them?"

"I can protect them."

"How?"

"They don't know who you are. Not really. I know your type. You're a drifter, a nobody, a man passing through. I've seen it before. You're running from something, which means you won't tell them who you are. And more importantly, they won't know where you are. I'll tell Mr. Brock I already asked them. He doesn't know that you're staying here. It's best this way."

Widow stared at Nora, and stayed quiet.

Franklin's jaw tightened. He said, "Be gone soon. After that, I can't protect them." He turned to leave.

Widow stopped him and asked, "You ever heard of Alex Hopper?"

"Who?"

"He came in riding one of the trains going into your railyard. About a year ago."

Franklin shook his head. "There are no trains coming in on that line. Not for people. Only for livestock."

"What about Wade Sutton?" Widow pressed. "You mentioned him the other day. Nora's husband. He went missing too. About the same time. Which is a strange coincidence. What do you know about him?"

"Rumor is that he skipped town. You should do the same. Or you might end up missing too."

Widow let the words hang in the air. Franklin climbed back into his truck and closed the door with a kind of finality. He took the gear out of Park, gassed the engine. The truck roared to life, backed out of the driveway, and disappeared down the road.

Widow turned back to the house. Joanie was still surrounded by the girls, their laughter echoing across the farm. Nora hovered over them. She glanced up, her eyes meeting Widow's. She said nothing, but the gratitude was there. She realized Widow wasn't out asking about Hopper last night. He was getting Joanie back. Unlike her husband, Widow was there. He was present. He got things done. She felt safe with him. She felt something special.

CHAPTER 34

Widow didn't leave the next day. Or the one after that. He couldn't.

Instead, he stayed at the Sutton farm, staying busy, staying useful. The days passed in a blur of hammer strikes and heavy lifting, of dirt under his nails and sweat running down his back. He worked the land, repatched the roof after a hard rain revealed cracks in it, and fixed the hinges on the barn door that had been creaking ever since Nora could remember. Nora taught him how to tune up the tractor, which was his first interaction with it. His second was when he cut the grass with it. Halfway through, Nora brought him more fresh lemonade, in another sexy, low-cut summer dress. Jokingly, he asked her how many she owned. She replied with, "I thought you liked them?"

Widow said, "I like what's underneath better."

She took his empty lemonade glass, kissed him, and whispered, "You can see more of that tonight." She walked back to the house, leaving him in the hot sun. Widow was grateful that Nora had a spare straw hat to keep him from getting sunburned.

Widow lived the life of a farmer, a father, and a husband in the span of a week.

On the second day, Nora got tired of seeing Widow in the same outfit, so they went to town and bought some new clothes, more than one set. Nora had him try on various outfits. Most of them casual everyday wear. She didn't have him buying church clothes or anything. Widow felt awkward keeping his old clothes and buying new ones. She eased his tension by telling him she expected nothing from him. "These are just clothes you can keep in my closet," she said. "Whenever you're in town, they'll be here, waiting for you."

On the third day, the girls painted Widow's nails various colors of the rainbow. The next morning, he sat at a tiny child's table, where they played tea-time with him, which used to be Joanie's job. She sat next to him at the same table in a little bonnet of her own. She growled at him. "At least you get the blue bonnet," he said, referring to the pink one that Poppy insisted he wear. He couldn't fasten the ties around his head, so it was a balancing act just keeping it on.

At night, Widow made love to Nora. She snuggled up with him until she fell asleep. But he couldn't sleep. He got restless, not because of his urge to get back on the road, but because he anticipated reprisal from the Brocks. He feared it was coming. Everything was so good between him and Nora, between him and the girls. He had a taste of the good life. But a question lingered. It gnawed at the back of his mind.

When would the other shoe drop?

On sleepless nights, Widow kept watch, sitting on the porch with Nora's rifle across his lap. Joanie lay by his side, her ears twitching at every noise. Moonlight glowed, casting long shadows across the farm's quiet fields. The night air was cool, but Widow's eyes burned with focus. He never let himself relax—not fully—not with Franklin's warning echoing in his mind. He kept waiting for something to happen. An invasion. A night raid. Something. But nothing happened. Nothing ever came.

Six days had passed since Widow stopped at Violet and Poppy's lemonade stand, since Nora first pointed a rifle in his face. Now he slept next to her. He felt something he hadn't felt since the Navy. He felt that he belonged.

While in town one morning, they stopped by an electronics store. Widow picked up a security system—motion sensors, cameras, alarms, the works. Nora didn't think it was necessary, but Widow insisted.

Back at the farm, Widow installed everything. He climbed the rickety ladder again to mount wireless cameras at the corners of the house. Nora, with help from the girls, put motion sensors on the windows. Widow double-checked the one on the window in the girls' bedroom. By dusk, the system was fully operational. Nora watched him fiddle with downloading the app on her phone. She took over and learned how to use it herself.

He told her, "Now you can see everything, even when you're not here. It'll send alerts to your phone if anything trips the sensors." They were things she already figured, but she let him explain it all to her anyway.

Nora looked at her phone screen, scrolling through the recorded feeds. She smiled, then glanced up at him. She thanked him, feeling happy that he cared so much.

Widow shrugged and said, "I just want you to feel safe."

She touched his hand, gazed into his eyes, and said, "I do. We do."

Around noon, Widow walked down to the Graces'. He rang the doorbell. Martha answered, with hostility in her voice.

Widow asked to speak to Frank, who came out. Martha started to go back inside, but Widow asked her to step out onto the porch too.

Widow apologized for any misunderstandings between them. He gave them a peace offering in the form of an invite to dinner. They responded reluctantly, as he expected. So he asked them if they had ever had Hawaiian Kalua Pork. At first, it seemed they would refuse, but then Frank mentioned he was stationed in Honolulu once and liked the food he'd had there. Martha rolled her eyes and commented about Frank and some floozy he dated back then. It seemed this was a hot button for her. Frank reminded her that it was a long time ago, before they met.

To help Frank's side, Widow told Martha that the pork was slow-cooked for seven hours. Nora had already started it. And she was really looking forward to them coming by for a first-time dinner. Martha thought it over.

Eventually, they agreed to come over. Frank convinced Martha to try Hawaiian food, citing a New Year's resolution she'd failed so far, to try new things. They argued in front of Widow, but it was in an old-couple's way. It wasn't a relation-ship-ending argument; it was more like when couples bicker about something trivial.

At sunset, Widow sat on the porch, holding a mug of coffee and watching the girls play in the yard. Joanie lay at his feet. She'd already had enough playing. Violet and Poppy's energy seemed to know no bounds. At one point, Widow looked down at Joanie and said, "So this is the good life? I guess I can see what all the fuss is about." She glanced up at him and groaned.

That night the stars were brighter than they'd been in a while, and the air smelled like fresh-cut grass. Frank and Martha walked up the driveway. They had cleaned themselves up and dressed like they were going out on the town. Martha had fixed up her hair and wore makeup and earrings. Frank was clean-shaven, wearing trousers and a short-sleeved button shirt. His hair was combed.

Widow stood from the chair to greet them. He slipped his hands in his pockets, trying to seem casual, friendly. Joanie rose from her nap and stood next to him like she thought it was expected. He called to Nora that they were there, and she came out of the house. She too had changed clothes. Now she wore a flowing summer dress, and not a low-cut one. This one was a soft, muted blue. It set off her tanned skin. The dress seemed designed for her body. It had thin spaghetti straps that sat precisely on her shoulders, framing her collarbone and leaving her toned arms bare. The hem of the dress swayed just below her knees, light and airy, moving with every step she took. No way could someone confuse this dress as being too short, like the other ones Widow had seen her wear. Nora's hair cascaded in loose blonde waves around her face. She wore a thin silver bracelet that caught the starlight as she stepped out onto the porch.

Even dressed conservatively, Nora was stunning. Widow's mouth hung open, like aliens had caught him in a tractor beam and were sucking his soul out of his body. She was the kind of woman who was good for all occasions. He pictured them going to some traditional Navy ceremony. She would fit in with all the sailors' wives, yet be their envy.

Nora wore little makeup, and her lips had a soft shine. Simple but elegant, she'd somehow managed to look so good still have time to cook dinner. It caught Widow off guard. For a moment, he almost forgot the Graces were walking up the driveway.

Nora stopped on the porch next to Widow, waving to the Graces as they walked up. Widow leered at her like it was his first time seeing her. She saw his mouth hanging open, leaned into him, and whispered, "You've seen me naked. There's no reason to ogle me like that."

Widow shook it off, then whispered back, "I probably should've cleaned myself up for this too."

"Go do it after we greet them."

"That's not much time."

"Widow, I've seen you shower. You take less than fifteen minutes from shower to fully dressed."

She had a point. Widow could shower, shave, put on fresh clothes, and brush his teeth, all under twelve minutes. Plus, it wasn't Nora's fault he hadn't done that already. He'd known the Graces were coming; he just didn't want to get up from the chair on the porch.

Nora walked down the steps to greet the Graces. Widow followed her. Pleasantries were exchanged. Nora had Widow entertain them while she checked on the pork. She came back out and told them it was almost ready. She sent the girls to wash up and Widow went in to do the same. He came back out in one of his new outfits—a collared shirt and jeans.

Dinner was good. "Very tasty," Martha commented. Over the course of dinner, she opened up and treated Nora like they were the oldest of friends, even though the age gap between them was decades rather than years. Violet took credit for picking the fresh vegetables, and Poppy claimed that she handmade the cornbread. That was the word she used— handmade. She was so proud of it, not even Violet corrected her. Instead, Violet glanced at her mother and rolled her eyes, like they both shared the secret that they had made the cornbread. Also not true; Nora had made everything.

The Graces were polite, a little reserved in the beginning, but tensions thawed as the meal progressed.

After dinner, Nora gave Martha a tour of the house, staying out of the bedroom that had her camera equipment and lighting setups. They did tour Nora's sewing studio. Martha commented on the sewing machine and on the fabrics strewn about. "Oh, I like this," she said, running her fingers across an incomplete Hawaiian-style dress.

Nora smiled and thanked her for the compliment. They kept talking and got to know each other better.

Widow poured Frank a whiskey, and poured another coffee for himself. They retired to the porch while the women toured the house. They sat on porch chairs, looking out over the night. The girls took off running outside with Joanie in tow. They ran through the night with flashlights, pretending to lightsaber-fight, the flashlight beams crashing into each other and shining over the treetops.

Frank took a couple of cigars out of a shirt pocket. He offered one to Widow, who stared at it, debating. Frank said, "Take it. It's a Cuban."

Widow nodded and took it. Frank added, "Just don't tell the cops." They chuckled. Frank lit both cigars, puffing his intently. He surveyed the land and said, "This is a good farm. You've made a lot of progress sprucing it up, and just in a week. Pretty commendable."

"Nora gets the credit. I just went where she told me."

"She gives the orders and you follow, huh?"

A distant memory named Jaime Harper flashed through Widow's mind. He used to think that very same phrase about her. She was the only woman he had loved in the happily-ever-after sense. He had actually wanted to marry her. He remembered buying an engagement ring and everything.

Frank noticed Widow was in deep thought, and said, "I'm just horsing around. Didn't mean nothing by it."

"Nora's tough." Widow nodded, smiled, and puffed his cigar. "She really does all this all by herself. She's not the quitting type."

Frank nodded and said, "She's a woman with grit. I can see that just by living down the street."

Widow stayed quiet.

"Takes more than grit, though. Sometimes it takes luck," Frank added.

Just then two tractor trailers blasted through the crossroads. Both men stared at them and saw a trail of truck lights blur by. Frank said, "That's annoying."

"You get used to it," Widow said, and shrugged. After the truck noise died away, they were left in a stretch of silence, the sounds of the night filling the gaps. Crickets chirped in the fields, and highway vehicles rumbled in the distance.

"You know," Frank said, his voice low, "this place's got a history."

"What do you mean?" Widow asked.

Frank leaned back in his chair, the cigar dangling between his fingers. "You asked about some guy the other day. What's his name?"

"Hopper. Alex Hopper."

"Yeah. Funny thing, after we called the cops on you," Frank said, and put both hands up in front of his chest, like he was surrendering. "Which Martha did. I didn't do it. So don't be mad at me."

Widow stayed quiet.

Frank said, "I guess after the cop talked to you, he stopped by here, just to check in on us. Nice kid. Can't remember his name."

Torres, Widow thought.

"I got to talking with him. I mentioned that you asked about Alex Hopper. He seemed to light up when he heard that."

"What did he say?"

"Nothing. Just showed interest in it. Anyway, I told him something he didn't know. Apparently, he's new here. I never heard of this Hopper guy. But I know Nora's husband went missing," Frank said, paused, and puffed his cigar.

"And what happened?"

"Well, again, don't kill the messenger. People think he up and left Nora. But they didn't at the time. The cops believed her and there was a search. People looked all over Iron Crossing for him. They searched the river and the woods. No sign of him. But the cops found a body. It wasn't Wade. It turned out to be the remains of a guy who worked for Junior years ago. Rumor was, the guy crossed him somehow. Nobody knows what he did, but they killed him dead. Looked like a bear got to him."

"Are there bears in the Ozarks?"

Frank shrugged, and said, "There are, but they're black bears. And no black bear could've done the damage that this guy endured. Police said it was a grizzly, but we ain't got grizzlies here." He gulped some whiskey. "People say it was Junior that killed the guy. People say he threw him into a woodchipper. Because that's the only other thing to shred a guy like that. But that's all hearsay."

"You ever meet Brock, the father?" Widow asked.

"Met him once. He was bad news back then, but at least he was smart. Got out of the dirty stuff, went legit. His kid? Junior's got none of that. Just mean for the sake of being mean."

"How do you know he went legit?"

"I don't. But he's highly regarded now. Like a politician."

"What's Junior into? Drugs?"

Frank stared into the rest of his whiskey, and said, "It's best not to ask questions like that. Questions like that will get you killed. But if I had to guess, I'd say smuggling. Drugs, maybe weapons. Railroads make for a convenient delivery system." Frank grunted. "I mean, why not? If you need something moved quietly, Junior's your guy. But don't expect anyone around here to admit it. They're all in their own bubbles."

Widow stayed quiet, and just let his mind wander. They sat in a long silence, the weight of the conversation hanging between them. Then Frank changed the subject and said, "So, you were a Navy SEAL?"

Widow nodded.

Frank whistled softly. "Well, damn. Makes sense, the way you carry yourself." They reminisced about their Navy days after that. Frank did most of the talking.

CHAPTER 35

The same bright stars loomed over Franklin's secluded house, the trees dancing in the wind. Franklin's truck crunched over his gravel driveway, his truck's headlights cutting through the darkness before he killed the engine, parking in front of his house. He sat in the cab for a moment, fingers drumming the steering wheel to the ending of a country song. He was in a good mood because he felt that his Widow problem was solved. All he had to do was keep Junior on a tight leash, and they'd get through this. Eventually, they could come up with some plan to either include Junior's father, or, possibly, usurp him.

These were thoughts Franklin couldn't believe he was having. But when he was speaking with some of the switchmen, they had confided their dismay with the way things were being run. Brock was off doing elite rich-guy stuff while they were still here, running his smuggling empire. Brock was out of touch, was how one of them described it.

There was a window of opportunity here. Either Brock's empire could be split up or completely taken over. Junior's was still growing, but Franklin was here to help guide him.

Together, they could run things better than they were being run right now. Of course, these were just thoughts Franklin had swirling around in his head. He and Junior were still a long ways off from any sort of action plan.

Franklin hopped out of his truck and stared at his house. It loomed ahead, dark and still. He froze. Something was off, again. Titan and Apollo, his Dobermans, weren't at his door barking like they usually did. Last night he hadn't noticed until he was inside his house because he was preoccupied with a couple of switchmen. Tonight he was more alert. He'd learned his lesson. He'd even double-checked that his back-door was locked.

Franklin hung out the driver's side door of his truck, one foot on the rocker panel. He made himself as tall as he could and surveyed the windows of his house. He saw no movement. He called out to his dogs—nothing. They weren't scratching at the front door. No barking. Nothing from inside the house and nothing from the backyard. Just silence. Franklin frowned, and reached back into the truck's cab and took his gun from the console holster.

He stepped out of the truck, boots crunching on the gravel, and shut the door. He moved toward the house with his gun drawn. He stopped near his front door, noticing for the first time a bunch of pebbles on the ground under his doorbell. Then he remembered his cameras. He checked his phone, but there were no notifications. He opened the app and checked the cameras, and discovered that the one over the front door was dead.

Great, he thought. He knew something was wrong. Widow had better not be back for more, because this time, he'd shoot the guy. Which would be a shame, because Franklin liked him. Despite their being enemies, he respected Widow.

Franklin went to open the door, and realized it stood slightly ajar. His heart thumped in his chest. *Widow.* The thought snapped into his mind like a trap. He reached for his gun and eased the door open with his other hand, stepping inside.

The house smelled different. Not like it did when he left. The air carried a faint hint of cologne. It mixed with the usual scent of polished wood and cleaning chemicals. Franklin shoved the door the rest of the way open with his gun barrel. The door creaked on its hinges. The house was dimly lit by night-lights. He stepped forward. A lamp in the living room, the one next to the chair Widow had sat in, clicked on. He diverted his attention to the living room as he entered the house. He passed the bench and walked in through the foyer.

He stepped cautiously into the living room, his gun leading the way.

And then he saw him.

A man sat in the same leather armchair where Widow had perched the night before. He was leaned back, legs crossed, Franklin's expensive whiskey swirling in a glass in his hand. He appeared calm, almost amused, by Franklin's caution. He said, "Franklin, you seem on edge."

"Rourke," Franklin said, lowering his gun. "What're you doing here?"

Rourke gestured lazily with the glass. "Sit down, Franklin."

Franklin didn't move. He glanced back over his shoulder at the shadows he had passed in the foyer. Suddenly, an enormous figure stepped out of the darkness—a towering brute of a man. Maddix. One of Brock's personal enforcers, like Franklin, like Rourke—only Maddix was a giant of a man. He moved with quiet menace. He wore leather gloves, which Franklin didn't notice. He was too befuddled by this visit.

Then a thought occurred to him. He hadn't looked out the backyard windows. He took a glance, saw nothing, and swallowed hard. His voice wavered as he said, "Where's my dogs?"

"Don't worry about them," Rourke replied. "Sit."

Franklin hesitated, his gun half-raised. Maddix stepped into the room. He moved closer, until he stood in the shadows next to Franklin. The guy's sheer size seemed to shrink everything else in the room. Franklin lowered his gun slowly and sat on the sofa, his back stiff, every muscle in his body coiled like a spring. And he realized he was sitting right next to the bullet hole in the sofa, where Widow had shot it the night before.

Franklin stared at Rourke. His eyes teared up. He whispered, "Where's my dogs?"

"Give Maddix your gun," Rourke said. Franklin knew this scene. He'd damn near written the script. He'd been in Rourke's position before, and, more often than not, he'd had to kill someone.

Rourke stared at him. Maddix hovered over Franklin from beside the sofa. That's when Franklin remembered a crucial detail. Normally, when he was in Rourke's position, he'd already had a gun in hand, pointed at the guy in Franklin's position.

Franklin glanced at Rourke's hands. He'd seen the whiskey glass, but he'd missed the gun in Rourke's other hand. Rourke pointed it at Franklin, lazily. Franklin might've been faster than Rourke, but Rourke already had him in the line of fire.

Franklin reversed his gun and handed it over. Maddix took it and stepped around the sofa, stopped behind Franklin, and stood over him.

Rourke set the whiskey on the side table and leaned forward. He said, "Mr. Brock's not happy, Franklin."

Franklin blinked, his throat dry. He felt Maddix hovering behind him. "What do you mean?"

"Are you keeping secrets from us?"

"I don't know what you're talking about."

The shadows from a hallway behind Rourke shifted, and Collin Brock stepped into view. Franklin's eyes widened and his mouth gaped open. Brock circled the edge of the shadows, his tailored suit perfect, his eyes cold and calculating like a predator's.

"You disappoint me, Franklin," Brock said. His voice was low, steady, like the rumble of a far-off hurricane. Something was coming.

"Collin, I can explain—" Franklin started, but Maddix grabbed a tuft of his hair and slammed his head down on the coffee table, shattering the glass top. Maddix yanked Franklin's head back, revealing blood streaking down his face. Franklin's eyes peered toward Brock and Rourke, but he faced the ceiling.

"I hate being interrupted," Brock said. "We go back a long time. How many times have you seen this before? How many guys have you tuned up for me? Why would you think it'd be a good idea to steal from me?"

Regret clouded Franklin's face, only no one could see it because of the blood running down it like a river system. He said, "Collin, I'm sorry."

Brock's gaze bore into him. He said, "Three years. That's how long you and Junior have been running some kind of side hustle. Online gambling, is it? Dogfighting? That's the best I can figure."

"I—"

"Shut up," Brock snapped. "You thought I wouldn't notice? My trains. My resources. My money. You had my people out there, at my railyard, constructing some kind of underground bunker. And you thought I wouldn't notice? Is that where you're running this gambling thing from?"

Franklin had once been a Secret Service agent. He'd once sworn an oath to protect. He had pledged to take a bullet for his protectee. He was once fearless. Not now. Now, for the first time in his life, Franklin trembled in fear. Brock would kill him. He knew it. Like all the men who had faced the barrel of his gun on Brock's orders, he got desperate. He whispered, "It was Junior's idea."

The room was silent enough that everyone heard him. Brock laughed, coldly. "Junior couldn't run a lemonade stand without screwing it up. He could never have done this without help. Your help. You made this happen. You alone."

Rourke watched silently, his face unreadable, but there was a lot of disappointment there. Franklin was like a brother to him. Maddix hovered menacingly, emotionless like a statue, his fists clenching and unclenching—a fighter ready to go into the ring.

Franklin skipped over the first stages of grief, to acceptance. He figured Brock would kill him. But what he didn't know was when, because Brock liked to talk. And Brock wasn't done with him yet.

Brock leaned closer to Franklin and asked, "Don't you want to know how I found out? How I know so much?"

Franklin said nothing.

"Where's Camp?" Brock asked.

Franklin stared back at him blankly. "Who?"

"I spent a fortune on a guy to come in and find out what the hell's going on here. I sent him here to investigate. To audit. And now he's not answering my calls. He's not checked in. Where is he?"

"I got no idea—" Franklin said, and stopped. "Michael Walters?"

"Is that the name he gave you? His real name's Camp. He seemed like a good guy. I met him a handful of times. He came highly recommended by previous employers. Know who those are?"

Franklin spit blood in response. He turned his head and glared out the kitchen windows to the backyard. He didn't know it, but he caught a glimpse of his Dobermans. They had been shot dead and were clumped together in a pile by the backdoor.

"Camp's what they call an investigative auditor. He works for the cartels. He goes undercover and audits their books. He finds the thieves that're stealing. See, they deal with thieves all the time. The cartels really value Camp. And they're going to be angry when they find out he's missing. If he's dead, they'll want blood. They'll want the man who killed him to suffer and die," Brock said, and nodded to Maddix. The giant lumbered around the sofa, dragging Franklin over the arm and throwing him to the floor.

Franklin got back up on his knees. He threw his arms up, defensively, and said, "Wait! There's a guy!" Maybe there was hope. Maybe he could change their minds.

Maddix reared his arm back to start swinging at Franklin, but Brock put a hand up, stopped him, and asked, "What guy?"

"The guy who broke your son's arm. Maybe he killed Camp."

"What's his name?"

Franklin hesitated. His mind raced, searching for a way out. "Widow. It was him. He's been causing trouble since he got here."

"Widow," Brock said. "He got a first name?"

"Jack Widow. He's staying with a local woman, Nora Sutton."

Brock stroked his chin, like an idea was forming. Then he said, "You stole from me. You know, I don't know what it is with thieves. I mean, really. I give you jobs. I give you purpose. Look around. Look how good your life is. And it's all because of me. Yet, for some reason, you think you can just steal from me? You think you can manipulate my son? You twist him against me?"

It turned out Franklin was wrong. He wasn't at acceptance. He was at anger. He said, "Is that a joke? You never loved him! You've ignored him his whole life!" Franklin paused a beat. He breathed hard, knowing it might be his last breath. "You're a shitty father."

Brock's gaze turned colder. "You shouldn't have said that, old friend."

Rourke rose from the armchair and aimed the gun at Franklin, in case he tried anything. But there was nothing to try.

Brock looked at Maddix, and said, "Finish it." Maddix smirked, towering over Franklin, whose eyes widened in terror as the giant's fists pummeled down on him like sledgehammers. The first blow sent him sprawling onto the floor. The second left him gasping for air, blood pooling beneath him. The third and fourth sent him into unconsciousness. He never felt the next several blows. And by the end of it, Franklin was nothing but dead.

Rourke asked, "Want Maddix to take him out in the Ozarks and bury him?"

"No. Have our local friends in law enforcement clean this up. Tell them to look for the killer. This Widow guy. Tell them it sounds like he's been on a rampage. First he broke my son's arm, then he beat Franklin to death."

"Junior's going to be upset when he finds out."

Brock glanced at him, and said, "Yes. I forgot about my prodigal son. Better let him think it's true. The cops can call him after. Tell them to leave out that I'm here."

"Whatever they're doing down there in that bunker, maybe they'll do it to Widow?"

Brock nodded, said nothing.

Rourke added, "We could crash the party."

"This is why you're my number two, Rourke. Make it happen."

Rourke nodded, pulled out his phone, and called one of the local deputies.

CHAPTER 36

A deep, velvet-black night hovered over Nora's farm. Everything was quiet and still, except for the occasional trucks crossing paths at the highway's intersection. Crickets chirped across the fields. An owl perched on the barn roof, scanning the fields for mice. It hooted as if offering up bribes to the crickets to pinpoint any mice they came across.

The Graces had left a couple of hours earlier. The girls were fast asleep in their beds after another story Widow made up, one about a murder on board one of the ships he'd been on. Nora's eyes shot open wide at hearing him say murder. Poppy asked, "What does mooder mean?" This time Violet had no answer for her sister, because she didn't know either. Nora stared at Widow, begging him with her eyes to fix it. He told the girls that the word was Navy slang for man overboard. Then he weaved a tall tale about a sailor who went over the rails one night and into the ocean. He spun a yarn about him and others having to get in the water with lifeboats to locate the sailor. Eventually they located him; a pod of dolphins had found him.

Poppy asked, "What's a dolphin?"

"It's a really smart fish," Nora said, kissing each girl on the head. "Now it's time for sleep." The girls went to sleep after goodnights from Widow. By ten o'clock, Widow and Nora were in her bed. By eleven, they were both worn out and asleep. Joanie slept on the floor in the girls' room.

After midnight, the farm was as quiet as it ever got. But the silence was interrupted when Joanie jolted awake and barked. She heard tires on gravel, hopped to her feet, and ran to the foyer. She barked at the front door, then scurried through the house and out the doggie door. She ran around the house to the porch and barked the same warnings she had a week ago when Franklin was in the driveway.

Widow stirred at Joanie's barking. Unlike last time, he didn't dismiss Joanie's calls to action. Her barks set off a chain reaction in him, ripping through his body like an electric current. Instinctively, he hopped out of Nora's bed, skirted around it and grabbed the Glock, his fingers closing around the grip. He glanced down the hall, saw nothing but darkness. He scooped up his jeans, and slipped them on, leaving the rest of his clothes draped over a chair.

Nora stirred, blinking awake. She forced her eyes open and asked, "What is it?"

The motion sensor app chimed notifications on her phone, the soft ping alerting her that the front camera had recorded movement. The camera facing the driveway pinged after the one on the corner of the house. "Check it," Widow said.

Nora opened her phone and watched the video. It was grainy, and black and white, because of the night setting. The back corner camera video showed Joanie running out of the house to the front yard.

Widow leaned over her and watched the screen. Nora went to the second video. They saw a pair of headlights wash over the driveway, creeping closer to the house.

"Grab your rifle. I'm going out," he said, and went out into the darkness of the house, toward the front door.

Nora was up before he got there, putting her pajamas on quickly. She followed behind him with her rifle. They stopped in the foyer. She glanced over his shoulder, out the window. All they could see were two sets of headlights—cars, not trucks, judging by the headlight placements. Joanie's barking grew louder, more urgent, as the cars pulled into the driveway, past the spot where Widow broke Junior's arm.

Widow said, "Stay ready. If anyone comes into the house that's not me, shoot them."

Nora nodded. Widow clutched the doorknob and started to open it. But Nora grabbed him, pulled herself up to him, and kissed him hard. Then she released him, and out he went.

Widow descended the front steps, holding the Glock out of sight, down by his leg. His finger was on the trigger. He walked out as far as he dared, which was just behind Joanie. She barked at the headlights, which were on bright, blinding Widow.

Abruptly, the high beams switched to low, making it easier for Widow to see. But even before his eyes could adjust, he knew who they were. A sudden wash of blue flickered on from light bars and swept across the yard, bathing the farm in a surreal glow. Widow stopped short, his jaw tightening. "Cops," he said to himself.

Nora glowered, peering out the window past Widow. She saw the cops also. Two police cruisers had pulled into the driveway, lights flashing the moment they saw Widow. No sirens. Widow stood there, frozen. The Glock remained at his side, pointing at the ground. But he moved his finger off the trigger.

Suddenly, three more cop cars sped down the rural road and spilled onto the end of the driveway, all light bars flashing their blue lights. Joanie barked furiously. Widow stood there, motionless.

Five Iron Crossing deputies emerged from their cruisers—all the deputies the sheriff's department had. They drew their weapons. Widow recognized Torres and Dillard from earlier, at the library. Dillard—the older, jarhead deputy—took the lead. The other three deputies came in from the sides. They swarmed Widow in a matter of seconds. Each cop wore a bulletproof vest. They came out with two versions of AR-15s —which Widow recognized—Colt LE6920 and Smith & Wesson M&P15. Torres had one of the Colts. Dillard aimed his service carry at Widow, a Glock 19 like the one Widow held.

They surrounded his front view the same way they had at the library, like the top half of a clock face, from nine to three. They stayed twelve feet back. Dillard stepped a foot closer and shouted, "Drop the gun!"

Nora came out onto the porch, rifle in hand, but pointed at the ground. Joanie stood behind Widow, barking at the cops. Widow asked, "What's this about?"

"Drop the gun, or we'll shoot!" Dillard shouted.

Torres's face pleaded with Widow to do as he was told. Widow didn't hesitate any longer. He tossed the Glock away. A small dust cloud puffed around it from the impact on the gravel. Widow slow-raised his hands. "Okay, I'm unarmed."

Dillard glanced over Widow's shoulder at Nora standing on the porch, and shouted, "Recall your dog!"

Nora called Joanie back to the porch. Violet had gotten up, and stood in the hallway rubbing her eyes. She called out to her mom, asking what was going on. Nora ignored her and shouted at Joanie to return to the house.

Dillard stepped closer to Widow. The others stayed back. Joanie barked and snarled at him. Dillard moved his aim from Widow to Joanie. Nora shouted at Joanie again, calling her back to the house. Violet stood on the porch, watching the jarhead cop aim a gun at her dog. Poppy was up and out of bed, and standing behind her sister. Both girls stared at the cops, the guns, and at Joanie barking ferociously.

Dillard's finger was on the trigger, and he started to squeeze it.

Suddenly, Widow sidestepped, half-lunging between Dillard's gun and Joanie. He clamped a hand down over the Glock and redirected its aim ten degrees away. Dillard stopped, frozen, and stared into Widow's eyes.

"Don't shoot her! I'm cooperating!" Widow said, and glanced at Joanie. In a deep cop voice, he said, "Joanie, back!" The dog stopped barking, and heard Nora and the girls calling to her. She ran back to the porch and into the girls' arms.

Widow released Dillard's gun and backed away. The other deputies aimed their rifles at him. Three of them half-squeezed their triggers. But they knew if they fired their rifles, there was an unacceptable risk of hitting Dillard, so they stood down.

Dillard pointed the Glock back at Widow's chest. He looked angry, like he really wanted to pull the trigger. Widow saw it in his eyes. The guy was considering it. But he couldn't do it. Logic would indicate it was because Widow retreated, was unarmed, and was surrendering. But something else lingered there. It was like he fought back the urge to shoot Widow because he was under orders to take him alive. Widow had been in combat many times. He'd seen the look on a man's face when he had a violent urge, an itch he wanted to scratch, but orders prevented it.

Torres said, "Sir?" The other deputies glanced at him, like he wasn't on the same page as they were. Dillard glanced back at Torres, fury covering his face. Torres continued, "We should arrest him, sir."

Dillard breathed deeply, calmed himself, and turned back to Widow. He stepped to Widow, cuffs in hand, and said, "Jack Widow, you're under arrest." Dillard cuffed him, one thick wrist behind Widow's back, and then the other.

Widow asked, "For what?" From the porch, Joanie growled.

"For the murder of Wyatt Franklin."

"What?" Widow blurted out, shocked. "Franklin's dead?"

Dillard shoved Widow forward, and gestured for one of the deputies to take possession of him. But Torres stepped up first and took Widow by the forearm.

Dillard walked over to Widow's tossed Glock, took out a pair of plastic gloves, and put them on. He scooped up the Glock and ejected the magazine. He examined it, counting the bullets. He said, "You're missing a bullet."

Widow stayed quiet.

Dillard said, "Witnesses say they saw you on a motorcycle at the scene. We've got a bullet from his house. I bet it was fired from this Glock."

"Was he shot to death?" Widow asked.

"No."

"Then I didn't shoot him."

"Don't matter. That bullet puts you at his house," Dillard said, walked up to Widow, and stood inches from his face. "Someone beat Franklin to death. Judging by the wounds, it was someone big. Someone with brute force. A maniac. That's how I would describe the perpetrator." Dillard looked Widow up and down. "Are you a maniac, Mr. Widow?"

Widow stayed quiet.

Nora leaned her rifle against the wall, came down the steps and started to protest, but one of the other deputies got between her and Widow. He said, "Ma'am, stay back."

Another warned, "Don't obstruct justice."

Nora didn't move. "This has got to be a mistake!" Joanie barked wildly, but stayed back on the porch with the girls. The deputies with Nora got distracted by Joanie's barking. They glanced at the porch to make sure the dog was staying out of the way. Nora pushed past them and ran to Widow. Torres stopped pulling him away. Nora got up on her tippy-toes and kissed him. "I know you didn't do this!" she said.

Widow smiled at her, and said, "Nora, take the girls and go to the Graces'. It's not safe to stay here."

She hesitated, tears brimming in her eyes. She said, "Widow—"

"Go," he said sharply. "Take Joanie and go. For me."

Dillard said, "Put him in the back of a car, already."

Torres said, "Yes, sir!" He started to pull Widow away.

But Widow didn't budge. For Torres, it was like trying to pull an oak tree out of the ground with his bare hands. Widow stared at Dillard and said, "I'm innocent."

Dillard said, "Take it up with the judge. Court opens at 8 a.m." He nodded at another deputy, who came over and took

Widow's other forearm. Together, he and Torres escorted Widow away. The other deputy wanted him in the back of his cruiser, but Torres jerked Widow toward his. The deputy eyeballed Torres, who said, "I got him."

Nora stared after them. Her voice breaking, she called out, "We'll come to the station and bail you out!"

Torres stopped Widow at his cruiser, leaned him against the car, and searched him. He found Widow's passport, bank card, and burner phone. Widow's toothbrush wasn't in his pocket like it usually was; it was perched in a toothbrush holder next to Nora's, by the sink in her bathroom.

Dillard shook his head, and said, "Jail's closed to visitors. It's after hours."

Joanie continued barking at the officers. Widow looked over his shoulder as Torres shoved him into the backseat of a cruiser. He whispered to Joanie, wishing she could hear him. "Take care of them."

The door slammed shut, cutting him off from Nora, the girls, and the life he'd been sampling. Torres climbed into the driver's seat, putting Widow's belongings on the passenger seat next to him, and started to pull away. The flashing blue lights cast eerie shadows across the faces of the ladies Widow had come to know. He watched as the farm faded into the distance.

CHAPTER 37

It was just after midnight when Nora watched them put Widow into the cruiser and drive away with him. Dillard and another deputy stuck around and talked with her. Dillard asked her questions about Widow, their relationship, Franklin, and any other details she might know. She refused to answer any questions. They started to leave, but she asked a question: "Don't you need to impound my bike?"

Dillard said, "What's that?"

She stood on the porch, rifle resting behind her against the wall. The girls stood in the open doorway, holding tight onto Joanie's neck. Joanie snarled at Dillard. Nora said, "You said witnesses saw Widow on a motorcycle. My motorcycle. Don't you need to impound it?"

Dillard glanced at the other deputies. They glanced back. Then he smiled and said, "Oh yes, we need to get that."

"It's in the barn," Nora said, wiping tears away from her face. "I can take you back there."

"No, don't trouble yourself about it. It's the middle of the night."

"It's just right there, behind the house."

"We ain't got a truck to haul it. I'll send someone by in the morning to pick it up," Dillard said, smiled, and left.

Nora scratched her head. Something felt off. *Why wouldn't they take it now?* She wondered. It seemed like a breach of protocol to just leave it, uncollected and unguarded.

She watched as the deputies got into their cars and sped off. Light bars switched off as they headed back down her rural road.

Martha couldn't sleep. She watched from her bedroom window as the blue lights flashed, washing over her lawn and then switching off one by one as they passed her house. *What in the world is going on down at Nora's?* she asked herself. Then she asked it out loud to Frank, as she often did. But he wasn't listening. She glanced back at him. He was sound asleep on his side of their bed.

Nora tore through the farmhouse, frenzied but orderly, grabbing everything she could think of. Clothes, cash, and a few precious keepsakes she couldn't leave behind, thinking she might not come back for a while. She packed stuff into her suitcase, which was open on her bed. She glanced up and saw her reflection staring back at her in the mirror, behind a ring light. Widow was right. She should've left long ago. She saw it now. This was the final straw for her, the one that broke the camel's back. Wade was gone. And Widow's fate was unknown. She could lose him. He could be gone forever.

Nora teared up just thinking about it. He had come into her life a week ago, and now he was everything to her. She didn't want to lose him.

The old suitcase would barely stay closed after she shoved toiletries into it. Her hands shook, but she couldn't afford to stop. Widow was gone, taken by the deputies, and she knew it wouldn't end there. It must have something to do with Junior. She had to help Widow. But first she had to take the girls somewhere safe. They were exposed at the farm.

The Brocks never forgave, and they never forgot.

She glanced over her shoulder at the girls, who stood in the doorway, wide-eyed and silent. Poppy clutched a stuffed animal like a lifeline, while Violet kept hugging her. They were sleepy and confused. Violet was worried. She understood a little more than Poppy did. Nora knew Violet was worried because she wasn't asking any questions. But the questions were swirling in her head.

"It's okay, girls," Nora said, her voice wavering. "We're going to figure this out. Go grab your bags and pack some clothes."

"Māmā …" Violet began, her voice delicate, like it could break.

"Now, Violet!" Nora snapped, and immediately regretted it. She put her hands over her face and took a deep breath. "Please, honey. Take your sister and do as I ask. Okay?"

Violet nodded and dragged Poppy—and Poppy's stuffed animal—with her back to their room.

Nora finished packing and couldn't close her suitcase. She started to remove stuff, but suddenly Joanie ran to the backdoor and growled, ears pinned back, hackles raised. She ran out the doggie door and barked just as ferociously as she had at the deputies. Nora ignored her, but the barking got louder and louder. Then Nora heard noises in the backyard. She left her suitcase wide open and went around to the kitchen. The hair on her arms stood up as she moved to the window. She froze in horror, staring out the window into her backyard.

A huge orange light danced wildly against the darkness. The barn. It was a roaring fire.

"No," she gasped.

The flames spread fast, licking up the sides of the old wooden structure. Flares shot out onto the animal pens, just missing wooden posts. The dry summer breeze fed the inferno, making it significantly worse. Wood from the roof cracked as the heat split the boards. The sound shook her into action. Nora ran out of the kitchen, leaving the girls behind.

The fire blazed on. The horses kicked at their stall doors, neighing frantically. Nora could hear them. Joanie barked at the animals in the outside pens, trying to get them to run away from the flames. Black smoke filled the night. Nora ran through billows of it, coughing along the way. She reached the barn door, which was still intact. The roof was blazing. More of the wood splintered and cracked.

Nora took a deep breath and wrenched the door open. One of the horses bolted past her, knocking her on her butt. She coughed and gasped. Joanie kept barking outside, near the pens. Nora pushed herself up and got to her feet. The other horse was kicking and screaming. It was stuck inside the barn. Nora took another deep breath and held it. She ran into the barn. Smoke smacked her in the face. Flames engulfed the roof now. A support beam blazed above her. It cracked and fell to the ground, crashing into the empty horse stall. Nora crouch-walked to the other stall. Her horse was desperately trying to get out. Nora grabbed the door and pulled it open wide. The horse ran out in a panic. Flames had burnt half its tail off.

Nora coughed and pushed through the thick smoke, back out the door. Just behind her, another burning beam crashed to the ground. She had gotten her horse out just in the nick of time, before they both were trapped inside. But she wasn't home-free yet. Fire flared out from the barn's side and from the roof. It ignited the goat pen. Joanie scratched at the gate, desperately, trying to free her friends.

Nora ran to the goat pen and opened the gate. The goats stampeded out and ran off into the fields. Next, she opened the sheep pen and the pig pen. Then she chased the chickens out of their coop. At the end of it, most of Nora's animals were free, running around the back of the farm.

At the Graces' house, Frank rubbed his eyes and yawned. He and Martha were standing at their bedroom window. He stared at the black smoke filling the sky. He knew something wasn't right, and panic set in. This time Martha wasn't guilty of crying wolf when she woke him up; it looked serious. They left their bedroom and went out onto the front porch. They peered at the back of Nora's property, saw the smoke and the raging flames.

"Should I call the fire department?" Martha asked, like she wanted permission.

"Yes! Go! Do it now!" Frank shouted. She ran back into the house to search for her phone. Frank hurriedly threw on some shoes and some clothes—including his Navy hat; he hardly went anywhere without it. The shoes were required so he could run down there to help, but the hat was necessary to boost his abilities. Imagination or not, he felt stronger with it on.

Frank turned to go back into the house, but paused. He saw something else at the Sutton farm. He stepped farther out onto the porch and tilted his head. He squinted his eyes, which weren't so good anymore, but the firelight lit up Nora's farm with an orange glow. He saw something that made his heart skip a beat.

Junior's black Raptor was parked in the driveway of Nora's farm. "Oh no!" he said.

"What is it?" Martha called from the living room. She searched her bag for her phone. "What happened?"

"You better call the police too!" Frank said, and went inside to get his rifle.

Nora and Joanie entered their house. Nora called out to the girls but got no answer. A draft blew in through the kitchen, like she'd left a window open somewhere. She passed through the kitchen, Joanie on her heels. As she turned in to the hallway, she saw them—four men standing there, in the middle of her living room.

The men were dressed in all black—t-shirts, jeans, and cowboy boots. Three were big country guys in masks—and not ski masks. They wore black devil-masks, like something out of a Mardi Gras nightmare parade. Tattoos covered the visible skin of their necks and arms. They had handguns. Behind them the front door hung open. It creaked from the wind.

One of them pointed a camera at Nora, recording her reaction. Her children were being held by one big guy, his hands covering their mouths. Both girls kicked and pounded their little fists into his thighs, which did nothing. It didn't even irritate him.

The first time Nora saw Widow flashed across her mind. She remembered thinking he could crush her girls' skulls with his bare hands, and at the same time. So could the guy who held them now.

The one with the camera sidestepped, panning the room like he was a cinematographer trying to get Nora in the right shot.

The fourth man was different than the other three. He was no big country boy, but he was their leader. He wore a gold devil-mask, and his arm was in a cast. It was Junior.

Joanie recognized him by his scent. She recognized the others from their scents as well. She knew them from her time in their kennel. She snarled at the men. focusing on the big one holding the girls. Junior's good hand held a strange-looking handgun. Nora didn't recognize it. Joanie started to lunge at the men, but Junior shot her first.

Nora screamed out. "No!" But it was too late. A projectile fired out of Junior's gun and hit Joanie in the neck. She fell to the ground shrieking and crying, but within seconds she was out cold. No more noise from her but snoring.

Junior said, "Relax, it's an animal tranquilizer. We're not here to kill her, or you. We got plans for your dog. We got plans for you and your girls."

"What're you going to do to us?" Nora asked.

Junior handed the tranquilizer gun off to one of the other men. He circled Nora and said, "Smile! You're going to be a star!" Junior gestured to the camera. "You're all going to be stars! We're filming a very special event. You'll see. I don't want to spoil it."

In Nora's driveway, Frank stood at the back of Junior's Raptor. He crept past it and up to the porch. He saw the figures of four masked men through the open doorway. They were taunting Nora. Frank fished his phone out and called the number Widow had given him. He put the phone to his ear and listened to it ring and ring. No answer.

Martha waited back in their driveway for the cops and firemen. Frank had told her to stay behind. He had told her, *No matter what, stay there.*

Frank watched as the home invaders held Nora and her kids at gunpoint. He saw no sign of Widow.

Damn it, Widow! Where are you? he thought. He called again. Still, no answer. Frank had to intervene. He couldn't let these guys do whatever they planned to do to Nora and her girls. Widow or no Widow, he had to do something. Frank clicked off the phone, pocketed it, took a deep breath, and began sneaking up behind the masked men.

CHAPTER 38

Widow's burner phone buzzed on the seat next to Torres. The deputy glanced at it and said nothing. Widow sat cuffed and restless in the backseat of Torres's patrol car. The engine rumbled, pulsating faintly through the car frame. Torres drove in silence, his knuckles white on the wheel. He felt conflicted. Orders had been given. A superior had told him what to do. The hierarchy was clear. His job called for one thing. But his duty might be something else entirely.

A battle of right and wrong—or of truth and lies—waged in his mind. He glanced back at Widow in the rearview, hoping his prisoner wouldn't see it. But Widow was off somewhere else, having his own internal battle.

Why would they kill Franklin and blame me for it? Widow wondered.

He stared out the window, his eyes fixed on the dark countryside rolling past. His mind raced. Franklin was dead. That might be true. But Widow hadn't killed him.

His burner phone stopped ringing. Widow shifted his weight, the cuffs biting into his wrists. He asked, "Where we going?"

"I'm taking you to the station. You're going to jail," Torres paused a beat, letting his doubt show. "I'm sorry."

"You know I didn't kill anyone."

Torres faced forward, eyes on the road. He didn't answer.

"Torres," Widow said. "Something's not right. Can't you see it?"

Torres flicked his eyes to the rearview mirror. "Sorry, there's nothing I can do."

Defeated, Widow turned away and watched the landscape of quiet farms and green forests zoom by. The moon hung low, casting pale light over the rolling fields and dense trees. Everything was calm. The farms rested under a peaceful sky. The inhabitants slept, unaware of the crimes happening while they slumbered.

Torres adjusted the police radio. There was nothing but static over the line. He ignored it and drove on. A couple of minutes later, he fidgeted with the radio again. Widow noticed and asked, "What's wrong?"

"Nothing. Don't talk. It's best if you say nothing. You know your Miranda rights and all?"

"You never read them to me."

"You know what they are. Dillard'll read them to you at the jail."

"I thought you guys were supposed to read them to suspects the moment you arrest them?"

Torres said nothing to that, although he asked himself the same question. Dillard must've forgotten, he thought. He fidgeted with the police radio again. Nothing. All they heard was static. Then he said to himself, "That's weird."

"What's weird?"

"There's nothing. No one's saying anything."

"So? Slow night, maybe?"

"On a night when we arrest a murderer?"

"I'm not a murderer," Widow barked. *At least, I didn't kill Franklin*, he thought. "Besides, you already got me in the car. What else is there to say over the radio?"

"It's a lot more complicated than that. There's more that goes on after, behind the scenes. Usually, there's radio chatter for hours. But the others aren't saying anything."

Just then, Widow's burner phone buzzed again, urgently, screaming for someone to answer it. It hit Widow like a mortar shell to the chest: This was something urgent. Widow said, "Answer that! It could be important!"

Torres glanced at the burner phone. He picked it up, keeping one eye on the road, and checked the Caller ID. He said, "There's no name. It's just a number."

"What's the number?"

Reluctantly, Torres repeated the number. Widow pressed his head against the bulletproof plastic and spoke through air holes punched in it. He said, "Torres, listen to me. That's Nora's neighbor, Frank Grace. The one you met the other day. I gave Frank my number. Told him to call me in case of emergency. Something's not right! Answer him!"

"You were arrested, like…" Torres glanced at his watch, and said, "twenty minutes ago. They probably woke up from the commotion. That's why he's calling—to see what's going on."

"No! You're wrong. Something else is happening. He wouldn't just call me because he saw cop cars." Knowing the Graces even as little as he did, Widow knew Martha would insert herself into a situation with police at a neighbor's house. She wouldn't just have Frank call Widow. She'd go down to the scene.

Torres said nothing and just kept driving.

"Please, Torres! I'm telling you, something's happening!"

Torres remained quiet. Widow head-butted the plastic, hard. Startled, Torres glanced over his shoulder at Widow. He shouted, "Hey! You trying to get more charges added on?"

"Damn it, Torres!" Widow fell back onto the seat. He took a breath, trying to stay calm. He said, "Please. Call your boss on the radio. Just ask him. They should still be at the farm, right? They gotta collect the motorcycle. You know? The one that a supposed witness said they saw me on. And they gotta take a statement from Nora. Right? They must still be there. Just call him and check."

Widow's burner phone buzzed again, angrily, like a trapped bee buzzing to escape through a closed window. Widow stared at it through the bulletproof plastic. He ran a thousand scenarios through his head, trying to figure out a way to get to it. He could roll on his back and try to slip the handcuffs over his feet, to get his hands in front of him. Maybe he could kick out a window? Doubtful. That stuff really only worked in the movies. Police cruisers were designed to withstand that kind of escape attempt.

The phone buzzed. Torres saw Widow's expression in the rearview. He thought about Wade Sutton, Franklin, and the Brocks. He thought about the rumors of corruption. Why wasn't there much of an investigation into Wade's disappearance? Then he asked himself another question: Where was everyone? He was heading back to the station with a murder suspect, and not one of the other deputies was escorting him. He checked the mirrors. No one was with him. He did insist on taking Widow himself, but the other deputy had tried to take him in his own car. Why wasn't that guy following him?

Torres slowed the patrol car. He didn't realize he was doing it. He just took his foot off the gas and let the car coast to the shoulder. He put his foot on the brake and stopped there, just next to a ditch. The burner phone quit ringing.

Just then the clear night sky broke for incoming rain. A thunderclap boomed across the sky. It rolled and echoed. Clouds moved in over the landscape. Lightning flashed through the clouds. It began to rain. It was slow at first, but then it picked up to a consistent rhythm. It beat on the police car's roof.

Widow recognized the doubt on Torres' face. Widow said, "It's the Brocks. They killed Franklin and are trying to pin it on me."

Torres stared at Widow through the mirror. He asked, "Why?" Torres was torn. He had started looking into Alex Hopper and Wade Sutton, and realized something didn't add up. Maybe Widow was telling the truth.

Widow glanced out the passenger window. Rain fell against the glass. He thought for a moment, and a new fear awoke in the pit of his stomach. He looked back at Torres. "Junior, or the switchmen or whatever, wanted me out of the house. They knew they couldn't take me out alive, unless I was compelled to surrender. Got to be!"

"But why this way? I'm taking you to jail. Why would they want you locked up? If they intended to do you harm, then why not just shoot you?"

Widow thought for a moment. Torres was new and a little green, but curious, which was good. "Why do you think?"

Silence.

"Remember the bullet?" Widow asked. "Outside the window? With the footprints? Franklin did that. He left the bullet as a warning. He left it outside the bedroom of two little girls."

"So, you did murder him?"

"I didn't kill him. I talked to him, sure. But I didn't kill him," Widow said.

Torres stared out the windshield. The rain covered the glass, killing all the visibility ahead.

Widow said, "Remember the phone calls?"

Silence. The police radio clicked static. No one spoke. No police chatter. Widow asked, "Who called Wade the day he vanished?"

"Someone from Black River Rail."

"Who owns Black River Rail?"

"The Brocks."

"Who did Franklin work for?"

Torres paused a heavy beat, and said, "The Brocks. I see what you're saying. But why kill Franklin? Why frame you for it? Why get you arrested?"

"I told you. They wanted me out of the house," Widow said. Suddenly, lightning crackled across the sky, sending fractured light through the windshield. With the lightning, a realization crackled across Widow's mind. "Nora. The girls. They wanted me in cuffs so they could get to them easier. Their lives are in danger. We have to go back!"

Torres started to speak, but stopped. He grabbed the radio and clicked the receiver. He spoke into it. "Dillard, come in."

Static.

"What're you doing?" Widow asked.

"Let me check in with him. Maybe they're still at back at the farm."

A voice clicked on. "Torres? What's up?"

"Are you still processing evidence back at the farm?"

Silence for a long moment. The rain sounded through the cabin.

"What do you need?" Dillard asked.

"I'm on my way to the station with the suspect. I'm just wondering if you want me to book him myself, or wait for you."

The radio hissed static for another moment. Then Dillard said, "Why the hell do you have Widow? I asked Corin to take him."

"I took him."

Another long moment of hissing static passed. Then Dillard said, "Pull over to the side of the road and wait. I'll send Corin to take him from you."

Torres's eyes popped open wide. He stared at Widow in the rearview. He started to respond, but Widow asked, "Why would they want you to do that? Think about it."

Torres said nothing, unsure what to do. Widow said, "Let's go back!"

"Eddie?" Dillard called over the radio. "Give me your location."

Torres locked eyes with Widow, put his mouth to the radio, and started to relay his location. Abruptly, Widow's burner phone buzzed one more time. Torres froze with the radio to his mouth.

"Answer it!" Widow said.

Torres struggled for several seconds. He dropped the radio and grabbed the phone. He glanced at the incoming caller. It was Frank again. He clicked Answer and put the phone to his ear. "Hello?"

"Put it on speaker!" Widow said.

Torres clicked the speaker button and held the phone between them. He repeated, "Hello?"

"Frank? It's Widow!"

They heard breathing for a moment, and then a voice Widow didn't recognize asked, "Who you calling?" The line went dead.

"Call him back!" Widow said.

Torres repeated the call. The phone rang and rang. No answer.

"We have to get back there!" Widow said.

The radio crackled again. Dillard said, "Eddie, answer me!"

Torres reached up and switched the radio off. He looked at Widow and said, "This feels wrong to me. But I think you're right."

"Then let's go back!" Widow said.

Torres's phone blew up. He checked it. It was Dillard calling him. He ignored it and switched the car's windshield wipers on, U-turned, and headed back to the Sutton Farm.

CHAPTER 39

Rain hammered against the windshield. Visibility was low, so Torres flicked on his high beams. He sped along the rural roads, backtracking the way they had come, taking abrupt turns, forcing the car to glide for seconds at a time on the wet streets. Widow bumped against the passenger-side rear door. His hands and wrists hurt from being cuffed behind him the whole ride.

On the last road before the turnoff to Nora's, they saw headlights coming at them fast. It was a small convoy of vehicles going the opposite direction. The lead car had its high beams on, nearly blinding them in the heavy rain. Torres flicked his off and the lead vehicle in the convoy didn't return the favor. Torres and Widow both had to divert their eyes to the road directly in their own headlight beams to keep from being blinded. They passed the small convoy. Torres flipped his high beams back on and continued speeding to Nora's.

Widow tracked the convoy as it zoomed by. They flew by fast, but Widow grabbed a good look at one of the vehicles. It was a black Ford Raptor—Junior's truck. Flanking it, Widow wasn't sure, but he thought he saw the other police cruisers—

all four of them. Widow's stomach tightened, amplifying his worry.

They approached the Sutton farm's rural road. Torres kept his focus on driving. Widow leaned forward and looked up at the rainy sky. As they neared the Sutton farm, they both saw it and said nothing: A heavy plume of black smoke billowing into the night sky, above the trees where the farm was. Even with the low visibility, Widow pinpointed the fire's origin. It was at Nora's farm, which meant it was either the barn or the house—or both. Despite the rain, the fire from Nora's barn lit up the horizon like a beacon of destruction.

Torres turned onto the rural road leading to Nora's farm. As they drove, he blipped on his blue lights, sirens and all. He gritted his teeth and pressed the accelerator harder. The cruiser bounced over the uneven road. He swerved past a horse in the road. Widow recognized it as one of Nora's. It clopped on down the road, past the Graces' house.

A moment later, they skidded into Nora's driveway, kicking rocks over the spot where Widow first met Nora's girls at their lemonade stand. Widow stared through the windshield, ignoring the aches in his hands and wrists. He sighed in relief when he saw that the house was still standing. It was untouched by fire. The barn was a different story. Fire fully engulfed it. Animals ran frantically across the property. Two of the goats, whose names Widow had forgotten, grazed in the freshly cut grass off to the right of the driveway.

Torres threw the car into Park and switched off the sirens, but left the light bar on. It swirled blue light across the property. The light reflected through the rainfall. Torres jumped out of the cruiser—the rain instantly drenching him—stood with his door open and stared at the property. His eyes locked on the fiery barn. He wiped water from his eyes multiple times.

Widow leaned into the bulletproof plastic and shouted, "Uncuff me!"

Torres stumbled into the car's doorframe. He righted himself and hesitated, unsure of what to do, and filled with disbelief. He was flabbergasted that this was happening, that Widow was right. It was one thing to laugh behind the scenes with Freda about police corruption, about the Brocks being boogeymen. It was another thing entirely to come face-to-face with the horror of it—to the truth of it.

Torres snapped out of it and opened the rear door. Widow slid across the bench and out of the car. He turned around. Torres fumbled with the keys in the rain, but finally got Widow unlocked.

Widow flexed his hands and wrists, then he cracked his knuckles. The rain beat down on him. He was still shirtless. The cold rain pelted his skin. He blinked twice as much as normal just to get it out of his eyes.

"That convoy that passed us, I think it was Junior and his guys. They did this. Had to be them," Widow called out.

"Do you think they took Mrs. Sutton and the girls?"

"One step at a time. Let's check the house first," Widow said, because he didn't want to think about the alternative. His fear right then was finding Nora and the girls dead in the house. And if that happened, it'd take a lot more than armed cops to stop him from tearing the whole town apart.

"Stay behind me," Torres said, drawing his gun. Widow nodded, as he was unarmed. He thought about asking if Torres had a spare gun, but he figured he wouldn't get one. Not yet.

The walked through the rain, crunching across the gravel. Widow noticed something. No Joanie. She wasn't barking.

There was no sign of her. He clenched his fists. He was certain Junior took the girls, but not sure about Joanie.

They advanced farther up the driveway to the grass. It was slow going because of the low visibility, plus Torres was going slow because of the uncertainty of the danger ahead, as his training had taught him.

Widow's eyes scanned the yard and the house. Everything was wet. Suddenly, he saw it and his heart sank. About fifteen feet in front of them, there was a body sprawled in the grass. It was Martha Grace. She lay motionless, her clothes soaked in rain and blood. Torres got to her first. He knelt down to check her pulse, but Widow could see she was dead. She had been shot, three to the chest. Chunks of flesh and bone were on the ground underneath her.

Widow stepped past Torres, heading to the front porch. The house's front door creaked open slowly, behind the insect screen door. The wind blew it back and forth. The house lights lit up the porch. Widow could see another dead body. Torres was still searching Martha for a pulse that wasn't there, but Widow moved on.

Frank Grace was sprawled out across the front steps. A Remington Model 7400 rifle lay beside him—his hunting rifle, useless to him now. Frank had seen the flames, and, like the good man he was, had come running to help Nora and the girls.

They had shot him to death. Blood leaked out of bullet holes in his chest and gut. He had gotten a few shots off. Bullet casings from his rifle lay beside him. Widow knelt beside him and grabbed the rifle, eased it out of Frank's grip. He checked it. The gun was empty.

Frank's Navy hat had fallen off his head and landed on the top step. Widow picked it up and put it over Frank's face. He whispered, "Rest easy, Chief. You've crossed the bar. And they've crossed the line. Now I'm going to cross them out. I promise you that."

Torres joined him on the porch. "Oh God! Another one!"

Widow's voice was low and furious. He said, "Let's check the house."

Torres swallowed hard. He was visibly shaken, but he held it together. Widow rested Frank's hunting rifle beside his body and led the way, changing Torres' plans of going first. But Torres didn't argue. They stepped onto the porch, the wood slick under their boots. Widow jerked open the screen door and pushed through the front door, the hinges creaking. Inside, the house was silent. No barking and no voices. The emptiness was deafening.

There were wet, muddy boot prints all over Nora's floors, too many to cipher through. Widow didn't stop. He didn't go slowly. He ran through the house fast. All of Nora's guns were gone. Either Junior had taken them, because guns not traceable back to him were always useful, or he had tossed them out into the yard somewhere. Maybe his crew took the guns out of the house before Nora came back in. Widow knew they had drawn her out of the house before they broke in, because why else set the barn on fire? It was the distraction needed to get her to come outside.

Widow came back out of Nora's bedroom, the last room he checked. He had slipped on a black t-shirt while he was in there, which immediately started to cling to his wet body. His muscles showed through it by the time he got to the living room. Torres was still in there, stuck on the number of men's boot prints. Maybe he was trying to figure if any of them belonged to Dillard or the other cops he thought were his friends.

"They're not here," Widow said.

"Then you're right. They took them," Torres said, "But where?"

"I know where. The Black River Rail yard," Widow said, thinking about the hill he saw out there seven days earlier. It had the barbwire fence around it and the satellite dishes. Whatever they were up to underneath that hill, they were going to do it to Nora. Widow would bet money on it.

Torres didn't question it. Widow had proven himself so far. They exited the porch quickly, heading back to the cruiser. Widow started to get in the backseat, but Torres said, "In the front."

Widow climbed in through the passenger-side front door and scooped his belongings up off the seat—passport, burner phone, and bank card. He pocketed them and slid into the seat as Torres put the car in gear.

The cruiser reversed and roared back down the driveway, spinning out at the road. Torres might've been green, but he was a hell of a driver. Widow respected that. It made sense to him. When he thought about it, he figured the cops out here probably didn't get a lot of real-world shootouts. But they drove a lot.

Forgetting who he was speaking to, Widow said, "Take the highway! It's faster!" Torres said nothing, but was already heading to the crossroads. The rain had gotten much worse. It beat down on the concrete like artillery fire. Hail pounded the pavement.

"Better flip on the siren, driving in this. Be careful turning. The trucks barrel through here all the time. The last thing we need is to die in a car wreck," Widow said.

Torres flipped the siren back on. He stopped at the intersection and looked both ways, but the rain pummeled down thick and heavy. A copious mist filled the air, like a smokescreen. It was hard to see anything. They couldn't hear much either. If a tractor-trailer was blasting towards them, there was no sound over the rain. They could barely hear the siren.

So far, no trucks or any other vehicles were plowing through the crossroads. Which was weird, but understandable because of the conditions. Torres eased out into the intersection, to the point of no return.

Widow saw them first. Suddenly, three sets of headlights flipped on, like the drivers had been waiting, concealed by the heavy rain. The cars came from three directions. And they had flashing blue lights.

Torres saw them too, but too late. Three Iron Crossing police cruisers, their light bars strobing in the rain, accelerated toward them, trying to ram into the sides and front of the car. Torres spun the wheel to the left and gassed it, trying to dodge the collisions. It half-worked. The other cruisers slammed into various parts of Torres' car, but not the way they had planned.

Torres' cruiser went off the road and into a ditch. The passenger side was pinned to the ditch. The back tires were off the pavement. Widow was okay. No injuries. He looked at Torres, who was also okay. A trickle of blood streamed down his forehead. He had hit it against the steering wheel, but the cut was superficial.

Dillard pulled up behind Torres and Widow, so police cruisers boxed them in from every angle. Not the way Dillard had planned, but good enough.

The rain obscured the figures emerging from the other cruisers. Dillard got out, his Glock raised, flanked by three deputies armed with AR-15 rifles. They trained their weapons on the cruiser from the four points of a compass. But the west point had to adjust because Torres' car was in the ditch. They approached the car.

Torres tensed, one hand on the steering wheel, the other on his gun. He drew it and placed it on his lap. He looked at Widow and asked, "What now?"

"Can you reverse and get us out of here?"

Torres reversed the gear and hit the gas, but the rear tires spun. One kicked up muddy dirt from the ditch, the other spun in the air. "We're stuck."

Widow stayed quiet, stared into his side mirror. He saw the cop from the west closing in on the rear bumper. *Objects are closer than they appear*, a warning on the glass read.

The others moved up on Torres' side. Widow tried his door and the handle moved, but the door was pressed up against the ditch. He could only get it open far enough to let in the cold, wet air.

Dillard's voice boomed over the rain. He shouted, "Eddie, step out of the vehicle!"

Nothing happened. Then he shouted, "What're you doing? You've got a killer in there!"

Torres exchanged a glance with Widow. Widow nodded slightly, reading the fear and doubt in Torres' eyes. "We're going to have to make a run for it. I can't get out on my side. You'll have to lead the way."

"Run for it?" Torres asked, worried. "I could talk to them. Try and reason with them."

Widow shook his head. "That'll get us both killed."

Torres thought for a second and, without telling Widow what he was planning, he opened the door and stepped out. The dome light came on, exposing Widow's position. So he ducked down, trying to make himself as small as possible, which was a herculean task at best. Luckily, none of the cops were searching the car for him. Not yet. Right now, they had Torres, armed, to deal with.

Torres raised his gun slightly but didn't aim it at any of them. The rain soaked through his uniform again, instantly.

"What the hell is this, Dillard?" Torres shouted over the storm.

Dillard approached cautiously, his gun steady. "You're in over your head, Eddie. Widow's a murderer. You should've brought him straight to us."

"He didn't kill anyone!" Torres snapped. "But I can't say the same about you!"

"What's that supposed to mean?"

"You killed the Graces, those people back there! I saw the bodies!"

Dillard clenched his teeth, like he was having his own internal conflict. His face twisted to an expression somewhere between mockery and regret, like some distant part of him was still good. "You don't have a clue what you're talking about!" he shouted. "That was the switchmen. I didn't do that!"

Torres said nothing just inched toward them but also stepped farther out into the road. He was leading them away from the cruiser, away from Widow. "Either way, they're dead!"

"We didn't kill them. Let me explain, Eddie," Dillard shouted over the hammering rain. The other cops closed in. Two at

Dillard's back, tracking Torres. The fourth came closer to Widow's door, aiming his rifle into the cabin.

He wasn't pulling the trigger. None of them were. *Why weren't they?* Widow wondered. Even with the low visibility, they could shoot into the vehicle and kill him—end of story.

"Eddie, we've been running an undercover op. We want to take the Brocks down. That's why we've been helping Junior. He's a small fish. We want his father."

"That's a lie!" Torres shouted, and aimed his Glock at Dillard. No more pretending. He didn't need any more evidence. It was clear. Dillard and the others were all on the Brock payroll. He was the only true cop in Iron Crossing.

Dillard recognized the look on Torres' face. He knew. Torres wasn't as stupid as he had thought. So, Dillard smiled. He sympathized. He said, "Look at you. You've grown some balls, kid. That's good. But it's going to get you killed. Now, give us Widow! I'm not going to ask again!"

Widow flicked the dome light off, leaned over the center console, and reached for the control panel on Torres' door. He buzzed his window down and sat back. He listened to the exchange from the passenger seat, his mind working fast. The west deputy noticed the dome light flick off. He moved to cover the cruiser. His AR-15 was aimed directly at Widow, only he didn't know it.

The rain provided Widow with some concealment, but that wouldn't matter if all four cops decided to shoot into the cruiser. If they riddled the car with bullets, Widow would catch some. No question. He was a sitting duck. He had to get out.

Listening to the conversation, and seeing how the bad cops were treating the situation with kid gloves, meaning they weren't just shooting into the cruiser, Widow realized they wanted him alive.

"I can't hand Widow over!" Torres paused and raised his gun, aiming it at Dillard. "When I raised my hand to swear an oath, I meant it."

"Don't be stupid, Eddie! Oaths don't pay bills!" Dillard said, stepping closer, and holding his aim on Torres. "You're outgunned and out of your depth! Stand down! Final warning!"

Torres hesitated—his aim shaky, his grip slipping, his resolve weakening. He didn't know what to do. He glanced back into his cruiser to see Widow. But he saw no one. Dillard didn't wait. He stepped closer, fast, his Glock trained on Torres' chest. He fired twice, one bullet slamming into Torres' vest, the second penetrating his shoulder. Torres fell back with a grunt, dropping his weapon. His Glock skidded across the wet pavement, falling nearly out of sight in the mist.

"Get Widow!" Dillard barked at the other deputies. He glanced at them, only able to see the closest one through the rain. They all heard him clear as day. The deputies hopped to it, advancing on the cruiser, their rifles raised. The west deputy was on the ditch side of the cruiser. The others were on the street side. They all aimed into the darkness of the cabin.

Dillard looked back to Torres. But he wasn't there, not in the spot where he'd fallen. Dillard scanned the ground. He saw the wet blood trail from Torres' shoulder. Dillard followed it a few feet into the mist, and saw Torres dragging himself across the concrete.

"Where are you going?" Dillard asked, tauntingly. He stepped right over to Torres' feet and slowly followed him, aiming a kill shot at the back of Torres' head.

One of the cops on the front side of the cruiser stepped around the car, reaching for the rear driver-side door handle. Widow watched from the darkness. He realized they thought he was still in cuffs in the backseat. They didn't know that Torres had moved him to the front passenger side.

The one deputy had nearly pulled the handle when the one behind him spoke. "Isn't Widow supposed to be extremely dangerous?" He asked, scared.

Dillard huffed, stopped over Torres, and barked, "He's hand-cuffed and unarmed. Grab him so we can go before the fire department shows up."

The deputy gripping the car door handle wrenched it open and aimed his weapon inside. But he saw nothing. He fumbled for a good long second and pulled a flashlight out of his belt. He clicked it on. The beam fell over an empty bench. He flicked the beam across to the front seats. There was nothing. Then he noticed the passenger window was rolled all the way down.

The west deputy saw everything and started to ask what was happening, only he never got the chance. He never got the chance to do anything again but look to the trees because he heard a noise. It sounded like someone running through the mud.

The west deputy glanced right at the tree line. A large shadow ran at him. It was Widow.

Widow slammed a heavy rock across the cop's face, cracking open his skull in one massive blow. The west deputy tumbled backward against the cruiser's trunk lid. He was dead before he rolled off onto the ground. The other two deputies heard the thud and spun around to see what was happening. The flashlight beam caught the horror of their partner's face.

In a flash, Widow scooped up the dead cop's AR-15, a Smith & Wesson M&P15, which was chambered with 5.56 NATO bullets—deadly rounds—but then again, most rounds in the hands of a man like Widow were deadly.

Dillard followed Torres, menacingly, aiming at the back of his head. He glanced up and saw that Torres was crawling toward his Glock, which was still several feet away. Dillard lowered his aim, going for a bullet into Torres' leg. It would slow him down. But it was really to satisfy those urges—the dark ones that Dillard hid within himself.

Before he could fire, he heard the commotion back at Torres' car. He looked back. "What's going on?" he called out.

Before they answered, the two other deputies trained their rifles on the dark shadow that had just killed the west deputy. They fired through the cruiser's windows and into the sheet metal, aiming at Widow.

The deputies fired riotously. They shot up the car. Bullets sprayed wildly into the darkness and the mist. Several bullets tore through their dead partner. If half his face hadn't already been smashed in by Widow's blow with the heavy rock, he would be dead now.

They fired blindly into Widow's last known position. The thing was, Widow was no longer in that position. After Widow grabbed the M&P15, he dodged right and hid behind the front wheel well for cover. The other deputies fired into the rear. The flashlight beam shook with the gunshots, which was a major mistake on the part of the deputies. The flashlight gave away their positions.

Widow waited for them to stop firing. He came back up, tried to aim over the car's roof. But the front wheel was jammed into the ditch in such a way that the back of the car was lopsided. He couldn't get both of them. So he hopped onto the hood of the cruiser and rushed up to the apex of the driver's side. He aimed the M&P15.

The deputies heard him. They glanced to the front of the vehicle. The flashlight beam shone through the rain, making Widow's form glimmer. He shot both cops dead before the beam could blind him. The rear deputy got it first; Widow shot him twice. The M&P15 boomed through the rain. Two bullets ripped through the deputy's face before he had a second thought.

Widow flicked the rifle and aimed at the flashlight beam. He shot the next deputy three times. The first round hit his vest, knocking the flashlight out of his hands. It clattered to the concrete. Widow put two more in the guy's neck and face. He fell back dead. The flashlight rolled on the pavement until the beam washed over where the west deputy's face used to be.

Dillard spun toward the commotion, his eyes widened. But not from hearing gunfire. Not from seeing his dead partners. His eyes widened because he heard another gunshot. A bullet slammed into his bulletproof vest. The force pushed him off his feet and onto his butt. The pain hit him like a mule kick to the chest. He heaved in agony. Slumped over the pavement, he gazed back up and saw a nightmarish vision.

Widow emerged through the rain and mist, like something out of a horror movie. He aimed down the M&P15's sights at Dillard.

Dillard forced himself to stay in the fight. He scrambled to get back up. He fumbled for his gun, twisted on his knees, and tried to shoot back at Widow. Only it was all for nothing. Widow was too fast. And Dillard was too slow.

Widow shot him again, hitting Dillard square in the chest. The bulletproof vest didn't stop the 5.56 NATO rounds. It helped mitigate the damage, but he was hit. Blood gurgled in his throat. He coughed and gasped.

Widow stopped over him and kicked Dillard's gun away. He aimed the M&P15 rifle at Dillard's face. The jarhead deputy's eyes widened in terror. "Don't—don't kill me," he begged.

Widow stared at him, emotionless. He stayed quiet.

Dillard pleaded, "I can tell you where they are!"

"I already know," Widow said coldly.

Behind him, Torres groaned, dragging himself upright. "Widow, don't kill him."

"Why not?"

"He should face justice."

Widow hesitated, his finger hovering over the trigger. Dillard raised his only working hand; he had lost feeling in the other. He covered his face with it, expecting a bullet. When it didn't come, he looked at Widow. Widow looked back at him and said, "BANG!"

Dillard shuddered, thinking it was the end. But it wasn't. Widow lowered the M&P15, and, nodding toward Torres, said, "You're lucky he lived, or I would've killed you." Widow took Dillard's handcuffs and cuffed him with them.

Widow trail-carried the M&P15 and went to Torres. He helped him to his feet, checking that he was good enough to stand. He gave him Dillard's handcuff keys, and said, "Call it in. Get help. Whatever you gotta do, but I'm going after Nora and the girls."

Widow left Torres there in the rain and mist. He ran back to the fallen deputies, grabbed the keys from one of them and commandeered his police cruiser, racking the seat all the way back. He tore out of the crossroads, blue lights flashing and siren wailing. He headed back to Black River Rail yard.

CHAPTER 40

The police cruiser's high beams prismed through the rain, blurring the outline of the highway ahead. Widow drove fast and reckless anyway. He didn't care about the risk. His seatbelt was buckled, which was more than enough precaution for him. He had to get to Nora and the girls. No matter the cost. He drove with one hand on the steering wheel, the other resting on the gearshift. The rifle lay on the passenger seat. He had no idea how many bullets were left because he hadn't checked it, which was something he nearly always did. But he didn't care. He'd use them all to save the girls. Everyone who got in his way would get a bullet. And if he ran out, they would get whatever weapons he could procure on site.

The Black River Rail yard loomed in the distance. The wipers swiped across the windshield rhythmically, filling the silence in the car. *Nora and the girls better still be alive.* Widow was headed for either a rescue or a recovery. If it was the latter, then there would be blood.

Suddenly, his burner phone buzzed in his pocket. Widow fished it out and glanced at it, an unknown number flashing across the screen. He hit the speaker button and held the phone in front of him.

"Hello?"

"Widow," a familiar voice, trying to sound menacing, said. "You've been busy. You're supposed to be in custody."

The voice belonged to Junior. Widow didn't react, didn't blink, just kept driving. Most of his brain concentrated on the road, but a small part concentrated on thoughts of strangling Junior to death with his bare hands.

Junior sneered, "I tried to call Dillard. No answer. Then I tried the other deputies. Still no answer. Did you kill them all? I bet you did. Seems like wherever you go, people die. Look at what happened to Nora's old neighbors." He paused, letting his words sink in. "And Franklin? Dead too. You've really got a way with people, don't you?"

Widow kept his voice steady. He said, "Don't worry. You're next."

Junior said. "Do you know where I am?"

"Sure do. You're at the railyard. Probably in the bunker under that hill."

Junior paused, surprised Widow knew where he was. "Good. I want you here. Don't you understand? You're the main attraction tonight."

Widow stayed quiet. He imagined a chilling but overconfident grin on Junior's face. The guy sounded insane. But what did he mean by main attraction?

"Meet the switchmen at our service gate. Do you know where it is?"

"I know."

"Good. Come alone. Ditch any weapons you have. And Widow, I mean it. No weapons. Not even a toothpick. Or I'll throw these ladies to the wolves," Junior said, and smiled because he wasn't bluffing. He didn't have any wolves, but he had something better in store for them.

With that, the line clicked dead.

Widow turned off the main highway, the cruiser's headlights illuminating a rusted sign that read: *Private Property*. He paused, buzzed down the window. Rain pelted him in the face. He reached across the center console, grabbed the rifle, and tossed it out into the rain. He buzzed the window back up and turned onto the service road. It was the same one that the Greengate Hauling trucker used when he gave Widow a ride. The road turned into a gravelly service drive, leading into the shadowy heart of the railyard. Widow saw the same huge metal sign he had seen seven days ago. It was still chained between two rusty poles. It read: *Black River Rail & Stockyard.*

Widow stopped in front of it, switched from high beams to low. The headlamps were pointed at the sign, like two eyeballs locked onto it.

Widow killed the engine and stepped out into the rain.

Three switchmen waited near the sign. They carried the same cattle prods as they had seven days ago. One thing about them that was completely different was they wore devil-masks, like from a lavish Mardi Gras ball.

One of them had a big movie camera, sealed up in plastic to protect it from the rain. He circled Widow like he was filming him. Widow didn't know what the hell was going on.

The other switchmen didn't speak. They just surrounded him. One gestured for him to raise his hands. Widow raised them and stood steady. One of the switchmen stepped close to him and frisked him. He patted every inch of Widow, looking for weapons, but found nothing but Widow's passport, bankcard, and the burner phone. He left the passport and bankcard, but took the burner phone. The switchman pocketed it.

"Move," another switchman barked, shoving Widow forward with the butt of his cattle prod. He didn't ignite it.

Widow walked, his boots crunching on wet gravel. Heavy rain cascaded off his shoulders. The railyard spread out ahead, lit with harsh floodlights. Freight cars stood in rows, shadowed by the skeletal remains of rusting machinery. The smell of oil and decay lingered in the damp air. They could've been the same cars he'd already seen, or new ones. He had no idea.

As he pushed forward, two figures stepped out from the shadows. One was a huge guy, bigger than Widow. He was dressed in a rain slicker. His facial features under the hood were something to behold. He looked like he'd been hit in the face by a truck; his features were so rigid. He had a boxer's nose. It looked like it had been broken and reset and then broken and reset again. He was pushing something. It was a wheelbarrow. And he didn't look happy to be there.

The other figure was Junior. No question. He had the same wiry build, all sharp edges and expensive clothes that hung loose on his scrawny frame. He was wearing a rain slicker too. But Widow saw his suit sleeve hanging over the cast from his broken arm. Even in the rain, he carried himself with that same cocky swagger, the kind that spoiled rich kids had.

There was something different about him. He wore a gold devil-mask. It gleamed in the dim light, catching every droplet of rain like a cruel, shining beacon. The way it reflected the light made it look almost alive, as if it were glowing faintly, like molten metal cooling after coming out of a forge.

Junior held a gun. It wasn't a gun Widow recognized.

It was a strange-looking handgun. A long needle was visible in the barrel. It was a tranquilizer gun. "Thanks for coming, Widow," Junior said, grinning under the mask. He glanced at the camera, which was now a few feet from Widow's face.

Without warning, Junior raised the gun and shot Widow in the neck. The dart hit like a really bad bee sting. But seconds later it hurt like he'd been punched by a bolt gun, the kind they use to kill cattle. Widow yanked the dart out and stared at the needle head. The tip was bloody from his neck. The tranquilizer worked fast. His knees buckled, the world spinning in spirals of darkness and light. The last thing he saw was Junior's gold mask tilting in amusement.

Then nothing.

The switchmen picked Widow's body up off the ground. Maddix helped. They dumped Widow into the wheelbarrow, and hauled him off to the Iron Ring.

CHAPTER 41

arsh lights burned above him. Cameras clicked from various positions around the cavern. Widow opened his eyes but squinted under the lights. He lay on his back, his legs dangling off whatever object he was lying on. His head throbbed, and his vision blurred as he tried to make sense of his surroundings. The cold, rusted metal beneath him and the wet animal smell in the air rocked his senses. He felt dazed, unsure of where he was. He fought to clear his eyes, but everything he saw danced and shuddered, so he kept them closed for the moment.

Widow knew he was indoors. He listened to the sounds. Voices spoke somewhere above him. They rumbled and echoed. Animals growled and snarled. He heard dogs, and other animals that he couldn't identify. He heard one dog whimpering and then barking. It sounded like Joanie.

The human murmurs merged with the animal sounds, creating a chaotic cacophony that echoed around him. It felt like he was in some kind of chamber with multiple levels. The storm outside raged, its relentless rain pounding against the distant roof. Though the sound seemed far away, it also resonated close, reverberating around him like a haunting reminder of the outside world.

Above Widow, a motor whirred and a metal sheet slip out of a wall and covered a large hole in the roof, that acted as a skylight. Rain leaked through the holes and cracks in the sheet from high above. It slowly dropped down around him. He caught a couple of drops on his face. It hit his lips. He knew it was water.

Widow forced his eyes open and stared up, to where a ceiling should be. The lights blurred his vision worse. So, he focused on one blurry object off to his right, perched in a shadow. As his eyes sharpened, he saw the object was a camera. It was embedded in the rock.

Widow wondered how long he'd been out? Slowly, he tilted his head and scanned his surroundings. He was in a chamber, some kind of circular pit. The walls were high, lined with rock and broken bricks. Huge iron beams lined the floors and the walls. He continued tracing them. They weren't just beams. They were old iron rails that looked like they had been ripped from decommissioned railroad tracks and built into the cavern to keep the walls supported.

The cavern was enormous. Sounds from above echoed like the inside of a jet hangar. But near the bottom the sound was more contained, like in an orchestra pit.

This was the Iron Ring. Only Widow didn't know that was what it was called.

Widow twisted, trying to get up, but he was stuck in something, like being in a bathtub that was several sizes too small. Then he realized his hands were cuffed again. He rolled from one side to the other and tumbled out of the small tub. He fell hard against the floor. It was dirt and more rock. It was like the dirt was dusted over a rock floor.

The tub Widow fell out of wasn't a tub at all. It was an old, rusty wheelbarrow. The barrow clanged against the rock floor. The sound echoed up into the upper floors of the chamber. The cameras on the wall buzzed to life and focused on Widow.

Widow pushed himself up, his boots scraping against the rock floor. Some good news was that his vision was back. But that was offset by the pounding in his head. He felt like he had been hit by a truck.

A cruel drum beat in his head. It grew louder and louder, like he had swallowed a drum set. Suddenly, he realized it wasn't in his head. His sensitivity was at an eleven. Probably from whatever sedative was in that tranquilizer dart. He heard whispers. But they thumped in his head like the bass from Junior's Raptor the first time it passed him.

"He's awake."

"Cue the music."

Widow glanced up and saw a catwalk above him. It was just high enough that no man could vertically jump to it, but low enough to be within Nora's reach if she was standing on his shoulders.

As Widow's eyes adjusted to the lights above him, he saw that it wasn't the only catwalk. There were various tracks of metal catwalks. Some seemed to cross over into other sections of the chamber. Widow was not an architect, but he figured the pit he was in wasn't the only one. There seemed to be others behind the thick rock walls.

Widow caught a glimpse of large movie cameras—three of them—mounted on crude metal rigs like the catwalk. They weren't like the cameras embedded in the rocks. These were expensive cameras; not IMAX, but definitely listed somewhere on a sheet of camera models used in the movie industry.

Suddenly, spotlights clicked on and zoomed to life. They illuminated the pit around him. Widow glanced around. It looked like a gladiator arena. Then the spotlights narrowed their cone of light onto him. The music played like the opening theme to some kind of violent game show.

Several men stood above him on a catwalk. Another spotlight whipped around and lit up one of them. Widow focused on him, and then the light lit up the others. Four of the men wore devil masks. The first one was wearing a gold devil-mask—Junior. Widow saw the cast on his arm. Junior's devil-mask gleamed in the lights. He was flanked by switchmen armed with cattle prods. One of them held another camera. He stood in front of Junior, filming him for something, like a promo for an upcoming event.

From the shadows behind the camera, Widow saw three more men. One was a huge giant of a man, bigger than Widow. The guy probably stood around six feet, six inches tall—or taller—and his chest and shoulders were massive. He wore no mask. He leaned against the railing and peered down at Widow. Widow recognized one of the other two men. It was Collin Brock. It was obvious; he looked like his son, only older, and a little plumper in the waist. Plus, he carried himself with that above-everyone-else bluster. Widow didn't know the other guy, but he was some kind of right-hand man. Widow had seen the type before. Franklin had been the same type. And they killed him. Widow didn't know exactly who killed him, but Collin Brock was suddenly in Iron Crossing, a place he supposedly hadn't visited in years, and once he came back, Franklin was murdered. That couldn't be a coincidence.

Collin Brock grinned at his son from behind the cameraman. He gave him two thumbs up. The man beamed like he was proud of his son. They shared a father-and-son moment for the first time in Junior's life. It was like they had always been bonded. Twenty years of having an absentee father disappeared. Junior's memories of Franklin's care were wiped away with two approving thumbs from his father.

Brock whispered, "This is your show, son. I'm proud of you. Go do your thing. I'll watch. We won't interfere." Rourke stood behind Brock and nodded his approval as well, like the two of them were good buddies watching Junior's baseball game. It was twisted and deranged. But how else would a crime boss react to his son cutting his own path?

Widow wouldn't know. He had never met his father—some drifter who had swept into town, slept with his mother, and sailed out again. Widow didn't have any shared experiences with his father, but he was following in his footsteps.

Junior turned to the cameraman, spreading his arms out and making big gestures like the host of a TV show. He spouted an opener about his disturbing gambling event. He said, "Deranged viewers, tonight's event promises to be our biggest yet! If you've not bet already, place your bets now! We've got a man known to us as Widow. He's a natural brawler, unlike the others you've seen so far. He's about to battle the king of the Iron Ring!" Junior paused, like he was stopping for cheers, only there were none.

Brock watched from the shadows, cheering his son on. Two demented men, father and son, sharing in a demented game. Junior spoke with extra confidence, like he was being seen by his father for the first time. Which was ironic, since he wore a mask.

Rourke and Maddix stood near him, leaning on the rails and peering down at Widow. All the men who ran Brock's operations were here, and accounted for. They stood over the Iron

Ring like gods overseeing the youngest god's creation of death and carnage.

Widow barely heard Junior, because Junior walked the length of the catwalk as he spoke. The cameraman walked backwards. One of the switchmen guided him with his hand on the guy's shoulder. Junior rambled on like a news anchor on location.

Widow studied the chamber. There was a whole section of it covered in darkness. He started there, thinking something bad was going to come from that area. So far, nothing had, so he gazed around. He'd seen most of it already. Then he examined the walls, wondering if he could climb out. The walls were all brick, iron beams, and rock. There were large gaps in the brick. He looked at the floor and saw loose bricks that had fallen out of the walls. Then he noticed something else and stopped. It was under his boot. He squinted to see it. It made him shudder. He was standing on a pile of bones. There was dried-up meat still on the bones. Most of them were animal bones, but not just any animal bones. He saw skulls of all kinds littering the floor. There were large cats, buffalo, and even gorilla skulls. He saw a broken bull horn. The pointy end had dried blood on it.

Before Widow had time to question it, Junior stopped in the middle of the catwalk. He looked down at Widow. Suddenly, his voice crackled over a speaker somewhere in the chamber.

"This is Jack Widow. Our challenger. Widow, I want you to know that the betting market is still going. So far, this is the most money we've had on the platform. Guess what your odds are?"

Widow stared up at Junior. He shouted expletives at Junior, which the audience on their screens at home couldn't hear.

Junior gestured angry fists at one of the switchmen. The guy hopped to action, scrambled over to the railing and lowered a boom microphone, down closer to Widow.

Junior apologized to his audience and to Widow. Widow said, "Where are they?"

Junior looked at the camera, and asked, "Where are who?"

"Nora and the girls! What have you done with them?"

"I wouldn't worry about them," Junior looked at the camera, and said, "Guys, if you want to see the fate of a hot mom and her two girls, make sure you purchase the Iron Ring's Top Tier Package with Bonus Content. And stay tuned right after this match to see it happen. It's only for the most deranged of you out there. Do you have the stomach to watch?"

"What the hell is this?" Widow shouted. But the switchman was already pulling up Widow's boom mic.

Junior faced the camera and said, "Widow's handcuffed. Now, that's not going to be fair, is it? So let's change that." He turned to Widow and held out the handcuff keys. He jingled them, tauntingly, like Widow was a kid. Then he tossed them. They dropped into the darkest part of the chamber. The men on the catwalk all watched, eyes wide, mouths agape.

Widow went to the edge of the darkness, unsure how he was supposed to locate a small handcuff key in the shadows. Then he heard it. Something rumbled in the darkness. Something big. He pressed forward, shuffling his boots around, hoping to hear the jungle of a key under them.

Suddenly, the spotlights fell on Widow, lighting him up. One of the lights veered away from him, formed a cone, and lit up a large, trapped beast. From behind a gate, the beast locked hungry eyes on Widow. It roared a guttural growl, drool dripping from its teeth. There was something wrong with the teeth. They weren't white, like bone. They glinted in the spotlight's beam. They were silver, and razor-sharp.

The creature snarled, then growled louder, more menacingly than before. The growl was primal. It echoed in the enclosed space. Suddenly, a motor hummed to life and chains clanked. The links rose up and it folded in on itself, like a garage door.

Widow stood there horrified. He couldn't move. The beast's massive shape moved out of the shadows.

"Widow, the challenger, versus the reigning king of the Iron Ring, Bearzerker," Junior said, then he clicked the mute button on his microphone for the audience on the dark web. But for Widow, he said, "You shouldn't have killed Franklin!"

A behemoth of a grizzly bear stepped out into the chamber. Its claws were massive, like shovels, ready to scoop out Widow's insides. Like its teeth, the claws were fitted with razor-sharp steel.

Its metal claws, long and curved, raked the rock floor, making the screeching sound of metal on stone and leaving gouges in its wake. Its sheer size seemed impossible, its powerful shoulders rolling with each deliberate step. The bear's eyes, deep pools of primal instinct, glinted with a ferocity that was both terrifying and mesmerizing.

Widow stepped back, slowly, but he hit something hard and tripped, landing on his butt. The monster bear lurched forward, slow and ominous. It could attack him now, and rip him to shreds. But it seemed to know that. It lingered, like it preferred to play with its food.

Widow glanced down at what tripped him. It was a human skull. Then he saw there were more of them, scattered about the dark part of the chamber—the bear's den. More skulls and human bones were piled around the inner lair, beyond the gate.

It dawned on Widow that one of them was probably Alex Hopper, the TikToker, the reason Widow had followed the Ghost Line.

The bear roared at Widow, and tracked toward him, slow and lumbering, its head heavy. Widow shuffled back, and away from the skull. He froze for an instant. A silver handcuff key glinted at him from under a collarbone. The bear got within striking distance, walking on all fours. Abruptly, it put all its weight on three legs and swiped a massive paw at Widow. He rolled and dodged, going for the key. He scooped it up and scrambled to his feet. He ran away from the bear and back to the center of the chamber.

The men on the catwalk laughed and cheered.

Widow jammed the key into the keyhole on the cuffs and freed himself. He tossed the handcuffs and key away. They were useless to him. The bear moved closer. Widow didn't flinch, though every instinct in his body screamed at him to run. But where? There was nowhere to run to. Raindrops leaked through the roof above and dripped between them. The bear roared again, its breath visible in the chilly air, and charged.

Widow dove out of the way. He came up and spun around. Gravel and grit covered some of his skin. The men above groaned, like they were watching a sporting event. This was like a sick boxing match to them.

Grizzly bears are fast. Reportedly, they can run up to speeds of forty miles per hour. Which meant Widow wouldn't outrun it anyway. Not many land creatures could. But this bear was at least fifteen hundred pounds of monstrosity. The Iron Ring was large, but it was an enclosed space. The bear didn't have the room to get up to its top speed. And turning around proved to be easier for Widow than for the bear, but this discovery gave Widow little comfort as he couldn't dodge out of the way forever.

The bear looped around and charged again. Widow ran to a far wall, put his back to it. At the last second, he dove to the side, narrowly avoiding the bear's charge. Bearzerker slammed into the wall, dislodging a couple of bricks. The grizzly shook it off like it was nothing. The creature had probably rammed into these walls dozens of times. It would explain all the loose bricks on the ground.

Widow waited. The grizzly roared, and charged at him again. Widow knelt and scooped up a couple of bricks from the ground. He hurled one at the bear's face. The brick slammed into the bear's snout and shattered into dusty fragments. It was a long way from a killing blow, but it caused pain. The bear roared in fury. Widow threw the second brick. It slammed into the bear's face. The brick shattered into another cloud of dust and rocks, momentarily stunning the animal, but it didn't stop it.

From above, the men's laughter echoed, taunting Widow. He glanced up at Junior. The gold devil-mask reflected back him. Widow couldn't see Junior's face, but he felt the stare of satisfaction, like Junior was enjoying every second of Widow's misery.

Widow shouted, "You think I killed Franklin?"

"You did, and you'll die for it!" Junior shouted back.

Bearzerker stopped charging, having learned that it led to crashing into walls. It stalked close to Widow and swiped at him with a massive paw. Widow dodged, but the grizzly was cunning. It did a double swipe. One claw passed over Widow, but Widow couldn't get away fast enough to escape the second swipe. The bear's razor-sharp claws raked down

Widow's chest, ripping through cotton and skin. Blood soaked through the shirt.

Widow scrambled away and grabbed his chest. The wound was deep enough to hurt and bleed, but it wasn't fatal. The claws had cut into his dermis, leaving long, jagged streaks of pain and raw, bleeding flesh beneath the torn shirt. The wounds burned as air hit the exposed nerves.

Widow stumbled backward, his hand pressed against his chest to slow the bleeding, his breath coming in sharp gasps. The grizzly was toying with him, wearing him down. He assessed the injury quickly. No muscles torn, no vital organs hit—just enough damage scare him that he might not walk away from this fight.

Widow had never lost a fight before. Not with human opponents. But this was no human opponent. This was a hundred thousand years of brute force, forged by nature, versus a Navy SEAL. Widow began accepting a harsh truth.

He was going to die.

CHAPTER 42

Thousands of people all over the world watched their monitors, hiding behind VPNs and various layers of security. They watched on the dark web as Widow barely stood his ground against Bearzerker. It had been an intense fight so far. A lot of the regular viewers were shocked that Widow lasted longer than so many of the wild animals the Iron Ring had offered previously on its pay-per-view streaming show.

The odds against Widow were ninety-five to one. But they had started at ninety-nine to one. In the last several minutes, people were actually placing bets on Widow to win.

Most viewers saw it as a losing bet. Some even got bored watching the battle, like it was a foregone conclusion that Bearzerker would rip Widow to shreds. A smaller sliver of the deranged viewers still wanted more. They were bored with Bearzerker. Some of them skipped right over to the feed that showed Nora and the girls.

Animal musk and old blood smells filled the chamber next to the Iron Ring. The red dots on the cameras embedded into the rock walls flickered like fireflies in the dim light, the cameras capturing the moments of terror as they unfolded. Nora's heart raced, each thud a deafening echo in her chest as she crouched with her girls in a corner. Her arms squeezed tight around Violet and Poppy, as if forming a protective shield. The girls' small bodies trembled against her.

They had no idea what was happening on the other side of the chamber walls. But they heard the terrifying roars of a grizzly bear. The sound was unmistakable, like a train blasting its horn in a dark tunnel.

Nora repeated the same phrase to the girls, over and over: "Widow's coming for us. Widow's coming for us." She rocked them, saying it like the words of a spell. She repeated it as if saying it would produce him.

Joanie was there with them. She wasn't trembling like they were, like she had the last time she was here, in the cage. She wanted to tremble with them. But her instincts kicked in. She had to protect them at all costs, which meant she couldn't afford to be afraid.

She stood at the forefront of the chamber, her body taut and bristling, a low growl rumbling deep in her chest. Her ears pinned back, her eyes fixed on a massive metal gate. Darkness shrouded whatever was behind the gate. Joanie—and Nora—knew it was some kind of animal, perhaps multiple animals. They knew it because of the sounds—shuffling claws on rock, guttural breaths, and the occasional eerie, raucous laugh.

It was the laughing that made no sense to them. They couldn't figure out what animal made that cackling laughter. It was sinister, almost evil.

Suddenly, they knew what animal made that sound. Several overhead lights hummed and clicked on, lighting the chamber, but dimly. The animals behind the gate were clearly visible in the shadows. She braved a peek. It was something that she wished she'd never done.

Hyenas gamboled and toe-tapped from side to side, like trapped wolves waiting for dinner. They cackled and shuffled. Their black eyes stared back at Nora and the girls. Drool pooled around their mouths, dripping off their sharp yellow teeth.

They danced in and out of the shadows, going from full display to silhouettes. The dim lights revealed shaggy coats with thick muscles rippling beneath. The light reflected in their eyes, giving them a yellow glow. They paced restlessly, snarling and snapping like they'd not been fed in days, which they hadn't.

Poppy sobbed. "I wanna go home."

Violet whispered, "Māmā... what're they?"

Nora pulled her daughters in as tight as she could. She whispered, "Don't look." The girls obeyed her, but she couldn't heed her own warning. Her eyes stayed glued to the gate. She couldn't stop looking.

Joanie growled and barked at the hyenas, their lips wet, mouths chomping. Joanie's barking bounced off the cavern walls. She barked to warn the creatures to stay back, stay away from her family. The hyenas cackled back at her with a chorus of croaky laughter, their tones warped and unnatural. Their calls echoed in the chamber, like twisted sounds of madness.

Nora's skin crawled.

"Widow's coming for us," she muttered again under her breath. But she knew that was a lie. Her mind raced, searching for escape options. The pit was empty. She scanned the floor for anything that could be used as a weapon, but there was nothing there but sticks. Then the truth slapped her in the face. Another rack of lights hummed to life above her. She saw the sticks weren't sticks at all. They were bones.

"Oh God!" she whispered, clapping a hand over her mouth. She didn't want her girls to hear the fear in her voice.

The pit had no way of escape. It was designed with cruel precision. The pit wasn't just a prison—it would be their tomb.

The hyena's pack leader paced close to the gate. Its frame hulked over Joanie. It was larger than the others, with patchy fur and numerous scars. The creature's yellow eyes locked onto Joanie. Its lips curled back to reveal teeth that seemed too large for its mouth. Its low growl vibrated through the chamber like a rumbling engine.

Joanie didn't back down. She barked again, pushing her power to the limits. The pack leader tilted its head, as if sizing her up. Then it laughed—a monstrous, mocking sound.

Nora stared at the cameras. Someone was watching her. Why? She didn't understand. All she knew for sure was they were safe as along as that gate stayed closed.

Then came the sound that sank all hope.

Clang. Clang.

A mechanical sound groaned. Nora glanced at the hyenas. The gate juddered. Something was moving it. Somewhere above the wall, wheels turned and an engine cranked.

The hyenas went wild, throwing themselves at each other with excitement. They climbed over one another to get at the gate.

Nora's breath clogged in her throat. She clenched her fingers on the girls' clothes, like she could pull them in closer. But she couldn't. There wasn't a millimeter of space between them. Her heart pounded so hard it felt like it might burst out of her chest. Joanie stood between the girls and the hyenas. She stood fearless. She would die for them.

Another clang echoed in the chamber. The gate began to shift, its hinges creaking ominously. It was rising.

Nora glanced back at the cameras again. She knew someone was watching. She knew with absolute certainty. The sick watchers were enjoying this. And suddenly it occurred to her. A question. Is this what happened to Wade?

The gate rattled.

Another metallic clang echoed through the pit. The cameras' red lights blinked in unison. The gate shuddered, and then whirred ominously as it sped up. The gate began to rise, inch by inch. The metal ground against the rock wall as the gate retracted.

The gate kept rising.

And the hyenas laughed.

CHAPTER 43

Widow panted. He was out of breath, out of energy, and out of time. He was going to die in the Iron Ring. A monstrous grizzly bear stared at him with dark, menacing eyes. Nothing behind them but a single thought, a single urge—to kill.

Junior had modified the creature with metal teeth and claws, like something out of a horror book. Widow asked himself a question. Why stop there, why stop at just the teeth and the claws? The answer: Junior probably didn't.

In the SEALs, candidates have to go through rigorous training conditions—enduring extremes of physical and mental stress that push their bodies and minds far beyond normal human limits. To aid in maintaining these extraordinary capabilities, SEALs are rumored to undergo experimental enhancement therapies.

These therapies include cutting-edge techniques like hyperbaric oxygen treatment to accelerate healing, blood plasma replacements to reduce recovery times, and neural stimulation devices to boost cognitive reflexes under duress. Speculatively, some reports suggest that micro-dosing with nootropics is employed to heighten focus and memory recall during high-stakes missions. Other more controversial theories include regenerative stem-cell therapies for rapid muscle and tissue repair or the use of gene-editing technologies like CRISPR to improve endurance and resistance to diseases.

The line between science fiction and reality blurs with stories of SEALs being injected with compounds that allow them to hold their breath longer underwater or even withstand extreme cold without shivering. While much of this remains unconfirmed, these advancements symbolize the relentless pursuit of making elite warriors even more extraordinary.

To Widow, some of the supposed enhancements and experimental therapies weren't rumors at all. They were fact. He was given such therapies back in his day. So why not do the same to this bear? If Junior had it modified to look more terrifying, maybe he went even further.

Widow thought this because the grizzly seemed more malicious, more bloodthirsty, than any he'd encountered in the wild. For all he knew, Junior had experimented on the animal with steroids, adrenaline, and maybe even narcotics. He suspected the latter the most because of the look in the bear's eyes. It stared back at him from a deep place of madness—a horrific killing machine. The evidence was all around him—all the bones of its kills—animals and humans.

Widow wasn't going to beat the bear. His only hope was to escape it. He'd already scanned the Iron Ring. He'd run the gauntlet around it. The best he could figure, there were two ways out—up or through.

Widow either had to climb out or bust out. Back in the grizzly's den, Widow saw a set of massive double doors. The doors were how they got the bear into the Iron Ring to begin with.

There appeared to be no way to climb out. He remembered hearing that grizzlies were excellent climbers. So, if there had been a way to climb out, the bear would've found it already.

So, Widow decided to try the door. But first, Widow would have to get past the beast. That was proving difficult. He would dart left, then dance back right, to try to run past the bear. But Bearzerker was smart. He might fall for Widow's tricks once or twice. Not three times.

The only thing that slowed it down was hitting it with bricks. However, each brick to its face enraged it even more. The other problem was that eventually, Widow would run out of bricks. And once he did, the bear would rip him to shreds and make it worse than it would've been if he had just submitted.

Widow scooped up two more loose bricks. He chunked one at the bear. It busted over the creature's snout again. This brick didn't crumble like the others. It really hurt the bear. It paused a long beat, and Widow shot to the side and began to run to the den. But the bear stood up on its hind legs and roared at him.

Before, it had been toying with him, playing with its food. But now it was done with all that. Widow had enraged it to the point where all it saw was red.

He heard Junior and the others cheering on the bear.

"Kill him! Kill him!"

Suddenly, Widow thought of a third way out—speaking. Ballots over bullets. The pen was mightier than the sword, and all that. Words over violence—or in this case, words and a brick.

Widow grabbed the last brick near him and shouted at Junior, "I didn't kill Franklin!"

"Yes, you did! The cops arrested you for it!"

"I didn't kill him! Collin killed Franklin!" Widow said, and backed as far away as he could.

"The cops arrested you for it!" Junior called out.

"Did they arrest me because I killed Franklin? Or did your father pay them to pin it on me?"

Junior turned to his father. He stared at him through the gold devil-mask. "What's he talking about?"

"He's just making shit up! He's desperate!"

Junior didn't buy it. Something about the way his dad ignored and dismissed him for all of those years. "What's he talking about?" Junior repeated.

"Come on?" Brock said. Rourke sensed the tension and put a hand near his gun, which was on a belt holster under his coat. Maddix saw the move and stood up from the railing. He got behind Brock.

The camera got up close to Junior's face, as the switchman had been instructed to keep the camera rolling no matter what. But Junior pushed it aside and ripped off the gold devil-mask. He stared into his father's eyes. Tears streamed down his face. "Did you kill Franklin?"

Brock stared at his son. Apathetically, he said, "Son, he came between us."

Fury and emotion swept over Junior. He shouted, "But he was there for me! He was like a father to me!" Junior paused a long beat, then added, "He was more of a father than you ever were!" Junior grabbed a gun from the closest switch-man's belt holster and shot his father. And so the fray began. Like a Shakespearean scene, a war between a father's forces and a son's ignited.

Brock stumbled back against the rails. Rourke went for his gun. Junior shot him too. Two bullets. One tore through his chest, the second splattered his brains out into the air. Fragments of brain matter slopped to the ground.

Bearzerker stopped feet from Widow. He sniffed the air, turned and looked up. The men on the catwalk plunged into an all-out brawl. Guns went off. Cattle prods ignited. Punches were thrown.

Widow seized the moment. He grabbed another loose brick, only this time it was from the wall. He looked up at the catwalk, reared back like a pitcher on the mound, and threw it. The brick flew through the air and nailed Brock right in the head. He stumbled back, still clutching his bullet wound, and fell off the catwalk. He fell fifteen feet and slammed onto the rock floor. Blood trickled out of his mouth. He scrambled upright.

Brock stared at Widow. Then he saw Bearzerker. The grizzly slowly approached him.

Widow scrambled for another loose brick. He jerked two more out of the wall. Maddix leaned over the railing, calling out to his boss, trying to figure out a way to get down to him. Widow gave him one. He threw the brick at the large man. The brick broke across his face, like it had the bear's, only it did wound Maddix. Maddix's nose broke on impact and he was blinded by the dust. He stumbled over the railing and landed hard on the rocks below. He landed between Brock and the bear.

Maddix wiped the dust from his eyes and stood up. He stared at the bear. And the bear stared back, its eyes wide with delight. It salivated at the thought of tearing into the big man. Maddix began cowering. He glanced at Widow, then he glanced at a dark shadow on the wall. Widow looked at it too, and saw something he had missed before. It was a door. It was crude and built into the wall. The rocks and brick camouflaged it. That was how they had gotten him down there.

Widow waited for Maddix to go for his gun. Only he never did. He didn't go for it because he didn't have one. Widow saw the man's fingers. They were too thick to fit inside the trigger housing of most standard handguns.

Maddix ran for the door. He grabbed at the handle, and jerked and pulled. It was locked.

Bearzerker walked toward him, salivating the whole way. Maddix spun around and tried to do what Widow had done. He picked up a brick and threw it at the bear. But the bear had learned from its mistakes chasing Widow around the Iron Ring. It swiped the brick out of the air. The brick broke apart on impact.

Maddix screamed right before the bear mauled him to death.

Junior won the fight on the catwalk. He shot two switchmen who were obviously loyal to Brock. One of Junior's men got shot in the skirmish. Junior made the only remaining switchman swear loyalty to him. He let the guy keep his cattle prod, but not his firearm.

Junior surveyed the Iron Ring. He saw that his father was still alive. And that wasn't going to work for him. He wasn't done with his father. So he ordered the last switchman down to get his father. The switchman hesitated. "Alone, boss?" he asked. "But... Bearzerker?"

"Use the cattle prod!" Junior shouted. Then he scooped up the camera and took control of it.

The switchman took his cattle prod and ran down the stairs to enter the Iron Ring.

Maddix's gruesome death gave Widow time to take action. He ran past the bear while it was devouring Maddix, and entered the bear's den.

He slammed into the double doors and jerked back on the handles. But the doors didn't budge. They were locked from the outside.

Widow gave up on the doors. He didn't want to waste time and get cornered in the bear's den. Standing over all of those human bones, he realized the bear hadn't been dragging humans into the den to eat them. They had gotten trapped in there, trying the same thing he just did.

The bear's den was much bigger than it looked from the outside. There was another thing about it that he'd missed before, a second room. There was a large hole in the wall, with bars across it, like bars on a window. Inside there was a set of stairs going up. And there was a second door leading into another chamber. Widow tried the door. It was also locked.

The second room wasn't empty. Widow saw a man lying face down on the floor. He was gaunt with lily-white skin, like he hadn't seen the sun in months. He was all bones and sinew.

Widow thought the man looked dead. But he wasn't dead, and he slowly stood up. The man was emaciated, his skin stretched tight. His veins bulged everywhere. His hair was matted. He hadn't bathed in weeks. His clothes were old and tattered. They were so dirty, it was impossible to tell their original colors. Then Widow noticed the form of the clothes. They were scrubs, like a doctor would wear. Words were stitched into the fabric, just above a torn pocket, above the right breast. Widow couldn't read the words.

The emaciated man's pale eyes stared blankly at Widow. Widow saw the animal claw and teeth marks covering his body, scars for life. The scar sizes ranged from canines to large animals. Maybe even the bear. Two fingers were gone from the guy's left hand.

The man was a prisoner, like the bear. A long chain ran from the ceiling and attached to a collar around his neck. He stood up and shuffled over to Widow.

Widow glanced back out through the den's opening. The bear had finished off the last of Maddix. Slowly, it lumbered over to Brock, who had crawled into a corner.

But then Bearzerker noticed a trespasser was in its den. It changed course and slowly sauntered over to its den, toward Widow. He turned back to the side door into the man's cell. Widow shook the handle. It was also locked. The door rattled on its hinges. It was looser, weaker. There were dents in it, big ones. They were bear-head-sized. It looked like the bear had rammed this door before, although it wouldn't fit through the doorway even if it could knock the door down.

The emaciated man slowly walked to the window. Widow shouted at him. "Open the door!"

The man stopped just near the window. He slowly looked at the door. Widow shouted at the man again, asking him to unlock the door. But the man just stood there, unfazed, like he was dead inside.

Widow backed into the den. He was out of time. The bear's massive head was already in the opening. It hunkered down to move further into the space. It roared at Widow. Maddix's blood dripped from its silver fangs.

Widow had run out of bricks back in the chamber, so he picked up a skull. It was human. He stared at it. For an instant, he wondered if it belonged to Alex Hopper?

The bear moved in closer. It was within striking distance now. At any moment, it would swipe at Widow, tearing his throat out before eating him alive.

Just then, Widow glanced at the emaciated man. He leaned into the bars, watching the horror—still unfazed, still dead to the world.

Widow saw what was stitched into the fabric of the man's shirt. It was the name of the veterinarian's office Nora had taken him to, the one where he helped the girls put a flyer up on the bulletin board of missing pets.

Under the name of the clinic, there was another name.

Widow said, "Wade Sutton?"

The emaciated man snapped to life, like he hadn't heard that name in so long, he'd almost forgotten it. He stared at Widow. Widow said, "Nora and your girls are going to die if we don't help them!"

Wade stared blankly.

The bear swiped a massive blow at Widow. Widow put the skull up to block it. The bear's paw smashed the skull into fragments, but missed Widow. The next one wouldn't miss. The bear reared up for another strike.

Widow called out, desperately. If he was going to die, Wade was the only chance left to save Nora and the girls. "Wade! Save Poppy! Save Violet!" Widow shut his eyes tight, ready to die.

Long seconds passed and nothing happened. Widow opened his eyes. Wade had stuck his hand through the bars. His arm extended all the way out. And Bearzerker was licking his hand.

Wade tousled the bear's fur with his two-fingered hand. The massive grizzly closed its eyes and grunted like it was a big dog.

Widow put it all together in his mind. And it made sense. Wade was a veterinarian. He left his house one day, headed to work, when he got an urgent call. They needed a veterinarian for emergency work on some livestock. So, he went.

Only it was a lie.

Junior had tricked him into coming to the Black River Rail yard. They needed a veterinarian to care for their fighters, their products, the animals. Wade had been captive for a whole year.

Bearzerker was also a prisoner. They sedated him, operated on him. Probably forced Wade to stick those metal claws and teeth on, surgically. And in that time, Bearzerker bonded with Wade. They were brothers in captivity.

Wade probably lost those fingers by refusing to do the operations at first. So Junior had his men take a finger until he agreed. Wade had been in this deep dark hole for so long, he probably wasn't even sure who he was anymore.

Just then, the grizzly roared in pain. Electrical currents zapped through it. Its fur smoked. The bear spun around. It shifted to one side and crouched against a wall. The last switchman had been standing behind the bear. He had zapped the bear with one of those cattle prods.

The bear stared at him. Then it glared at the cattle prod, like it knew this weapon, and hated it. They must have cattle-prodded the beast a lot.

Behind him was Junior, holding the camera. He pointed the camera at the inside of the den. But he also pointed a gun at Widow. He held a Glock 19 in his right hand. Because of the cast on his arm, he had to angle himself so the weapon could point where he wanted it to point. He said, "You're still alive! That's good! The show must go on! You know?"

The bear roared in pain as the switchman shocked it into submission with the cattle prod. The switchman shocked it and stopped, shocked it and stopped. He repeated the pauses, like he was waterboarding it for information. But really, it was because he enjoyed it.

In the pauses between the bear's roars, Widow heard Joanie barking somewhere in the caverns. He also heard the faint sound of screaming. It sounded like a woman, or two little girls.

Junior sneered at Widow, diabolically. He said, "I want to get you back on camera. Just now, before I pointed this camera at you, I checked my phone. And you know what? The bets have doubled. And your odds went up. I can't believe it. It's sixty-forty now. You're still favored to lose. But Widow, you're turning out to be a star. I might have to keep you around. Like I did Nora's husband there. What do you think about that?"

The look on his face was something truly rare. Widow had seen it before. But not often. Widow said, "You're insane!"

Junior barked, "Come on out of there!" Widow walked forward, past the bear and the torture. As he exited the den, Junior moved away, making sure to stay out of Widow's reach.

Widow was covered in blood and sweat. Both were his own. Blood dried on the claw marks down his chest. Junior moved, his back now to the bear. "Keep going! Back to your corner! We'll have to reset!"

But Widow didn't move. He glanced down behind Junior. And he stepped forward. Junior twisted, angling the Glock to point at Widow. But Widow sidestepped, out of its line of fire. Junior stepped back and angled again. Widow repeated the moves, driving Junior back. "What the hell are you doing?" Junior asked. He dropped the camera. It clattered on the ground. He switched the Glock to his left hand, giving himself freedom of movement with it. Now, he could aim at Widow from every angle. Only it was too late.

Suddenly, Collin Brock stabbed his son in the calf with the broken bull horn. The tip skewered Junior's calf muscle. He shrieked like a child. He spun around and shot his father in the head. The bullet blew part of Brock's brains out onto the floor under his ear.

Junior stood over his dead father and stared down at him, no remorse on his face. He felt happy about it. It was over twenty years coming. He had done it. But in that few seconds of relief, he'd forgotten about Widow.

Junior spun back around too late. Widow was right there in front of him. He towered over Junior. Time seemed to slow down. The switchman kept zapping Bearzerker behind Junior. In between currents, Widow heard the girls shouting and screaming close by.

Junior began to move the Glock to Widow.

Widow caught the Glock on its arc back around to point at him. He clamped a hand down on it, preventing Junior from moving it. He grabbed Junior around the throat with his other hand and squeezed. He lifted Junior up off the ground. He didn't rip the Glock from Junior. Instead, he twisted Junior's hand forward. Junior fought against Widow with all his strength. But Widow was much stronger. He folded Junior's forearm in such a way it snapped and broke, like a twig, like his other arm had. And Widow didn't stop.

Junior pleaded, but no words came out of his mouth because Widow strangled him with his other hand. Widow folded Junior's arm back and pointed the Glock at his head.

Widow stared into Junior's eyes and pulled the trigger with Junior's own finger. The Glock fired. The gunshot echoed in the chamber. It was loud and undeniable. The bullet traveled a fraction of a second before it exited out the back of Junior's head. Like father, like son. Blood and brains splattered out and across a large iron beam.

Widow dropped the lifeless body. It crumbled to the floor like a heap of bones, landing in such a way that Junior faced his dead father. A rotten family tree destroyed.

The switchman stopped shocking the bear. He stepped back to see who Junior shot with the Glock. But Junior wasn't standing there holding it. Junior was dead.

Widow stared at the switchman. It was the same one he met seven days ago. He had already taken a cattle prod from this guy once. But he wasn't going to do it again, because he didn't have to.

The switchman froze when he heard the grizzly growling behind him. He spun around and saw Bearzerker staring at him. It growled in anger. Its breath huffed out in big puffs of vapory exhalations. The bear glanced at the cattle prod. The switchman tossed the prod away. He put his hands up and began begging the bear for mercy. But mercy wasn't on the menu. The switchman was.

The bear tore him to shreds.

CHAPTER 44

The dark web viewers lost camera feeds for the main event. But they'd paid for the bonus event as well, which was promised to be particularly gruesome. Depraved viewers watched from all over the world. They salivated over their computer monitors and smartphones to see the mayhem they had been promised.

The hyenas were loose. They surrounded Nora and the girls in the other pit. Nora and the girls huddled together as closely as they could. Joanie stood out in front of them. She barked and growled at the hyenas.

Suddenly, the pack leader charged at Nora. Joanie launched herself at the large beast. Two others came in and clamped their jaws down on Joanie's legs. Three others joined in. The pack leader got Joanie by the neck and squeezed hard. Huge teeth punctured the dog's neck and legs. Each hyena jerked and pulled in opposite directions. They were tearing Joanie apart, limb from limb. Blood seeped out of her wounds. She cried and moaned in pain. Things around her started to go dark. She lost a lot blood in seconds. The pain was unbearable. Her brain was switching off.

The pack leader let go of her. Joanie collapsed into a clump of blood and pain. Two of the others stayed with her, sniffing her and licking her blood, preparing to consume their biggest meal in days.

The pack leader moved to Nora and the girls. Two others joined it. They flanked both of its blind spots. Nora and the girls weren't escaping. They would be the main course.

Nora pushed the girls behind her. She shoved them against the wall and pressed in front of them like a human shield, like a sacrifice. Violet and Poppy held onto her legs and shivered in terror.

The pack leader glanced at one of the other hyenas. It seemed to nod, like it was giving an attack order. Joanie wailed in pain. The hyenas laughed and snapped their jaws. One of the hyenas charged at Nora. It clamped its jaws on her arm. She cried out in pain. The teeth cut deep. The beast ripped her away from the girls. She punched and kicked, but the beast overwhelmed her and dragged her away from them.

The pack leader and the other hyena crept in closer to the girls. Violet and Poppy were on their feet, eyes closed tight. Each squeezed the other's hand.

The pack leader laughed. They all followed suit. It closed in and sniffed the girls. It went from Violet to Poppy and back again. The pack leader got first bite. It was picking out the one it wanted. Nora screamed and fought against the one chomping down on her arm.

The pack leader reared back and lunged at Poppy.

The pack leader's head exploded just before it clenched its teeth around Poppy's throat. It exploded a fraction of a second after a gunshot rang out. Followed by two more, and with them, two of the other hyenas' heads exploded.

Three shots fired from the Glock in Widow's hand had killed them. The pack leader went first. The backup one went next. And the third hovered over Nora. All dead.

Widow rushed into the pit from a massive double door that had been pulled open.

The two hyenas chewing on Joanie released her and spun around to see their brothers dead on the ground. They charged at the girls, but Widow stood between them. He aimed the Glock and fired. It clicked empty. He dropped it and prepared to fight the hyenas with his bare hands.

But he didn't need to because just then, one of the hyenas was flung to the right by a massive bear paw. Bearzerker had followed Widow into the pit. The other hyena tried to scramble away from the bear, but it got the metal jaws.

Nora scrambled to her girls, the three of them cowering in terror of the grizzly.

Widow threw his arms around them, hugged them tight in a bear hug. He said, "It's okay. He's with me."

Confused, Nora hugged him back, like he was the last man on earth. She cried in his arms. Violet and Poppy hugged his legs, crying with their mother. They held each other a long time.

But reality set in. And Widow knew he wasn't the last man on earth. He whispered to them, "Everything's going to be okay."

Violet whispered, "Joanie. What about Joanie?"

Widow released the girls. He looked back at Joanie. They all did. Nora stared in horror and disbelief. An emaciated man knelt over Joanie. There was bullet-shot chain, broken, dangling from a collar around his neck.

Widow let go of Nora and the girls, joined the emaciated man. Nora's mouth hung open wide. Finally, she said, "Wade?"

But the emaciated man didn't recognize his own name. He stared at the bloody mess that used to be his dog. He wasn't even sure he recognized her.

Wade whispered to Widow. "Can save her. Need gauze. Bandages, and…" He hesitated, his hollow eyes scanning Nora for the first time, like he knew her. "Adrenaline… epinephrine shot. Need jump-start her heart. Stabilizer for blood loss."

Widow asked, "Where can I get that stuff?"

Wade slowly looked back at the door, past Bearzerker devouring a hyena. He said, "Room down hall has stuff."

"I'll carry her. We'll follow you," Widow said. He scooped Joanie up. Her head hung off his arm like a sock with a baseball stuffed in it. Her blood covered him. Wade led the way and the others followed. Nora carried Poppy and held hands with Violet.

They took Joanie to an operating table in another room. The room was probably where Junior had forced Wade to operate on the bear. There were tons of animal medicines and an array of operating equipment.

Widow laid Joanie on a table and Wade went to work. Nora cried on Widow's shoulder part of the time, over her dog and over discovering her husband was alive. It was a shock to her system. They called the police, only got no answer.

An hour later, ambulances and fire trucks were there. Two hours later, the rain slowed and the state police showed up, since there were no functioning local police.

CHAPTER 45

Widow slept in a jail cell for three of the longest nights of his life.

The cell wasn't for him. It was just an empty cell at the Iron Crossing sheriff's office. No one had charged him with a crime. Not yet. The jail was empty. The whole office was empty. The only deputy still active in Iron Crossing was Eddie Torres, and he was recovering at Brock's General Hospital.

Widow slept in a cell because the local hotels were all booked up. Motels too. Even the local bed and breakfasts had no space. Various state and federal law enforcement agents had flooded Iron Crossing, booking up everything that had a spare bed. There were no more rooms to be found.

There was a large mess to clean up. Evidence needed to be sorted. Jurisdictions stood on a razor's edge. Conflicting interests fought over who would get what. Law enforcement agencies from all across the US had a stake in the Brocks. There was a lot to piece together, a lot of questions to answer.

It turned out Collin Brock's company was a front for smuggling. They smuggled things from all kinds of illegal industries—drugs, guns, people, and livestock. And that was just Black River Rail. Brock had his fingers in a lot of other criminal pies. His businesses stretched across Missouri, and beyond.

The FBI was there. The ATF. The Missouri State Police. The DEA expressed interest because of some connection to drug cartels in Mexico. Officers from Fish and Wildlife Service. Even the railroad police departments sent agents. Clean-up would take months. Maybe years. There was a lot to sort through. Everything from bank records to large wild animals.

The Wildlife officers asked Widow several times if he was certain there was a grizzly bear, because they couldn't find it. "There are no grizzlies living in the Ozarks," the officers told him. Widow told them there was a grizzly. There was no hiding it. It was on film, on the internet. And there was plenty of evidence of bones, left behind by Bearzerker. The thing Widow didn't mention was that once they escaped the Iron Ring, they left a large garage door open. It was the entrance to the loading center at the back of Junior's hill.

Widow and the others watched as Wade said goodbye to the grizzly. He hugged the bear and shoed it off. They watched as the bear ran out into the rain, into the woods.

Years and years would go by. Hunters and hikers would claim to have seen traces of a grizzly living in the Ozarks. They'd find animal bodies, mauled and partially eaten by some massive creature. Fisherman on the rivers would claim to find gigantic bear tracks near the banks. The state would offer a reward for the live capture of the grizzly. Talented trackers would come from all over the state and hunt for it, but no one would ever find it.

Eventually, the bear became an urban legend. It got to the point where tourists would claim to have seen it. Local news headlines would read: *Another Bearzerker Sighting Near Shady Grove*. It got to be like seeing Bigfoot.

The railroad tracks known as Route 67, dubbed the ghost line by trainhoppers, was closed completely. The railroad police had it condemned and the tracks removed. Eventually, grass and forest grew over the long section of trail where it went through the Ozarks, leaving it as a distant memory.

In the future, there would undoubtedly be prosecutions and convictions. State prosecutors would argue with federal ones as to who got to go first. Lawyers from every state west of the Mississippi River would come crawling to defend wealthy clients. Low-level guys would get no lawyers and probably strike plea deals.

Junior was a different story. The FBI didn't know what to make of the horrors of the Iron Ring. But they would investigate it even though Junior was dead. For now, they shut down the websites.

Thousands of deranged viewers from all over the world kept logging in, only to see an FBI Closure page. It warned that the site they were trying to access had been seized due to criminal activity. Eventually, some of the deranged viewers were tracked through their IP addresses, and arrested. Others were never found.

Widow wasn't sure about the future of the investigations. He wanted no part of them. He only stuck around for three reasons—Nora, and the girls. The doctors checked Widow over. It turned out he was lucky. He didn't need stitches for his bear claw gashes; they would heal on their own. The doctors prescribed him painkillers and an ointment to put on the wounds three times a day. The rest of his injuries were superficial.

The girls had no physical wounds, but the psychological ones were potentially catastrophic. Widow wasn't sure. The girls were so young, they might forget all of it.

At the hospital, Nora was a trainwreck. Along with her physical wounds, Nora had been traumatized by the hyena attack on her and her girls, and the possibility of them bearing emotional scars for life. Not only that, but Nora had spent a year thinking her husband had run off, but the whole time he had been tortured and held prisoner just miles from their farm.

After the doctors examined Widow, he waited for Nora and the girls lose track of him, then slipped out of the ER. On his way out, he stopped at the receptionist desk, under the large portrait of Collin Brock he'd seen before. The same young receptionist was there, the one he'd met a few days ago. This time she was going off her shift. He asked her about Torres. She directed him to a room on the fourth floor, the same floor as Junior's hospital suite. Widow rode the elevator up and found Torres recovering from shoulder surgery in a room on the opposite end of the hall from where Widow had seen Junior's men.

Torres was bandaged up, but lucid. Freda from the library was there, holding Torres' hand. She wiped tears from her face, smearing her makeup. Widow got there while she was confessing to Torres that when she heard the news he'd been shot, she feared that he would die. She admitted to not wanting to lose him. Torres was all smiles for a guy who'd been betrayed by his entire department and shot in the shoulder, all in the same night.

Widow stopped in the doorway to wait for them to finish their intense exchange. At one point, Torres joked, "If I knew all I had to do to bring us together was take a bullet, I would've got shot a long time ago."

Freda laughed. Widow waited a beat, then tapped on the door. Torres and Freda glanced at him. He said, "Hey there. Am I interrupting?"

"No! Come in!" Torres said, and pushed himself up to offer a hand for Widow to shake. He grimaced from a sharp pain that rocketed through his shoulder. But he stood his ground. So, Widow took his hand and shook it. They chatted, and exchanged words of gratitude.

Torres revealed that he had been unofficial investigating the disappearances of Wade Sutton and also Alex Hopper. Only he ran into problems verifying the TikToker. He found out why. Alex's real name wasn't Alex Hopper. It was Alexander Kovalenko. He was a Ukrainian refuge from the war. His parents have been searching for him. Torres mentioned that the FBI would contact them. They still couldn't confirm that he had fallen victim to the Iron Ring, but Widow imagined his bones were in their among the others.

Widow convinced Torres to change the official story to leave out his name. By the time the authorities started interviewing witnesses, word had gotten around and no one seemed to recall the name of the giant stranger.

Widow asked if Torres knew a place he could stay for a few nights. He didn't think it was right to stay at the Sutton farm, not with Wade being alive. Widow figured it was best for Nora and the girls that he not be there. He was a complication they didn't need at the moment. He wasn't sure where he stood, and he didn't want to return to the farm. It didn't feel right.

But Widow couldn't leave, either. There were things unsaid that he wanted to say. So, Torres offered the jail. It had a cot, shower, sink and toilet. No one was using the cells at the moment. Plus, the department was going to be closed now. Nobody knew when or if it would reopen.

Widow stayed in the cell and waited to see if he'd hear from Nora. He wrote off his toothbrush as a casualty of war—or love. He had left it in Nora's bathroom in a cup next to her toothbrush, ten feet from the bed they had shared for seven nights. It was where part of him would belong forever.

Widow left the hospital without saying a word to Nora, but he left a trail. He knew that if she wanted to find him, she could.

Widow bought a new foldable toothbrush from the general store. He used the soap in the cell to shower and wash his hair. He brushed his teeth over the jail sink. And he slept on the hard cot for three nights—hoping, waiting. But she never came. Widow gave up on hearing from her, which he accepted as *that's life*.

Still, he needed to tell her how he felt. It ate at him to just walk away. Widow decided to leave her a note. He figured it was best. He could say what he needed to and leave it to her if she wanted to read it or not.

So, on the third morning, Widow sat at Dillard's desk with official Iron Crossing Sheriff's Department stationery and one of Dillard's pens. Dillard wasn't going to need it anymore. He was going to jail for the rest of his life.

Widow sat for two hours staring at the blank page. Eight scrunched-up balls of paper lay across the desk—the rejects. On each, he had written long messages without any coherent plan. They were just confessions of his feelings for her. On one he wrote a terrible poem about her. On another, he doodled pictures. He felt stupid, like he was back in high school trying to write a note to a girl who didn't even know he existed.

Finally, satisfied with the note he had written for Nora, Widow left the sheriff's office. He hitched a ride out to the highway near Nora's farm, keeping his options open. The driver tried to chat with him but he just stared out the window. He looked over at the Graces' farm. And then he saw the Sutton farm. There was an SUV he didn't recognize parked in the driveway. The old barn had burned to the ground. Nothing was left but a pile of rubble. Somewhere in the rubble was Nora's old Honda motorcycle. It probably was worth nothing now, unless some of the parts could be salvaged. Judging by the damage to the barn, Widow doubted it.

The animals were gone. Nora had scrambled together some local farmers to come by and round them up. There was nowhere to keep them on her property. Not until it could be restored. If that was her plan.

At the crossroads, the driver stopped and looked both ways. He let two tractor-trailers go first. Which wasn't really up to him, since they both blasted through the intersection.

A year later, this problem would be solved because the state would finally get around to reinstalling the two stop signs.

The driver started to head south, but Widow said, "Wait!" The driver stopped the car and Widow hopped out. He thanked the driver for the ride, and said he was going the other way. He got out in the middle of the crossroads and jogged back to Nora's farm. He stood at the end of the driveway for a long time, staring at the house, second-guessing himself.

Widow walked up the driveway. He passed the spot where he first met Violet and Poppy at their lemonade stand. He passed the spot where Nora had pointed her rifle in his direction. A smile crept over his face at the thought of her in a bikini, threatening him with the rifle.

Widow thought about seeing Joanie running through the yard, barking at unwanted visitors. He threaded past the SUV parked in the driveway. A rental tag hung off the rearview mirror. Widow walked up the steps to the porch. The note was folded up in his back pocket. He opened the screen door and raised his hand to knock. He heard voices inside the house. There was some laughter, which was a good sign.

Widow decided not to knock. He just stood there a long second. Then he took out the note. Nora's name was scrawled on the outside. He stuffed it into the doorjamb, released the screen door. It snapped shut. He went back down the steps. Just then, he heard a dog barking. He turned around and saw Joanie scrambling from around the side of the house. She struggled to run to him.

Joanie was wrapped in bandages from her various wounds but she seemed okay. She walked crooked, but Wade had been able to save her. She spent two days in the animal hospital where Wade had worked. They took care of the rest.

Widow knelt and petted the dog. She wagged her tail and licked his hands. "Good girl," he told her.

"Hello? Can I help you?" a voice asked from the porch.

Widow stood up, his eyes glassy from holding back tears. A woman was standing on the porch. She was about fifteen years older than Widow, maybe more. She was beautiful in a wildflower kind of way. She wore a Hawaiian dress, flowing and colorful. She had dark hair with gray strands. Her face was friendly and warm. She looked just like Nora, only with darker skin. She held Widow's note in her hand.

Widow said, "Sorry to bother you, ma'am. I was just leaving." He smiled at her and turned away.

"Wait!" She said, and looked at the note, then back at Widow. "You're him? The guy my daughter told us about?"

Widow said, "I'm nobody, ma'am." A man stepped out behind Nora's mother. He was a little older than her. He was Nora's father. It was obvious. They had the same eyes. Probably had the same hair color once too. Now her father had gray hair, but Widow could imagine it was blond when he was younger.

Her father was tall and lean. He said, "Can we help you?"

"I was just leaving," Widow said.

"It's him. The guy Nora told us about," Nora's mother said.

"Widow?" Nora's father asked.

Widow said, "It's me."

"We're so happy to meet you! We're Nora's parents," her mother said. Both parents smiled big. They came down off the porch and hugged Widow. They thanked him for a long minute. They tried to get him to come inside, but Widow told them he really couldn't. They accepted it. He left them there.

Nora's parents went back into the house. Widow walked back down the driveway, and Joanie followed him. She barked and barked for him to return. Widow tried shooing her away, but she kept following him.

Suddenly he heard a voice. "Widow?" He looked back. It was Nora. She stood behind her parents' rented SUV. She wore a new summer dress, or at least it wasn't one he'd seen before. She looked beautiful. She had a couple of bandages over her eyebrow, to cover a single stitch. One of her forearms was wrapped up tight in bandages. It was where the hyena had bitten her. Otherwise, she looked pretty much back to normal.

A tear fell from her eye as she stared at him. "Are you leaving?"

Widow looked away, tried to put on a tough face for her. He said, "Yeah." His voice broke just a bit.

"Without saying goodbye?"

"I was..." he said, and choked up. "I left a note in the door. Your mother must've gotten it."

"Oh," she said, glancing back at the house. Her parents had gone back inside, but her mother watched from a window. Nora couldn't see her, but she knew her mother was there. "Well, where are you going?"

Widow shrugged and said, "I don't know."

Nora walked to him, stopping just inches away. He could've grabbed her and pulled her to him. "Want me to give you a ride?" she asked.

Widow could get a ride with her. They could just drive and never come back. He wanted to. He wanted to say so many things to her. "That's not necessary."

"So, that's it?"

Widow stayed quiet. He stared at her, into her eyes. He wanted to tell her how he felt. But he couldn't.

"They took Wade to Kansas City. Better doctors there for him," she said.

"Yeah?"

"Yeah. He's in really bad shape. They say most of it's psychological. The doctors said the physical toll will heal in a month or so. Not the emotional and mental trauma. That'll take some time."

"I'm glad he's alive. This should've never happened to begin with. But at least he'll survive. That's a good thing."

"You know, he never did speak to me and the girls. It was like he didn't even know us anymore."

"Will he recover?"

She paused a beat and looked at the house, then back to Widow. "The doctors say so. It'll take time. But he will make a full recovery. And he'll probably need months of therapy. Maybe years."

Widow nodded. Unable to say what he needed to say, he slowly backed away, like he was going to leave.

"The girls are inside," Nora blurted out to stop him.

Widow froze. He smiled. "Tell them I will miss them."

"Don't you want to tell them yourself?"

Widow stayed quiet.

"They love you, you know," she said, and stepped close to him. Her eyes were as glassy as his.

Widow stared into her eyes, and eternal sadness stared back at him. He swallowed hard and tried to speak. But the words wouldn't come out.

Nora threw her arms around him. She kissed him passionately. He kissed her back. "Widow, I…" she paused, searching for the right words.

Widow interrupted her. "I know. Me too."

"We could go somewhere. Together. We could take the girls."

Widow stared down at her. "Is that what you want?" he asked. She froze, staring back at him, conflicted.

Tell me that's what you want. And we'll do it. I'll go with you… Widow thought. They stood there for a long moment, caught in their emotions. The sun beamed down over the farm.

Joanie sat there, wagging her tail, confused as to what exactly was happening.

Eventually, reality set in. It seeped into Nora's mind. And she let go of him. She pulled back, trembling, and looked at him tearfully. "I want to go with you," Nora said. "But I can't."

A deep pain cut through Widow, worse than the massive bear claws had. He knew. He stepped back from her, and said, "It's okay. You got a good life. I want you to be happy. I want the girls to have the life they were meant to. The one you started here."

She held his hands and said, "Wait here. They'll want to see you. Let them say goodbye?"

Widow nodded.

Nora eased away, like she was slipping away from him forever. She went back to the porch, called Joanie to follow. They climbed the steps. Nora looked back at Widow. He stood there, waiting. She looked at him like it was the last time she'd ever see him. She smiled, and went inside. Joanie followed. Moments later, she came back out with Violet and Poppy.

But Widow was gone.

"Where is he, Māmā?" Violet asked.

Nora stepped out into the driveway. The girls followed. Joanie shuffled out past them. She sniffed the gravel where Widow had stood. Nora walked to the end of the driveway with the girls. She cupped a hand over her eyes to block out the sun. She looked around, down the rural road, and at the crossroads. No sign of Widow.

Her mother came out of the house and met her in the driveway. She put a hand on Nora's shoulder like she used to do when Nora was a little girl. She handed Nora the note.

Nora took it and walked away from them, back to the house. The girls played with Joanie like they were hunting for Widow. Nora opened the note and read it.

It read like a page ripped out of a screenplay for a famous movie, with the characters' names and everything.

Rick:
"I'm saying it because it's true. Inside of us, we both know you belong with Victor. You're part of his work, the thing that keeps him going. If that plane leaves the ground and you're not with him, you'll regret it. Maybe not today, maybe not tomorrow, but soon, and for the rest of your life."

Rick:
"We'll always have Paris."

At the bottom it read:

We'll always have Casablanca,
Widow

A WORD FROM SCOTT

Thank you for reading THE GHOST LINE. You got this far—I'm guessing that you enjoyed Widow.

The story continues…

The next book in the series is THE MIDNIGHT MEMORY, coming in 2024!

To find out more, sign up for the Scott Blade Book Club and get notified of upcoming new releases. Go to ScottBlade.com

GET JACK WIDOW KINDLE BOXSET

Did you know you can get a Widow book free when you buy the eBoxSet on Kindle? Buy three Widow eBooks for the price of two.

THE MIDNIGHT MEMORY: A PREVIEW

SOME MEMORIES DON'T FADE. SOME WON'T LET GO. SOME DEMAND JUSTICE.

Coming 2025

(Actual cover to be revealed in 2025)

THE MIDNIGHT MEMORY: A BLURB

Some memories don't fade. Some won't let go. Some demand justice.

Jack Widow, a drifter with an unshakable moral code and a violent past of his own, is no stranger to the strange and dangerous. But even he can't ignore the eerie sight of an elderly man wandering barefoot along a desolate Nebraska road in the dead of night—dressed in pajamas and clutching a loaded shotgun.

The man is lost, confused, and shooting at someone who isn't there. Widow intervenes, taking him back to his family, only to uncover a haunting mystery: the man suffers from dementia and every night at midnight, he's pulled back into a violent memory—one that might reveal a long-buried crime.

Determined to get to the truth, Widow delves into the man's dark past, uncovering secrets that might lead to a dangerous crime family. What Widow finds will test his limits and put him on a collision course with those desperate to protect their dark legacy at any cost.

A thrilling tale of justice, redemption, and a relentless pursuit of truth, *The Midnight Memory* will keep you up all night.

Preorder now and follow Jack Widow into a mystery where past memories refuse to stay buried.

Readers are saying about Scott Blade and the Jack Widow series...

★ ★ ★ ★ ★ Scott Blade's Jack Widow is so good, my biggest complaint is having to wait for the next one!

A SPECIAL OFFER

Get your copy of Night Swim: a Jack Widow Novella.
Available only at ScottBlade.com

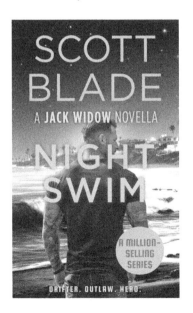

NIGHT SWIM: A BLURB

Under the cover of night, Widow swims through dangerous waters to rescue an FBI agent from a death sentence.

A blown cover for an FBI agent means a death sentence, unless Widow can stop it.

Under cover of darkness along the Malibu coast, Widow takes a night swim. It's meant to be soothing and stress-relieving.

Instead, Widow's night swim turns deadly with the echo of gunshots over open water. A covert FBI operation is blown apart, leaving only blood in the water and a lone undercover agent exposed to a den of lethal international criminals. From the quiet night swim to a high-stakes criminal party at a mega millionaire's beach house, Widow faces grave danger to warn her.

Widow, the drifter who stands for justice, emerges from the waves. With literally nothing but his resolve, he faces unbelievable odds. Time is running out, the enemy is within reach, and for Widow, stealth and cunning are his only weapons.

In this pulse-pounding Widow novella, the line between the hunter and the hunted blurs in a deadly game of espionage and survival.

THE SCOTT BLADE
BOOK CLUB

Fostering a connection with my readers is the highlight of my writing journey. Rest assured, I'm not one to crowd your inbox. You'll only hear from me when there's exciting news to share—like a fresh release hitting the shelves or a can't-miss promotion.

If you're just stepping into the world of Jack Widow, consider this your official invite to the Scott Blade Book Club. As a welcome gift, you'll receive the Night Swim: A Widow Novella in the starter kit.

By joining, you'll gain access to a trove of exclusive content, including free stories, special deals, bonus material, and the latest updates on upcoming Widow thrillers.

Ready to dive in? Visit ScottBlade.com to sign up and begin your immersion into the Widow universe.

THE NOMADVELIST

NOMAD + NOVELIST = NOMADVELIST

Scott Blade is a Nomadvelist, a drifter and author of the breakout Jack Widow series. Scott travels the world, hitchhiking, drinking coffee, and writing.

Jack Widow has sold over a million copies.

Visit @: ScottBlade.com

Contact @: scott@scottblade.com

Follow @:

Facebook.com/ScottBladeAuthor

Bookbub.com/profile/scott-blade

Amazon.com/Scott-Blade/e/B00AU7ZRS8

66720386R00287